MW00787820

HEAD LIKE A HOLE

ANDREW VAN WEY

head like a hole

A Novel of Horror

andrew van wey

Head Like a Hole is a work of fiction. The characters, incidents, and dialogue are products of the author's warped imagination and should obviously not be construed as real. Any resemblance to actual events or persons, living or dead, is entirely coincidental. Furthermore, any resemblance to actual events should be documented for science.

Cover Design: Damonza | Damonza.com
Interior Images: Deposit Photo | Depositphoto.com
Editing: Bodie Dykstra | Bdediting.com
ISBN-13: 978-1-956050-04-2 (hardcover)
ISBN-13: 978-1-956050-05-9 (paperback)

V.12.4.22

Visit the author online: andrewvanwey.com

part one

Come As You Are

chapter one

There's something about tract housing that gives Anwar the creeps.

Perhaps it's the identical streets, coordinated names like Rose Way becoming Ivy Lane or merging into West Tulip Court. Perhaps it's the size of the trees and their species, the blue palo verde and desert ironwoods, all pruned and carefully spaced. Or perhaps it's the houses, their emerald lawns and fences, their fountains and rustic gates. Each home cozy on its own yet gaudy when compressed together, an assembly line of American perfection. The only distinguishing feature, he realizes, is the cars parked in the driveways.

"Blue Tesla, black Range Rover, black Tesla, blue... Subaru. Here we go."

The GPS chimes his arrival at 1414 Marigold Drive. He circles around and parks the rental car across the street. He collects his notebook and tablet from the passenger side. He pops out two Xanax and swallows them dry.

He checks his watch: 2:40 p.m. A few minutes to gather his thoughts.

On most days and most interviews, he wouldn't be nervous. At forty, Anwar Fariz is a veteran of journalism's changing trenches. He's seen it all, from the local rags to the national newspapers collapsing around him. Even now, on the internet, where his old colleagues once laughed and sneered before eventually calling him up, asking questions like, "Can you really make money at this podcasting thing?"

And it turns out you can, if you find the right niche and kick over a few rocks.

If you're willing to get dirty.

2:41.

Last year, his true crime podcast *Suburban Murders* brought in a half million in advertising. His spinoff, *Small Town Sex Crimes,* was nominated for an Ambie. He has a meeting with Spotify next month and is confident they'll ask for an exclusive. He just needs something fresh to get them hungry.

2:42.

Which is why he's here in Arizona, the spring sun warm through the Camry's windshield as the Xanax settles his heart. He takes out two recorders.

The first, a silver microcassette, he tests and slips into his pocket.

The second, a tiny digital recorder with a wired mic, he slips under his shirt and threads up his sleeve.

2:43.

He waits until a boy with red hair and freckles bicycles past. He knows that a brown person in a car has a tendency to draw eyes, especially in these planned communities. But if his timing is right, he shouldn't be here for more than a few hours.

She'll be arriving any minute.

And bringing her kids.

2:44.

The key to getting a good interview, Anwar has discovered, is the element of surprise. Catch the interviewee off guard, then give them an opportunity to recover. Explain there are deadlines, due dates, and it's now or never. Don't they want a chance to correct the record?

She'll never know that he booked this plane ticket last month. Or that his list of questions is nearly one hundred long. And she won't need to hear about the private investigator he hired to learn her routine. No reason to tell her such things.

2:45 p.m.

Here comes her silver Jeep, the only car on the street.

As she turns into the driveway, he catches a glimpse of her dark hair pulled back in a ponytail and the shadow of a scar on her cheek. Hoisting groceries and a child's gym bag, she unloads, a pair of baseball shoes dangling. Two kids explode from the back seat, twins in third grade and with energy to spare. The girl swings a backpack laden with books. The boy runs and jumps over the fence, doubling back to open the gate for his mom.

And now, watching her lock up the car and head past a lawn strewn with toys, Anwar feels a moment of pity for Megan Collings, forty-six, artist of minor acclaim and mother of two.

She has no idea her past is about to catch up with her.

chapter two

Shoving the dirty uniforms into the washer, Megan is overcome by the cold tickle that's plagued her for weeks: something is off, something discordant and wrong.

She chalks it up to middle age. To a sense of melancholy her friends say sometimes comes with these years. Still, it persists, following her to the kitchen, where she starts preparing dinner. She'll try an old recipe tonight, stuffed chicken with a side of Olivier salad. Yes, that might cheer her up.

As she cuts the carrots, a spike of loneliness slides into her thoughts. She has friends, yes, many close friends. She has patrons of her art who have funded this house. She has this view of the mountains in bloom.

But her parents...

Sometimes she wishes she could call them. To ask them questions and gather advice. To commiserate with them on days when things fall apart. And to tell them she's sorry; she understands it now. Parents aren't perfect, but they do what they can.

She slices the chicken breast and presses it flat on the plastic block.

Perhaps Symon and Sofiy will think of her cooking someday, long after the baseball practices are over and the parent-teacher conferences have finished. Maybe that's what immortality is: remembering the tastes of your youth while feeding your children.

Then a chill blooms and spreads through her body. The knife slides from her fingers.

Her gaze turns to the knocking and the shadow beyond the front door. The mailman always uses the bell.

The man she finds standing on her porch is a stranger, a few years younger, a bit scruffy and rough at the edges. He has sharp eyes and the flat smile of a snake. Even before he speaks, Megan senses a gravity, someone who comes bearing bad news.

Still, she smiles and says, "Can I help you?"

He introduces himself as Anwar Fariz, a producer of award-winning podcasts. He passes his card through the gap in the door. Beyond, the neighborhood is quiet, the kind of warm afternoon that chases the children indoors until evening.

Anwar says, "It's okay if you've never heard of me."

"To be honest, I'm more of an audiobook listener." She turns the card over. There's his company, *TANGLED PRODUCTIONS, LLC*, and a little microphone crossed with a magnifying glass and a pair of muddy footprints. "But I'll be sure to pass this on to my husband. He's a true crime junkie."

"I hear that a lot," Anwar says. "But I think you'd be interested in my newest project. Actually, that's why I'm here."

She finds her head tilting. First, when he puts his hand on the doorjamb, leaning like he's just chatting with an old pal. Then his lips part to say something that hits her in a place of deep memory.

"It's about Oksana Samarina."

Megan's throat dries and constricts. It takes every muscle, every cell in her body, to keep her face a flat mask of indifference. She says, "I'm sorry, who?"

Anwar's smile turns into a smirk. He makes a *tsk-tsk* sound punctuated with a derisive flare of his nostrils. He leans in, closer, his fingers tapping a worn, blue notebook close to his chest. That's Inspector Gadget on the cover.

That notebook... She hasn't seen it in decades.

"C'mon, Mrs. Collings. Megan Collings, Megan *Monroe*, from Stonefield, Connecticut. You went to the Tenbury School, class of ninety-four."

Megan finds her voice and offers Anwar a smile. "I'm sorry, were we classmates?"

That serpentine grin widens his face. "No, I'm a product of public education, I'm afraid."

He glances beyond her, to the twins settling into their video games, some new thing about defending a castle from zombies and aliens. She says, "Symon, feet off the table."

"Sorry, Mom."

It's just the pause she needs to regain her balance. That name and that notebook. They knocked the breath from her chest. "I'm sorry, what is it you said you're here for?"

She needs to hear the name again, to know that it wasn't a series of misfiring neurons and her overworked mind.

"Oksana Samarina," he repeats, leaning in so close she can smell his mint gum and the sweat of a long drive.

He knows. God help her, he *knows.* And that's why he's here.

She breathes deep, touching the V-neck of her tennis top where her chest heaves and her heart drums. Objectively, she knows her figure can be distracting. At Sofiy and Symon's baseball practice, she always catches a few glances from the dads. And a few glares from the moms. She even blushed today when a teen in the stands asked his friends, "Dude, who's the MILF?"

But Anwar's beady eyes stay locked on hers, scouring every inch of her face for recognition. For the first time in years, she's aware of the scar.

It's starting to itch.

With a sigh, she opens the door and gestures to the cool air and the shade. "Mr. Fariz, I think you should come in."

chapter three

From the outside, the house looked like any other Tudor revival in the Windy Sage Village. Inside, Anwar has to admit, it's quite a nice home. The layout is vaulted and filled with warm desert light. A half dozen paintings hang from slate walls. Despite the scattered Legos and toys, the living room is spacious and comfy. The view through the back offers a breathtaking panorama of the McDowell Mountains rising from the desert in bloom.

Before Anwar even notices the children, Megan says, "Kids, I'm going to be visiting with someone very important in the kitchen. So, DND time, right? What does that mean?"

"Do not disturb," Symon says.

"Don't worry, Mom. We got you," Sofiy adds.

Megan smiles. "You got me? No, no, missy, I got you."

She gives her daughter a kiss on her head and pushes her son's hat over his eyes. He fumbles with the Xbox controller. "Mom, I'm gonna die."

"Not without my permission. But your character might."

The kitchen is semi-open, and like much of the house, its utility impresses Anwar. Megan hooks her finger into the wall, sliding a partition out and closing it off from the dining area and beyond. Smaller, but still half the size of Anwar's whole Westwood condo. He really is getting robbed in L.A.

"Please have a seat," she says. "What can I get you to drink?"

Anwar settles on a sparkling water, privately inventorying the contents of her fridge. Glass bottles of juice and fresh vegetables. The kind of beer and white wine he only buys on special occasions. She's come a long way from her penniless art student days.

But not far enough.

He waits until she's served herself white wine in a cup painted by her kids and signed *MOMMY'S MAGIC MUG*. He sits at the kitchen table, a bright tiled thing of Mexican mosaics. He savors the details: her trembling hand, her delayed composure, the calm facade ready to crumble. Over the years he's developed an instinct for these interviews. He can almost tell which ones will make a hit podcast by the rusty tang in his mouth.

It tastes like adrenaline.

It tastes like fear.

"So, how do you know Oksana?" she asks in a breezy voice.

Anwar sips the sparkling water. In his experience it's best to start slow. Let the interviewee believe you know everything. Give them silence and they'll tell you so much.

So he takes out the old notebook and places it on the kitchen table. It sits there, binding frayed, the once-colorful Inspector Gadget cover worn down by the decades.

But its contents are ageless.

When he found the notebook after his mother's funeral, he almost tossed it. She had never cared for his career, never encouraged his pursuit of a good story, never asked what he was chasing. And all he cared about was selling her house, paying off her medical debts, and keeping what little remained, which wasn't much. But it turned out that notebook might be the most valuable thing she owned.

So he waits, fingers drumming the blue cover, *tap, tap, tap*.

After a pregnant silence, he says, "You know who this belonged to."

"I do."

"And who was that?"

"Detective Nolan."

He nods. "Then you know what's inside."

She gulps down some wine. "Nothing good for me."

His gaze drifts to the wide window, where a buzzard circles over the foothills.

She asks, "So, how did you get it?"

"Graham Nolan was my uncle. Kind of the black sheep of the family. My mom always said he was the worst kind of brother. He wasn't mean or rude; he just hardly existed. But here it is, proof that he did exist, and quite a bit more."

Megan studies him, her gaze that of a predator posing as a house pet. Even her scar seems sharper in this light. For a moment he wonders why she never bothered to have it smoothed out by surgery. She could certainly afford it with what her paintings sold for.

"Anyway, this turned up at our house sometime after he went missing. Looks like he mailed it to her, thinking she'd read it and go to the cops. That's what the last entry implied. But she never did. Maybe she skimmed it and got bored. It's pretty dry up front, doesn't quite grab you, which I've found is important. People have short attention spans these days. But I went through it, cover to cover. What I read didn't make sense. At least, not until I started lining up dates and photos."

He reaches into his bag and places a black book upon the table. On the cover, a crimson marlin leaps from the water above a school's gold crest and the words *Veritas Vitæ Magistra*.

"Truth is the teacher of life," she whispers.

"Lovely motto. I always wonder if fancy schools choose these Latin phrases out of a catalog or something."

He drinks the sparkling water, the crisp lime and carbonation a balm for his throat. He always forgets how dry the desert is.

"Right," he says. "Dates and photos."

He opens the yearbook, carefully turning to the proper page as he'd practiced. When you're breaking a subject, presentation matters. If he lays out the right facts, he won't need to ask for her story.

She'll beg to tell him.

"It's a good picture, isn't it?" He taps the black and white photo.

Five kids—well, legally adults—so smooth-faced and moody they could pass for a grunge band. Flannel jackets hang loose around low-rise jeans. A midriff shirt is paired with a plaid skirt. Curtain hair and at least two pairs of Doc Martens.

There, at the edge with her *Ugly Kid Joe* T-shirt and patch jeans, Megan's younger self looks back.

Anwar says, "You know, overalls on a lady are severely underrated. That fashion needs a rebound."

He waits as the ice crackles in his glass. Not even a smile, damn. Well, time to pour some vinegar in with the sugar.

"Chunhee Chang," he says, his finger tapping the young woman with fierce eyes. "That business in New Hampshire was awful. Same with Desiree Chastain and Tom Frenning. And that old boyfriend of yours, Adam, funny how he vanished around the time my uncle went missing. Or the fact that two houses burned down in two years, both places you were connected to."

Her eyes have grown cold. "There's nothing funny about that."

"Maybe not. But there is a story there, waiting to be told. Your story."

He reaches into his jacket and takes out a silver recorder. He places it beside the yearbook and gives it a friendly tap.

"Everyone's on digital these days, but I still like tape. Maybe it's a generational thing. Who knows? My point is, this is what I do: I reach back into the past and I dig. See, most of us are bad at covering our tracks. And that look you keep giving me—like you're trying to hide what we both know—that look needs to stop."

She swallows. "I'm not sure what you're talking about."

He rises, the chair squeaking against the Italian tiling. "You want to play dumb? Fine. I've done my research. Maybe the police will be more interested in what my uncle had to say."

He starts gathering his things. Another trick he's learned: feigned offense breaks down stubborn doors. People want to be heard, especially when they've been misheard, misquoted, and misunderstood. It's why we relive old arguments in the shower until we've won.

She gestures, palm out. "Please... That's not what I meant." She closes her eyes, focusing on her words. "Please, just sit. You have to understand, this is all sudden. I haven't thought of them in years."

Anwar smooths his jacket and settles back into the chair. Privately, he's smiling. But outwardly, he lets his eyes scrunch into a hesitant scowl, cautious and skeptical to this audience of one.

Because it always starts with that number, doesn't it? One. One little journal. One nagging question. And one answer from her leading on to more questions and answers that he can sell to an audience of millions.

And yeah, he'll return the tape recorder to the table between them. He'll even start it and stop it, promising her that some details are best kept off the record.

But he knows the truth. It's another prop for the performance. He's been wired up with a second mic since he turned off the engine. He's been recording since he knocked on her door.

Anwar taps the journal. "Look, I've already read my uncle's story. Tell me what happened to your friends." Then he taps the tape recorder between them. "I want to hear your version. Don't you think people should know your side of the story?"

"No," she says.

"No?"

She sips her white wine, eyes drifting to the window and that warm cobalt sky. Two more vultures have started circling.

"No. It's not my story, but I'll tell it if that's what you want. It's hers. And it's a love story."

part two

I'll Never Get Over You (Getting Over Me)

chapter four

Autumn 1996

Crab season ended a few weeks ago, but Louis Harding didn't care. He had a good spot in the cove and a dozen pots to check. He knew the game warden slept in on the weekend.

As the motorboat sputtered out of the harbor and up the coast, the might of the Atlantic reminded Louis that he was alone. The sea spray and gray waves, those rocky shores to his left. The rare sail on the horizon. Yes, he was glad to be by himself.

New England was becoming crowded these days. The New Yorkers encroached from the southwest and the Beantown crowd spread down from the northeast. Even a trip to the supermarket was a chore, cars all jostling for spots, foreign products on the shelves, and pretentious coffee shops sprouting up. There was talk of a Starbucks moving in, and that really set him off something else. What kind of idiot pays two bucks for a coffee?

The same that would pay double for crabs at the farmers market as long as he writes *LOCALLY SOURCED* on their shells. Rich idiots, he thought. That's who.

So he'd woken up at four, stopped by the Dunkin' Donuts for some bear claws and some black coffee at seventy-nine cents. He sipped from his thermos, guiding the motorboat northeast, hoping the ocean was generous.

It turned out it wasn't.

The first pot was near empty, just a few juvenile crabs. The ones that followed were even worse. Hoisting the empty frame into the boat, Louis took a moment to study his placement. He'd been coming to Bresden Bay for thirty-odd years; he knew the water's secrets. There were the triplets, three sea stacks a half mile offshore and covered in bird shit. There was the rocky arch, known to the locals as the Eye of the Needle. Louis had even threaded it a few times when he'd gotten sauced and a little too cocky.

And up ahead of the bow was his favorite cove, the gray sea funneling to turquoise eddies where caves dotted the headlands like ravenous mouths. There, he would find his remaining crab pots full; he was sure of it.

But he didn't.

By the sixth pot, he was certain of one of two things: some other fisherman had found his secret spot or someone had emptied his pots. Either way, he was pissed and caffeinated and properly cold. With each wet rope and empty pot, a new curse flew past his lips.

Then came the last pot, and he told himself this was the good one. He felt resistance as he hoisted it up. When the cage neared the surface, he smiled. It was teeming with crabs. Dozens of legs and claws and shells all rolling and crawling over each other. His lucky day.

Until he emptied the pot.

On any other morning, the scream that left his lips would have embarrassed him, both in its intensity and pitch. He was a man, dammit, a New England man, and a fisherman too. He wasn't supposed to shriek and scamper off to the far side of the boat.

But Louis's heart was racing, his eyes scouring the pile of crabs all turning and sliding and clacking over each other.

Because of that thing underneath...

He told himself it was just some pale rubber. Maybe a silver net of some sort all tangled against it. Or a doll. Those silver-gray clumps, they couldn't be hair...

Could they?

Slowly, carefully, he inched his way back to the mound of scattering crabs. Damn, had he really leapt all that way?

Yes, because you know what you saw, a little part of him whispered. *Your mind understands what you're still trying to deny.*

There, beneath a mound of crabs, was a woman.

Well, part of her. Just a head and some piece of ruined torso, skin patchy and mottled with sand.

With shaking hands, he gripped the gaff, using the hook to brush crabs from the corpse. He was scared of touching her flesh, worried he might mark it or defile it. The whole thing looked gelatinous and tender. He knew he'd have to involve thc police. They'd ask questions, like, "Why are you out here?" and "What are you doing?" There'd be no way to avoid the fact that he was crabbing off-season.

Last he checked, the fine was a few hundred bucks. Hell, he didn't have that in his checking account. And today's haul wouldn't even cover the table fee at the farmers market.

Especially if people learned what his crabs had been eating.

Another brush with the gaff and the crabs fell away. He sighed, studying the remains of this woman, something hurting deep in his heart. A matte of gray hair concealed her face. Her chin glistened. Mealy skin and sallow cheeks made her age impossible to determine.

And the piece of her torso—if it could be called that at all—was an odd bulb beneath her neck. An oblong stump of sealed flesh where barnacles and algae clung to her skin, little forests of life growing from death.

Something struck him as odd about that stump. A memory of childhood action figures he'd pulled apart. The little knots where a figure's neck joined a body, allowing articulation and movement.

Christ, he wasn't looking at a person, but a mannequin of some sort. Some head with a bulbous neck that fit into a body, posable perhaps, and draped in the latest fashion. Hell, she probably came from a damn mall.

Chuckling to himself, Louis reached out with the gaff and brushed the last crab from her face. Its claw snatched at her hair, peeling back that silver matte like rotten curtains, revealing a mud-freckled face, pale and wet and quivering with life.

The woman opened her right eye.

chapter five

Louis screamed again, this time so loud it scared off the greedy gulls floating nearby and waiting for chum. He didn't hear their wings beating in the wind, nor the clatter of the gaff against the gunwale as it fell overboard. He didn't hear the slosh of the water. All he heard was the beating of his heart, a drumming so high in his throat he thought he might see the bear claws and coffee again.

Her eye. The dead woman's eye, it was open.

It was looking at him.

Beneath matted hair, her cheeks stretched and her forehead wrinkled. Indentations formed near her jawline. And her cold, blue eye rotated and scanned the small boat.

He felt... What did he feel? Trapped and repulsed. Every muscle in his body screamed to get away. From her. From the boat itself. *Don't think. Just jump overboard and swim for the shore.* He could make it perhaps. He could...

And yet, there was a compulsion growing under his skin, fishhooks dragging him toward her, closer to this shivering, shaking *thing* he'd dredged up.

This thing that was—impossibly—alive, her eye wide and imploring: *Come. Come closer...*

Louis was distantly aware that he was crawling, the crabs parting for him, pushing up against the sides of the boat in two rising mounds.

They skittered over each other and dropped into the water, *plop, plop, plop*.

Their world was below.

And his world? It receded to a dim hallway, a tunnel of damp wood and shells. All he could see was the woman's head at the far end, her eye a lighthouse, blinking and beckoning. *Closer now... Closer.*

A gurgle passed her turgid lips. Her nostrils flared. Dark tears spilled down her cheeks.

Come closer and closer...

The lump beneath her neck swelled and fluttered. Something inside pressed against milky skin. Small lungs, he realized. Like an infant taking its first breath. Yes, this was life that he'd found, impossible life that shouldn't be breathing. And yet he knew it was happening with a certainty so pure it charged his thoughts and shivered his skin. He was no longer sleepwalking through life but was now fully awake.

Then he was there, at the end of the tunnel, the end of the boat and within inches of her; he'd crawled the whole way.

He found himself unsure what to call it. She was more than a mere head and far less than a body. A quarter torso? And her skin. From the far side of the boat, her flesh looked ready to slide off with a touch. Now, so close, he saw strength within her, an inner light that warmed his skin and softened his fears. Not beauty or lust but something comforting and safe. A glowing stove on a cold, snowy night.

There was no longer the boat or the bay. No arches or sea caves whistling with winds. There was only this woman and her puckering lips.

Lips trying to form something, he realized. She was trying to speak.

"Can... Can you hear me?" His quaky voice startled him, rejuvenating his doubt. *You're in a boat, Lou. You're talking to some* thing *you've pulled up with the crabs. Think, Lou. Think.* "Ma'am, give me a sign if you understand."

Her neck muscles strained. Was that a nod? Hard to tell, but definitely a reaction. "Nod if you can hear me." Could a head nod without its torso attached? Could a neck move without most of its spine? He had to be sure. "Okay, give me a blink if—"

She blinked. Just once, but a long, slow blink as she met his gaze. Which meant her ears worked. Which meant she understood.

"Oh man. Oh sweet Jesus, this is some weird shit. Lady, what'n the hell happened to you?"

A gurgle from her throat as foam poured past her lips. Her gray tongue traced ruined teeth flecked with seaweed. With a crunch, a sea snail tumbled from her mouth.

"Help..."

It was the first word she spoke to Louis. And it was beautiful.

"Help?" he repeated. "Lady, you need some serious fucking help, that's for damn sure. Okay, we'll, uh... We'll get you back to shore and then... Well, I'll tell 'em I found you all... messed-up like, okay?"

Saying it all out loud loosened the spell that'd come over him. Suddenly, he had a plan, steps to follow, a sequence of actions one after another. She might die if he didn't act fast. But if she lived, well, he'd be the local hero. They might put him on TV. Hell, he could do the talk show circuit, stop by Maury Povich and Ricki Lake, perhaps sell the rights to this story.

"Help..."

"Yeah, I'm gonna help you, sweetie. Don't you worry." He glanced back at the motor, a few crabs still scurrying about the far side. Could she make it back to the harbor?

"Help..." Her tongue circled her lips again, eyes darting down and blinking, darting down and blinking.

"Wait... You're telling me something, aren't you?" He squatted beside her and brushed the matted hair from her face. He could see her other eye now, and it almost drove him away once again.

A starfish bloomed from the socket. Clutched like a gem in a ring, her left eye glared back, lidless and milky.

Louis choked down his fear. This poor woman, she needed him now.

And yeah, he had to admit, there was a certain beauty to her. An antique charm, dusty and dim yet stunning once cleaned and polished. "What are you telling me?"

"Help..." Her eyes flicked down to her lips, then back up to him.

Her jaw clicked as her mouth stretched open. Pink fissures split her cheeks. "Help..."

Stomach coiling, Louis watched another snail tumble from her mouth.

"You... You got them things stuck in your mouth, don't you?"

She gave him a long, slow blink. Yes.

"And, uh, you want me to get it out?"

Another long, slow blink. He could get lost in those blue-gray eyes. But he had work to do unblocking her throat. She was probably close to choking. And if she died on him, what then? How the hell would he explain any of this?

He stretched out a hand, and her mouth opened to receive it. He could see them inside, the barnacles and snails all clinging to her cheeks and blocking her air. He had to help or she'd choke.

Hooking a finger, he scraped a snail free from her cheek. He reached in for another. Something shifted deeper inside, an anemone taking up most of her tongue. He noticed her back teeth a half second too late.

They were coral and shells, a whole jagged reef.

The bite caught the meat of his finger, dug in and ground like rusty gears. The pain was so sudden, so precise, so buckling that he had to squeeze his hips to keep his bladder from emptying. With a sharp tug, he tore his finger free as ruby foam drooled from her lips. He stuffed his hand under his armpit, too scared to look at what was left. Maybe bone and half the skin if he was lucky.

"Goddammit! You... *bitch*. You bit the shit out of me."

Fury overwhelmed him, tore him backward and narrowed his perception to that dim hall. With his left hand—his *good* hand—he grabbed that head by her silvery hair and hoisted her up like Perseus with Medusa.

He flung her back into the sea.

Silence.

The cool breeze.

The sloshing water.

And Louis, chest heaving, ears ringing as the pain in his finger throbbed something fierce. He listened to the soothing click of the crabs. He let the rocking boat comfort him. Far off, shorebirds cried in the bitter bay wind.

Then he heard something else too. Yes, a wet murmur surfaced, like a radio sinking through the inky-black depths. A broadcast, just for him.

It took all of his courage to release his finger from his armpit. He knew it was ruined without even looking.

What he did not know yet, what he sensed on an instinctual level, a cellular level, was that something was making its way into his own rivers and streams. A small armada had penetrated his body's defenses, moved through torn flesh and entered his veins. There, it rode the fast currents of his circulatory system, up the veins and arteries and into his brain, dropping their own hooks into his thoughts, fusing with them and growing, growing until he could feel the sweat crawling down the back of his neck, the heat of this new kindled furnace burning within, and a screeching hiss, like those modems dialing into the internet. A furious connection in a voice too beautiful to ignore.

Please, don't leave me, she whispered. *Please, just follow my words.*

So that's what he did.

In the November wind, Louis Harding stripped off his clothes, vaulted overboard, and dove into the bitter black depths.

chapter six

The nightmares began that November.

Megan crouched among the cindering ruins of her home, scooping ankle-deep ash with a shovel as embers warmed her bare feet. She was naked but wasn't ashamed. She didn't shy away from her reflection in the smoky hall mirror. Instead, she let her arms drift out, fingertips tracing the blackened contours of these walls and rooms she ran through as a child.

First the den, where her father once studied his stock market charts, a bourbon in hand, while Phil Collins's voice filled the air.

Next the sitting room, where her mother hosted her monthly book club, chairs circling the coffee table, wine and crudités platters spread out before them.

Then the entryway, with the grandfather clock and family pictures: her father's hairline silvering and retreating, her mother's hard lines setting in, and Megan's smile shrinking from the broad, toothy laugh of elementary school to the flat line that marked her middle and high school years. There she stood at the end, robed in the crimson and gold of her boarding school's colors, her graduation cap tilted, her parents at both sides.

It was that photograph that clinched Megan's gut and whispered a cold truth: *This isn't real. Your parents neither framed nor hung such a photo.*

They died before the film was developed.

Charred floorboards crunched underfoot. Ash swirled like the season's first snow. In a smoldering corner, a power strip packed with too many plugs belched black ribbons of smoke.

But it was the door that drew Megan's eyes. Twin amber doors stood proud amidst the hazy ruin, unburned and unmarred. She drew closer, hesitating at this perfect threshold.

No such doors had been a part of her family's house.

The fire that had consumed the two-story colonial in Stonefield, Connecticut, burned so hot it ignited the meadow shared with her neighbors. Or so she was told. She never saw the damage from the inside, only the heap weeks later, bulldozed and stacked in dumpsters to be hauled off. It had occurred to her then that she was breathing the very ashes of her childhood, her home, her family.

By summer's end the kids in town had started whispering as she passed.

"Don't let her drive your car or she'll crash it and split your head open."

"Don't let her into your house or she'll burn it down while you sleep."

But not all had been burned. Not here.

There were still these impossible doors, a pair of healthy teeth amidst a mouthful of coal. Few things unsettled her more than these doors that did not belong.

And yet, drawing closer to the wood, she sensed a great schism beyond. The sounds of her childhood sleepovers—the horror movies and late-night gossip that felt so important—seeped through the cracks and the gaps.

She might find her friends down there, blankets over their faces, a scary movie painting the walls in cool VHS blue.

Or her mother, descending the stairs, a bowl of popcorn in hand. "Brought you kids a snack."

Or her father, his reading glasses high on his nose, a cordless phone in his hand. "Girls, someone said a prank call just came from this number."

So there she stood, teetering against two worlds, her hand drawn to that spotless knob.

Open the door.

She might even find a smile and some laughter. Those times before the bad grades and the boarding school. Before all the arguments and fights. Before she grew up, grew into a woman who saw only the flaws in her strict parents and wished they would just go away.

Open the door.

She might find it down there, all those moments burned and bulldozed and trucked off to yesterday's landfill to rot into the earth.

This is my gift. Now open the door.

And Megan said, "No."

Her fingers retracted. The warm ash slid beneath her feet as she stepped away. Her lips made little gasps. "No, no, no."

Because something was crawling up those stairs, going *thumpity thump thump*. Something was rising on the other side of the door. Something that dripped salt water and murmured like the sea.

And then, with a crash of breaking wood, it knocked.

Megan's world furled at its edges. The ashen beams smoothed into brick and exposed pipes. Blackened windows became clear paneled glass. And her hands no longer hovered over a knob but were now fumbling at her tangled sheets, pulling herself free from the bed. She was home, in her brick loft apartment, the afternoon cool through the industrial windows. She was safe.

And judging by the angle of the light, it was the afternoon.

Megan checked her bedside alarm clock, but no numbers flashed in the empty display. The batteries were out. Not good.

Thumpity thump thump. That was her door.

She hurried across the loft, squeezing between two paintings that stood unfinished for months. She tripped over the tarp underneath, catching herself and wiping sleep from her eyes. Then she unlocked the front door.

"Let me guess, you overslept."

Corey stood there, two coffees in hand as a disappointed sigh left his lips. He handed her a cup and stepped in.

"No," she said. "Well, maybe. The batteries went out."

There wasn't enough time to shower so she squeezed into a pair of distressed jeans and started brushing her teeth. At twenty-one, she was finally shedding the grunge look she wore in high school. Still, fashion was low on her list of priorities. She favored comfort these days.

"Ah, yes, the batteries." Corey stopped by the bed, where the alarm clock's cord was unplugged. "You know they have an invention called electricity. It comes in through the wall and travels down cables." He plugged the alarm clock in, and it blinked: *12:00*. "I've heard it can even power a microwave."

"Yeah, and it can also start fires." She passed by the bed, unplugging the alarm clock once again before sitting on her couch and starting in on her makeup. "Besides, I'd miss your wake-up calls."

"Is that what it's called when I bang on your door for ten minutes? Your landlord hates me."

"Mr. Fallson? He hates everyone. One of the perks of cheap rent."

Corey glanced at the TV, the lamps, the stereo, all unplugged. "Yes, cheap rent and the roaming packs of pit bulls."

"They're friendly if you don't look them in the eye."

While Megan quickly applied her makeup, Corey settled on a stool by her paintings, regarding the small splashes of dark colors against the empty white canvas. He ran a finger over a dry brush. "I see these are coming along. By next summer you might have another three inches."

"Hey, you can't rush inspiration."

He sipped his cold coffee. "No, you certainly cannot."

chapter seven

O'Bannon's bar was a pity project squatting at the wrong end of a strip mall in terminal decline. The drinks were cheap, the fights rare, and the last customers wouldn't shuffle out for another few hours. Megan suspected the place was a front for the mob. How many Irish people cooked perfect Italian?

Most of all, it was a decent gig for struggling students. As long as Corey poured the drinks and Megan carried them, and someone kept the drunks away from the darts, the O'Bannons didn't care what their employees did in their downtime.

Last fall, they'd all watched the O.J. trial live, Senior dozing off in the corner while Junior grumbled, "He did it. Trust me, it's in the eyes. That son of a bitch did it and got away."

Tonight, Junior was talking business with some serious men in from Queens. Which meant Megan had time to catch up on some assignments. She peeled an L7 sticker from a sheet and affixed it to the front of her Strathmore sketchbook. She sharpened her pencil and turned the pages, skimming past her professor's notes, their suggestions to try harder, that she had talent but she needed to take risks.

"You and those books," Corey said, toweling down the pint glasses and stacking them behind the bar. "You don't ever worry someone's going to take a sneak peek?"

Megan was almost done shading in the door from her dream. That amber wood. That gold knob. She said, "It's really not that exciting."

He began mixing a whiskey sour. "An artist's diary, that's like the holy grail of insider information. I could make a small fortune selling the secrets of the female mind. It'd be like Bridget James."

"Bridget *Jones*." Megan closed her sketchbook and slid it into her bag under the bar. She began collecting the bowls of half-eaten pretzels, the damp napkins. "And it's not a diary. It's more for taking inventory of my thoughts."

"Ah, that headshrinker stuff."

Wiping down the sticky bar, Megan winced. She regretted sharing her ongoing therapy with Corey. Ever since she started working at O'Bannon's, they'd built up a flirtatious banter, culminating in a series of hookups this summer and a relationship neither quite understood.

"Yeah, headshrinker stuff," she repeated and carried the whiskey sour off to table five.

Her therapy routine hadn't stopped their hookups—Corey was a good lover, after all, and nice on the eyes—but it made things occasionally awkward. Somedays, he treated her as if he was handling nitroglycerin. Sometimes, he asked how she *really* felt. Once, when they were tipsy and frisky in bed, he had asked her which personality he was inside. She laughed and bit his shoulder and cried quietly later.

Perhaps therapy made men uncomfortable. So much else about women did.

She hated that her thoughts were discordant. Or that her head sometimes felt like it would crack open. The crescent scar running from her temple, down through her eyebrow, and circling back across her cheek was a constant reminder: she had been broken and was still putting the pieces back together.

And yet, she didn't want to be treated differently. Was there some sort of happy medium? One where they could hook up without the seesaw of attraction and repulsion? A friend with benefits, like that Alanis Morissette line?

Tray empty, she made a quick lap of the bar. It was a slow Saturday at O'Bannon's, only a handful of blue-collar regulars nursing their drinks. Senior was playing cards with some Hells Angels, his cane leaning against the booth. The tip jar was thin with cash, mostly ones and a few precious fives. If she finished her duties, she could get some drawing in before they closed out. Perhaps catch up on another overdue assignment.

Or she could shoot the shit at the bar with Corey.

"Hey, I'm sorry if that came off as rude." He stacked the used ashtrays and gave her an apologetic look. "I'm an idiot. It was a dumb joke. Heck, my sister's in therapy. Doesn't make her weird or anything." Then he smiled that smile that either curled her toes or rolled her eyes. "It just makes her crazy."

She reached for her bag. "I'm going to take my fifteen."

Deee-Lite's "Groove is in the Heart" buzzed over the stereo's tinny speakers, the bouncy samples and lively lyrics a sharp contrast to the dim, half-empty bar. She was almost to the door when she spotted Old Jack alone at his regular booth, arms folded under his corduroy blazer, head resting atop them. He was passed out again.

Damn.

"Hey, Jack," she whispered. "Let's get you home, okay?"

She helped him up, his arm clutching his shoulder. Beneath a suit two decades out of fashion, she could feel the shape of the old featherweight boxer who'd taken too many hits and still tried to drink like a young man.

She swiped a pair of fives from the tip jar as they stumbled past. Old Jack's head lolled and his eyes snapped open. "Oh, Megan, sweet Megan, when will this young lad get a dance with you, love?"

He gave her a buoyant grin and made a clumsy pirouette as the song reached its chorus. She caught him and steered him toward the door. "Sorry, Jack, dancing's not in my bones."

Outside, she poured him into the cab and paid the driver with the fives from the tip jar. Old Jack was fast asleep as it drove off. She tightened her jacket against the wind off the Delaware River. Above, plump clouds threatened snow but hadn't yet followed through.

She found the old chair in the alleyway and sucked down a cigarette. She twirled her pencil and opened her sketchbook. Soon, she was lighting a new cigarette off the old one, waiting for inspiration to strike.

By the end of the second cigarette, her pencil gave the drawing vague shape. Some smoldering beams here, a charred set of stairs. Her therapist had encouraged her to focus on symbols lately, and she wondered what that meant.

Did her razor-cut hair mean she was secretly a boy? Did her chipped nail polish and safety-pinned jeans mean she no longer cared? And were her dark hoodies signs of angst and rebellion? Her parents had believed so.

But no. This was just who she was. Or who she'd become after two years of art school and a mind like a scratched record. She started on a third cigarette and added crosshatching to the burned window screen.

Art school. That had been her idea, her dream, and one that was now ending. After four semesters of mediocre grades, she'd gotten herself kicked out. But she'd stuck around Philadelphia, keeping this job at O'Bannon's and planning to re-enroll in the spring.

If only she could improve her portfolio.

And yet the pencil hesitated. Something stayed her nervous hand. "C'mon, keep drawing," she muttered.

The pencil stopped moving.

So this was her life: the bar, the sketchbook she struggled to fill, and a few friends she could count on one hand. Her advisor believed she was creatively blocked. Her therapist believed she was depressed. Her parents had never believed in such thoughts.

Discipline. Determination. Dedication before God. These were their cures so often prescribed.

Closing her eyes, she could see it now.

Her father, handing her the boarding school pamphlet. "I went there myself. You'd be a legacy student."

Her mother, crying as the car pulled away from the campus.

Her suitcases, sitting in the dorm room as she took in the silence.

The Tenbury School. Why the hell had that popped into her head?

She didn't realize she was crying until the tear dampened the paper. Damn, that was a half-decent sketch. She crumpled the ruined drawing and dropped it in the dumpster.

Then she stopped in her tracks.

It took her brain a slow beat to recognize the man standing at the end of the alley. Not because she didn't know his face, but because she last saw him two years and several hundred miles away. The center-parted hair, the broad shoulders of a lacrosse player. Perhaps it was the clouds and the lighting, but his freckles had faded, leaving him with a pale hue.

But it was the hands and the posture that struck her as odd. Adam never used to stuff his hands in his pockets; he could hardly keep them off her in high school. Adam never used to slouch.

"Hey, Meg. They said you'd be out here." He gestured back to the bar. "So, it's sure been a while, hasn't it?"

She didn't say the first word she thought of. Nor the next half dozen. She filtered through her emotions. First the fury, all those letters she'd written and sent without a response. All the long-distance calls. She'd even set him up with a Lycos account and paid for three months of service. He never replied, claiming email was too complicated for him.

Which was a bullshit excuse. They'd both taken a computer course their senior year.

Now here he stood, yesterday's specter, his tired face a reflection of her own.

"Adam Verhooven," she said, the nostalgia tugging at her lips. "What the hell are you doing in Philly?"

His smile matched her own, a thing of shared history. "Megan Monroe. Well, I came to see you."

chapter eight

Megan dipped into O'Bannon's, spotting Junior by the bar, telling jokes to a pair of tired strippers. His eyes were fighting a battle not to look down at their chests.

"I'm taking my break," she called out from the door.

Junior's face scrunched in confusion. "I thought you just did."

"That was a smoke break. I'm hungry."

"You fucking kids. You want a break? Fine, you're fired. Is that enough time?"

"Thanks, Junior." She gave him a wink.

Corey grinned; he knew Junior's routine. But he didn't know Adam, and his grin faded. Was that a flash of something nervous in Corey's eyes? Damn, she thought, maybe he was starting to catch feelings. She'd have to dial it back.

Adam followed her across the parking lot to a Friendly's where the host knew her and gave her a discount. Despite the weather, she had a sweet tooth and ordered a sundae with their coffee. When the mugs came, Adam dumped in creamer and three packets of sugar. His hands didn't stop shaking.

"Look, before anything else, I just want to say that I'm sorry." He tilted the mug back and drained a quarter of the cup. "I let you drift away. That wasn't right."

"You 'let me drift away'?" Her toes curled and her jaw tightened.

"What, like we were a pair of boats tied together? Jesus, only you could make it sound mutual."

His faltering gaze emboldened her, unearthing frustrations she'd buried and forgotten. The scar on her forehead throbbed. Some days it actually pulsed like a vein. And just like that, all her goodwill was gone.

"Adam, you didn't let me drift away. It wasn't like, 'Oops, where'd she go?' You flat out cut cord, zero effort, no contact."

She could see her words landing like bee stings, each one bringing a twitch to his cheek and a wince to his eyes. He kept his head low, nodding. And somehow that meek look spiked her anger.

She continued, "And what was it, anyway? Like, was it the distance? Did you meet someone else? 'Cause you never told me. Or maybe you just never told me the truth."

"The truth." He chuckled.

"Yeah, that thing people share with each other."

"The truth is... It's complicated."

"Only if you make it."

He didn't answer for some time, so she let the silence linger. Two years of pent-up frustration and it had all poured forth. All those weekends spent riding the bus to Providence and back, failing her classes and trying to save their relationship. She had done everything to make it work after high school. Sure, there had been boyfriends after him, even ones she had loved. But a *first* love? Well, nothing ever felt as intense. Nothing ever would.

Where was the confident young man who danced at the formal? The all-star lacrosse player? The captain of the rifle club? Whoever this Adam was before her, something had weakened him, worn him down.

Then his eyes flicked up to her face. No, she realized, to her scar.

"The truth is, it was hard to see you," he said. "After the fire, the accident, that whole rotten summer. You were... different. Scattered and unfocused."

She swallowed. "Brain damage tends to do that."

"I'm not sure I can apologize enough for leaving."

"That's one way to keep from trying." She crisscrossed her straw's wrapper. Over the years she had armored herself with a disdain for the openly joyful. She made it a habit to never smile for a photo. She shrugged often and echoed Bart Simpson's "whatever." If she wasn't outwardly happy, she could never be hurt.

At least, that was what she told herself.

"Hey." He reached out and touched her wrist. "I'm really sorry."

And that was it. Three little words, so simple they were almost silly to her ears. Why had she given them so much weight?

"So, how's Brown?" she asked. "Did they let you into the Skull and Bones yet?"

"There's no Skull and Bones at Brown," he said with a sad smile. "Or maybe there is. I don't know. I never really got into the Greek thing while I was there."

She tilted her head. "While you were there?"

He stirred his coffee. Someone at the next booth over lit up a cigarette. Megan considered bumming one but decided to wait until after the sundae. God, she needed the sugar.

"I dropped out over the summer." Adam leaned in. "Actually, no, that's not true. I got expelled last spring. I didn't tell my parents until the summer. Figured maybe I'd get back in on appeal, but that didn't work out."

"I'm sure the girls' volleyball team is really bummed."

It was a cheap shot, one she regretted the moment it left her lips. Dammit, why couldn't she just be mad and move on? Why was this bottled anger turning into pity and toxic nostalgia?

"Sorry," she said. "I got kicked out too."

He scoffed. "Out of PhilArts? No shit?"

"No shit."

"Drugs?"

She could feel her armor cracking. "Grades."

"Grades? For real?"

"Okay, first off, art school is hard work. My parents didn't give me a trust fund and a legacy at Brown. I've got a full-time course load and a full-time job. You try that."

He held out his hands apologetically, denim jacket all floppy. "No, I'm... I'm sorry. What I meant was that you were always an A student. I'm just surprised, that's all."

"Yeah, well, it's like you said: I was scattered and unfocused." She put a little too much salt in her words. "Besides, people change."

He studied his mug. "Yeah, people change."

The waitress brought Megan's sundae, which she promptly dug into. She might have offered Adam a bite but she was hungry and she couldn't afford a full meal, even with the discount. Besides, she had to get back, and this trip down memory lane was giving her a dissonant anxiety.

"Meg, I need to ask you something." The vinyl booth groaned as he scooted closer.

"Ah, there it is." She pointed a chocolaty spoon at him. "So what, you drove all the way out here to open old wounds?"

"Actually, it was my aunt's funeral in Lancaster. Figured I'd stop by."

"I'm sorry to hear that." Another chink in her armor. "Still driving the Grand Cherokee?"

"I've got a 4Runner now."

"Yeah, of course you do."

He sighed and placed his hands flat on the table. Had his fingernails always been bitten that close? Some of them looked almost raw. No, she remembered those fingers and how they once knew her skin.

"Look, Meg, I want you to know that I really am sorry."

"Yeah, Adam, and I want you to know I'm really over it."

"I don't blame you. I was an asshole. Worse, I was a coward."

The armor was softening. Maybe it was the sugar. Or maybe it was the fact that she had been trying to hurt him, and yet all she was doing was showing him how much she still hurt.

"You were the last person I thought I'd see this evening," she said. "But it's nice to see you, Adam."

Something flickered in his eyes. His posture rose. He didn't smile, not outwardly, but there was the shadow of the boy she'd kissed beneath the fall trees, the boy she'd danced with at winter formal, the boy she'd snuck out of her dorm to meet in the spring woods and fool around with.

"It's nice to see you too, Meg."

It was a curious thing, this deflation. As if they were back in the senior lounge, the crack of ping-pong games in the background as they ate ice cream sandwiches and studied for the SATs. As they planned their futures together.

She laid down her spoon. "You said you needed to ask me something. So, what is it?"

He hesitated, smiling and shaking his head. "It's going to sound silly, but..." He turned, making sure the waitress was out of earshot and the table beside them had cleared out. "Have you been having any strange dreams?"

chapter nine

Adam knew she was lying.

He told her about his recurring dream but went light on the details. Like the fact that each dream started with them making love and ended with her as a corpse. And that in each dream something wet always squeezed the back of his neck.

But she listened, her spoon reducing the sundae bite by bite. It wasn't often your ex had started dreaming about you. Or if it was, he suspected it wasn't healthy.

"So, we've been hooking up in your dreams." She pushed the empty sundae bowl away. "And you drove out here to tell me. Any other old feelings you want to stir up? Maybe go over our biggest fights?"

"I'm not..." He squeezed his neck as the tension headache formed. "I'm just wondering if you've been having any weird dreams."

She cleared her throat. "Well, if you're asking if I'm getting laid in my sleep, you'll have to use your imagination."

He realized he was staring at her, studying her intently. "No, that's not it. It's more like a feeling." He cast another glance around the diner. All those ears potentially listening. All those eyes that could watch. "I don't know how to describe it."

"You're an English major, Adam. Try it," she said, then corrected herself. "*Were* an English major."

He held his tongue and considered it. Recently, he'd read that women were an average of seven years more emotionally mature than men of a similar age. It tracked with his experiences at Brown. So he took a risk and told her.

About the body in his bed, hers yet something else too.

About when he slid inside, he felt connected to something *other*.

And about how certain songs always flashed through his mind before his eyes opened.

He could tell he was losing her.

She shook her head and said no, she didn't remember her dreams, and if she did, they meant nothing. He stole a few glances at her scar, pleased that it was starting to match her skin tone. He liked the idea of new tissue healing old wounds. He hoped it was the same with her heart.

It wasn't fair what she'd been through. What he'd done.

"You're sure you haven't had any odd thoughts?" he asked, pushing the question.

"Let's rewind. I was in a coma for two weeks. My parents died in a house fire I can't remember. I'm an artist. I have a thousand odd thoughts every day. But you asked about dreams."

"You're right. I did." Another sip of his coffee. "But you're doing okay?"

She watched her crinkled straw slowly unfold. "Yeah, sure. Being a barback and taking junior college courses to revive my GPA is just where I wanted to be. Oh, you remember my grandmother, right?"

"Yeah, how is she?"

"I wouldn't know 'cause she hasn't talked to me since the fire. Which she blames me for. Which, of course, was probably my fault since it began in my room. So yeah, that's a fun one playing on the mental tape deck." She opened her chain wallet and pulled out some cash. "Look, I've gotta get back to work."

He tried to pay but she insisted. In the end, she covered the food and he left a nice tip. Near the register, she fed the cigarette vending machine some quarters and fished out a pack of Parliament Lights.

He said, "You know, I could never figure out how you stayed so skinny with what you eat."

"What do you mean?"

"The sundaes." He was trying to be affable and friendly but sensed she read it as rude. "You used to eat them by the dozen and you still look great."

She glanced back at the table, as if his observation unsettled her. "That's funny. I haven't had one in years."

They walked across the strip mall parking lot and back to the bar. Despite Philadelphia's history, Adam found a latent misery etched into the bricks of the vacant row houses, the graveled lots with their rusty jalopies and Bill Clinton-stickered fenders. Even the trees here seemed defeated.

They said their goodbyes outside O'Bannon's, a handshake turning into an awkward hug. Adam wasn't sure if he initiated it or not. God, why did he gum up around her? She walked inside, waving to the bartender and a few patrons.

And like that, she was gone. A reminder of all the good he had broken.

Preferring not to entrust his 4Runner to a grotty lot, Adam had parked in front of a Blockbuster Video where posters for *Independence Day* promised alien destruction. He had mixed feelings about the past half hour, mostly because of the lies he'd mixed in with his truths. There was no funeral in Lancaster, no deceased aunt. And the bar, he'd been waiting outside for a few hours, working up the courage. Yes, he knew how creepy it sounded, but it wasn't like that.

If he was wrong about this feeling, well, he might be losing his mind.

And if he was right? He wasn't sure what it meant. Only that he was in danger. She was as well.

Maybe they all were.

But she'd lied too, hadn't she? It had been a few years, but he remembered her tell. She fidgeted whenever she was avoiding the truth.

And she'd been playing with her straw the whole meal.

His other major lie, he supposed, was a lie of omission. He said his dreams had shaken him, scared him so much he needed to look her up.

He wasn't alone.

Stopping at the payphone outside the Blockbuster, he pulled out his address book and flipped to the ABC section. His thumb slid down the list, stopping at *Chang, Chunhee*, and several scratched-off long-distance numbers. He dropped in a few quarters, dialed, and then held his breath.

Megan wasn't the only one still angry at him.

chapter ten

In the mint-blue halls of Kappa Alpha Theta, a Pepto Bismol-pink phone rang a dozen times before a hand finally picked it up. That hand was Cindy Simon's, a sophomore hurrying between the showers and her room, eager to join the festivities along fraternity row. This was her first term in the house, and as a spring pledge, she was the phone bitch for the floor. If the older sisters saw her passing it up, she could get another demerit. She already had one for sleeping through the house meeting last week.

Cindy could tell it was a man before he spoke. There was the hum of a busy street. Guys often called from payphones after dark. Women usually waited until they were home.

"I'm sorry, who?" she asked after the caller said the name. It was probably the wrong number.

"Chun-*hee*." The caller repeated it louder as if she didn't understand. "Chunhee Chang. Tell her it's Adam from Tenbury."

"Okay, I'm like ninety-nine percent sure there's about zero people here named Chun-li or whatever, so... wrong number."

She was about to hang up when he said, "She's... Is there a Chinese girl in your house?"

Was it June? One of the juniors who had been friendly during rush but turned total bitch during pledge. Now that Cindy was in the house and paying dues, June hardly regarded her. Just another hot-shit upperclassman, heading off to the bars with her legal ID. Always acting like it was a huge burden to grab a bottle of Midori or Goldschlägger, no matter how much Cindy offered to pay.

She could hang up, she supposed. Pretend the connection was bad. But the caller sounded older as well, so he'd probably redial. Damn, she was still shivering and wet.

"Okay, Adam from Tansborough, give me a sec."

"Tenbury—"

It took her a few minutes to find the one Asian girl in the house, upstairs in the treasurer's study, a highlighter in hand and an accounting textbook before her. The CD player belted out No Mercy's "Where Do You Go," June's head bobbing to the synths and Latin guitar. Cindy liked that song and wondered if she could tape it. She'd read a Dale Carnegie book that said asking for favors made others like you.

She forgot all that when June turned and shouted, "What the fuck? You scared the hell out of me."

"Sorry, but I think there's a phone call for you."

June regarded her as if this news was confusing, those thin eyebrows rising. "Okay, so? Hello, who's the caller?"

"A guy. I don't know."

"Wow, that really narrows it down," June said. "Useless."

"Wait, it's Alex or Adam or... Is your real name Chunhee?"

June blanched. "Where'd you hear that?"

"He asked for Chunhee. He kind of, like, described you. I wasn't sure if it's a prank call or—"

"Just... Never mind. I'll get it."

While June paused her CD, Cindy stole a glance around the room. Sorority leadership all got third-floor singles, and she realized she'd never seen one before. It was larger than she expected. Plenty of room on the walls for posters of Tom Petty and the Beastie Boys. Plenty of floorspace for beanbag chairs. Lucky girl, she even had a TV-VCR combo. But June's view was worse than Cindy's, just the trees and a rusty fire escape barely clinging to the brick.

Shivering, Cindy followed June downstairs, retrieving the toiletry basket she'd left by the phone. "I think Chunhee's a beautiful name," she said. "It's super unique."

Again, June studied her for just a second longer, and Cindy hoped this might be it; she might be breaking through and making a friend.

Then June's brown eyes hardened and she said, "If I wanted your opinion, I'd ask for it."

And that was that.

She shuffled down the hall to the Pepto-pink phone, and Cindy went back to her triple, where her roommates were probably pre-partying before heading out.

She paused at her door. She didn't mean to eavesdrop, not intentionally, but there was something odd in June's posture as she answered the phone. She gathered the cord and dragged it around the corner to the nook by the window. Occasionally, she waved her hand as if lecturing someone. And Chunhee, was that her old name? The sorority composite always listed her as June.

"Okay, so what? You think she's lying?" June was trying to whisper but was just speaking deeper. "I don't know, maybe she's still mental. Who fucking cares?"

Cindy knew she should give June some privacy, but hell, she was curious so she lingered. She could see June's reflection in the window, fingers curling the phone cord, tighter and tighter.

"Yeah, as if!" June said. "And that's my point. You're making a big deal out of nothing."

Another pause. The last of the shower dripped down Cindy's neck and beaded between her robe and her shoulders.

June sighed. "Look, I don't know what it was, okay? But you tripping out over some dream, maybe that just made me nervous. Like it's contagious or something."

Cindy considered doubling back to the bathroom to pretend she'd left something behind. Yet she stood there, frozen. June had been quite rude, hadn't she? But maybe there was more to her. Cindy hoped so.

Or maybe she was just a bitch.

"Yes, Adam, I'm sure. I'm absolutely sure, okay? The rest of us, we've moved on. All except you. So get a clue and keep it together. I dunno, act like you're normal or something. In fact, don't call me again."

There was a clack of the handset hitting the switch hook a little too hard, then the clink of the bell. Cindy hurried to her room, surprised to discover that her roommates were already gone and a note was taped to the mirror: *Grabbing snacks at the student union, C U at Omega.*

Damn, she always hated heading out solo. Yes, she knew she was pretty—or rather, she was cute and petite—and guys always seemed compelled to help her. Still, whenever she arrived alone, she felt like her legs were too short and her arms dangled too long.

She was toweling off when a knock echoed out. If that was June, had she caught her listening in? Maybe. And if so, was there a code of conduct against it? Probably. There were codes against everything.

She opened the door to find June there, just as expected. What confused her was the softness in June's eyes. "Hey. Candy, right?"

"Cindy," she said. So much for tight sisterhood. "What's up?"

June nodded. "Back there, I was a bit of a thundercunt, wasn't I?"

Cindy blinked. Was this another trick? Like the final day of pledge month, when she was told she didn't make it. When she was sent crying from the house to do the dawn walk of shame. Then, when she found the whole sorority hiding in the bushes, giggling and holding up her new jacket with her letters and nickname, an official sister of Kappa Alpha Theta.

She said, "Maybe?"

"No, definitely. That was rude of me and I'm sorry." June's eyes scoured Cindy's messy room. "You going to the Turkey Trot parties?"

Cindy responded a bit too eagerly. "We're starting at Omega and working our way down the row."

June nodded as if that plan made sense. "You're skipping SAE, right?"

Cindy had heard the rumors about things slipped into red plastic cups and some bros who got a little too rough. "Yeah, totally skipping."

"Good. They're scrubs." June flashed a smile that wiped the bitterness away. "Let's walk over together, okay? I'll introduce you to a few of the guys."

"Really? That'd be great."

June glanced at Cindy's bed, where three separate blouses and tops were laid out. She pointed to the one on the left. "Wear the crop top. You've got the stomach for it. But definitely leave the jacket."

"It's kind of cold out."

"Oh it's freezing, for sure. But that gives you an excuse to borrow some cute guy's jacket."

It was Cindy's turn to nod and smile, and she did so, feeling both self-conscious and excited. She had so much to learn from her big sister.

She never noticed that June's knees were shaking.

chapter eleven

Louis Harding lived in a nine-hundred-square-foot prefab at the southern edge of the economically stagnant Marshfield Port. His neighbor's dog Beatrice was barking when he pulled up, shivering and near hypothermic. He gave the dog a dismissive wave, but that scruffy mutt just kept growling and yapping from the other side of the chain link.

It took him two tries to unlock the trunk of his Ford Taurus. His right hand was swaddled in so much torn T-shirt and duct tape it looked like a boxing glove. He didn't dare look underneath. And his left hand, well, he'd dived into the depths, grabbing that damn head with it before swimming back up. Now most of his fingers were numb.

He had considered stopping off at the doctor, but then something curious had occurred: a slight buzzing at the base of his neck, and a tingling, like a great sneeze teasing his eyes. Parts of the drive felt so distant. And then he was here.

Louis studied the boat bag in his trunk, its Velcro straps and shifting contents inside. Had any of this really happened? Had he really found that *thing* out in the cove?

A warm wind blew through the trees, rattling the dead leaves and settling around him. A buzzing grew behind him, a radio between stations. Here it came, that same voice he'd heard on the boat, the one that guided him overboard and down into the water.

Quick, she whispered. *Close the trunk and take us inside. We need to feed.*

So he hoisted the boat bag and started up the old stairs.

Objectively, Louis knew that the head in his bag posed numerous problems. To start with, it was alive and it damn well shouldn't be. Nothing could hold its breath for so long. And what'n the hell was that thing under her neck? Some sort of sack for her organs? Were those gills he saw there, all opening and closing? And her little webbed hands, so small and withdrawn they resembled twigs. Was she some fucking mermaid? And that didn't begin to explain how she could whisper without moving her lips.

A broadcast for an audience of one.

A special audience, she whispered. *Now hurry, Louis. Up the steps and onto your porch. Go, now. Take us inside.*

The whole thing gave him the creeps.

And yet, he felt compelled to help her. He'd never seen anything sadder and more beautiful than that head sunk in the shadowy depths. Like finding the biggest, blackest pearl of them all.

Louis, hurry. Hurry please. Open the door and help us warm up.

Inside, he unlaced his boots and stripped off his damp clothes. He locked the door behind him. He wasn't expecting company—he only had a few friends, and none of them close—yet he needed a moment to process this discovery. He didn't want his ex-wife barging in.

He placed the bag in the center of the living room, where the thing inside was stirring. He could see her pressing up against the PVC tarpaulin sides, moving as best as she could. He'd have to open it soon, but first he went to the bathroom to check on his finger.

No, let us out now. Louis, listen to me.

There was a splice in his thoughts. He found himself halfway back to the bag before he could stop, turn around, and tend to his wound. Why the hell wasn't he driving to the hospital?

Because we don't need medicine. We need each other.

"No, no, I *do* need a doctor," he said, as much to himself as the errant murmur bouncing inside his skull. "I think you degloved my finger. I'll probably lose it."

As he spoke, he took several steps. Not toward the bathroom where his first aid kit was, but back to the center of the living room.

Where the bag was now shaking and scooting.

He was halfway done unzipping it when his mind revolted, flashing bright neon letters in front of his eyes: *Stop. Call the police. You have one chance to tell them right now. No one will care about illegal crab pots when they see what you found. You'll make the five o'clock news.*

Warm fingers caressed the back of his neck. He turned but no one was there. Of course not. This was his home, had been for decades. These days the only touch his skin knew was his own.

We are hungry and tired. Our warmth is fading away. Please, Louis. Please. Help us recover, and we'll take care of your finger.

"Awww, shoot." Louis could see it all receding into the fog of his mind: his face in the newspapers, the interviews on cable, the award for his bravery in saving this... well, whatever she was.

Then that future was gone, consumed by her sweet, rattling voice. He unzipped the bag and tilted it over, spilling the thing onto the floor. He covered his nose and tried not to vomit.

Outdoors, in the cool light of the cove, the woman's head and the fleshy bulb beneath had been suffused with watery life, skin like the meat of a fish. Here, inside and lit from new angles, he saw more than he wished. His mind absorbed it in pieces, assembling each one at a time.

The rockweed and red dulse speckling her hair.

A few leeches falling from her forehead.

And the starfish he'd seen earlier, it was blooming out from her left eye socket, like it lived inside and was trying to escape.

The sea had grown through her. Or maybe, he sensed, she'd grown into the sea. Whatever it was, it didn't make a lick of damn sense.

"God almighty," he said. "What in the hell happened to you, missus?"

She made a wet choking sound, her jaw clicking as if trying to set itself back into the socket. "Don't know... Can't remember." Her throat stretched, the skin so thin he could see something like vocal cords beneath it, weak and exhausted.

Tucked in a fold of gray flesh, metal glinted.

A gold chain.

She was choking, he realized. The necklace was restricting her air.

He found a pair of wire cutters in the garage and hurried back. Cautiously, he parted her folded skin, nose wrinkling at the lichen. There it was, a gold necklace dug tight as if she'd grown around it.

Steadying his damaged finger, he clipped through the soft chain, unthreading it from the fold. "All right, lady, maybe that'll help."

No words left her lips, just a wet straining. Yet he heard her speak into his heart and into his mind. One word with three syllables. Her name, he realized.

Oksana.

It was the most beautiful name he'd ever heard.

chapter twelve

Oksana was hungry, she told him. She was weak and she needed to feed. She didn't speak. Not with her vocal cords or lips, but in buzzing whispers that slid through his thoughts, like roots probing the rocks and soil of his mind. It was a wholly strange sensation, one he was aware of yet regarded at a subconscious level, no different than discovering a new wrinkle on his skin, a new gray hair among many.

Oksana was starving, she said, so he went to the kitchen. He found some leftover pizza, a can of tuna he'd mixed with mayonnaise and bell peppers. He pulled some Lunchables from the back, remnants from when his nephew stayed with him last summer. He was certain they were so packed with preservatives they never expired.

He grabbed a paper plate but realized it was too casual. A guest should eat only off the best. He found his Newcor dinnerware and silverware from the cupboard. He stacked the stoneware plate with left-overs and added a Hostess cupcake for dessert. He cracked open a Mr. Pibb.

When carried out together, the meal struck him as so pathetic that he hesitated. Here he was, a middle-aged man with his best years behind him, presenting an offering unworthy of what he'd discovered.

Eat... Food... Tired...

"How do you want me to do this?" he asked. The head had fallen to her right side. "Should I just put it in front of you, or...?"

Feed me.

So that was what he did.

First, he tried to prop the head so it was upright, but the bulb beneath the neck looked tender and soft. He was worried it might pop. He knew that babies had a soft spot on their head where the bone hadn't fused. Once, when he'd first held his new nephew, he'd felt a shameful compulsion to find that spongy skin and press it with his thumbs.

He didn't feel that now. This compulsion was different, tender. Hearing her voice was like the world had let him in on a secret.

Let them both in, together.

The solution was simple. He leaned her head and the fleshy bulb beneath it at a slant against the boat bag. He placed a few dogeared Dean Koontz novels against her ears to keep her upright. All the while she studied him, that healthy blue eye blinking and curious, the gray eye fused with the starfish, always open, always glaring.

"So, I'm just, uh... Well, ma'am, I'm just gonna feed you now."

Oksana. My name is Oksana.

"Okay, Oksana." The name tasted sweet on his tongue, like blackberries from his grandmother's garden. "Well, here's your food."

He started with the tuna a la bell pepper he'd made last night while watching Jerry Springer. He added extra salt and pepper. He brought the spoon to her mouth. When her lips stretched to receive it, the stench moistened his eyes and twisted his gut. He stifled another gag with the back of his forearm, eyeing those teeth of coral and shells.

She bit down, scraping against metal. A weak gulp, then a grimace, and she spat it back up.

"Okay, let's try something else."

Next was the hunk of reheated pizza he'd cut into pieces. Again, her teeth clattered against metal. She chewed. She swallowed. Then she spat it up.

After that came some crackers and cheese and whatever meat was in the Lunchables. None of it stayed down. Her eyes fluttered. She was losing color.

"I'm sorry. I don't know what else to give you." It occurred to him he was apologizing to a head found in a crab pot. He would have laughed, but the needles in his finger were making him woozy.

Her face strained, jaw tensing as those vocal cords vibrated beneath thin skin. The fleshy bulb rose. Was she taking a breath? Was she trying to speak?

"Life," she murmured.

"What... What is it?"

"Life."

Her gaze shifted from his eyes to the spoon in his hand. No, he realized. To that wounded finger seeping crimson through the cloth.

"Life," she repeated. "Give... Life."

He scooted back, heart racing. She wanted his finger. That bite she'd taken on the boat, that must have jumpstarted something. Now she was hungry for more.

"No, no, no. I don't think that's a good idea. I, uh... Just no."

He tried another spoonful of tuna, but her lips sealed tight and her neck twisted to the right. All the while her stare pierced him, that one beautiful eye blinking, the other glaring from the starfish's grasp.

This was wrong. All of it, wrong. He needed fresh air.

He was halfway to the door when his nape tightened and sweat beaded his back. Her alto whispers bore into his thoughts, staggering him. He gripped his old La-Z-Boy to steady the world.

YOU GET BACK OVER HERE AND TAKE YOUR SACRAMENT. LOUIS. LOUIS JEREMIAH HARDING, YOU LISTEN TO ME.

That was his grandmother here, behind him. The Estée Lauder perfume she lathered herself in every Sunday filled his raw nostrils. Wrinkled fingers seized his wrist. The living room was no longer his but his grandmother's. Her collectible plates lined the walls.

DON'T YOU DARE BRING YOUR FILTHY BONES BACK TO MY HOUSE. YOU TURN AROUND, LOUIS. YOU TAKE YOUR SACRAMENT AND LET HIM INTO YOUR HEART.

No. He didn't want to turn around. He did not want to take anything from Father Harris with his halitosis and greedy fingers. That wolf who lectured his flock about sin and pawed at young flesh. That lecher with the secrets he made Louis keep.

Yet Louis knew Father Harris was dead. He'd pissed on that old pederast's grave.

His grandmother's voice merged with Father Harris's and Oksana's, sharp blades sliding through his soft thoughts, stiffening every cell in his body and clamping his eyes. He was no longer an adult on the wrong side of fifty. He was eleven, in this very room, a knot in his throat as he stuttered to explain why he wasn't comfortable at church.

WITHOUT HIS GRACE IN YOUR HEART, YOU'RE A VAGRANT TO HEAVEN. ANOTHER NOTHING SPAT FROM A LONG LINE OF NOBODIES. YOU GO TO HIM, LOUIS. YOU LET HIM INTO YOUR HEART AND BE GRATEFUL.

And then it was all gone, his grandmother's firm grip and Father Harris's soft touch. He was here, alone in *his* house. He felt nothing on his skin, only his own fingers digging into the La-Z-Boy's fabric.

Then came her soft whisper.

Turn around, Oksana said. *Come back, Louis. It can all go away. We can get rid of it together. You won't ever be afraid.*

She knew. Somehow, she'd rummaged through his old thoughts and found a few rotten sins at his core. He braced himself against the La-Z-Boy. Her voice was a warm beacon in the storm of his shame. That fireplace, forever safe and inviting.

Yes, he turned around. Yes, he unraveled the bandaged finger. Not *his* bandaged finger, because he knew he needed to be distant now, to take this new sacrament, or to give it, perhaps. Flesh of his flesh, blood of his blood. And yes, he placed his ruined finger into her waiting mouth.

He screamed when she bit down. He didn't stop screaming until her lips reached his knuckle.

chapter thirteen

On Wednesday, after her biweekly therapy appointment, Megan descended into the subway, riding toward Broad Street's Avenue of the Arts. She kept a book in her hands and her portfolio snug between her knees. She tried to ignore the old woman resting her head against her shoulder. Every few minutes the train rattled, rousing the old woman, who apologized in Spanish. Thirty seconds later, her head was back, warm against Megan.

Careful not to disturb her, Megan unzipped and double-checked her portfolio. Here it was, her overdue sketches and designs, her academic plan and application for readmission. Six months of work labeled and readied for the committee. She had so much riding on this afternoon.

And yet that same doubt scratched at her thoughts.

You're a fake; you're a fraud. Another art poser, slides in your pocket and a broken brain in your skull.

With a rumble, the train left the station and entered the tunnel. A moment later, she felt deceleration and the squealing of brakes. Passengers leaned as the train lurched to a halt. The lights blinked, on off, on off.

"Uh, ladies and gentlemen, your safety is our priority," the conductor's voice buzzed overhead. "We're giving the train ahead some extra space. We'll get moving again here shortly."

Megan returned to her book, a library copy of *Into the Wild*. Before her accident, reading was one of her joys. After, it had become a chore, her focus fleeting, her interest scattered. She often found herself rereading entire chapters with little memory of what happened. It didn't help that she struggled to relate to the main character, Christopher McCandless, a nomadic young man who wandered his way up to Alaska and died in a bus.

McCandless had a family. She had fractured recollections and regrets.

McCandless had a college fund. Megan had student debt.

But this was required reading next semester, so she flipped to the photo section to refresh her attention. Funny, she thought. McCandless must have attended her boarding school. That was the Tenbury School's wrought-iron gate.

Another blink of the lights and the scratching black shadows. The car rumbled and stopped.

No, that wasn't McCandless smiling back from this black and white photo before her.

This was Chunhee Chang, Megan's old friend.

Her cap and gown glimmered oily on the page. Her lips were upturned in a smirk. She was giving the school's sign the middle finger, a graduation tradition seniors called the Final Goodbye. Megan couldn't remember if she'd done it herself but suspected she had.

Chunhee... That shy, quiet girl. They'd befriended each other their freshman year when they'd been partnered on the track team. But this didn't make any sense.

A hiss of static as the driver mumbled another apology. The connecting car door rattled open and shut. Stomach knotting, Megan turned the page, finger tracing the border of another impossible photo.

Here stood a long shelf of books she knew well, the school library. There was Chunhee and Adam, papers scattered at the table after hours of study hall. Megan had tutored her roommate in English while the other girl taught her biology. They'd giggled at anatomical parts in hushed voices.

Her roommate. What was that curious girl's name?

Olivia... No, Octavia perhaps.

Someone clattered and clacked down the dark aisle, a sour rot filling the car. Megan did her best to ignore it, shifting so her book got some dim light from the bulbs in the tunnel. Now she found herself looking at a full-color picture that tightened her stomach.

At the edge of a bathroom sat a once-white tub now dripping crimson. A shower curtain hung spattered with rubies. Red ribbons oozed onto the tiles. Salty iron coated her tongue as the words *HUNGRY* and *LIFE* flashed deep in her mind.

No, not now. Not today. She didn't have time for a panic attack or whatever else her wounded mind had decided to serve up. She had her hearing in an hour. She pressed her knees tight against her portfolio.

Turning the page, she found the image repeating. Another turn, and there it was again: the same photo of some unknown slaughter. The word *FEED* sliced through her mind.

Except it wasn't *exactly* the same photo. No, something had changed. She had to put the book to her face just to find it.

There, at the edge of the tub, where the curtain met porcelain, three fingers clutched the rim. No, those weren't fingers, she realized. Not quite.

They were the arms of a starfish.

And they were wriggling.

"Spare some change?"

Megan didn't know what happened first: the filthy fingers that groped at her book or the scream that flew from her lips. She gave a sharp kick and felt her Chuck Taylors connect with something soft.

There was a groan, low and muffled, followed by the clacking of wheels and the clattering of cans. A tin cup glistened, spilling coins. Someone was shouting now, a torso wriggling and twisting, its hands slapping about. A makeshift dolly rolled down the train car.

"Aw, Christ, lady. The hell is wrong with you?"

The man's voice was raspy, one that spoke of late-stage cancer; his eyes gleamed with betrayal. Megan was horrified to discover she had kicked a vagrant with no legs and one arm. A cardboard sign hung by twine from his neck: *WOUNDED VET NEED HELP GOD BLESS.*

"Ah Jesus, lady. Ah God almighty."

The passengers were staring now, alternating between Megan and the homeless man but not wanting to touch him. Wormlike, he wriggled onto his chest, inching forward and cursing. He used his one arm to push himself upright.

She had to do something. He was a human and deserved dignity. She reached out to hoist him, but he batted her hands away. "Don't touch me. Don't."

She scooped up the coins and dropped them into his cup. Another passenger returned the dolly. Megan apologized but he waved her off, using the handrail to hoist himself onto the dolly. His wheels squeaked as he rolled down the car.

She pinched her temples and slunk into her seat.

What the hell was wrong with her? Had she really just done that? The train came to a stop and the speaker mumbled her station. She grabbed her book and exited as quick as she could.

She did not grab her portfolio.

chapter fourteen

It wasn't the worst day of her life, but it was in the top five. And the committee hadn't even made their assessment yet.

Earlier, she had shed tears of frustration while the station agent took down her phone number. He promised to call if someone turned in her portfolio. Or if the cleaning crews found it at the end of the night. Still, she had her slides from the spring semester, half-finished projects now filling the pull-down screen.

"Ms. Monroe, is everything all right?"

Megan blinked, and the world resolved itself, shadows and light sliding off hazy surfaces. Here was the conference table before her, and the appeals committee seated around it. The assistant dean of admissions, the chair of the department, her advisor, and the ombudsman. The slide projector fan hummed as they waited.

But that portfolio, damn. She'd stayed up all night to add some new content. Perhaps that explained it; she was exhausted and crashing. Yes, it had to. It must.

"I'm sorry," she said. "It's been a weird kind of... time."

"Ms. Monroe," her advisor repeated. "Please, take a seat for a moment. We'll get some water. Stephanie?"

The student assistant scurried from the conference room. Megan considered her advisor, his corduroy jacket, his dockers rolled up at the cuffs. He looked like a nervous ferret, she thought. Odd, how the appeals committee were all staring at her.

Like she'd said something displeasing.

She said, "I'm so sorry. I lost my train of thought for a moment. Where was I?"

The members regarded each other nervously, deferring to the chairwoman. "You were walking us through your latest designs. Specifically, how they pertained to your application for readmission."

"Right. Of course."

The student assistant returned with a glass of water. Megan took a sip, then another, hoping it would wash away the briny taste on her tongue. She used the silence to gather her thoughts.

Yes, her designs.

She clicked the remote, advancing the slide projector. Colors filled the screen, a surrealist-expressionist piece she'd made her freshman spring titled *Prozac Fixes Everything*. She guided them through her inspirations, from Dali to Basquiat.

Another click. Slide six: a charcoal sketch from her figure studies course last fall. Two nude bodies merged together, their skin dripping like wax.

Another click. A sculpture she'd formed out of rope. Then another click.

The ombudsman yawned. She was losing them fast.

"I know I don't have my most recent work here, but this next one should give you an idea of the direction I hope to explore."

She advanced to the next slide. Instead of the clack of the slide tray, a different noise filled her ears: the click of a camera shutter and the winding of film.

And an accented voice, saying, "*Tri. Dva. Odeen.* Cheese."

Megan's words caught in her throat.

She knew slide twelve by heart. It was the plein air pastoral she painted in April. The lilac-tinted clouds. The silver rivers like veins through the landscape.

But this wasn't slide twelve.

Instead, a photograph of her and her high school friends now filled the screen. Chunhee and Adam, Tommy and Desi. They were all standing on a lawn before a white chapel and smiling.

Megan knew that chapel. Twice a week they'd been required to dress in their best and attend service. Three words were etched into the stone arch above the doors: *Veritas Vitæ Magistra.*

"Truth is the teacher of life," she whispered.

Then the photo was gone and she was here, staring at the committee. Her advisor leaned in. "I'm confused. Is that the title of this work?" He gestured to the pastoral landscape on-screen.

"No." Megan shook it off. "Well, sort of. It's a placeholder."

After a deep sigh, he raised a finger. "Would you give us a moment?"

The assistant dean of admissions and the chairwoman conferred. The ombudsman scribbled a few notes while Megan sipped water to steady her heart.

That photograph of the chapel, why had it slid right into her thoughts? She could still feel the spring breeze in her hair, blazers warmed by the sun. The smell of the fresh-cut grass on the quad. The ringing bells, summoning the students to vespers.

And that girl behind the camera, the one counting down, "*Tri. Dva. Odeen.*" Megan knew that voice as well as her own.

So why couldn't she remember her face?

Ophelia... No, Orianna, or—

"Ms. Monroe." Her advisor cleared his throat. "As you've discovered, PhilArts is a tight community. We may lack the resources of RISD or Pratt, but we still produce more working artists than any other institution. We view our students as an investment in potential. Your talent has never been the issue. Rather, it's your dedication, your commitment to your fellow artists. And, in turn, to yourself."

"Yes, sir. I understand."

"Do you?"

She wasn't sure what else she could say. She'd played the part of the repentant student, hoping they'd see she was redoubling her efforts and catching up on assignments. She'd spent weeks honing her personal statement. She meant every word. This was her last chance, her *only* chance. Without readmission, what was she, really? Just a dropout carrying drinks for the boozehounds at the edge of the city.

Chunhee's face in her book.

The Tenbury School.

The dreams of fire now night after night.

Was this how madness happened? First slowly and then all at once?

She could always play the pity card, she supposed. Her parents' death, the car accident. They might buy some sympathy with the committee. And yet, it felt ghoulish to dig it all up as a means to an end.

Which was why she sighed inwardly when the assistant dean did just that.

"Megan, we understand the past two years have been a challenge. Focusing on academics after suffering a loss in your family. Or an injury such as..." He made a hesitant gesture to her face. "My point is, we're not insensitive to our students' unique situations."

"But we don't want to exacerbate them either," her advisor said.

"No, sir. Of course not."

Now the chairwoman spoke. "Ms. Monroe, despite your portfolio's absence, this committee will recommend that you be given a second chance—"

"Oh, thank you."

"Please, let me finish. Readmission is not our decision alone. Dean Henry oversees such matters. I would urge you to meet with him. You can reference this meeting, our recommendation here, but ultimately it's his approval you'll need to rejoin us next semester."

"Yes, absolutely. I'll stop by his office."

Her advisor shook his head. "Dean Henry isn't on campus this week. And since next week is Thanksgiving vacation, well, I would say time is of the essence. You're familiar with Gallery ZoLo, yes?"

Megan swallowed. Every student was both familiar with and frightened of Gallery ZoLo. Its monthly soirees featured a who's who of local artists. Twice a year they cleared their sandstone walls to show the works of promising students and faculty. Wineglasses were clutched and hors d'oeuvres picked at while critics roamed, their reviews often scathing and cruel. But every now and then, a diamond was discovered. Megan still dreamed of transforming herself into that diamond.

"We're not saying it's mandatory," the chairwoman said, yet her smile said it was. "However, it would help your chances. Dean Henry is more... approachable at such events."

"Just look for the man with a fedora and a martini," her advisor added. "But wait until he's on his second or third."

Two years of working at O'Bannon's had taught Megan a few truths about life: business might start in an office or a conference room, but it was usually sealed over drinks.

"Gallery ZoLo, third martini," she said. "Got it."

The committee stood, the chairwoman offering a slight nod. "Good luck, Ms. Monroe. Perhaps we'll see you this spring."

chapter fifteen

Tom Frenning, twenty-one, was a Gemini born in the year of the dragon. His palm held a curious twist to his lifeline. He had been told his aura was blue. These facts meant little to him. But to Desiree, they explained everything about her boyfriend.

She unrolled a Starscroll horoscope and flattened it against the desk. Tom tuned her out as she reviewed their lucky numbers.

"Oh, and here's something," she said, squinting at the red paper. "'A certain someone has taken notice of you. Their eye is fixed and their heart determined. Scornful thoughts merit cautious actions.' Huh."

Desiree was a Scorpio, which meant that she was passionate and assertive and full of ambition. It also meant she could blame any mistakes on the alignment of some stars. There was a certain deterministic appeal to horoscopes, Tom suspected. A Get Out of Jail Free card for the spiritually inclined.

She asked, "Are you having scornful thoughts now?"

"Yes, several." He nudged his glasses up and focused on the computer monitor. "Like why did editorial get new computers and we're stuck with these?" He gave the old Mac Performa a smack.

Of course, he'd also read Scorpios and Geminis were highly incompatible. Perhaps that explained why Desiree was bothering him here, at the student newspaper, and not reviewing her notes for finals in a few weeks. She was at nine units this term; she could sleepwalk to Christmas vacation. He was at fifteen. But it was his job as production editor for the *Spartan Gazette* that now reddened his eyes. He could only stare at the computer monitor for so long.

"Oooh, and here's Wednesday." She pushed aside a mouse and traced the horoscope's words with a black fingernail. "'Alliances that haven't fared well should be avoided. Relationships that are flowering should be paid special attention.' Do you think we're faring well, as an alliance? Are we flowering?"

"I think you're a massive distraction. Our alliance is in shambles."

He moved the mouse, clicking the digitized photo of Princess Diana and dragging it into the above-the-fold cut. He clicked the photo credit beneath and aligned the text. He centered the headline: *Royal Split; Di Divorce Almost Settled.*

Good. He had most of the front page laid out for December's biweekly. Just a few articles remained. Michael Jackson and his wife announcing the birth of their kid. Did that go in the *Entertainment* section or under *People*? Another article about Tickle Me Elmos flying off shelves before Christmas. Some company out in California was letting resellers auction them on the World Wide Web.

"You used to be more fun." Desiree rolled up the horoscope and slid it back into the plastic wrap. "At least one of us takes our future seriously."

He knew she was kidding, but after six years together, he also knew when to back off. "Look, I'm not saying I don't take our future seriously. But c'mon, vending machine fortunes are one step away from Bat Boy and the *Weekly World News.*"

"I like Bat Boy. And it's not a fortune. It's a horoscope."

"Ah, forgive me." He dragged an article about the new Hubble telescope to the fourth page. "Here, make yourself useful and roll up something good." He gave his backpack a nudge with his foot. "I got a fresh eighth."

"Useful? Not." Chair squeaking, she stood up and gave Tom a kiss atop his beanie and mousy brown hair. "I've gotta tinkle."

She squeezed past the staff boxes where the latest articles jutted out, red revisions across black text. She turned left at the copy machine. This summer, university IT had installed ethernet connections and a new combination printer-scanner. Some of the staff were even submitting articles by email, a practice his boss thought unprofessional but Tom embraced. The *Spartan Gazette*, with its readership of hungover students and overcritical professors, wasn't exactly *The Washington Post*. Nor was he a Woodward or Bernstein.

But maybe someday, Tom thought.

He reached into his JanSport backpack and fished out some Zig-Zags and weed. He'd pre-crushed the bud this morning in anticipation of this moment. He tamped it down, licked the paper, and admired his work. A pretty good little spliff to celebrate another issue on time.

Now he just needed to finish by eight.

Tucking the spliff behind his ear, Tom finalized the layout. He enjoyed his time at the newspaper. He believed in the power of the printed word, even if more of it was winding up on-screen. He embraced new technology, arguing they should get QuarkXPress for every computer. His boss, Professor Atwell, had approved only one installation, which Tom was currently testing, hopeful that next year they'd finally catch up with the future.

Which was why the glitch on-screen bothered him.

When the layout program froze, it usually left little traces of the windows and buttons. Tom could drag and resize it, creating a mess of repeating boxes and borders. Not here.

He clicked and double-clicked, but the newspaper's layout remained locked in place. He started to panic. When was the last time he'd pressed save?

Then the images refreshed.

Michael Jackson with his wife Debbie. A pair of shoppers fighting over a Tickle Me Elmo. Princess Diana, looking tired and forlorn. Every photo vanished, replaced by slowly loading boxes.

Leaning in, Tom squinted as the bitmap images resolved, pixel by pixel, line by line. A flash of shame as he recalled all the nude pictures he'd watched load in similar ways. God bless Pamela Anderson.

This wasn't tan flesh on-screen but undulating shadows. And the pictures were all the same.

Shit, a virus.

Tom held the power button, praying he wasn't too late. Once, back in high school, he'd thought he was loading *Doom 2* onto the library computer. It had turned out to be a zip bomb, endlessly expanding until it took up the whole hard drive and had to be reformatted.

Here, the screen crackled with static as the power winked off. Okay, crisis averted. He caught his tired reflection in the dark glass.

Was there someone there, behind him? Warm fingers slid along his shoulder. A ribbon of light played down the screen. He turned, but there was nothing, no one, just the new copy machine.

Which clicked and sputtered to life.

chapter sixteen

Tom held his breath as the copy machine's light moved under the lid, creaking and whining from one end to the other. Warm toner suffused the air. With a click, the printer spat a page into the tray.

Then it started over again. Another slide of the light. Another fresh page.

It was just someone sending in an article, of course. He had told the staff to put it in the *Shared* folder, not the *Print* folder, but networked computing wasn't perfect. Or easy.

It was on its sixth page when Tom picked up the sheets.

Black pages. Each of them a sea of warm ink.

This was a lot of toner being wasted. His boss would be mad.

Tom scanned the print queue on-screen. Page 7 of 999. He mashed stop until the machine rumbled, spitting out a half-finished page of inky darkness.

No, not totally dark.

There was something midway down the printout. Something formed of crosshatches and little comic book dots. A man's shape stood draped in shadows.

Tom opened the photocopier's lid, eyeing the scanning area and platen glass. There was nothing here, no paper or book. Nothing to scan.

He thumbed through the other pages, starting back at the beginning. There it was, so faint he hardly noticed it. On page three, the man's form had moved forward, as if stepping into soft light. On page four, there were shoulders, a nose, and two circles that formed cheeks. On five, the shadows slid back further, revealing a beanie and scruffy hair.

Tom instinctively touched the FUCT beanie on his own head.

With a clatter of plastic gears and metal springs, the copy machine resumed. A fresh page slid out. Then another. And others after that.

Tom took the warm pages, scouring the near-total blackness and what was emerging.

By the eleventh page, he understood. This was him, here, in the center of the shadows. Like stepping out of a dark closet and into the light. Each page revealed more of his features in crosshatches and dots. On fifteen, he could see shoulders. On eighteen, he realized his printed hands were holding a gray rectangle mid-chest. That was a piece of paper he was clutching. He was looking at himself holding this very page.

And his face...

One of his eyes was empty, just a dripping black hole.

But it wasn't this realization that dried his tongue and tightened his bowels.

It was the two shapes that gripped his printed shoulders. Twin things of jagged claws and tentacles, a writhing mass of wormy ribbons and fingers.

He thumbed past another page, and another. With each, the tentacled thing resolved, a massive smudge only a shade lighter than the oozing darkness surrounding them both. Thick, glistening ropes coiled and squeezed. Brambled veins stretched and twisted. Suckers opened and closed.

Tink. Click.

Silence flooded the newspaper office as the copier stopped. His heart fluttered against his throat. Who was doing this? One of the freshmen, perhaps. They must have hidden a camera connected to a computer. One of the Apple QuickTakes or a Canon EOS checked out from the photo department. A prank, it had to be.

Tinkity click. Tinkity click.

No. There was something beyond the copier now. Something bumping against the window, just past the blinds.

Tinkity, tinkity, click.

It took every ounce of his willpower to reach for the blind wand. There would be no tentacled thing at the window, he told himself. No shadowed form with damp breath on his neck. With tenuous fingers, he twisted the wand, bathing the newspaper room in amber light.

There was the campus quad, the fountain and statues. There was the bell tower and the fiery ivy climbing its walls.

And here was a snail inching its way up the glass. A crimson trail oozed behind it, viscous and bubbly. That thumb-sized body, the glistening foot, the caramel shell tapping against glass. This wasn't a fragile snail found munching grass around campus.

It was a whelk snail. He had spent most of his childhood stomping around tide pools and shores. This shouldn't be here.

More whelks oozed up the glass. Some as small as pennies, a few the size of his fist. All of them leaving foamy ribbons behind, turning the light through the window a sick shade of amber.

Tinkity, tinkity, click. Tinkity, tinkity, click.

Stomach roiling, he tapped the window where the whelk's glistening foot met the glass. The slimy flesh parted, revealing something that had no business being in a snail.

An eye blinked back at Tom.

It gazed around, gray pupil dilating and fixating on him. They all blinked now. All the snails glaring in through the glass.

Next came the wet buzzing noise, an incessant hum that drove him backward and into the shelf. Old newspapers spilled to the floor. The buzzing penetrated him, both terrible and familiar, a forgotten song sung out of tune between stations. It permeated his senses until it was deafening and blinding and all that he knew.

He spilled over reams of paper and folded chairs. He didn't remember running or leaving the newspaper office, but here he was now, out in the hall, the door slamming behind him as he gasped for breath. Down the hall, the elevator opened, and out stepped Professor Atwell, the chief editor and his boss.

"Tom?" The professor took in his young production editor, one of the few students trusted with a key. "Everything okay?"

"It's a really weird thing." Tom gestured back to the door. "We should call Facilities."

"Facilities?" Professor Atwell's gaze drifted from Tom's eyes to his ear. "Ah. Having fun with the old laughing cabbage?"

What the hell was he talking about? Then Tom remembered the joint. He plucked it from behind his ear and stuck it in his pocket so fast it could've been a magic trick. Too late today.

"No, I mean... It's the window."

"The window?"

Tom keyed back into the newspaper office. Gone were the snails and the amber-tinted glass. Only tiny flakes of dried slime remained, fluttering and crumbling in the autumn breeze.

"There were..."

"There were what, Tom?"

Saying there were snails on the window—snails with *eyes*—wouldn't boost his standing with his boss. He had never been Professor Atwell's first choice for production editor, but that student dropped out over the summer. This wasn't helping.

So he said, "Nothing. Never mind."

That was when Desiree returned from the restroom, pale and shaking and clutching her purse to her chest. A dirty smear marred her neck. Her sopping Doc Martens left puddles on the floor.

"Tom," she said, ignoring Professor Atwell. "I need to go home. Now."

chapter seventeen

Desiree showered back at their apartment, insisting that Tom keep the bathroom door open and stay in the same room. It was overkill perhaps, but she didn't care. Her heart was still racing and her tongue tasted like rust. She didn't trust her senses. Not after what happened in the bathroom.

"Okay, so let me get this straight," Tom said, taking a seat on the toilet while she toweled off. "You got stuck in the stall and you couldn't get out."

"I didn't get stuck. I..." The words lingered between her mind and her mouth. She told herself to walk through it, one step at a time. "I opened the stall door. I washed my hands at the sink. I stepped into the hall but then I was back."

"Back where?"

"Back in the bathroom stall."

The steam was fogging his glasses so he removed them, his soft eyes studying her. God how she loved them. "What was it, like a stroke?"

"Like a reset or something. Each time I left, it started over. Back in the stall, back in the stall. Tom, I wasn't stroking out."

"No, of course not." He wiped his glasses. "Okay. So then you climbed over and broke a pipe?"

"The fire sprinkler." She could still feel the metal snap as she tried to climb out, the brackish black water dripping down her skin. The panic. "But it wasn't like that. It was..."

He tilted his head, his way of saying she might as well be speaking in tongues. Maybe she was. Her memory was transmuting into something else now, frustration and an undercurrent of doubt. A vague haze hung over it all.

"It was what?" he asked.

It was beyond reason, she told herself. Beyond explanation. She knew her words would just tilt his head further, until his face would split into a grin and he'd laugh, saying she was being silly, she had a wild imagination, and it was all in her head.

And maybe it had been. But fuck, it felt so *real*.

"Desi, what was it?"

"Nothing," she said. "You know how I hate small spaces? It was probably that. God, I'm so embarrassed."

Tom didn't say anything. Instead, he lit up his joint and cracked the window, blowing smoke into the cool air. He offered her a drag but she declined. She was in the wrong headspace to get faded.

What a fool, she told herself. Despite the dark clothes and her occasional goth fashion, she was easily rattled. On Halloween they'd taken mushrooms and wandered over to the video store. They'd rented two movies—Pink Floyd's *The Wall* and something called *In the Mouth of Madness*. By the time they were peaking, her giggles had turned quiet, the walls were breathing, and the carpet was starting to unravel. She spent the evening snuggled so close to Tom that he complained she gave him bruises.

A flashback, yes. That was what occurred in the bathroom. She'd read on a GeoCities page that they could happen years later.

But the rotten feet shuffling into the next stall...

That putrid smell...

And when she had peeked through the gap at the stall door, she knew what she'd seen. Megan and Adam and Chunhee in the mirror. And Tom. Tom, wandering around the bathroom and bumping into things.

Tom, missing his eyes.

She applied lotion to her arms and began her makeup routine. It felt nice to refresh, like she got a do-over on the day.

Tom exhaled a final, skunky cloud and closed the window. His soft eyes glistened with concern. "Yeah, so I also saw something I can't quite explain."

She lowered the eyeliner. "Like what?"

AN HOUR later they were dining beneath the orange roof of their local Howard Johnson's. The pot had given Tom the munchies and Desiree wanted to be someplace open, someplace public where others could see her.

She stirred her milkshake as Tom described the glitches, the photocopier, the snails on the window. By the time he finished, she was at the edge of the booth.

"That's what it was like," she said. "I mean, not the same, but that feeling of dread. Like I'd forgotten some assignment or left the heater on."

Tom poked at his ham and cheese melt. "Funny, those printouts got me thinking."

"Thinking about what?"

"Megan."

Desi stiffened as that name hung between them, heavy and awkward. At the neighboring booth, a boy poked his head over and studied the pair. This young woman with dark lipstick and black nails, her short bangs and heroin chic fashion. This skater across from her, the Caesar-cut hair and Alien Workshop hoodie. What an odd couple. And she supposed that was why it worked out between them for so long.

Still, it sometimes felt like they were speaking two different languages. "Megan," she said. "I'm not following."

"She used to make those weird sketches, right?" Tom traced his finger on the table. "You know, the kind of stuff you see in a bad trip. That's what those printouts looked like."

"What, was she, like, faxing them to you?"

"No. I don't think so. I mean... why would she?"

"Megan," she repeated, more to herself than to Tom. "Whatever happened with her and Adam?"

"Same thing that happens to most high school couples: they split up."

"Not us."

"Babe, we're not most couples." He gave her a wink with those piercing eyes.

She slipped her left foot out of her shoe and rested it on his lap, where he started rubbing her toes. The boy from the neighboring booth was peeking over again, head bobbing up and down. She stuck out her tongue, the barbell piercing glistening under the fluorescent lights. Wide-eyed, the boy ducked back into his booth.

"How do you know they split up?"

Tom shrugged. "Darnell told me."

"Darnell?"

"From Tenbury. Basketball player, dormed in Harpsburg, sold us Ritalin during finals."

She nodded. It was coming back to her, but only just. "For a stoner, you have the memory of the FBI."

"Word." He started in on her ankle, working the tension out with his palm. "Anyway, Darnell roadie'd for Cypress Hill, who were in Philly for Lollapalooza in June, I think. Or maybe July. He said he bumped into Megan at some bar, that she still had that scar and seemed kind of muddled."

"Poor girl," she said. "Do you think we should call her? In case this is... I don't know, something more?"

He shook his head, fingers really digging into her foot. "No. No way. We're different people now. I wouldn't even know where to start."

Desiree's eyes drifted down to her salad. "Sometimes I like to think that school never existed."

Tom let out a grim chuckle. "Most of us do."

"Not you."

He leaned across the table and stole a sip of her shake. "Boarding school wasn't that bad. Everyone always bitched about studying and curfews and their dorm parents, blah blah blah. Yeah, that sucked, but it made college a breeze. I got the hard partying out of my system."

"You got the whole school's partying out of your system."

"You're clowning, but it worked." He spooned out the last of her shake.

Sometimes she envied her boyfriend. It was different for guys. Sure, they had reputations, but they could shed them like old clothes over the summer and become something new. Women had labels that stuck.

She had entered Tenbury as a sophomore, wearing scrunchies and colorful blazers picked out by her mom. As a kid, she idolized Punky Brewster. As a teen, Clarissa Darling. At Tenbury, she became a chameleon, drifting from one clique to another.

First, it was the candy ravers, but she hated spending every weekend searching for warehouse parties in Bridgeport or New Haven.

Then the rich girls grabbed her for a term, but she didn't like being judgmental about money.

For a month she dated Ernesto, a student from Venezuela, and her Spanish really took off. After they broke up, she floated around, joking that she was like Switzerland, neutral and friendly to all.

Then the rumors began.

She was easy with guys, they said. She'd give a mean blowjob for a ride to Manhattan. Apparently, she'd gotten out of detention by jerking off Coach Dawson.

It was bullshit, of course, but it clung to her, somehow both a virgin and the school slut. Her inner thighs still bore the scars of the X-Acto she'd dragged across just to feel anything other than shame. Sometimes Tom kissed those scars and it all went away.

"You're going to your dark place again, aren't you?" he asked.

Desiree gave the waitress a flat smile as she dropped off the bill. Tom tried to pay but she insisted and left ten dollars.

"Hey, look at me." Tom reached across the table and took her hands. He'd always liked her soft skin, telling her he could find a new freckle every time. He said, "That was then, this is now. We did what we needed to do, okay? If we had to do it all over, I'd do the same thing."

"But you think she's okay? Megan, did Darnell say she seemed happy?"

"Happy? Life isn't *Barney & Friends*. I mean, who's really happy? But she's alive, right? That's good enough."

Adam and Megan, she thought. Chunhee as well. Friends relegated to another life, faces blurring with each passing season. She was starting to understand the truth of it all: most friends didn't grow older and closer.

They simply grew apart.

And Oksana...

Desiree's back stiffened. Funny, she hadn't thought of that name in so long it felt odd and unpracticed.

She needed to do something.

She reached into her purse and took out her cellular phone. At a mere six ounces, the Motorola MicroTac was a thing of slim convenience. The boy in the next booth was back, his eyes widening as she extended the phone's antenna and flipped down the mouthpiece to reveal the dial pad.

"What are you doing?" Tom asked.

"Calling her."

"Calling who?"

"You know who." She whispered, "Megan."

The boy in the next booth wasn't the only one with wide eyes now. "Okay, first, hit pause, 'cause you're bugging out." Tom's voice dropped an octave. "And second, like, what if they're listening in?"

"Who?"

"The FBI, the police. *They*. That phone, it's just, like, radio waves and stuff. Anyone with a scanner can hear your calls."

"You're tripping. Who has a scanner?"

"Uh, RadioShack has an entire section. Do you seriously not know how this works?"

Her thumb hovered over the green LED display. The phone was a gift from her father, for emergencies only. Lately, it felt like a leash. The only time it rang was when her mother was tipsy and wanted to gossip or complain about Desiree's brother. Plus, it was expensive to use, especially when roaming.

But still, she wanted to know. She needed to hear it was nothing. Just a vague fear with no roots in the truth. Maybe she really was becoming her parents.

Tom said, "Seriously, what are we going to do? Like, get the band back together? Relive the glory days? Not a chance. Adam's probably captain of the rowing team or whatever. Last I heard, Chunhee rushed a sorority. People move on. We should as well."

"And Oksana?"

Tom blinked as recognition flickered in his green eyes. "Fuck Oksana."

There was a little gasp as the boy watching them sank, his nose sliding along the booth divider. Desiree closed her phone.

"Forget it. I'm being silly." Then she stood up, taking her purse with her. "I've got to tinkle."

She didn't dare enter the bathroom alone, not after today. But she did linger by the payphones, watching Tom flip through his newspaper back at the booth.

She opened her phone.

It took three calls to three different 411 services. First, the NYNEX for New England. Next, Southern New England Telephone, which handled Connecticut. Then she was passed off to Bell Atlantic, which handled the region from Pennsylvania down to Virginia. They produced four Philadelphia numbers matching the name Megan Monroe.

Desiree called every one.

Two hundred and fifty miles away, in a former candle factory subdivided into loft apartments, Megan Monroe was painting for the first time in months. Inspiration had struck and her muse guided her fingers, sweeping the brush across canvas after canvas. She'd been at this all week and only stopped to fuel up on caffeine.

Basking in Eddie Vedder's baritone vocals, she realized Pearl Jam's *Vitalogy* had played through at least three times. Funny how fast time passed in the throes of creation. She sipped her coffee and stepped back to study her work.

Four canvases, each a progression from dark abstraction to bold, bright constructions. Her most recently finished painting, an aggressive explosion of images pulled from her dreams. A cindering woman, skin cracked and leaking magma, pressed an open palm against the center of the canvas. Mirroring her on the other side stood a woman of cool blues, her skin liquid, organs formed from seaweed and kelp, a conch shell for a heart.

Megan put her coffee on the stool, unsure what her fifth painting would be, certain only that she would discover it along the way like she had with the others. She cleaned her paintbrushes, humming along to the chorus of "Nothingman."

She gave little thought to the stack of sketches she'd penciled lately. The snails chasing a scared dog. The car made of soft flesh sliding down a jagged cliff.

And she gave little thought to these ideas and where they came from, only that for two years and six months, they hadn't come at all. And now they flooded her, too much to contain. Her only fear in this moment was that she might run out of paint.

She did not hear the phone ringing on the other side of the loft. Her answering machine, a simple thing with micro-cassettes and no greeting, recorded a few seconds of silence before the battery died and the caller was disconnected.

chapter eighteen

Now

Anwar's gaze drifts to the tape recorder on the table between them, the light blinking red as the microphone captures his subject's words. He sips his sparkling water, waiting for Megan to continue.

She doesn't.

Her eyes have taken on a misty glaze, rife with nostalgia. He envisions this Arizona kitchen stretching and fraying and curving backward in time, transforming into some artist's loft visible only to her. He can almost see the brickwork and paint. He can almost smell the incense and coffee.

That's the power of memory, he supposes. Every one is unique, carved into neurons and strengthened through emotions and senses. It's why so many adults never move past the music of their youth.

And it's also his stock-in-trade.

The little clues through which the truth can be triangulated, tracked down, and resurrected. Perhaps even punished. There is something here his listeners will devour. He can feel his mind pawing at them greedily.

If only he can cut through her bullshit.

In the living room, the twins have moved on from video games to TV, where Jeff Goldblum is guiding curious viewers through the wonders of ice cream. Anwar takes another sip, letting the awkward silence drag on.

Still, dead air is a crime, so he licks his lips and says, “Did you ever hear from her?”

Megan’s smile fades. “From Desiree?”

Anwar nods. “Or Tom.”

She shakes her head. “No. Not really. Just a few words...”

Rochester, he realizes. He’d read about that mess in his uncle’s journal. But he’s getting too far ahead.

He asks, “Do you miss them?”

The question scrunches her eyes and softens her features. She’s quite beautiful, he thinks. Far prettier in middle age than some of his acquaintances chasing their youth through endless facelifts and injections, only to end up stretched and uncanny. He admires a woman who wears some of her miles.

“Do I miss them?” she repeats. “Do you miss your friends? The ones you traded albums with? The ones you stayed up with until dawn talking to, trading secrets, trying to figure out the big heavies of life?”

“Big heavies of life?” He smirks. “I don’t know, Mrs. Collings. My high school was different. Small town, Muslim name. And 9/11 didn’t help. Sure, I had a few friends, but none I keep up with. Most days I was just happy not to be called a terrorist.”

He reminds himself this is her interview and he’s wasting tape. Perhaps his recollection warmed her, because she looks at him as if she’s truly seeing him for the first time. It feels like a soft hug.

“I’m sorry that was your experience,” she says. “Kids can be terribly cruel.”

Now there’s a juicy quote, he thinks. He can already hear it on the audio trailer, punctuated by ominous music, perhaps overlapping with a coroner’s report, a press conference, or a guilty verdict. Yes, he suspects this might not be an episode but a limited series.

Still, more work to be done.

“And to answer your question,” Megan says, “of course I miss them. I like to think we’re the sum total of all those who helped us or hurt us or simply shared our life for a moment. I revisit the past often these days. But I couldn’t back then.”

“Because of the distance?”

“Because I wasn’t ready.” She taps her temple. “When your skull has been cracked against a steering wheel, you tend to think a bit slow. I wish I could have warned them back then."

"Warned them about what?"

She smiles her coy smile. For a moment he wonders if she knows more about this visit than she's letting on. But how could she? No, he's in control here. He has the journal. He has the dual recorders and the element of surprise. He has enough of the truth to piece it together.

All he needs is her confession on tape.

"Warned them about what?" he repeats.

Her eyes drift to the window and the warm desert mountains verdant with spring grass and wildflowers in bloom. "I wish I could have warned them about the storm that was coming."

part three

All That She Wants

chapter nineteen

1996

Detective Graham Nolan, a husky forty-five, stepped out of his Ford Bronco and straightened his cap. He gave himself a moment to let his instincts rouse themselves from slumber. He hadn't considered himself a proper detective in a few years, not since Boston. He'd made peace with that fact. Bristol County was placid, its residents amiable. Most craved the same quiet he moved here to enjoy now that his pension was flowing.

His neighbor pulled double duty as a dentist and a substitute teacher. His computer repairman was also the local butcher. The mayor, who lived down the street, was also the church deacon and the local mechanic. Finding him was just a matter of driving down Main Street, which only took a few minutes.

Occasionally, Graham assisted in tracking down runaways, usually love-sick teenagers in the throes of rebellion or the occasional sundowning senior. Most wandered back on their own.

But a missing dog? What was he, Ace Ventura?

So here he was, standing on Bill Hodgson's back porch, listening and taking notes and trying to give him the benefit of the doubt. Bill was his dentist's half-brother, and he owed him a favor for fixing a loose crown. Bill's wife Lorie had died last spring and he'd been on the bottle for months. Graham was three years sober himself, but he still got the cravings.

"I'm telling you, she didn't like him, not one bit," Bill said, his breath all minty. "She can sense it, you know? Dogs are like that. They sense the good in us."

Graham nodded, his pen scratching out notes. *Neighbor: Louis Harding. Dog: Beatrice. Time of disappearance: overnight.*

"Walk me through this, Bill." Graham gave a tilt of his head to the chain-link fence bounding the property. "You went to bed sometime around midnight, right? You let Beatrice out but you didn't let her back in."

"She always barks. That's how she lets me know when she's done her business."

They followed the weed-tangled fence, the deadfall and leaves knee-high in some places. They passed the shadow of Lorie's garden, rusty tomato cages, and a woodshed with a dangerous lean. Graham felt bad for judging Bill, but dammit, man, couldn't he at least try a little?

He asked, "So she didn't bark to be let in?"

"No, sir. Not once."

"And if she had, you would've been awake to hear it?"

Bill blinked, eyes falling down to his boots. Perhaps he sensed what Graham was getting at. "I always hear her. She's got a loud bark."

Graham took a moment to straighten his cap. People at the edge of communities often clammed up around detectives, and he found the old Red Sox hat humanized him. Plus, it gave them something to bitch about when the Sox inevitably lost.

"What I mean is, were you awake?"

Bill swallowed. "I might've been snoozing."

Snoozing with a bellyful of schnapps, Graham thought. Or whatever was on discount at the Market Basket. But what he said was, "So you never heard her bark to be let in. And when you woke up in the a.m., she was gone?"

Bill nodded vigorously. "Stolen. Taken right out of my yard. I'm telling you, he had it out for her."

There it was again, that fixation on his neighbor. As far back as Graham could remember, Louis and Bill had been at each other. Two locals who grew up together, about the same age. Perhaps some high school slight they'd never resolved. Small towns were like that; rivalries festered.

Graham said, "Let's check for some holes. Maybe she tunneled her way out."

"Already done that."

"Humor me, Bill."

They walked the rest of the fence, Bill kicking a few piles of leaves, Graham taking note of the occasional rusty beer can or rotting lawn chair.

He pitied Bill, of course, and he might have offered some encouragement, some advice, or a ride to his weekly AA meeting, but it seemed Bill was still in denial of his demons. Graham knew his own demons too well. They lived in the pediatric cancer ward.

A butterfly fluttered past, brushing that dark thought from Graham's mind and landing on the fence where the chain link met the gate. There was a fork latch and no lock. "Bill, was that open or closed when you woke up this morning?"

"Closed, of course."

Graham used a stick to lift the fork latch. It wouldn't have taken much force to raise it. Nor was it out of a dog's reach. "Bill, this is probably a dumb question, but did Beatrice ever open the gate on her own?"

Bill scratched his ear. "Well, she ain't got fingers, so I can't imagine how."

"Like, with her nose or something."

Bill blinked and studied Graham as if he'd started speaking Norwegian.

"Forget that I asked."

He opened the gate and they stepped out into the driveway. If Bill was right and someone had stolen his dog, they could've been standing right here. Graham bent down, touching where the reedy grass ended and the gravel began.

Bill asked, "So, are you gonna dust for prints or something?"

Graham stifled a chuckle. With the rise of cable TV and shows like *COPS* and *Law & Order*, it seemed like every Tom, Dick, and Harry knew what his job entailed and how it was done.

"It was dewy this morning," he said. "Latent prints would be a hard pull, especially off chain link. We'd get a lot of false positives too. Like a gardener or something."

Bill laughed. "No gardeners, that's for sure."

"Or the utility man reading the meter." Graham pointed to the side of the house. "You got any plastic baggies? A Ziploc or something?"

Bill's eyes gleamed. "What, you found some evidence?"

Graham flashed a sidelong glance that Bill took for annoyance. God, he was getting grumpy in middle age. Still, it did the trick and Bill shuffled off to the house. Graham didn't need bags; he had a few in his jacket. What he needed was some quiet.

Sometimes, he could sense where a perp might place themselves. Where they would stand or how they might sit. What they'd be doing with their hands or their body. It wasn't a superpower or anything unnatural like some people made it out to be. It was just empathy and imagination, things often dismissed by other cops.

The fence, the gravel, the gate. He had doubts about Bill's story, but if someone wanted the dog, they'd have stood right here. He squatted and looked up at the latch. Bingo. There, pinched between the gate post and frame, where the fork met the nut and bolt, hung something small and fibrous and fluttering in the breeze.

Graham took out his compact collection kit. He removed a pair of tweezers and a one-inch resealable bag. Carefully, slowly, he plucked the clump of fibers and dropped it into the bag. Then he held it up to the sunlight.

It was blue fabric, cotton perhaps, like a piece of torn shirt. It could have been Bill's or Lorie's or anyone's. It could have hung there for years, trapped between the steel nut and bolt.

But his instinct said it was something to consider.

Bill was returning now with a whole box of Ziplocs. "Didn't know how many you needed."

Graham held up a finger. "Bill, stop. Just stop right there."

Bill froze, the gravel grinding beneath his boots. Not three feet away between them, Graham caught a glimpse of something mixed in with the stones and the pebbles. He scooted forward, studying the driveway.

"I'm freezing, boss," Bill said, trying to hold steady but failing.

Graham smelled the scent of fiery bourbon on Bill's breath. He must have imbibed a little inside.

That smell, shit. No, not the bourbon, but something else. He'd caught a foul whiff just before and had seen something dry by the gate, sharp yet different than the gravel. He crawled on all fours, careful where he placed his palms and his knees.

"Still freezing."

"Just... stay there, Bill."

Graham was so close to the gravel he could smell it again, his nose stinging with the tang of salt and meat, something starting to rot. There it was, a jagged, pinkish clump about the size of chewed gum and dry at its edges.

"What the hell is that?" Bill asked as Graham lifted the clump with his tweezers. Something red jutted out.

"Looks like some fish and bell peppers," Graham said, sniffing it and wincing. "Smells like it too. Bill, you been making any tuna sandwiches lately?"

Bill shook his head. "Nah, not tuna. Can't stand the stuff. Just PB and J's."

chapter twenty

Louis hardly recognized his own reflection when he passed the hall mirror, so he pried it from the wall and tossed it into the closet. The sunken eyes, the sallow cheeks, the mottled spots that began at the nape of his neck and now spread like a collar of roots. He told himself not to scratch it, but he still found himself doing so reflexively, itching with a finger he no longer possessed.

And his hand...

At first he didn't dare unravel the clothed bandages. After a day he worked up the courage to peek underneath. Oksana had chewed right through him, of course, leaving nothing past the knuckle. He couldn't even pick his nose properly now.

But she had been satisfied and quiet, her words no longer digging around in his brain. The headaches subsided, for a time.

She slept for a whole day after the first feeding, her normal eye closed, that starfish-clutched eye open and rolled up to the whites. For a while he worried she might have died. Then came the crackling and crunching from inside her mouth.

She was grinding her teeth in her sleep. He found it endearing.

When she finally woke, she spoke to him, first without words and then slowly, carefully, enunciating each command with lips that were riper, more full of life. A pink flush had bloomed in her cheeks. Even her hair seemed curlier, thicker, less matted. He had a compulsion to comb it, which he did, placing her in his lap like a sickly infant. He could feel her little heart beating, *pitter pat*, and her lungs heaving as she spoke.

"I need food, Louis. *Real* food. I need to heal and get better."

He knew what she wanted but lacked the strength to give more of himself. He tried to think, but an odd fog had descended over the house and followed him room to room. He hadn't left home in several days.

"I'm sorry, I can't give you any more," he whispered. "I need my fingers. I... I think I've got some sort of infection."

Tenderly, he plucked dry seaweed from her scalp. The bulb beneath her neck had shrunk, those twig-like arms and gills retracting into soft skin. The leeches and barnacles were shedding like dried scabs. He swore little vellus hairs were sprouting as he brushed out her tangles.

"You want me to get better, don't you?" She turned her eyes up to him. "I know you do. You care about me, Louis. I can see it in your eyes. A great kindness shines inside you."

It was a curious thing, these soft words that she spoke. Earlier, he'd struggled to understand her at times. The coral and shells and snails all crowding her mouth. Now he caught glimpses of a pink tongue, a few perfect white teeth, and no coral in sight.

She was healing all right.

"Please, Louis. Please. All I've had is what the sea brought to me. Bottom feeders, that's all I've tasted. Louis, do me this one kindness and I will repay you tenfold. You hold a great treasure here, in your lap."

It made sense, he supposed, in an odd sort of way. She needed more life to consume. But another finger? God, it would hurt something fierce.

Then the fog of his mind lifted, and he heard his neighbor's dog barking again and again.

Oksana didn't complain when he fed it to her, dead but still warm and cut into pieces. She chewed, greedy and grateful. He could feel her little lungs expanding, her heart beating heavy and fast. He wondered where it all went.

Did she have a stomach down there? Some sort of digestive system?

Or did she simply absorb it all, the muscle and the fat, the fur and the bone?

Over the next several hours, she rested. He watched her, entranced as little dark tendrils stretched their way out from that bulb. She no longer ground her teeth but burbled and wheezed. He could see tiny bones sprouting from the tendrils, like a plant ready to be potted.

He was wrong, he realized. She wasn't just healing. She was growing.

Then someone knocked at the door.

chapter twenty-one

Graham rapped his knuckles and waited. He just wanted to talk to Bill's neighbor, maybe see if he'd heard anything strange. Yeah, Bill filled him in on their feud over the years: Lorie's favorite northern red oak that bordered their yards until Louis cut it down, how Bill claimed Louis was dumping oil into the storm drain and called the county, petty grievances that grew into hostilities and the occasional threat.

But taking Bill's dog?

It didn't feel right. Not a provocation but an escalation, out of character for these kinds of spats.

Still, he knocked again and waited.

He could hear a shuffling from within the old house. The murmur of a voice trying to speak quietly but drawing attention. He took a peek through the window and saw a shadow lumber off to the back and then return.

Graham's cop instinct lit up when the door opened, revealing a haggard man he recognized as Louis, but only just. Like Bill, Louis was one of those fellows that struggled in life. He was drawing disability from an accident at the paper mill years ago. He kept a small booth at the farmers market where he sold fish or crabs or the occasional basket of scallops. He always seemed to be breathing too hard.

"Afternoon, Louis. How you doing today?"

Louis nodded, keeping the door half closed. The lights were off behind him, giving the modest house a musty feel, a dim cave of depression. Graham wondered how long it'd been since Louis had heard a kind word or felt the touch of another. A part of his heart started to ache.

But that cop sense, it was vibrating now, sparkling bright.

"Yeah, I'm doing fine, Officer. Afraid you caught me during my afternoon nap."

"I hear you. Nothing like a siesta."

Yet Louis looked like he hadn't slept in a week. His clothes hung off him as if he was in the throes of a crash diet. And his neck, was that some sort of infection rimming his collar? Perhaps sensing this, he lifted his left hand, zipping the jacket up to his Adam's apple.

"Well, I'm sure sorry to disturb you. So listen, this is a weird one, but your neighbor's dog has gone missing."

"Beatrice?" Louis touched his chin with his left hand. His right was still stuffed in his pocket. "Haven't seen that old pooch in ages. She's still around?"

Curious, Graham thought, and flipped his notebook back a few pages. "She is. Well, she was. One of your neighbors, they told me otherwise. Something about a recent altercation?"

Louis shifted, eyes drifting to his feet. "Well, I may have shouted a few things the other week from this porch. Never meant a thing by it. Just hot air I should've held in. You sure she's missing?"

Graham adjusted his cap and pushed back his thinning hair. "Eh, she's probably just out for a stroll. You know how hunting dogs get when they see a squirrel. They'll be three counties away before they realize they've left the yard."

Louis chuckled a little too loud. "Yep. Yep. That they do."

"Anyways, I'm just doing my duty to the community. You mind if I come in? That's a cold wind off the bay."

"Actually, things are a bit—"

Graham made a spot judgment and gave the door a push. He was already inside before Louis could finish. He didn't know what he sensed, not exactly, just that something was amiss and Louis was being shifty. If he could get this thing resolved between the two men, he could get back to the station, back to doing what he enjoyed most, which was a whole lot of nothing. Besides, he didn't like the way Louis was keeping the door between them and his right hand stuffed in his pocket.

"You sure you're feeling okay? You look a bit under the weather, if you don't mind me saying."

Louis closed the door. "Well, I've been getting these headaches. Come on awful fast and leave just as quick."

"You been to St. Mary's?"

He shook his head. "I go to the V.A. over in New London. They take care of me. Uncle Sam, he's always happy to charge me fifty bucks for some aspirin."

"Yeah, I hear you. But don't be afraid to push back and get that head of yours taken care of. Squeaky wheel and all."

It was a curious thing. For a moment something like fear flashed across Louis's face. Was it something Graham had said? His instincts were all over the map here, tugging him in discordant directions. Yeah, Louis was lying or holding back, but that didn't mean he was lying about the questions at hand. Maybe there was just a ganja plant in the next room or a cable descrambler on the TV. And hell, Graham didn't care about either.

"So Bill's dog, Beatrice. Last time you saw her was...?"

"Umm, maybe two weeks back. Maybe longer. Kinda hard to recall specifics. She was barking, barking, always barking."

"That's gotta be a pain."

Louis nodded. "Sure is. I tell him, 'Dogs and children oughta be seen and not heard.'"

"I hear you." Even if Graham didn't agree with him, rapport was important. And Louis's right hand still stuffed in his pocket was making Graham nervous. "Here, hold this for me real quick."

He practically shoved his notebook into Louis's chest, but the man reacted swift with his left hand. Graham tried to cover by passing off his ballpoint pen as well, but the same thing happened again. Louis was hiding something in his right hand, but now it was obvious.

So, Graham called his bluff. He reached into his jacket and pulled out his business cards. He went to peel one off but spilled them all onto the floor.

"Ah, shucks." He made a show of bending down to retrieve them. "Let me give you my card, in case you think of anything."

It wasn't much, but it was enough. Louis's right hand slid out of his pocket while Graham squatted. He caught a glimpse of a bandage, some gauze and medical tape all wrapped tight around his index finger.

Or rather, where his index finger should be.

Graham scooped up a few cards, mind rewinding to the fibers caught in the gate's latch bolt. They'd been navy blue, hadn't they? Or a faded black?

But Louis's bandage was white and speckled red.

Graham collected the last of the business cards. "What happened to your finger?"

"Oh, this?" Louis regarded his right hand with hesitation. "Fishing accident, out in the bay."

"Christ, whatchya after, piranhas?"

There was an odd desperation to Louis's laugh. A little too forceful. "It was the propellor. I, uh, well, I was trying to fix it. Then it started up on its own. Chop suey."

"You need to be more careful. You show that to the V.A.?"

"Oh yeah, sure. Charged me fifty bucks for more aspirin." Louis studied the business card with his left hand, stuffing the right one back in his pocket.

Maybe that was all this was, Graham thought. An embarrassing way to lose a finger and nothing else. He'd met plenty of men like Louis and Bill. Men who kept their problems to themselves, thinking perhaps it made them weak to take help. Hell, maybe he was the bully here, pushing his way into this house on the basis of a neighbor's words and a vague suspicion. He should probably get going.

And yet...

"Can I trouble you for an aspirin? I had a little too much fun last night and I've been paying it off all afternoon." Graham rubbed his temple for show.

It was as if every muscle in Louis's body momentarily froze. Then he recovered as quickly and said, "Yeah, let me fetch you some. Hold tight."

He ambled off to the bathroom, passing a boat bag by the closet and giving it a quick glance. This was it. Graham went into the kitchen, fetching a glass from the counter and some water from the sink. He used the time to inventory it all: the messy pots and pans, the dinner table with room for only two. Road atlases and notes lay on the counter near a phone book open to the T section with a circled name and address.

He turned off the faucet, calling out to Louis, "You going on a trip?"

Then something caught his eye and tightened his gut.

There in the trash bin, beneath a pile of crumpled newspapers, some old Lunchables, and a crushed Mr. Pibb, were several empty cans of tuna. It wasn't a smoking gun, these cans.

But the leather collar beneath it was.

Carefully, slowly, quietly, he lifted it out of the trash, the tag rotating and glinting in the light.

Beatrice.

Graham's hand slid into his jacket, where a steerhide holster held his Glock 19. He turned as he drew, his only mistake.

Louis must have snuck up on him, must have sensed something and doubled back. He was there at the threshold of the kitchen, a ball-peen hammer raised high and falling. Graham saw it coming a half second too late.

He didn't feel the impact of the hammer's face against his. Nor the smack of the cool kitchen floor. There was a flash of light. Then darkness wormed in from the edge of his vision. He had time to wonder two things before the shadows consumed him.

What was in that bag Louis was carrying?

And why was he whispering to it?

chapter twenty-two

Megan knew she was underdressed the moment she entered ZoLo Gallery. These were not her people. They wore turtlenecks beneath blazers, pastel jackets and plaid pants. Their clothes that were distressed had been done so out of fashion and not length of use. Someone in a tuxedo passed out sushi by a white chocolate fountain.

She lingered a moment near the bathroom to straighten her hair in the payphone reflection. A headache struck her like a hammer blow, but she pushed past it, ignoring the scared girl looking back. *Keep it together.*

She found Dean Henry easily enough. He was the silver-haired man in the loud patterned jacket and a Burberry scarf that hung a little too long. He wore John Lennon glasses and the righteous smile formed over decades of lectures. A grinning cadre surrounded him. She drifted close enough to catch the end of a conversation about movie posters and the recent death of Saul Bass.

Dean Henry plucked a fresh martini off a passing server's tray, swinging his gaze toward Megan. Recognition flashed in his eyes. Shit, time to plead her case.

"Dean Henry." She gave him a wave that felt almost childish. "I don't mean to be a bother, but I was hoping I could have a word."

He sipped his martini while the cadre studied Megan. The youngest was probably in his mid-thirties, the oldest perhaps double. They reminded her of lizards sunning themselves on rocks, faces upturned. Was this the future she wanted? Meandering around a gallery and coolly eyeing sculptures while shrimp cocktails warmed under lights? Quietly laughing at jokes?

"Ah, yes, Ms. Monroe." He switched his martini to his left hand so he could gesture with his right. "I present another one of our hard-working artists. I confess, sometimes I envy them. They don't have to mingle with you vipers and beg for your money. Life's far simpler and more focused."

A round of polite chuckles from the lizards. A septuagenarian in a kimono turned to Megan and asked, "And what's your medium, dear? What inspires you?"

Megan swallowed. "At the moment I'm into painting."

"Oils?" asked a man with a purple vest.

"Acrylics mostly." She sensed by the man's nod and the tilt of his chin that her answer displeased him. "But I work with oils too, when I can afford them."

"Ah, a true starving art student," the older woman said. "Don't let Darren shame you for acrylics. Hockney himself favors them."

"*Hack*ney," the man in the purple vest said over his drink. Everyone chuckled.

"Mmm, perhaps," Dean Henry said. "Though I suspect we'd all finger-paint for a taste of Hockney's success. Now, if you'll excuse me..."

With a practiced smile and a smooth gesture, Dean Henry found Megan's back with his palm. Her heart drummed as he guided her to a quieter part of the gallery.

"I see the committee steered you in my direction," he said. "How fortunate. Tell me, what was their decision? Walk me through it."

Megan had practiced answers and lined them up in her head. Now she found herself stammering at first, then speaking and building up speed. He nodded, as if it all made sense. And yet, concern narrowed his eyes and wrinkled his forehead. That jovial warmth he shined on the others was cooling.

"And you're never going to believe this," she said, already regretting her choice of words. "But the other day, I left my portfolio on the subway."

He took a deep sip from his martini. "No bother. I've seen enough of your work to get a taste."

Megan swallowed. "You have?"

"Of course. Your surrealist pieces, your landscapes last spring—those Hudson Valley pastorals. There were others, too, from a trip to the Finger Lakes, if I recall."

Megan nodded, impressed. She'd spent a week outside Auburn, camping on the shore of the Owasco with Corey and some friends. She'd studied the light on the trees and the water, painting several triptychs of the landscape at different times of day.

"They were... adequate."

The word landed like a punch. "Adequate?"

"They displayed excellent skill, of course. Craft has never been your weakness. But they were lacking something, yes? Come, let us look."

He walked her to a wall where five paintings hung, each the same three-foot by two-foot vertical shape. They bore similar compositions and motifs: two women, a sword, and a man being restrained in the throes of decapitation.

"Judith beheading Holofernes," Dean Henry continued. "The seductress-assassin who inspired countless brushes, from Botticelli to Caravaggio, from Goya to Klimt. A contrast of beauty and violence, youth and death. Some artists focus on the seducer, emphasizing her low-slung clothes, her breasts, her nude form. Others, her aggression, the slice of her sword across the general's throat, the noble resolve upon her face, willing to do whatever it took to protect her city from destruction."

Megan nodded throughout it, familiar with the story. She found it empowering. She had even hoped to make her own someday, when she was a better artist and could do the subject justice.

"My point—just so you don't think I'm rambling—is that great artists take risks. Tell me what you see before you."

Megan's eyes darted about the five canvases, the five variations on the same subject yet each radically different. She focused on the one in the middle, a mixed medium oil and newspaper collage intermixed with Polaroid pictures. Here, the sword-wielding Judith was a pudgy brunette, fully nude and raising the blade to her own throat and slicing.

Behind her, Holofernes was depicted as a newscaster, his heads repeating along a wall of TVs. The title: *Self-Portrait (Sorry I'm Such a Mess).*

"It's so… striking," Megan said. "She updated it."

Megan recognized the woman depicting Judith and cutting her own throat. She'd passed her earlier by the restroom. Now she was talking with two others by a metal sculpture of a blue ant.

"Striking indeed. Ms. Dabner channeled the trauma of her suicide attempt and made the story of Holofernes her own." Dean Henry gestured to the painting on the far right. "And here, Mr. Patel has recontextualized the subject through a Hindu lens. Skanda and his six severed heads replace Holofernes and his one. Tough work for the sword, except for six-armed Kali. Doesn't she seem pleased with her vengeance?"

Megan nodded, amazed by the detail in Patel's painting. The interplay of shadows and light. Kali's glistening indigo skin. The range of expressions on Skanda's severed heads, from fury and horror to apathy and acceptance.

"You have excellent technique, Ms. Monroe. You're more skilled with a brush than many of the artists on these walls. But tell me, what do you see in these paintings? What do you feel?"

Megan swallowed. "I see bravery."

"Yes, precisely. They are brave. We must be fearless, as artists. We must confront what truly scares us." He was so animated now she worried the martini might spill. "For Ms. Dabner, that was the fear of her body and how the media judges full-figured women. For Mr. Patel, it was the weight of cultural traditions and his crumbling faith. What scares you, Ms. Monroe?"

My broken mind.

My parents burning.

The Tenbury School.

But she said, "I don't know."

"Yes. Or perhaps you don't want to." He finished his martini. "When you applied for admission, your portfolio was excellent for its place in your trajectory, which was a senior, in high school. But has it progressed? Have you been brave these past two and a half years?"

She forced herself to speak past the lump in her throat. "No. Not really."

His eyes sparkled. And damn him, he was right. She hated to admit it, but the man bore a hole straight into her heart. She'd been holding back.

"Your work is lovely and adequate, yes, your technique acceptable. Your paintings would look wonderful upon the walls of a hotel or a hospital or... *wherever*. But greatness only comes from the balance of the eye and the heart. Unless you can be honest with yourself, unless you can be brave and take risks, then I'm afraid there's little any of us can do for your journey."

Megan told herself not to get misty-eyed. She blinked and forced a smile to her face. This man, he wasn't standing in her way; she understood that now. None of them were. She couldn't move forward because she was still holding back.

Then a name came to her, first soft and foggy at the edges, then clarifying in cool light.

Not Ophelia or Octavia; not Olivia or Orianna.

"Oksana," she said.

Dean Henry's gray eyebrows scrunched. "Come again?"

"No, you're right," she said. "Thank you."

And then she turned and left him standing right there, martini in hand. She left the gallery and let the crisp air wash over her.

She knew what she had to do now, but it scared her.

Because it was so far away.

chapter twenty-three

Graham Nolan had been knocked unconscious three times in his life. Once, when he was fifteen and mouthed off to the school bully. Next, when he was twenty-one and on R&R in Bangkok, sauced and bitter about how the Vietnam War was turning out. He'd cracked a joke about French surrenders and a Frenchman cracked a bottle of Singha over his head.

Waking up on Louis's kitchen floor was the third time, which he counted as his most embarrassing. He was older now; things hurt worse and took longer to heal. The shin splints from jogging, the bruises from boxing at the gym. Mostly, he knew better than this. He should never have turned his back on a person of interest.

A suspect, shit. Was that what Louis had become?

When he found the butchered remains in the bathtub, he knew the answer. The crimson-spattered tiles, the ruby-stained curtain, the knives. He called dispatch and told them to come over, but discreetly and without lights. He didn't want Bill to see what had happened to his dog.

Fifteen minutes later and the house was humming with county police. Bill paced outside, giving some poor deputy an earful and demanding to be let in.

Inside, Graham sat as a paramedic flashed lights in his eyes. His tongue circled a rough patch on his incisor. Damn, he'd knocked that crown loose again, perhaps falling on the kitchen tile.

Or perhaps the hammer. It was all sorts of fuzzy.

"Yep, you can feel where it grazed your temporal bone. Here, hold your finger." The paramedic motioned to keep the bandage tight on Graham's scalp while he finished dressing the wound. "Lucky guy. You should grab some lottery tickets on your way home."

"It's this stupid hat," said Rourke, the sheriff's lieutenant. He handed the Red Sox cap back, now scuffed and bloodied from the hammer strike. "I keep telling you that curse is real."

Graham picked at the frayed stitching. "Yeah, or maybe that curse just saved my life."

He'd gotten plenty of crap at the station about the Curse of the Bambino, beginning when the Red Sox sold Babe Ruth in 1918 and hadn't won a World Series since.

Rourke squeezed Graham's shoulder. "I don't think that's how curses work." Then he gestured, *Come talk to me later*, before returning to get briefed by the others.

It amused Graham that so many cops fit into a small house. Perhaps it was boredom and a sense of community violation. Little happened here in Bristol County. Now forensics was out in full force and animal control was taking poor Beatrice off in a bag.

A bag, he thought, recalling what Louis had been carrying. And what he was talking to.

Had he really seen that bag move in the fractured moments before darkness? Had he really heard someone talk back?

No, of course not. It was like the paramedic told him: he was concussed; his brain was wounded; he couldn't trust his senses right now.

And yet...

Graham shook it off. The paramedic told him to head over to St. Mary's for a CT scan. He promised him he would, knowing full well he wouldn't. He hated getting slid into those machines, even if it was only his head.

Cleared by the paramedic with a warning to take it easy, Graham found Rourke outside, breaking the news to Bill Hodgson by the curb. The man's tear-streaked cheeks glistened in the gloaming.

"I was right." He wiped his nose down his sleeve, leaving a wet trail.

"I told you, he always had it out for her. Dogs sense the good in people. They *know*. Beatrice, bless her, she never sensed anything good in him, not a lick. That's why she always barked."

Rourke and Graham shared a glance while Bill sobbed into his hands. Graham flagged down another cop and got Bill some tissues. He gave the man a moment to compose himself, touching the tender lump forming on his own head under the bandage.

While Bill worked his way through a few tissues, Graham asked, "My head's still swimming, so if I ask you the same question twice, you'll have to forgive. Bill, we both know Louis is a few candles short of a birthday cake, but did you do anything to provoke him?"

"Hell no. You go check his garage. You'll find my lawnmower in there. Lent it to him last spring and he still hasn't returned it. I've been nothing but nice to him."

Yeah, that tracked with what Graham had gleamed through community gossip. The usual small-town frustrations that festered over the years.

But killing Beatrice, then assaulting an officer and fleeing... This had gone from a neighborhood spat to multiple felonies. What a pluperfect fuckup.

Of course Graham made a few fumbles of his own. He'd pushed his way into Louis's house, perhaps a little too forceful. With the right legal counsel, Louis might argue he'd been coerced. Of course, Graham could claim exigent circumstances, Bill's suspicion, the wound on his hand.

No, not just a wound, he thought. The man was missing a whole finger.

Graham's instinct was tingling again. "Bill, did Louis tell you how he injured his finger?"

Bill blinked. "You saw that too?"

"Looked like the whole thing got chopped to the knuckle."

"Yeah, he said it was an accident out in the bay. Something about catching in a crab pot."

"A crab pot, not a propeller?"

Bill shook his head. "No, I saw him when he came home too. He was wet, like he'd fallen overboard and was still drying off." Something narrowed in Bill's eyes. "He was carrying a bag. Like clutching it all close to his chest and talking to it."

Graham tensed. He was about to ask the question when Rourke did it for them. "What was he saying?"

"Just mumbling, you know? Like how you'd talk to a baby."

Fifteen minutes later the animal control officers and first responders were clearing out. The neighbors still watched, either from their warm houses or from their cold porches, occasionally chatting with each other. Someone brought hot cocoa out to Bill and the others.

Once Bill was out of earshot, Rourke and Graham conferred by the cruiser. "Well, they haven't found the rest of poor Beatrice," Rourke said. "But it looks like Louis did a fair bit of cooking. You know that's a delicacy in some places?"

Graham nodded. He'd seen that and worse in the jungles outside Nha Trang. Pits filled with human bones sucked clean. The VC had eaten anything to survive and keep fighting. The Americans were choppering in burgers and fries. That was when he first knew it was over. They had no idea what they were up against.

Which was how he felt now. No idea. Just the fog of war and a feeling that he was missing a bigger picture.

Rourke said, "You mentioned Louis had some maps and directions. They didn't find any, so he must've taken 'em. Anything else you can think of?"

"Yeah, he had a phone book too, but I didn't get a good look."

"White pages or yellow?"

Graham closed his eyes. "It was the white pages, T section. Can you grab one from the neighbors?"

Rourke waved that deputy over and gave the order. A minute later the deputy returned, holding the phone book and smiling. They opened it, the deputy leaning in, excited to be a part of the action.

Graham studied the four columns of the TE–TH section on the right page. "It was somewhere in the left middle." He traced a finger down the thin paper, indicating the range that ran from *TEAK, Donna* to *THOMPSON, Jim*. But it didn't look right. "Wait, no. It was the business white pages."

He flipped further back, *Team Builders, LLC* to *Thorstein*

Plumbing. He could almost see the yellow highlight, somewhere on the left two columns, near the center.

"I think it was around here." He indicated in the general range of *Techsoft Training Videos* to *Terry Point Mobile Homes*. "Sorry, that's as good as I've got."

Rourke considered the page and turned to the deputy. "I want you to get a photocopy of this page, then cross reference every business name and see if Louis works there. Or if he did and was recently fired. Maybe he's got an axe to grind or something."

The deputy gulped. "You... want me to call them?"

"Well, don't advertise it. Be subtle."

Phone book in hand, the deputy hurried off.

Graham thumbed his journal, studying his notes, but none of it made sense. Rourke glanced at the Inspector Gadget cover, said, "Thought I told you to get a proper notepad."

Graham closed it. "It works as well as any other."

"Blue ain't your color. I'll have Nancy get you a real one from supplies." Rourke thumbed his duty belt. "So that bag you both mentioned, that's making me nervous. Do you think we've got some sort of Unabomber on our hands? Or maybe Louis's planning to go postal?"

"I'm not sure." And it was the truth. Graham tried to avoid speculation, but that was all he was working with now. That, and a concussion.

"What I mean is, do you think he's got some sort of target?"

"We should probably treat it as such. But I don't know..." Graham ran a finger from the brim of his cap to the rip the hammer had left in the side. Damn, he'd have to buy a new one.

"Don't know what?"

He swallowed. The sun was setting and the shadows were growing long. He'd spent half his day in this forlorn neighborhood and he couldn't wait to get home. What began as a favor was now a full-blown clusterfuck.

Graham said, "That bag, it didn't seem like some sort of weapon."

"Well, forgive the wording, but what'd it strike you as?"

"It's weird, but the way he was holding it, it was almost protective."

chapter twenty-four

"So what you're really asking is, 'Can I borrow your car?'"

Corey squeezed the damp rag and wiped down the bar. A few happy-hour regulars nursed pints near the dart board. Someone had fed the jukebox a few quarters, speakers buzzing out the chorus of Collective Soul's "December." It seemed so cozy in O'Bannon's that Megan was starting to doubt her tenuous plan.

Because it wasn't much of a plan, was it? Just a hunch she was chasing.

"Yes," she said. "So can I borrow it?"

"To drive to your old boarding school." He crossed his arms and added, "All because of some dreams?"

"They're not dreams if I'm awake."

He nodded a goodbye to a customer and retrieved a dollar bill from under the empty Budweiser. "And let me guess: one of those boarding school friends includes an ex you still have feelings for."

"I don't have feelings for Adam," she said. "Except anger."

Corey raised an eyebrow. "So yeah, feelings."

He was only three years older than Megan, but the pain behind his eyes made it seem closer to ten. She had told him they weren't a couple, insisting after each hookup that nothing had changed. Yet she knew he secretly hoped that someday it might. Still, he respected her space and never pushed it.

She said, "Look, I'm sorry I'm so fucked in the head. I don't know, maybe this trip will help."

"How so?"

"You know how you get a bill you can't pay so you just keep ignoring it? And the fees and interest build up? I've been doing that for two and a half years. Something happened, and I think it's connected to that school."

"Yeah, your parents died and you nearly drove yourself off a cliff. Meg, you're an artist. You say it all the time: a few demons come with the turf. And maybe... I don't know, maybe it's part of your charm." The way he looked at her now broke a little piece of her heart. God, she really was misleading him.

Junior hauled a keg in from the rear. "Ah, Megan, you're early. Help clean the pinball. Some shitbird stuffed gum in the coin slot."

"Sorry, Junior, I need to scram for a day or two."

"Scram? Take the whole week then. You're fucking fired."

"No, Junior, I'm not fucking fired."

"Fine. But you owe Corey. Poor guy's so smitten he'll cover your shift."

Corey blushed and slid her his car keys, a little rubber troll with green hair dangling from the ring. "Do you have enough money for gas?"

Her voice caught in her throat so she nodded. She needed this kindness, yet she felt unworthy. If she could just break through this mental block, perhaps she could finally move on. Perhaps she could be better.

"You okay to drive?"

She lied and nodded that she was.

"Page me if you need anything." Corey smiled and added, "Good luck, Megan."

THIRTY MINUTES LATER, she pulled the Isuzu Trooper up to the gas station and killed the engine. She had done it; she had driven for the first time since the crash.

She had taken lefts and rights at first, double- and triple-checking her blind spots and mirrors. She drove slow and stayed to the right, the car rattling, her heart beating its way up into her throat. She signaled early and often. After weaving around the neighborhood, she followed South Columbus and turned into the Sunoco station.

Now her hands finally stopped trembling. She wasn't sure how she felt. Triumphant, yes, but also like a failure. She was twenty-one; she should have her own set of wheels. She shouldn't be scared of the road.

It was just a car, after all.

Yet the reflection of that crescent scar bisecting her brow and forehead said otherwise. A flash of her father teaching her to drive while she was home for the holidays. His mustache rising as he said, "A car is a tool as well as a weapon. Every driver needs to respect that."

According to the police report, she had disrespected this rule.

She'd gotten drunk and gotten behind the wheel, and it had cost her a few weeks of her life. Her graduation, the parties, the final week with her parents, all swallowed by a hole born from one stupid mistake.

The moon rising over dark waters.

The whistling wind through a pair of creaking amber doors.

The rattling gravel as the tires left the road.

With a click, the pump stopped. Her gas tank was full. She knew she couldn't undo her past. But maybe she could try to move forward.

Inside the station, she bought a road atlas for Pennsylvania and another for Greater New England. She laid them out on the dashboard and studied the routes, a Jolt Cola cold between her knees.

She found Corey's cassettes loose in the center console, settling on something labeled *Summer '94 Mixtape* and pushed it in. Scott Weiland's smoky vocals filled the interior as "Interstate Love Song" started up. She smiled because she knew every word. The album had come out at the end of her senior year at the Tenbury School.

Which was where she was now headed.

chapter twenty-five

In his youth Graham had been broad-shouldered and barrel-chested. By his late forties he'd gone a bit soggy, a fact he was reminded of every time he squeezed behind a desk at the station. On most mornings he could count the cops present on one hand. Not today.

Word of Louis's deeds had spread as they did in small communities. Everyone offered their own theories. Louis was starving and had eaten poor Beatrice. Louis had finally snapped as Bill long promised. That Louis had assaulted an officer seemed to bother everyone, except Graham, who just wanted Louis to turn himself in before things escalated.

Which was what it felt like some of the younger cops were hoping for.

"It'd be a shame if Old Louie got a back-of-the-cruiser tune-up," Deputy Harris was telling Second Deputy Tomlin. "Graham gets the first five minutes, of course."

"Oh, what a pair of Don Johnsons." Rourke's voice boomed in the crowded room and stiffened the deputies' backs. "Folks, any talk of rough stuff and you'll be passing out parking tickets until spring. You want to scuff your knuckles, go join the staties, clear?"

Every head nodded, even the accountant's.

Rourke sidled up to Graham's temporary desk. "We got my granddaughter one of those oversized teddy bears for Christmas. She has tea parties with it. Always makes me chuckle, that big bear and that small table, all the other tiny animals around it. You remind me of that bear."

Graham pushed aside a report he'd just finished signing. "Yeah, well, I don't shit in the woods, so you're out of luck, LT."

Rourke took a seat on a stack of boxed paper. He gave a nod toward the packed room. "It's been a while since I've seen it this busy. Everyone's curious, including the press. How're you holding up?"

Graham gave his hat a tap. "Fine."

Which was a lie. The headache had persisted overnight and into the morning, never quite relenting. He'd vomited twice. Mostly, there was a faint haze, as if someone had streaked his glasses with Vaseline.

Rourke leaned closer. "Look, if you need some time off—"

Graham waved it away. "Working through it helps. Besides, I want to be the one to cuff Louis. Maybe I can get an explanation out of him. He seemed reasonable, just scared."

"Reasonable until he tried to flatten your melon."

"I overplayed my hand. Probably scared him."

"Now you're doing his attorney's job, making excuses."

It was true. Louis had assaulted an officer, butchered a dog, lied, and fled the scene of a crime. He was a felon; his actions were indefensible.

And yet, Graham had spent years around criminals—real criminals—and Louis didn't strike him as one. His instincts murmured that there was more to this than a neighborly dispute gone sour.

"Here's something for you." Rourke placed an evidence bag on the desk. "They found it in the bathroom, thought maybe it came from the dog, like a fancy tag or something."

Graham hoisted the baggie up to the light, studying the necklace inside. "That'd be one hell of a tag."

"Bill said it wasn't Beatrice's."

"This is a woman's necklace." Graham thumbed the bag, the dirty gold catching the light along the intricate links as he worked his way down the pendant. "Any word on whether Louis has a lady friend?"

Rourke sipped his coffee. "Stranger things have happened."

"If he did, he might be headed that way."

Graham turned the pendant over. The gold formed something like a flower or a bouquet, several vines merging into a cluster of petals. It was detailed, precise. Whoever made this had skill.

He smiled. "Look at this: hallmarks."

THREE PHONE CALLS, two jewelers, and an hour later, Graham entered Putnam & Sons to the jingle of a bell on the door's handle. The young woman behind the display case already had her eyes fixed on him. "Grandpa, that cop's here."

Graham smirked. "How'd you know I'm a cop?"

She blinked at him. "You walk with purpose. No one walks like that unless they're a cop or they're going to rob us."

She was right, of course. Graham knew he still had that old soldier's march in his bones. "Well, that's my Indian name, He Who Walks With Purpose."

The woman chewed her gum and pierced him with a bored stare. She cleared space behind the display case for her grandfather, who was pulling out a stool on his side.

"Fetch us some water, dear," the old man said, and off she went, into the back. When she was out of earshot, he shook his head. "Kids these days."

Graham liked the old man. He was probably close to eighty, his head egg smooth and speckled, his nose a beak over an explosion of white mustache. He reminded Graham of a proud walrus.

The old man placed a black velvet tray on the display case. "So, let's have a peek at this necklace of yours."

Graham laid the evidence bag in the tray, eliciting a raised eyebrow from the jeweler. "Should my attorney be present?"

"No, sir. We're just trying to track down some details. This was found at a crime scene."

"I'll be on my best behavior then." He gave Graham a wink and put the loupe to his right eye. He lifted the evidence bag with his tweezers. For a moment he just tilted and twisted his head, occasionally sniffling and clearing his throat.

Graham glanced around the old jewelry store, the rings and necklaces, the earrings and broaches. He knew he was in a true craftsman's place when he could taste the crisp air. Cheap metal smelled, but real gold had no odor.

The jeweler's mustache twitched. "Yep, yep, I remember this piece. Made it a few years ago in, oh, probably the spring."

"Really? You're sure of that?"

"Well, I'm sure that I made it. Those're my hallmarks." He lowered the loupe. "As for when exactly, I'll have to check the receipts. How long've you got?"

"As long as you can give."

The young woman returned with one glass of water and placed it between Graham and the old jeweler. He studied her for a moment, then asked, "Where's the other glass?"

"I thought you only said *a* glass."

"Why would..." The jeweler sighed and gave his best God Grant Me the Strength smile. "Go pull the receipts for ninety-one through ninety-five."

She scoffed. "That's, like, a *lot* of years."

"And I suspect it'll be a lot of receipts as well."

The young woman let out a long sigh and shuffled off to the back again. The jeweler pointed past Graham to the Putnam & Sons sign hanging over the door. "And she wonders why it doesn't say 'and granddaughters' yet."

Graham had expected the receipts to come out in a pile, perhaps paper-clipped if he was lucky. The old jeweler surprised him yet again. They were kept in thick binders, each order placed in its own plastic page with pockets and Polaroids beside them. It reminded him of a baseball card collector. Or his young nephew Omar with his precious comics.

The jeweler's tongue circled his dry lips while he flipped through the pages. Partway through the binder for 1994, his tongue stopped. He hooked a finger inside and withdrew a Polaroid, comparing it to a piece of yellow carbon paper and nodding.

"Yep, here we go. Spring of ninety-four. I was off by a little, but not much. Looks like the design was submitted in late April and delivered in

June. Rush order too. Sometimes that means they forgot an anniversary present."

The jeweler placed the binder on the counter between them, turning to the yellow intake form. The ballpoint pen had left faint markings in the paper, but Graham could see where the man's hand was pointing. "Eighteen-karat gold," he said. "That's quite the order."

"I usually remember those customers, but today I'm drawing a blank. Fortunately, we keep meticulous records. Kelly, take note." He gave a sidelong glance to his granddaughter, who was nose deep in a *Rolling Stone*, a tired-eyed Sheryl Crow staring back from the cover.

After fumbling with the plastic flap, he retrieved several carbon copies and unfolded them. They described the nature of the work, the quality of materials, the estimated cost and deposit.

Graham squinted, studying the name atop the page. "What's that here? Og-zenna—"

"Ok-sa-na," the old jeweler said. "Oksana Samarina."

Graham squinted at the scratched handwriting. "You can read that?"

"Had eighty-some years of practice."

His granddaughter silently mouthed, *Ninety*.

Graham asked, "Do you have Ms. Samarina's address or a phone number perhaps? I'd like to notify her, see if she's missing a necklace."

Or if she's harboring a fugitive, he thought. It was a stretch, but then again, so was the thought of Louis eating his neighbor's dog. It'd been a weird couple of days.

"Yep, insurance would have our head if we didn't. I got it here, somewhere."

While the old jeweler reached into the plastic envelope, Graham's eyes traced the sketch of the pendant's design. His senses were tingling again. He was pleased to see his assessment at the station was right: there was something floral about the pendant. Not a bouquet or a bundle. Rather, it resembled a cross section of a sunflower. He asked, "What is that, a daisy?"

"Mugwort," the jeweler said, pointing to his own notes, where he'd scribbled down the customer's request. "Also known as wormwood."

"You mean like in absinthe?"

The old jeweler shrugged. "That's what the customer wanted. Beats me what it all means."

It was the young woman who spoke, without even looking up from her magazine. "'And the third angel sounded his trumpet as a great star, blazing like a torch, fell from the sky upon a third of the rivers and springs, turning the world's water into bitter oil.'"

Both men studied her for a moment, not quite sure what they'd heard or why she'd said it. She returned their stare, gum moving from one cheek to the next.

"Book of Revelations, hello." She tapped her fingers on the counter. "The name of the fallen star is Wormwood."

chapter twenty-six

Louis didn't understand her instructions, but he followed them anyway; she was usually right.

Like when she'd told him not to let the cop into their house. Which he'd done.

Like when she'd told him not to turn his back or fetch that aspirin. Which he also did.

And like when she'd said to swing hard with the hammer and he'd held back because...

Because... why? Because he wasn't a killer.

Now her words clawed inside his mind. *You said you'd do anything for me. Louis, you promised.*

Here, behind the wheel of his idling Ford Taurus, Louis closed his eyes and tried to plug his ears for a moment. He'd known Oksana for a week, but it felt like his whole life. She was in him, inside, all intermixed with his thoughts and scratched over his past. When he envisioned his ex-wife, all he saw was a soft mannequin scrubbed of her features. When he thought of his neighbor Bill, it was just the shadow of the high school bully who shoved him in lockers.

Mostly, when he thought of tomorrow, all he saw was Oksana.

Or, rather, what she was becoming.

"You sure this is the right place?" he asked, glancing at the long lawns and ivied buildings, the trees all planned and precise. Past a sign for Parking and Admissions, he could see a statue garden and something like a sunken amphitheater. A pond lay to their left, lined with gas lamps flickering in the morning fog. Behind them, the metal sign squeaked from the arched gate, the Tenbury School.

What kind of school was this?

The rich kind, he thought as they drove a slow lap through the campus. It was quiet, the parking spaces empty, the buildings dark. A group of deer munched on some hedges by a building named Harpsburg Manor.

Louis felt that buzzing, like caterpillars crawling across the backs of his eyes. Oksana wanted something.

He fumbled with the boat bag, unzipping it and gagging as a wave of rot bloomed. He rolled down the window, caught between the cold and the stench.

"This is the place," she gurgled. "Bottom floor. Stacksss..."

He tried to ignore the way her lips split vertically on S sounds. Or how her jaw was coming loose and drooping to the left. He eyed those tendrils stretching up the edge of the boat bag and forming a lattice of bone. A dozen shards digging their way into the bag's fabric.

Like it was some sort of nest or cocoon.

And yet her face...

He stole another glance. Her cheeks were flush and dimpled, her hair a hint of copper. Even the once ochre skin and the spine of the starfish fused with her eye were now a soft peach. She was molting, perhaps.

Louis sucked in the fresh air as they cruised past a white chapel and a building with high windows and a wide oaken door. Tannhauser Literacy Center.

"Sssstop," she hissed. "Inside... Downstairs... Stacksss..."

He surveilled the dim building. He didn't want to go in. He didn't belong here, not with his rusty Ford Taurus. Not in the same clothes he wore when he slept in the back seat. And not in this condition.

He knew he had done something too, something terrible that he couldn't explain. When he tried to focus on the *why*, all he saw was a red bathtub and his carving knife. Shame knotted his thoughts and coiled the back of his neck. What was he doing?

"I've got to go pee."

Then the caterpillars squirmed behind his eyes.

YOU SCARED MAN LOUIS YOU CRAVEN SLINK YOU NEVER FINISH ANYTHING YOU JUST DRIFT JUST FUMBLE AND FALL AND FAIL AND AT YOU WE LAUGH THE WHOLE FAMILY LAUGHS AT THE FOOL WHO DOESN'T KNOW WHAT HE IS.

Louis dug his thumbs into his ears and cupped his hands. He tried to bring his knees to his chest and curl up, but the steering wheel blocked him. Gasping, he folded in on himself.

He was suddenly nine again, his grandmother's golem crashing around his subconscious, screaming that he was no good for his mother, no good for God, no good for anyone. His grandmother was behind him now. He could smell her hairspray and the Estée Lauder she rubbed on her wrinkles.

Then Oksana's voice, a honeyed whisper beside him, the only warmth in this car. *You can do it, Louis. Please... You promised you'd help.*

And like that, the echoing golem receded.

He would help her, yes, because she helped him. There was a word for such a thing. A big word he'd read in a magazine long ago.

Symbiotic.

Smiling, he parked by a sculpture of two open books and a planet between them. He turned off the ignition and zipped up the boat bag. He slung it over his shoulder.

Symbiotic, yes, that was what they were. And maybe someday a little bit more.

The Literacy Center was dim, its halls mostly shadows. A sign behind the glass read, *HAVE A HAPPY THANKSGIVING BREAK!* The doors were locked, of course. He hadn't seen a soul since he'd stepped foot on campus.

But this brick building was where she wanted to go, so he pressed his face against the glass, trying to suss out the interior. An open lobby with concrete stairs and frosted glass banisters. Huge windows looking out on a hilly forest they'd passed driving up. To the left, rows of shelving loomed over tables and desks. To the right, classrooms and offices, one of them lit up.

So he wasn't totally alone. Shit. He'd need to be careful.

He switched the boat bag to his left shoulder.

Why aren't we inside?

"It's locked," he whispered. "I don't think we can get in—"

IMPOTENT BOY LOOK AT HOW LIMP AND WEAK IT IS AREN'T YOU ASHAMED YOU'RE NOT A MAN BUT A WORM AND YOU CALL THIS AN ATTEMPT.

Louis, don't listen to her. You are brave, so very brave. See those windows down the hill? Those are classrooms. Maybe one of their windows is open.

He craned his head past the trees. She was right. The building was on a berm, and if he just followed a little irrigation path, he could connect with that statue garden below. He soon found a set of stairs that brought him along the far side of the structure. Decorative stones crunched underfoot. Cigarettes spiked a few ashtrays.

He tried the emergency door, but the handle didn't budge. He tried the windows next. Latched from the inside. Curtains drawn. He supposed he could grab a stone and smash one in, but if any place had an alarm, it'd be a rich school like this.

What's happening?

He ignored her. He had a sneaking suspicion there might be another door at the other end for fire code.

At first, he thought it was the gravel still crackling as he walked. But the sound followed him onto the grass. Then he saw it, little bones starting to poke through the bag's fabric. She was trying to get out.

I want to see...

The bag dimpled in a dozen places and started to split. She was tearing a peephole.

"There's another door," he whispered and carried the boat bag the rest of the way from the bottom. If the bag broke, he wasn't sure he could take much more of her smell. He needed a way inside.

He pulled and twisted the other door's handle, but the lock was tight and nothing budged. He could feel the caterpillars back behind his eyes, furious and scratching, and his grandmother's voice preparing to scream.

Then another voice broke the silence.

"Hey, down there."

Louis glanced up the slope to see a boxy woman wearing grass-stained overalls and a gardening tote on her hip. A pair of clippers and a spade jutted from her pockets.

She raised a walkie-talkie to her lips. "Never mind," she said. "It looks like I've found him."

chapter twenty-seven

Sandra was tired and cranky by the time the handyman finally arrived. Pete had called in sick yet again and she drew the short straw, covering his part of campus. Gardening, never her favorite. But she didn't complain 'cause Pete had a daughter with Down's and that wife with expensive tastes. Sometimes you just had to shut up and help out in this world.

Well, at least the handyman was here.

She spotted him wandering at the back side of the Literacy Center, poor fool. The campus was confusing, after all. They called dorms "houses" and "manors" and the class buildings "halls." They even named the grades "forms" and gave them different numbers.

Perhaps that was what the rich liked to do, she figured. Change common names and sneer when people said them wrong. Like her job title, which was technically an arboricultural engineer. But the kids all called her Groundskeeper Sandra, which she much preferred.

She waved at the handyman and went around the berm where the grassy slope wasn't as steep. She walkie-talkied Frank back at Facilities and Maintenance to tell him she'd found him.

From a distance, the handyman was handsome, a Brian Johnson if he'd maybe let himself go. Closer, and she realized her assessment had been generous; this guy was a mess.

"Thanks for hurrying over," she said, a bit too sarcastically perhaps, but the handyman just nodded and clutched his tool bag, shifting it to his back. "I hope you brought your voltmeter 'cause I can't figure out what the problem is."

"My... voltmeter?"

She gestured to the brick balcony above. Two of the lights were off. A third was now flickering. The handyman glanced upward as if just noticing the lights. Something about his oily gaze seemed off. A drunk, perhaps, or maybe a bit slow. She made sure to enunciate.

He grunted something, shifting the bag to the other shoulder. His right hand was curled, perhaps some form of palsy. But none of that mattered so long as he could climb a ladder and fix a few bulbs.

"The lights," she said. "My guess is it's the kids tossing rocks at 'em." She gestured with her thumb back toward campus. "Probably a nice place to hide a smoke after dark."

It was less a guess and more of a guarantee. She'd caught students doing all sorts of things out in the woods, from smoking spliffs to humping like bunnies. She never went looking, but it always gave her a chuckle when they tried to hide. She wasn't a narc. And the school didn't pay her nearly enough to circle back after she'd clocked out.

"Kids?" the man asked. "Like students?"

"Yeah, them or the rats. They like the indoors when it gets cold and end up nesting in the wires." He was an odd fellow, this handyman. "Anyways, maybe you could get up there, tell us what we're looking at fixing. Or if we should replace the panels with stronger glass."

The handyman swallowed. "I need... the bathroom."

Oh geez, was that why he was shaking? She'd had a bad taco in Hartford and it laid her out for a few days. He looked just as awful.

"Yeah, of course." She used her keys to open the back door to the Literacy Center and gestured past the stairwell. "Right there, buddy."

"Thanks."

As he shuffled in, she caught a glance of his fraying bag, something twig-like bumping up against it from inside. She swore something blinked.

No, silly thought.

As he did his business, her walkie-talkie blared in the stairwell,

Frank's voice coming in: "Sandra, could you repeat your last message? I was on the other line with Coleen. Over."

She was a bit too close to the bathrooms, so she turned the corner where the stone halls led past empty classrooms. "I don't recall. Probably just shooting the shit. Over."

She studied the student art lining the dark walls. One picture caught her eye: a psychedelic landscape, like the guy who painted those dripping clocks. A young woman curled up in the center, all cold and alone. Two shadows stretched out from a warm colonial house. Swirling in a tempest at the edges of the picture were report cards marked F, essays covered in red ink, crucifixes rising and pills spilling from bottles.

A bit melodramatic, wasn't it?

But then again, she remembered her high school days: every kiss was desperate and passionate, each moment the most meaningful ever. Life's volume, turned up to the max.

It was exhausting and she was glad those years were behind her.

"Sandra, I swore you said something about a handyman. Over."

She raised the walkie-talkie. "Yeah, I said I found him. Over."

There was the sound of the open mic, but no speaking. Then Frank said, "You sure? 'Cause I got a call from Bob Johnson saying they can't get anyone up here 'til tomorrow. Over."

She heard the words over the radio but processed each piece on a delay. The man's vague confusion, his shifty eyes, that floppy finger in the glove. Her conscious mind fumbled even though her gut knew the truth.

"Repeat. Over."

"Bob Johnson said he can't send a handyman until tomorrow. Over."

Christ, how could she have been so dumb? She turned the corner back to the stairwell and the bathroom, ready to rip this stranger a new one. Instead, she stopped in her tracks.

Sitting at the base of the stairs was the frayed bag he'd been carrying. The bag was open.

Something inside it was moving.

Peering at the zippered edge, she saw some sort of thorny nest, white twigs all intertwined. A few of them crackled like branches.

No, her subconscious whispered. Like blood-gorged veins and growing bones.

But it was the smell—oh Lord—a biting rot, redolent of sea caves and moss. She stifled a gag, eyeing the open bag and moving quickly to the emergency exit. She needed air.

Another sidelong glimpse, just enough to put a dent in her sanity and suck the wind past her lips. That was a woman's head in the bag, half cocooned by a lattice of bones. Her jaw was stretching and detaching. One eye bulged and came loose, clutched by a starfish.

The other eye was glaring at her.

Go. Get out. Now.

Sandra ran for the emergency exit. She did not see the man tucked into the alcove between the stairs and the door, his trembling arms lashing out and embracing her.

A man who wasn't here to fix the lights.

chapter twenty-eight

Shivering, Louis gave the limp body a shove down the embankment, watching it gain speed along the damp grass. It slid and struck the berm at the edge of the woods, tumbling ass over chest. For a single turn, he caught a glimpse of the groundskeeper's face, the ruined cave where Oksana had suckled and gnawed.

He knew they'd done something terrible and wrong. Gone and left another black mark on his soul. He observed his actions with disappointment and detachment, no different than when he'd tried Weight Watchers, counting every calorie and point only to find himself digging through the freezer for ice cream. He knew he was powerless to stop it.

And besides, Oksana needed it all, the lips and the teeth, the tongue and the jaw.

The body rolled to a stop in the woods. Good, he could hardly see her now. Just a tangle of autumn leaves and twigs and mud. If he was lucky, no one would notice her for weeks. If he was fortunate, they might get an early snow.

He used her keys to unlock the emergency door and stepped back into the stairwell. He took a moment to wipe a bloodstain off the wall.

The boat bag lay on its side, Oksana's head still stretching out like some terrible jack-in-the-box. She flexed her new mandible, letting it settle under her cheeks with a click. It occurred to Louis that he was watching something like a hermit crab trading out shells. It didn't make much sense, but love never did.

And that was what he was feeling now, love. Oksana chose him and he had a duty, an obligation. That was what a man did; he put those that he loved above himself.

So he picked her up and placed her back into the boat bag. The bone lattice had formed something of a bassinet. Louis suspected she was emerging from a larval stage now, nurtured by fresh food and a purpose he couldn't quite place.

"I remember... more," she said. Her voice was louder, less raspy, her lips more precise. "Take me to the library. Basement floor. Row twelve. There's an emergency entrance at the end of the hall. Use the..." Her tongue twisted and clicked. "K-K-Key."

He followed her directions down the long hall, taking one left and then a right. He had his doubts. But as soon as he unlocked the door, he could see she was correct. They were in some sort of basement area with metal shelves and books, all academic and oversized. At the far end, the main stairs led up to that library he'd glimpsed from the door.

He stepped soft, mindful of his work boots on the cold linoleum. He found row twelve, noting the black spines of uniform size, the text mostly crimson and gold.

These were yearbooks.

"Nineteen ninety-four." She spoke easier now, clearer. He suspected she was enjoying her new jaw. God, she'd made a mess when she'd consumed it.

Louis found the yearbook for 1994 and flipped through the pages. Just like he'd guessed, preppy kids in their blazers and blouses. Moneyed smiles and nice hair. Even a few names ending in *Junior* or *the Third*.

He didn't blame them, of course. Hell, if he'd spent his formative years at this place, his life might be different. He might like his reflection in the mirror.

But he never would have met Oksana.

"Turn the pages." Her head rose out of the bag on a column of tendons and bone. He thought of a centipede stretching for a leaf.

He flipped past the football and soccer teams. Past a mountain bike club and something called dressage. Holding guns and medals, the rifle club stared back from the page.

Further in, there were computer clubs and musical bands. A chess team and a group of Young Republicans in blazers and bowties. Each page featured a dozen or so students and a faculty supervisor frozen in black and white, the kids smiling from that liminal space between adolescence and young adulthood.

"Turn to the senior pages," she said. "Hurry."

He came to a section called Sixth Form Memories, where each student had their own page. Some had packed the space with photos and graphics, moments of their time at this school. Others had poetry or quotes interspersed.

What a long, strange trip it's been.

It's better to burn out than fade away.

Those who don't hear the music think the dancers are mad.

Turning the pages, he realized he didn't know Oksana's last name; he'd been too smitten to ask. But here it was at the top of the page, Oksana Samarina.

Below her name, Louis couldn't discern what he was seeing. Unlike the other senior pages, Oksana's was filled only with text. One long, massive block of nonstop writing covered the page.

There were sentences bolded, sentences italicized, words underlined or written in mixed cases. Only a quarter was English, and it made little sense, like those pronunciation guides found beside big dictionary words. The rest was in Cyrillic script, Eastern Slavic perhaps.

This wasn't for him, he realized. It was for Oksana.

Something was happening.

It began in her eye that was scanning the page, unblinking. Something intangible grew, a cold light glimmering brighter and brighter. He felt that familiar buzzing behind his own eyes, the caterpillars all squirming down a hot wire. He wanted to let the yearbook fall from his hands, yet he sensed a connection between the page and Oksana's expression. Was that awareness dawning on her cheeks? Was this some sort of epiphany?

Her eye scanned and scoured and devoured, not just the words but something they represented, some latent knowledge. Louis had a flash of a computer booting up, all that code shooting past and instructing it what to do next. He sensed himself standing at the edge of a great storm, rain spattering his face and the winds whistling with strength. He tasted the past.

In the adjacent stacks, moments streamed past the shelves like glimpses from a fast-moving train.

An Asian girl tearing up a Valentine's card and quietly crying.

Another flash of a woman's body pressed up against a young man's, their skin glistening in the moonlight as they slid under the sheets.

A third flash, a different woman in a study filled with mahogany shelves, her father shouting that if she wanted to go to art school, she could damn well pay for it herself.

They came faster now. A forest glowing blue. A metal cage melting. A gray hand floating among red foam at the grate of a storm drain.

The visions overwhelmed Louis, dark aisles birthing new sounds and smells, new memories and moments. Water and fire, laughter and screaming. He could only hold onto Oksana until his toes clenched and his sphincter tightened. The stacks became hissing shadows and wind.

And then it all passed.

He was here, in this library basement. He was holding a head in a bag as she finished reading. When she spoke, it was as if she'd found a new voice, her true voice, perfect and pure, like the closing note of a hymn.

"Page ninety, please. Sixth form destinations."

Woozy, he turned to page ninety. There was a listing of colleges the seniors would be attending in the fall. He recognized some by their sports teams. Division I universities he'd bet on or against and usually lost.

"Take it," she said. "Tear it out."

He ripped the pages, one after another until she told him to stop.

"Wait," she said. "Wait. Back."

He understood that she didn't mean turn back a page, but turn to the back of the yearbook. He licked his middle finger and thumb, flipped to near the end. He was getting used to life with fewer fingers.

There, at the very back, was a final picture beneath the caption *Tenbury Friends Forever*. Louis sensed he knew the five students in the picture; he'd caught glimpses of each when Oksana scanned those weird words. A mental backsplash that now fogged his own thoughts.

The students were standing before that gorgeous white chapel he'd driven past earlier. The sun was in their eyes, the wind blowing their hair. Two guys had their arms around each other, one with mousy brown hair, the other jet black and making a *hang loose* gesture with his hand. Three girls stood to their right, a blonde, a brunette, and an Asian girl with a quiet smile that struck Louis as impossibly sad.

chapter twenty-nine

One hundred and ninety-four miles to the northeast of Tenbury's Tannhauser Literacy Center, a young woman was taking part in her weekly ritual. Her heart raced. Her body quaked. Every toned muscle flexed and released. She swam in the training lane of the university's Olympic swimming pool, aiming to beat her best time for seventy-five laps.

She was well on her way.

Despite the coach's attempts to recruit her over the years, Chunhee "June" Chang was not on the swim team. These days, competitive sports repulsed her. She had been required to play them in high school, three seasons a year. She still cringed when she thought of the cliques, the locker room laughter, the girls who teased her, asking if it was true: did Asian pussy really go sideways?

She stole a breath between strokes and powered through another lap, turning her anger to sleek speed in the water. Here, she could burn off the past. Here, she could reach for the future. And if she pushed herself hard enough, she could become someone new.

It hit her in the middle of lap fifty-eight, a piercing memory clearer than all those dreams of the past several weeks. She could see her, Oksana. She could see Adam and Megan, Desi and Tom. She could see Desi's summer home on the coast, the dunes and the beachgrass, that old, tilted fence half swallowed by soft sand and jagged rocks.

Then something coiled around her foot.

She glanced down between strokes and spasmed. Seaweed hooked her ankle. She kicked and twisted and fought to disentangle her leg. Her hands flailed for the lane lines, fingers slipping off the plastic donuts.

Only they weren't donuts anymore; they were bones and teeth and hair all threaded together.

Gasping, June righted herself, toes skimming the bottom. Instead of firm tile and concrete, she slid through something wet and viscous. A crimson smear bloomed in the water and darkened her goggles. She kicked up, hands thrashing out and batting at the kelp probing its way up her legs, past her hips, and slipping beneath her swimsuit like unwanted fingers.

And then she was at the edge of the pool, screaming and hoisting herself out, tearing herself away from...

Away from what?

Her lane line was just red and white plastic. There was no bloody water, no seaweed clutching her flesh. This was just her swimming pool, its lanes empty and quiet. The other students had already gone home for Thanksgiving.

And she was alone.

TWO HUNDRED AND five miles to the west, where the wind off Lake Ontario was bitter and the clouds were gray with rain, two pairs of hands worked PlayStation controllers while a third rolled a fresh joint.

Desi had never taken an interest in video games, but with *Mortal Kombat 3*, something clicked. She had mastered the classic fighters and was getting proficient with the new ones, like Night Wolf and Sector. Still, her favorite was Kung Lao and his bladed hat. Currently, she was beating up Mileena, played by their neighbor Ray. Each new blow brought a further slouch to his shoulders, a picture of gaming frustration.

"Cheap... ass... whore," Ray grumbled, sinking into the papasan.

Desi grinned as she pummeled his character. To Tom, fighting games felt a bit simplistic. He preferred RPGs or the occasional shooter with crude humor, like *Duke Nukem 3D*. But *Mortal Kombat* made Desi happy, so he didn't mind her bogarting the TV when their friends came over.

But she was running out of friends to beat.

"Ah, you bitch," Ray groaned. "Just kill me now."

Tom licked the joint and used the lighter to seal it all up. He took a moment to test the airflow, satisfied. There was an extra-large pizza on the way and he hoped to be properly lifted when it arrived. It was the only way he could stomach pineapple and ham.

"A thousand curses upon such filth," Tom muttered.

"What?" Ray asked, his thumbs mashing the buttons.

"Nothing. Forget it."

He sparked up the joint, took a drag, and passed it to Maynard. One of the perks of living off campus was the freedom. The dorms were a ghost town over Thanksgiving break. Just a few international students stuck wandering the halls like zombies.

But here, if he got bored, he just needed to step outside the apartment. Turn left, and he could knock on Ray's door. Turn right, and he could grab Maynard. His boys were always up for no good.

Like this afternoon, when they'd distracted Desi so Tom could run to the jeweler and pick up the ring. He really hoped she'd say yes.

Maynard took a second drag, then a third and a fourth, violating the sacred puff-puff-pass, but Tom didn't mind. Weed was meant for good times, and good times were better when shared.

But now the TV had his attention.

With a flick of her fingers and a triple tap on the controller, Desi executed a perfect Fatality. Kung Lao sent his bladed hat spinning across the screen. Ray discarded the controller while his character's head left his shoulders in a spray of red pixels.

"All right," he proclaimed. "I'm done."

But Tom continued to stare.

That was Ray's character, Mileena, there on-screen. But that wasn't her head falling and landing with a crunch. That was a young woman he kept forgetting.

Oksana Samarina.

Her eyes were locked on his.

Tom leaned to the right, and her gaze followed his tilt. To the left, and the little pixel pupils tracked his lean. Damn, this weed was strong stuff.

Desi's scream broke his glazed stare.

She tossed the controller down and scooted up the couch, waving her fingers as if they'd been burnt. She gave the controller a kick, sending it spinning across the rug.

"Whoa, Desi, what the hell?" Maynard said, finally passing the joint to Ray.

"It... It was suckling my fingers," she said, squeezing her digits. Her eyes locked on Tom. What she said made no sense and yet he didn't doubt her, not one single word.

"The controller," she said, "it was licking my hand."

TWO HUNDRED AND fifty-four miles to the southeast, beneath the florescent lights of Balducci's, Adam waited with his mother while the cashier totaled up their groceries. There was the red wine and white, the warm cornbread and muffins. There were Styrofoam cups of organic cranberry sauce, fresh stuffing, and three kinds of pie.

Most of all there was the turkey, fifteen pounds of free-range meat all wrapped in plastic, butcher paper, and twine. He hoisted it up and placed it on the checkout counter, the conveyor belt groaning. He smiled at the cashier, a young woman he went to elementary school with but whom he pretended not to know.

"Honestly, I don't know what your father is thinking. He never finishes one pie, let alone three."

"Dad just likes his options, that's all."

"Well, he'll have his options: a heart attack, diabetes, cholesterol..." She took out her checkbook and continued the list.

Adam helped bag the groceries while the poor cashier got an earful of his mother's complaints. He gave her a sympathetic shrug. *Family. What can you do?*

He was placing the turkey in the bag when he felt it, a faint drumming under his fingers. No, under the paper and plastic wrap. Something moved inside the bird.

He licked his dry lips, studying the twine wrapping the turkey. That wasn't cheap string but an eighteen-karat gold chain.

"Adam?"

Slowly, carefully, he tugged on the gold chain, unraveling the knot. The butcher paper fell away from fifteen pounds of plastic-wrapped meat.

"Adam?"

This wasn't a turkey here on the counter; it was a lump of tumorous flesh. Pink muscle flexed alongside rows of chattering teeth. Nostrils flared and contracted. Bone slid past quivering skin. A low moan rose from gray lips as a nipple pressed against the shrink wrap.

"Adam?"

Adam shoved the sopping mass away, sending it tumbling to the floor where the cashier sprang back.

"Jesus, honey, what is it?" his mom asked. "What's wrong with the turkey?"

Nothing, he realized. No, everything. He squeezed his toes and felt his shoulders tense. He needed...

He needed what? He didn't know. Just that the walls were closing in and he needed to leave.

"Sorry, Mom, I've gotta go."

Then he hurried out of the market, his mother's shouts fading beneath his thoughts. He licked his lips, heart drumming deep in his chest as the sweet taste of Dr. Pepper lip gloss now danced on his tongue.

A taste he had forgotten.

chapter thirty

Old Paugussett Road meandered along the hills and hollows of the southern Taconics. It rambled past a colonial cemetery where vine-choked graves leaned, inscriptions long worn away. It wound beneath a mossy stone bridge carrying the murmur of freight trains. It abutted a pasture the boarding school kids often cut through on their nocturnal journeys in search of cigarettes or booze or adolescent adventure.

It was here, at this pasture's stone fence, that the headache hit Megan, seized her, forced her to pull off before she lost control of the Isuzu. She dug her thumbs into her temples while the turn signal went *tic-took, tic-took, tic-took*.

The memories assaulted her, a discordant symphony of senses. The tang of fresh-cut grass in the air. The salt and black pepper of her mother's pot roast. The touch of Adam's soft fingers over her sweater, her chest, her beating heart.

She was no longer in Corey's Isuzu. The seat underneath had become the Queen Anne chair that her mother called elegant but struck Megan as outdated. The gray car seat was now burgundy linen. She no longer clutched the steering wheel but held a fork in her left hand and a knife in her right. Across from her sat her parents, their dinner plates half empty. The meal was at midpoint, judging by the low level of her mother's wineglass.

"And where will you be heading in the fall, dear?" her mother asked, that sparkling stare shifting from Megan to the girl at her right.

"I'm not deciding yet, Mrs. Monroe." The girl spoke with an accent, both elegant and hoarse, soothing and scratching. Her skin bloomed with sunspots and rays. No one seemed to notice or care. "There are many dance schools to be choosing."

"Oksana's here on exchange, just for a semester," Megan said and smiled to her right. "But we're kind of hoping she'll stick around."

"You're *kind of* hoping, or you *are* hoping?" her father asked. He had finished chewing his asparagus and his tongue was now cleaning his teeth. He had that fierce look that she dreaded, a criticism that would turn into a lecture.

Not tonight, she thought. *Please not tonight.*

"You're either one or the other, not *kind of*. Heck, we had to pink slip one of our accountants today. We didn't *kind of* fire him—"

"Okay, Dad, I get it."

His eyes flashed behind his glasses. He was on his second bourbon and he'd been in the city on business all week. Why couldn't they just order pizza when she brought a friend home for the weekend? Why couldn't he stay at the company apartment a little longer?

"What is this 'stick around'?" Oksana asked. Whenever she was excited, she leaned forward. Megan found it endearing and smiled, but her friend's skin was blinding.

She said, "Stick around means to stay somewhere."

"Ah, I like this. Stick around."

Megan's father swirled his whiskey sour, placated for the moment. It wasn't lost on her that Oksana had distracted them with her question.

Megan's mother dabbed her lips with her napkin. "Surely your parents prefer having you closer to home. I've never been to Russia, but I can't imagine it's too different."

"Oksana's from Ukraine," Megan said. "And her parents..."

"My parents are... no more," Oksana said. "But my uncle, he likes that I travel, see the world. It is such a big and wonderful place, yes?"

"And dangerous," Megan's mother said. "For a pretty young thing like you."

"Mom, we're almost eighteen."

"Well, you'll always be our little girl."

Megan smoothed the napkin on her lap. The texture was too crinkly. And the fork in her hand felt brittle and thin.

"And this uncle of yours," Megan's father said, his eyebrows scrunching. "He doesn't worry about you?"

Megan couldn't see her guest's face, couldn't even look in that direction, and yet she sensed Oksana's smile radiating through time and memory. "I think all people worry. Especially caretakers of daughters, yes? It is, how do you say? Instinctual. Like, is in DNA."

It took a lot for Megan's father to nod, but that was what he was doing. His lips tightened and his eyes saw Oksana, as if he were seeing not his daughter's friend but a woman far wiser than her years.

Oksana must have sensed it, because she quickly said, "We are study Watson and Crick at school, so I make brag of my learning. Is that right? Make bragging?"

"Boast," Megan's mother corrected. "And it's not exactly polite to boast, but... cultural differences, I'm sure."

"Ah, I see."

"Well, I think it's impressive," her father said. "You moving halfway across the planet for a semester. We tried to get Megan to do a summer in London, but she wanted to work."

Megan found her voice so small, so quiet. "I needed the money."

A chuckle from her father. "Yeah, money for rap CDs and that skateboard."

There was a clink of fork scratching against plate. Megan was surprised to discover it came from her hands. Because she knew what was coming, what she was going to say next. And the consequences that would follow.

"No, I sold those CDs," she said. "And the skateboard. I needed the money because I'm going to art school."

Her father scowled as if he'd just bitten his tongue. Her mother's eyes hardened as she slowly drained her wine. Even Megan frowned, unable to meet their glares after saying her piece.

But not Oksana. Despite the radiance bursting from her skin, Megan could sense a smile in there, in the light, on the lips of her old roommate, her study partner, her friend whose name she had hardly spoken in years.

That warm hand squeezed hers.

Then it was over. Or never had been.

The edge of the dining table became the dashboard. That antique chair was just the driver's seat, old wrappers stuck in the cracks. No disappointed glares loomed, just the placid gaze of a few cows at the edge of their pasture.

There was no fork in her hand, just a Staedtler drawing pencil held between trembling fingers, tip broken against the sketchbook in her lap. She studied the page, the drawing, seeing it for the first time. She had no memory of this.

Even in its crude shape and quick design, Megan recognized the Tenbury campus. The jagged scribbles that made up the chapel. The crosshatches that filled in the lawn. And the library, most detailed of all, had been circled three times until the pencil tip broke.

Oksana. The Tenbury School. The library. There were answers there, something reaching out from her past. Something she shared with others, those friends who were once her whole world.

She pulled the car back onto the road. She drove toward the school.

She did not notice the truck passing her on the left. A red pickup, its bed covered with a tarp where landscaping supplies rattled about.

chapter thirty-one

The chapel bells echoed across campus, arching Megan's back on reflex and pulling her gaze to the red brick and white columns of Sprague Hall. She could almost see the students in the dining commons, their heads bowed for grace beneath the paintings of former headmasters. She could almost hear the clatter of warm plates leaving the kitchen while the staff barked orders at each other.

But not this week.

The Tenbury School was deserted, its parking lots mostly empty. After a few years at college, it struck her just how small the campus felt. Everyone had always acted like this hill was the center of the world.

She parked near the library and shook off her discomfort. She was no longer a student, no longer subject to the strict rules. She lit a cigarette to prove this to herself. She was an alumnus now, yes, and alumni were always welcome to visit their old home on the hill.

At least, that was what the donation requests always promised.

She stopped by the chapel, eyes taking in the bell tower, the arches. This was it, that picture from the slides. But it felt empty.

Because she and her friends weren't in it.

Maybe it wasn't the chapel, she thought, but that picture of them itself. Hadn't it been selected for the yearbook?

She found an ashtray near the entrance to the Literacy Center. The doors were locked, as she suspected, the lights dark and the halls dim. But not the library.

"Señorita Monroe?" asked a voice with a slight Castilian lisp. "*Que pasa?*"

Megan found herself smiling before she turned. Crossing the lawn between the dining hall and the library and carrying a brown lunch bag was Señora Cortez, her old Spanish teacher.

"*Hola*, Señora Cortez." Megan felt herself slipping back into student mode, worried about her pronunciation and conjugation. She'd taken four years of Spanish, three with this woman.

"I thought that was you," Señora Cortez said in Spanish, a smile splitting her freckled face. "What brings you back to campus?"

Señora Cortez was a no-nonsense Spaniard from Harlem, one of the youngest faculty members. She had joined in Megan's sophomore year, straight out of college and with a head full of tricks she was eager to try. She had ruffled a few feathers, insisting that her students address her in Spanish first, even outside the classroom.

"*Yo estoy...*"

Megan hesitated, remembering that the word for library was *biblioteca*. But what was the word for premonition? *La advertencia?* No, it was *la premonición*. And how could she say, *My yearbook was burned in the fire and I need to see the school's copy?*

"*Mi libro... fue quemado. Necesito...*"

"Relax, I'm just teasing you," Señora Cortez said as Megan fumbled her way through the explanation. "Here, hold my lunch while I unlock the door."

Megan took the brown paper bag, noting the weight of the contents and the little name with a heart dotting each I in her first name: *Kiki*.

"I didn't know the kitchen was open during vacation."

"It isn't." Señora Cortez grinned, opening the door and gesturing into the Literacy Center. "But the yearbook is on deadline, I need the overtime, and let's just say Gary has a thing for brunettes." She gave her former student a wink.

Scary Gary from the kitchen. Megan could see his tattoos, his long salt and pepper hair up in the net. Bootleg Megadeth buzzing from an old cassette deck by the industrial fridge. That toothpick forever stuck between his lips, never falling, no matter how loud he yelled at the student helpers to hurry up and bus the plates.

"I didn't know you two were a thing."

"Oh, he's definitely a thing. As for us?" She shrugged.

They continued through the Literacy Center, footsteps echoing out in the dark halls.

"Megan, I was so sorry to hear about your parents." Her eyes flicked to the scar. "And the accident, *que horrible! Mi más sentido pésame.*" She offered Megan a tender smile, something rarely seen in the classroom. "How are you holding up these days?"

So, word had spread. Megan suspected as much when the yearly Christmas card from the headmaster came with a personal note at the bottom: *Whatever we can do to help, please let us know.*

She shrugged and spoke her usual lie. "Oh, I'm doing fine."

She told Señora Cortez about everything getting lost in the fire, including her yearbook. She said this trip was for a college psychology assignment, which was enough. She knew liars tended to overexplain so she kept her reasons vague.

Then she mentioned her friends, including Oksana.

"*Dios mío*. Now there's a name I haven't thought of in a while." Señora Cortez paused by the water fountain as if she'd forgotten something. "Oksana, huh. So how's she doing? You keep in touch?"

"No, not really."

She wasn't sure how she could keep in touch, not after Oksana returned home. Maybe she'd left an address. But if so, it was just one more thing lost in the fire, consumed by the void that divided her life into *before* and *after*.

"That's too bad," Señora Cortez said. "You two were inseparable."

They arrived at the library, the late-November sun cool through its tall windows. Dusty portraits lined the walls, Poe and Hawthorne, Thoreau and Alcott. Their painted gazes fell upon books and card catalogs and the occasional computer.

"We keep the old yearbooks in the basement archives," Señora Cortez said. "We've started digitizing the past five years. Depending on how far back you want to go, we can pull microfilm."

"I don't think that'll be necessary."

She gestured up the stairs to a lit office. "I'll be working on this year's edition. Dean Schneider wants the cover to read, 'At Tenbury, nothing is Mission: Impossible.'"

Megan blinked. "That's pretty lame."

Señora Cortez mimed putting a gun to her head and pulling the trigger. Then she winked at Megan and walked up the stairs, her brown lunch bag in hand and that confident strut to her hips. It struck Megan that her teacher of three years was treating her not like a student but a woman, a peer, perhaps someone she could share a beer with. Was this what it meant to get older? If so, it wasn't too bad.

Downstairs, the basement lights buzzed and hummed and mostly blinked on. Only a few dark pools remained between the shelves of books. It didn't take Megan long to locate the section she needed and the spot for the yearbook. A part of her wasn't surprised at what she found.

An empty spot for 1994.

This was silly, she told herself. She had no real reason to be here, in this basement. It was just a blind compulsion, false nostalgia, her broken mind distracting her with the past to avoid addressing her present.

Which was in shambles.

She had failed out of art school. She was afraid and a fraud. Just another starving artist in an indifferent city, another pretender with a portfolio under her arms and fueled by delusions.

"Stupid," Megan mumbled. "There's nothing here. Go home."

But there was.

She was about to turn when she saw the yearbook, her graduation year on the spine. It rested on its side, a half section down among the 1960s. It was as if someone had just randomly discarded it.

And they had.

She could see smudges at its corners where rough fingers had turned the pages. The sticky outline of a hand, still glistening beneath the harsh florescent lighting. When she cracked the spine, she noticed it immediately.

Several pages were missing.

chapter thirty-two

Few things made Kiki Cortez happier than an empty campus during vacation. The dark hush that hung over the dorms at night. The dew-laden grass at daybreak, undisturbed by the feet of scurrying students. And the occasional fling with Gary.

Yes, he was crass and vulgar and ten years her elder. On paper, they had little in common. But they both spoke the same love language: a good meal, a nice drink, and a foreign movie on the VCR, preferably something that made her cry.

Last night, Gary had poached two bottles of merlot from the kitchen. Together, they cooked veal scallopini in her tiny apartment. They watched *City of Lost Children* and rolled around in her bed. He was always gone in the morning, which she appreciated. She stopped by the kitchen for a cereal brunch before heading to the yearbook office, discovering he'd left her a bag of leftovers and a note.

Something that put a blush to her cheeks and a spring in her step.

Then she'd forgotten it.

Oksana, she realized. That was why. When Megan said her name, it was like a cork had popped deep in her brain. So, here Kiki was, scrolling to the S section of the 1994 yearbook, letting the photos load one by one. Why the hell was it so hard to remember that girl's face?

Oksana was on exchange for the spring term, so she wouldn't have been on any teams or clubs in the fall or the winter. Kiki skipped those. To make publication in early June, the printer needed the yearbook's zip drives no later than April 1. The spring term always started the last week of March.

That didn't leave Oksana much time to wind up in the photos. Here she was, *SAMARINA, Oksana, '94. Files: 1. Pages: 1.* Huh. Not very many.

Kiki clicked open and waited for the zip drive to load. She had never wanted to teach Spanish at Tenbury, but some of the campus elders were concerned she lacked the experience to run the new computer media lab. Or, she suspected, they were concerned to see it run by a young woman with skin darker than frost.

They'd asked her to teach home economics instead.

As if.

When the page loaded, Kiki wasn't sure what she was seeing. Every senior was given one page to thank their family, their friends, to fill with precious quotes from their favorite bands. But unlike the pages that included in-jokes and the occasional sexual innuendo, Oksana's senior page was a grid of words.

Words that made little sense.

Some were italicized, some underlined or written in a mixed case. Only a quarter of it was English, many of the words phoneticized. The rest was Ukrainian; Kiki was certain of that. She had a vague memory of Oksana submitting it, insisting it was some sort of traditional poem.

"Is like a lullaby, but opposite," Oksana had said. "Not for sleeping but for the waking up."

The computer's screensaver blinked on, winged toasters flying diagonally down-screen, interspersed by the occasional piece of toast. Kiki blinked. Odd, the screensaver didn't start for fifteen minutes. Yet her eyes were dry and a sour paste coated her tongue. Had she been staring the whole time?

Shaking it off, she dug into the filing cabinet. For every photo that made it into the yearbook, there were a dozen that didn't. Sometimes it was a matter of being out of focus. Sometimes the subject was redundant. And despite the school's reputation for sports and its alumni's sizable donations, Kiki believed not every picture needed to include a group of rich Anglo boys in pads hoisting their trophies.

She found the section for 1993–1994 and flipped through the photos. Three-by-fives and four-by-sixes. The occasional eight-by-eleven. She turned them over, confirming the names on the back written in ballpoint pen.

Lisa Tower, with her Hampton's smile and lazy glare, a girl who had never heard no and probably never would. Jerome Brown, the towering basketball forward, that mask of subtle discomfort often worn by the inner-city students brought in on sports scholarship: *How the hell did I wind up at this place?*

And there, near the end, she came across the first instance of the name Oksana.

It was dated March 28 and professionally developed. A photo of the girl's track team at their first practice run on the trails. There was Megan in the front. Ashlee Travis coming up behind. And there at the edge was a bloom of light washing out the corner.

Kiki told herself it was overdeveloped. And she believed it too, until she came across a second picture.

Another black and white photo, the interior of Memorial Chapel balanced with the pews on both sides, the aisle splitting the image down the center and drawing the eye. Whoever shot it had a good sense of composition.

There at the left, five pews back, that same blurry radiance overwhelmed the edge of the picture, washing it out and rendering a dozen students into thin wisps of light. It was an artifact, a bad lens perhaps. Or the film had been improperly developed. Kiki had seen it all happen.

And yet...

The yearbook office felt too small, too dark. She turned on another lamp and dug further back in the files.

Here was a group photo of sixth-formers crossing Ford Lawn on the way to class, their blazers open, ties loosened, hair messy. Guys on the cusp of adulthood and trying to pretend they weren't preening for the camera. Girls all gangly and shy smiles.

And there it was again, a glare in the background, just out of focus.

She could see Megan and Adam, Chunhee and Desiree. That stoner Tom who somehow never got caught. No, that bloom of light wasn't part of the development process. It was walking beside them.

It was casting shadows on the grass.

chapter thirty-three

Megan closed the yearbook and rubbed the bridge of her nose. She was an idiot. Driving all this way here, and for what? More questions, more confusion, and all she had to show for it was a yearbook with missing pages.

Then she heard the chittering. She was no longer alone.

Tucking the yearbook under her arm, she scanned the row of old bookshelves. There were encyclopedias dating back to the last century, atlases of countries that no longer existed. It seemed like *National Geographic* took up a whole section.

And there was something else, too. A faint crunch and a wet slurp. Something squirmed beneath the open base of a shelf.

Squatting, Megan wasn't quite sure what she saw under the shelf. A pink and fleshy *thing*, like an infant's hand clutching a huge lump of dust. Gray string all tangled up in it. And that hand, was it squeezing?

Megan pressed her head to the floor, eyes level with the pink object.

And then the pink object looked back.

Megan found herself without words, without any clear understanding of the aberration. It held a single gray eye at the fleshy nexus of five dimpled fingers. She thought of tide pools and field trips to the Boston Aquarium. She thought of her grandfather's cancer.

But this starfish, it had mouths along its limbs, little slits that puckered and gulped in the shadows. It had jagged teeth glistening violet.

Because it had been chewing, she realized. That wasn't a clump of dust and some string. That was a dead rat it was clutching.

The starfish-thing glared and rose on its fingers, tenuously inching toward Megan. Its rear leg dragged the dead rat.

No, it wasn't dragging the rat, she realized numbly. It had burrowed into the skin and was sliding under the fur. It was consuming the rodent, fusing with it. Some of the fur was now pink.

A sudden scratching as little nails pawed about inside Megan's mind. She lurched to the right and knocked several books from the shelf. Somehow, she sensed that as impossible as it was, the source of her headache was the starfish-thing before her.

A thing now wobbling closer on wet fingers.

—GAVE YOU A CHOICE AND YOU REJECTED IT YOU COWARD YOU SLUT YOU'RE NO DAUGHTER OF OURS NO FRIEND NO ONE WORTH CARING FOR YOU STAY OUT OF OUR WAY AND—

Dragging the dead rat, the starfish-thing wriggled closer, closer. It raised dimpled fingers, those slits opening to shout maddening insults. That furious gray eye that never blinked and never stopped glaring. Numbed, Megan felt herself slipping down a hole. She was tired and confused. If she shut her eyes, she might just fall asleep here, on her feet, leaning against the dark shelves. If she let herself blink, she might sleep forever.

She did not blink.

Instead, she grabbed something off the shelf and she threw it. The book was a rarely used thirteenth edition of *The Chicago Manual of Style*. It weighed over two and a half pounds.

Flipping spine over fore-edge, it struck the starfish-thing and the rat, sending them rolling beneath the shelves and leaving a glistening streak on the floor. Megan felt a severing as the headache released. She could move now; she could think. She knew what to do.

She grabbed another thick book and hurried to *The Chicago Manual of Style*, kicking it over. The pages were dampened, brown and viscous. Wincing, she wiped her wet thumb on her jeans.

The starfish-thing was gone.

Silence. Then she heard it, the skittering and *tickity-ticky* of little teeth a row over. She could hear a faint mewling too. She'd wounded the thing, whatever it was.

She reached the next row, finding little droplets it had left in its wake. The mewling grew too, a weak squeaking, like tape between wet fingers. She caught a glimpse between books on the shelf: broken fingers limping two rows away.

She ran three rows over, just in time to see it duck beneath the last shelf. That was it. There were no more rows, only the creme walls of the basement archives, the florescent lights painting it cool. She could see the crawling thing, the thing that shouldn't be. She had it now. She would capture it, kill it, study it, figure out—

No. She understood where it was going.

The radiator.

Where the wall met the cast-iron radiator lay a hole where a pipe once carried steam from a boiler. But they'd upgraded to central air a few years ago, building by building. Megan remembered the construction.

The hole wasn't large, but just large enough. Mewling and squeezing, the starfish-thing rose, corkscrewing its broken limbs and feeding itself into the darkness. The pink fingers closed around the eye, sliding inward. The rat followed, tail and hindquarters first. Then its body followed. The last thing Megan saw were its beady eyes bulging out of its face before the shadows devoured it. One eye was blue. The other was gray.

chapter thirty-four

Kiki sensed her former student was holding something back. Still, she didn't push it. It had been an odd afternoon. So when Megan returned to the office with the yearbook and pointed out the missing pages, Kiki tried to ignore the young woman's shaking leg.

"It looks like they tore out a chunk of the college section," Megan said. "Sorry."

"It happens. I caught a couple of third-formers using old Bible pages to roll tea into joints." Kiki laid the defiled yearbook by the computer. "They thought smoking Earl Grey got you buzzed."

She wasn't sure why she was telling Megan this, only that she liked the girl and she wanted to appear relatable. Most of the Tenbury teachers kept the students at a distance.

She loaded the missing yearbook pages onto her computer, the zip drive clicking away. Outside, crows were circling over the thicket that clutched the western slope of the campus forest. A few stubborn leaves rustled in the window, refusing to fall.

"Jay Brubaker," Megan finally said.

"Jay? What about him?"

"He started that rumor about the tea."

"No shit?" Kiki tilted her head, trying to remember the student.

She'd just crossed five years now and the faces were beginning to blur. Was this how it started?

"No shit," Megan said. "But it was oolong and oregano, not Earl Grey. He sold it to new students every fall. He said it worked best with a bottle of Robitussin."

Kiki grinned. "Boarding school kids are their own brand of wacky. I'm not even going to ask how you know."

Megan's smirk said that was for the best.

"Thankfully, we've got a box of spare yearbooks," Kiki continued. "So whatever they were smoking, the damage isn't permanent. At least not to our glorious historical records. Here's the first missing page."

Megan studied the fourteen-inch CRT display. The page was part of the yearbook's *Where We're Headed* section, where students listed their college acceptances and where they had enrolled for the coming fall.

It always struck Kiki as an odd inclusion, a bit snooty and pompous. She had asked about it when she first joined the faculty and was given a lecture on tradition and the definition of prep school: to prepare students for college. Still, it felt like an aristocratic practice, which she supposed it was, considering Tenbury's yearly tuition.

"Could you print these out?" Megan asked. "And the others as well."

"All the missing pages?"

Megan nodded.

"The laser printer's low on toner so it'll have to be dot matrix."

"Yeah, that's fine."

They waited while the printer squeaked and rumbled, the pins and ribbons striking the paper, squealing as the darker shades resolved themselves, line by line. Kiki tore off the perforated strips while other pages followed.

She watched her former student study the pages, perhaps searching for some answer the accident had obscured. She tried not to look at the scar, which wasn't as hideous as she heard but drew the eye's attention as it tracked down her face. She noticed a dark spot on Megan's leg where something brown had been wiped.

She wanted to ask Megan if she was okay—if she was *really* okay—but she remembered what it was like to be that young and independent, always struggling to prove to yourself you could make the transition into adulthood. Most of all, she wanted to tell her that things would get easier. Time doesn't heal everything but our scars give us strength.

But she stayed quiet.

Megan took the final page, something like recognition flickering in her eyes and a little puff of wind leaving her lips.

"What, did you see something there?" Kiki asked.

Megan blinked, that glimpse of recognition giving way to something like fear. "See what?"

"Whatever it is you're looking for."

"No. Not really." She folded up the pages and put them in her purse. "But thanks anyway."

They said their goodbyes and exchanged a friendly hug. Kiki told Megan she was one of the good ones and she wished her the best. It came easy to her lips; the truth always did.

Mostly, she wanted Megan to know that somebody cared, and that whatever Megan was after, there was no need to lie.

chapter thirty-five

Megan placed the printouts on the hood of the Isuzu, flattening the edges and studying the names. She'd left the yearbook with Señora Cortez but was confident she no longer needed it. She could see the patterns before her.

Five pages torn from the yearbook. Five names she recognized within each, including her own.

On page ninety-two was one half of the permanent couple, Tom Frenning. Page ninety-eight was the other half, Desiree Chastain, both attending the same college.

Page ninety-four was Adam, formerly at Brown.

Page ninety-five was Megan, formerly at the Philadelphia School of Art and Design.

Page ninety was Chunhee Chang, her list of acceptances so long it took up a third of the page. Megan could see them all sitting in Banecroft common room, cheering as Chunhee opened letter after letter. Rumor was she set a school record.

These were her friends, people she'd laughed with, cried with, thought of often and deeply. Yet she hadn't worked up the courage to call them in years. That debt of silence had hung too heavy, accumulating with each passing month.

What would they see in her now? A broken woman, a shell of the

Megan they once knew? Someone who once painted with passion and could now hardly finish a sketch?

Maybe that was all they would see.

But she still had to try.

She stuffed the pages into her bag and climbed into the Isuzu. She drove away from campus and into the sleepy town of West Bedford. She was pleased to discover that the arcade was still there, tucked between D'Angelo's Sandwiches and a Rite Aid.

She found the change machine inside and inserted five dollars. A group of sugared-up kids turned their attention from *Tekken* to her waterfall of quarters. She would need the change.

Outside, she fed the payphone some quarters. She clicked her pen and readied her forearm. She dialed 411. Two transfers later and the line rang at the other end, some one hundred ninety miles to the north.

It rang and it kept ringing.

Megan waited, unsure whether to spend the money and leave a message or hang up immediately if she got an answering machine. Then someone answered.

"Theta," squeaked a panting voice. "Hello?"

"Uh, hi there." Megan had hoped she'd recognize Chunhee's voice, but this wasn't it. "I'm looking for Chunhee Chang. Is this her... roommate?"

Was that how sororities worked? The 411 operator had insisted the only Chunhee Chang listed in Grafton County, New Hampshire, was at a place called Kappa Alpha Theta. Megan had laughed; she could hardly believe it.

But the woman on the other end of the phone said, "One moment." There was a clatter and the clomp of feet down a hallway.

Megan tried to imagine it: Chunhee, a sister in a sorority. Did she have to do keg stands or get eggs cracked over her head as a pledge? Did she have some sort of nickname? How far she had come from the quiet third former at Tenbury who avoided most people. Good for her.

"Okay, listen, I thought I told you don't fucking call me."

The voice stunned Megan. It was Chunhee, and yet it was forceful, her words decisive and strong.

"Oh, I'm so sorry," Megan said. "I didn't mean to bother you."

A pause, followed by a low gasp. "Meg?"

Megan cleared her throat. "Hey, Chunhee. Long time, right?"

"Meg, wow. I... I'm so sorry. I thought you were someone else. One sec."

Megan heard the squeak of a chair being dragged. Of course, it wasn't her roommate who'd answered; it was a hall phone. Perhaps sororities were no different than dorms.

"Wow, Meg, I'm so glad to hear from you. It's been, what, two years, hasn't it?"

"Since after graduation, right?"

"Yeah. Since after graduation."

The silence hung heavy and thick. Megan tried not to imagine the quarters she'd fed the phone for the call. Why was it so hard to talk to someone she'd known for her most formative years?

Because for some, those years were a deep well of torment. For some, those years were best forgotten.

"Listen, Meg, I should've kept in touch. That... Well, it was shitty of me, you know? It's just... I needed a clean break after Tenbury. I needed to start over, you know?"

Megan wasn't surprised to find herself nodding. The girls had been cruel to Chunhee, the guys mostly indifferent. Then, in her senior year, Chunhee had blossomed. She filled out in ways Megan envied, both petite and sharp, long-legged and thin-necked. She stopped slouching, stopped looking so scared. She still hid her smiles with her hand but their frequency increased.

"I'm really sorry, Meg."

Megan was surprised to find something wet sliding down her ruined cheek. She was smiling and crying.

"Yeah, I know," Megan said. "Me too. It's just... It's really good to hear your voice."

Chunhee sniffled. "Are you tearing up?"

Megan tried to tamp down the lump in her throat. She said a scratchy, "No."

They burst out laughing, fear and miles dissolving, just two friends connected by time and memory. And there was more, Megan sensed. A guilt to Chunhee's words, laden by the silence of years.

She had to defuse it, so she said, "So, you're a sorority slut now?"

Chunhee sniffled and laughed, a playful tone suffusing her words. "Correction, I am a sorority *treasurer*, a dean's list slut, and one badass bitch who interned for the Clinton campaign, thank you very much."

Megan could imagine Chunhee's planner, each hour filled out in different colors. "You've been wicked busy."

"Well, it's a long way from the Golden Wok."

"Not too long, I hope. I still dream of those egg rolls."

Chunhee's parents owned the Golden Wok, a chain of Chinese restaurants that ran along Interstate 95, from Bridgeport to Bangor. Like many immigrants, they never shed their accents, a fact that embarrassed Chunhee when they visited campus for Parents Weekend, bringing hundreds of free egg rolls and potstickers for the students. They had smiled and bowed and handed them out in little folded boxes, happy to play a part in their daughter's life. And yet, in their kindness, some kids found a new angle of torment. Megan once read a valentine passed around the classroom by giggling boys.

Chunhee, can I pork your hot dumplings? Me love you long time.

"Meg, how are you? I've been thinking about you a lot lately. God, I'm such a terrible friend. I never picked up the phone."

"No, it's okay. I could've called too." Megan leaned forward, letting her head rest against the cool glass of the phone booth. "I'm... Well, the truth is, I'm not too good, Chunhee."

"I'm so sorry."

Megan sensed there was something underneath. It wasn't just the lack of communication, but something deeper, something like guilt. "I need to tell you something and it's going to sound weird."

There was silence at the other end. Then Chunhee whispered, "Okay."

So Megan told her.

About her dismissal from college. About her fractured dreams over the years and the recent stress bleeding into her life. About the new ideas for her art, which had surged forth in interlocked visions, drawing her back to Tenbury.

And a girl named Oksana whom she barely remembered.

When she told her she'd found the torn yearbook, Chunhee said, "Wait, you were there today?"

"I'm still in West Bedford, outside the arcade. You know they have a Blockbuster now? Probably got it the week after we left."

Chunhee laughed, but Megan sensed it was a cover. She was thinking, considering something. "Could you make it up to Darrington?"

Megan checked her watch. It was well after two and the drive up to New Hampshire would take a few hours. She wasn't even sure how to get there. And poor Corey, he'd lent her his car and she was stretching his kindness.

Still...

"Meg, I really think we should talk, in person."

Megan found herself nodding at the urgency. "Yeah, of course."

"If you're in West Bedford, then just get to the I-91 and take it north. It's like two hundred miles or so. If you hit Canada, that's way too far."

"I've got some maps."

"Good. Here's my pager number. Put 911 after your number and I'll call you right back. Got a pen?"

Fingers trembling, Megan scribbled it all down on her forearm. There was something beneath this conversation; she could feel it. The hint of a promise, some itch that needed to be scratched but not over the phone.

She took a deep breath, afraid of what she was asking and the answer she might hear.

"Chunhee, did we... Did we do something terrible?"

Chunhee didn't answer, but the silence stretched on without a dismissal. Then, "Just hurry on up, okay? I'll tell you everything, I promise. I've been meaning to tell you for years."

And then she hung up.

chapter thirty-six

Graham found Ms. Samarina's apartment in Hartford's Upper Albany, on the second floor of a two-family brick walkup built at the turn of the century. He could smell cooking inside, coconut and chicken and pineapple, all carrying a delicious hint of the Caribbean. His finger hesitated over the doorbell.

He had considered calling Hartford PD to let them know he was tromping around in their field but decided against it. No need to bother them with small-town crap. Either Ms. Samarina knew Louis and she could point him out or Graham was straying past the edge of the map.

It turned out to be a bit of both.

"Oksana... Was she a Russian woman?" asked the Puerto Rican man filling out the apartment door. Behind him, kids scampered about while a woman cooked in the kitchen. The kind of chaos that often followed young parents between school and supper.

"Russian? I'm not sure," Graham said. "The last address I have listed this apartment."

"Yeah, she was before us," the man said. A wide-eyed toddler ambled up and wrapped her arms around her dad's legs, staring up at Graham. "We've been renting this unit... What is it—"

"Two years!" his wife shouted from the kitchen.

He gestured back. "Yeah, that. Some guy from the... What's it called? Consulate. Yeah, some guy came by looking for her."

"From the Russian consulate?" An errant possibility tugged at Graham's thoughts. He pulled a photocopied picture of Louis from his notebook, one they'd faxed to every police department in the state. "Was this him?"

The man studied the photocopy. In Graham's experience, recognition happened within the first few seconds. That he was still studying the picture after ten told him this was another dead end.

"Nah, the man was big, skinny. And no smiling, you know?" He returned the photocopy.

"No smiling, got it." Graham clipped his pen to his notebook. "Well, sorry to trouble you."

"Hey, maybe you can call them? I'll give you the number."

"You have it?"

The man was already off, back into the apartment and passing through the kitchen. He gave his wife a kiss and stole a pinch of something from the stove, dodging a playful smack of her wooden spoon. He stopped at a magnet-covered refrigerator and picked among the clippings.

Nearby, the toddler was peeking out from behind the door, her big brown eyes focused on Graham, sticky fingers tugging her curly hair. A flash of his daughter at that age, learning new words every day. He covered his face and played peek-a-boo, eliciting a giggle from the child.

"Here you go, officer man." The man passed Graham a business card. "Oh, and I was wrong. She's Ukrainian. Maybe go ask Mrs. King, downstairs. She owns this building. She might remember this woman."

"Thanks." Graham turned the card over. Sure enough, it was the Consulate General of Ukraine, New York City. He pocketed it, telling himself he'd call them later, maybe, if it somehow connected. For now, Louis was the priority. He needed to be brought in before he did something truly dumb.

Pausing at the stairs, Graham said, "You're a lucky man. Whatever your wife's cooking..." He kissed his fingers and blew, eliciting a deep chuckle from the man and a wide smile from the toddler.

"Yeah, don't we both know it."

Downstairs, Mrs. King proved to be friendly and helpful in the rare moments they heard each other. From outside her unit, the TV mumbled through the fire-resistant door. And inside now, it was hard to ignore the pounding piano and shrill violins that made up the theme song to *Murder, She Wrote.* Graham waited, hoping she would mute the TV, but soon he was speaking over Angela Lansbury and trying not to shout.

"Ms. Samarina," he repeated. "She lived upstairs, unit two. Or at least she did until a few years ago. I'm just trying to see if she... if we share a mutual acquaintance."

Mrs. King nodded her curly gray head, yet she wasn't really understanding him. He could see the cord of a hearing aid and figured the batteries were overdue to be changed.

"I'm sorry, Detective. No one lived there by that name." Her hand straightened the lace placemat on the end table. "Well, actually, hold your horses, dear. Sam-a-ree-na? You mean Oksana? That cute foreign girl?"

"I think she's Ukrainian," he said. He was thrown off by the words *cute* and *girl*, having imagined her closer to Louis's age. "Wait, how old is she?"

"Old? No, she's not very old." Mrs. King's wrinkled face nodded a few times. "She's a student, if I recall. Only stayed on weekends, and not every one."

"*Years*, Mrs. King. How many years old was she?"

"I don't know, maybe seventeen or eighteen."

"Wait, like a high school student?" Mrs. King's narrowing eyes told Graham she hadn't quite heard him. He raised his voice and said, "Ma'am, was she in high school?"

The question came at a lull between scenes on TV. Graham realized from her wince that he'd shouted.

"No, not a high school. It was one of those... Shoot, what are they called?"

"College?"

She shook her head again. "Boarding school."

Graham jotted down the notes as they came, telling himself not to get too attached to the answers. It was as he'd feared, more tertiary details but little to hold onto. But if he was lucky, maybe one or two would lead him to Louis, to an answer, to some sort of closure.

And yet, dark thoughts were pooling in his mind. Why did Louis have her pendant? In a house with hardly anything that wasn't decades old or scrounged from a yard sale, that gold necklace was too fine for Louis's tastes. Which meant he'd acquired it somehow, perhaps recently.

"Do you have any forwarding information for this, uh, Oksana Samarina? A phone number or an address?"

The old woman shook her head. "No. Her rent was always on time. Then, one day, nothing. No note, no check, no answer at the door. We had the locksmith open it up and there was her stuff, some clothes and a few books, but no Oksana."

His posture tensed. These new facts gave discomforting form to his fears. "Did you keep any of her possessions?"

"I'll see what we've got."

Mrs. King beckoned him into the living room and pointed to an old chair on the verge of collapse. Graham sat, minding his center of gravity. While she shuffled off to another room, he listened to a few minutes of *Murder, She Wrote*, trying to guess the episode based on the body they found. He marveled at how Jessica Fletcher's beloved Cabot Cove saw more murders than Pablo Escobar's Medellín.

Mrs. King tottered back in, carrying a small cardboard box. Graham asked, "That's it?"

"We furnished the room," Mrs. King said. "We washed the linen and donated it to the Salvation Army. You can check with the Ruizes."

He knew by its weight the box would be nearly empty but opened it anyway, sorting through the items at the bottom. An English-Ukrainian dictionary. A book of American expressions and idioms. A ticket stub for the Red Sox versus the California Angels at Fenway Park on April 24, 1994.

He unfolded an odd page, handwritten words and sentences both vertical and horizontal. Trying to read it made his head spin, so he refolded it and put it back.

At the very bottom lay a few musty old shirts, including a ringer with a fish and the name *Tenbury Track & Field*.

Tenbury.

T-section.

That vague fear in the dark basement of his imagination now coiled and took form. A Ukrainian girl, perhaps missing for over two years. A necklace found in Louis's house. And Louis, freaking out and hitting the road.

Shit, maybe the dead dog hadn't been the worst of it. Graham cursed himself. How the hell had he been so slow to make this connection?

Because he'd been too close, he supposed. Hadn't wanted to believe Louis was anything other than what the town had made him out to be: a local grump always down on his luck.

"Ma'am, could I borrow your phone book?"

Outside, Graham found the nearest payphone and used the department's calling card to dial the station. There were rumors they'd get issued fancy Nextel phones next year, but he had his doubts. When he got through to Lieutenant Rourke, his hands were shaking. Partly from the breeze, but also from what he'd found in Mrs. King's phone book.

The Tenbury School was on the middle-left column, that same page Louis had torn out.

"LT, it's Graham," he said . "How fast can we get a cadaver dog out to Louis's house?"

chapter thirty-seven

June was applying the last of her lipstick when the knock rattled her door. She lowered her music and called out to come in. Cindy stood in the hall, her bootcut dress pants below a shiny tube top, a lacy wrap topping it off. She looked like she'd gone through Express and grabbed half the sale rack. She looked nervous, poor girl.

June preferred black, which went with everything, including her hair. Recently, she'd started dying her tips blonde, which had horrified her parents, but whatever. She was working up the courage to go full platinum and put it up in small buns like that chick from No Doubt.

"You look cute," she said.

Cindy's eyes flashed and her body seemed to swell. "I do?"

June nodded. "I like your pants."

Cindy laughed. "I had to zip them with pliers. Don't let me eat too much or I'm hosed."

June turned off the music and dimmed her lighted mirror. She caught a glimpse of her reflection off the window. The confident posture, that practiced smile. If she smiled all the time, that meant she was always happy, didn't it? If she made perfect grades, that meant that everything was rock solid and steady. That was what others would think. And if they believed it, perhaps it was true.

Megan...

Hearing her old friend's voice had really knocked her off balance. She needed a drink, or several. And yet she'd also promised Cindy she'd buy her mojitos. She was underage, which meant she couldn't drive them home with even a drop of booze in her blood.

So, Diet Coke it would be. Until Megan arrived and they could get into the bottle of vanilla Stoli she kept in the mini fridge for special occasions.

Until she could tell Megan the truth.

Downstairs, the sorority halls were quiet, most of the sisters already gone for Thanksgiving. June preferred to wait until Wednesday. Every time she went home too early, she got pulled into working at the restaurant, where her parents paraded her around to the regulars, boasting about their Ivy League daughter and making her uncomfortable.

Outside, she locked the front door, remembering something her big sister had said when she first joined the sisterhood. "Strawberry daiquiri," she told Cindy. "That's the cue if you get uncomfortable tonight. If your date gets too handsy or you just want to bounce, say strawberry daiquiri in a sentence and we're Audi five thousand."

Cindy's eyes took on a playful sparkle. "Like a code?"

"Yeah, our secret code."

June clicked the remote, activating her Saab's engine and starting the seat warmers. It was cool out, but they could still crank up the heater, drop the top, and drive to the cantina with the wind in their hair.

It reminded her that she was alive.

ONE HOUR LATER, Cindy was finishing her second mojito, eyes twinkling and cheeks lightly flushed. Dennis, her date, was a sophomore who'd pledged Pi Kappa Alpha this spring. He dressed a little too preppy for June's taste, but he was polite and well mannered; he'd pulled Cindy's chair out and insisted on buying the first round of drinks.

June's own date, however...

"See, that's the thing about Tarantino, you know? Zero talent, all talk. *Reservoir Dogs* was basically a high school play. Anyone could have staged it. *Killing Zoe* was indulgent. I'll give him *Pulp Fiction*. That was okay."

Sal was a senior, a film major who had just returned after working as a P.A. on some Harrison Ford thriller. He wore a baker boy cap and a tightly wrapped scarf. He chain-smoked Djarums.

"Hold up. *Killing Zoe* wasn't Tarantino," Dennis said, leaning in. "It was someone else."

"It was Tarantino. Said so on the poster."

"No, it said, 'From the Creators of *Pulp Fiction*.' Tarantino produced it, but he didn't direct it."

Sal stubbed out the clove cigarette and immediately lit another. "Trust me, I've seen it five times."

"But I thought you didn't like it," Cindy said. "Who sees a movie five times if they hate it?"

"Ah, she's got you," Dennis said, pointing with a tortilla chip.

"It's called film *studies*. I don't like Bertolucci, but I've studied all his stuff. My point is, just 'cause some snooty frogs at Cannes gave Tarantino their dinky award doesn't mean he makes good cinema."

"You're impossible." Dennis shook his head. June noticed Cindy subtly mirroring her date's gestures and posture. So, the sides had been drawn and it was two against one. The question was where June would fall. On personality alone, it wasn't looking good for Sal.

He turned to her. "June, baby, please tell me you've got good taste."

Baby? Ugh. She washed the bad taste away with her cola. "I thought *Pulp Fiction* was fun. It was something different, you know?"

Sal let out a dramatic sigh. "Peasants, the lot of you."

Dennis whispered, "Don't get him started on *From Dusk Till Dawn*."

"Oh fuck that. See, here's the thing: you can't genre-swap mid-movie—"

While Sal's rant meandered from George Clooney to the superiority of the LaserDisc, June tuned him out. At least Cindy and Dennis were gelling. They exchanged bashful smiles, finding excuses to brush against one another. She was currently resting her hand on his thigh while he egged Sal on.

Dessert arrived and was ignored by the guys, who were now debating where French New Wave Cinema ended. Cindy dug into her slice of tres leches. June poked at her chocolate cake. Across the cantina, the mariachi band was starting up again, black and silver outfits glinting in the pastel uplighting. A pair of international students danced, really twirling each other around on the floor.

But it was the trumpet player who had June's attention. There was something about one of his eyes, something wrong. She squinted, telling herself it was the lighting.

Then, between notes, he lowered his trumpet and turned his gaze upon her.

His left eye was a scarlet hole ringed by puckering gray lips. Jesus, his left eye was a mouth. And it was whispering.

The words enveloped her, a damp breeze that reeked of sea spray and old, rotted wood.

—look at you pretending to be what you're not because you're not cool never have been you're not one of them always an outsider always different always lying to everyone to yourself because you're chunhee ching chong chunhee not june not some other name and everybody knows that you're not one of them Not One of Them NOT ONE OF THEM—

June removed her glasses and wiped each lens, counting to ten. It was one of hundreds of tricks she'd built up over those lonely years before college to steady her thoughts.

Sure enough, when the glasses returned to her face, there was no salty whisper, no gray mouth rimming the musician's left eye. Of course not. There was only this exhausting conversation about movies, a conversation she was staying at the edge of. Because what happened tonight at this cantina didn't matter. This date, it was just a favor for one of the younger sisters.

What mattered tonight was her conversation with Meg.

And what that might cost them.

"You're not eating?" Cindy asked. Her tres leches was already gone and June's fork had hardly touched the cake.

"Oh, sorry." June slid her fork through the creamy dark chocolate and into the moist cake. She cut off an end piece, making sure she included one of the chocolate shells.

She chewed and started to swallow.

"Look, all I'm saying is that Scorsese's best work is behind him." That was Sal, drilling his finger into the table to underscore the weight of this discussion. "*Goodfellas* aside, he hasn't done anything groundbreaking since *Raging Bull*. And *Casino*? Three hours, multiple voice-overs. I mean, the whole thing was just masturbatory."

June covered her mouth and coughed.

"Sorry," Sal said, finally noticing his date. "I get worked up over movies."

Cindy grinned. "Yeah, you think?"

June sipped her cola, tongue probing the sharp lump that was clinging to her inner cheek. She held the napkin to her mouth and spat a lump of cake inside.

And yet, the obstruction remained.

"Excuse me." She wheezed and stood up, taking the napkin and hurrying to the restroom.

Like at most popular drinking holes, the line for the women's room was five deep. The men's, however, was empty. June squeezed inside and cupped her hands under the faucet. She gulped down the water, coughing even harder when it hit her throat.

The water was briny.

Still, it softened up the gunk stuck to the inside of her cheeks. She spat sandy cake into the sink, chips clinking against the porcelain, *tinkity tink*.

No, not chocolate chips, she realized. Those were snails.

She stifled a gag as the water dissolved the rest of the cake, revealing sharp pieces of coral and shell.

Her stomach tightened and her body shuddered. That had been in her mouth, been so close to being swallowed. Gagging, she thrust her hands under the faucet and scrubbed them with soap. This was outrageous. This was...

The old pipes rumbled and burped. With a hiss of rusty water, dark lumps spurted from the faucet. There, coiling the drain like an old rope, lay a length of seaweed. Frayed leaves and glistening bulbs beaded it, the last strands still clogging the faucet. The water became a trickle.

Sandy cake clung to her tongue, so she gave the seaweed a quick tug, eliciting another rumble from the pipe. What the faucet belched forth now was no longer seaweed, not entirely.

The dark hair came first, a twisted braid growing thicker. The white shards quickly followed. Black hair threaded the kelp. She wasn't sure what she was looking at until they clinked upon the porcelain, little bones and beaks going *dink, dink, dink*. Beneath them, something pink and throbbing held it all together, the seaweed and hair, the beaks and the bones. Something with suckers and thorns.

The tentacle lashed out, seizing June by her wrist and coiling up her forearm. With a squeeze, it yanked her forward.

To the drain.

Which was now ringed with gray lips.

June watched, first numb and distant, then fully aware of what was happening. Tongue-like, the toothed tentacle slid down the drain, dragging behind it the lumpy seaweed and clumpy black hair, the bones and the beaks.

And her arm.

It was going to pull her into the drain, swallow her by her fingertips, or tear her arm from the socket.

So she screamed and kicked and buried her flat heels against the counter. She leaned back, pulling the tentacle, this terrible tug-of-war that shouldn't be. Pulling harder and losing.

She clamped her eyes shut. *Think... Think...*

Countless hours of physics homework flashed before her. Then it came: the Euler-Eytelwein equation. A rope's tension changes when angles are involved.

She dropped down onto the floor, used her swimmer's legs to press up against the underside of the sink's cabinet. She braced her thighs for an inverted squat and pushed out.

A rip and a sudden release snapped her head back, sent her sliding off the bathroom tiles. Gasping, she opened her eyes.

The tentacle was gone, leaving her right arm wet and scratched. Cindy stood at the bathroom door, wide-eyed and frozen. "Sis, what's going on?"

"I was just..." June crawled up, her words coming to a stop as she studied the empty, burbling sink. No kelp or hair. No beaks and bone held together by tentacled flesh. There were just a faucet and her chocolate cake-spattered napkin.

"Strawberry daiquiri?" Cindy asked.

"Yeah." June nodded. "Strawberry fucking daiquiri."

chapter thirty-eight

In the cantina, Dennis and Sal's great debate was shifting from cinema to sports. They hardly noticed that their dates were leaving until their jackets were on and June dropped a twenty on the table. By then it was too late, but that was okay. In the grand scheme of things, there would be other dinners, other dates, and other one-sided discussions. They had their whole lives ahead of them; they all seemed to know it.

June didn't remember to lower the Saab's top on the drive back to campus. She had told Cindy she'd dropped a ring in the sink, had gotten her hand stuck in the drain trying to retrieve it. Cindy didn't buy it, but she pretended to, and June was grateful for that small mercy.

The sharp beaks.

Those puckering suckers.

That mariachi player with his empty left eye.

June white-knuckled the steering wheel. Why was it all falling apart these past several weeks?

Cindy tuned the radio to a disco station and bobbed her shoulders, trying to lighten the mood. She said, "Anyways, don't trip. They were a pair of scrubs, weren't they?"

June shrugged. "Dennis seemed nice."

"Nice by proximity, but I need a larger sample size. God, Sal...

Could you imagine hooking up? He'd probably keep a log and critique it."

"He'd probably wear his scarf."

"That ratty thing swaying around like an old elephant trunk while he's all naked and thrusting? There's an image." She raised her nose and took on Sal's inflection. "Mmm, yes, missionary, a most rudimentary position. I much prefer the Gutenberg pile driver."

"The Gutenberg pile driver?"

Cindy shrugged and held her hand out the window, making little wave motions in the cool air. June felt the laughter building between them. Then she was dabbing her eyes, trying to steer while wiping that mental image from her mind. Perhaps, in another life, that was how her night with Sal was proceeding. No wonder some of the sisters preferred much older guys.

Back at the house, June locked the front door. Cindy called out from the dining room, "Hey! Thanks for coming. Sorry it was such a bummer."

June shook her head. "I'm just having an off night."

"Well, if you get bored, I'll be in the rec room. Maybe we can watch a movie and change our majors to film."

June smiled. "Actually, I've got an old friend coming by. If you hear a knock at the door—"

"Yeah, sure. I'll let them in."

June wanted to say more, to offer her younger sister some encouragement, some words to help her keep pushing forward. Words she had craved but were rarely offered. Yet she sensed Cindy didn't need them. She was already taking advantage of the house's emptiness, sliding into the kitchen and retrieving a tub of ice cream from the industrial freezer.

"Good night, Cindy."

"Night, sis."

Upstairs, June turned on her light and closed the door. She knew she didn't have to lock it, but her mind drifted back to those Saturday nights in Tenbury common rooms, the TV and the rented horror videos, the nervous giggles and screams.

Slumber Party Massacre.

Cutting Class.

Maniac.

She shivered at the cool air, thinking of that bottle of vanilla Stoli in her mini fridge. Perhaps she could plant a warm buzz in her gut until Meg arrived. Yes, that would help her unwind.

She did not notice the window and how it was slightly open.

She made it as far as her desk before her feet stopped on their own. Something sat upon her bed, a thing that didn't belong.

It was a dirty tarp bundled into a mound and twisted together at the top like a hastily wrapped present. It was crinkling and slowly coming undone. Yellow twine slid through the holes, pulled from within.

Then it all fell open.

Numbly, June perceived her sanity fracturing, a rending tear as the impossible unfolded before her. A matte of dark hair. A widening grin. A head rising on branches of tendon and bone. A single eye glared at her, covetous and seething. She sensed a great instinct to scream, to run, to flee and do it now, *now*, NOW!

She did not sense the man behind her, a man who had waited in the shadowy nook formed by her door and her dresser. A man whose stubby hands wrapped around her, silencing her hopes of screaming and fleeing, and squeezed the wind from her lungs.

chapter thirty-nine

Louis knew he was a bad man who'd done terrible things with his heart and his hands. He had lied and hurt and done even worse. And yet, he didn't quite care. It was love that compelled him, and it was true what they said: it filled your body with warmth; it made you move mountains; love conquered all.

Like a fisherman of lore, the tides had brought him a mermaid. His affection had lifted her from a watery grave. His mighty blood had nourished her, given her strength. And now he had gifted her this: a new body.

With a crimson hand, he wiped his face. With all the sawing and cutting done, there was still the mess to contend with. He wished he'd swapped out his boots for that landscaper's galoshes. But then, he supposed, he would've made a ruckus creeping up the fire escape and into this bedroom. There really was no such thing as perfection.

Except when it came to Oksana.

Still, Louis had his doubts about the... *procedure*. He was no surgeon and he had only seven fingers to work with after this afternoon's feeding. His hands trembled to keep the saw straight and angle the hedge clippers. He followed her instructions, clipping and tugging and opening it all up.

Now he stepped back to admire the work. His part in this reshaping was finished. Hers was beginning.

With faint crunches, the bony roots beneath Oksana's neck grafted into this new body. Her one eye darted about, guiding a vast, internal rearrangement. A damp shudder as her neck-sack settled into the fissure he'd carved in the donor. He glimpsed something within, a gnarled and knotted heart drumming in furious rhythm, faster and faster. He averted his eyes and fell to his knees, unworthy of such splendor.

"You are beautiful," he whispered. "So... perfect."

And it was true. From the shoulders up, Oksana had really come into herself. As her cheeks had healed, they took on a soft cream seen on cherubs in the most glorious art. Her gums had grown rosy, her teeth pearly and straight. Now even her neck was settling into the raw socket, life pulsing through her body's new veins and smoothing the wounds.

Like a puppet on leery strings, Oksana rose from the wet bed.

"Please, take it slow," he whispered. "You need to rest."

She flexed the other girl's right hand, rotating it in a small circle. It was her hand now, he supposed. No different than a donated kidney. Perhaps she could teach him this trick, help him grow new fingers, thicken his hairline, or spackle some wrinkles. Was it too much to ask?

She extended a leg and wiggled her toes. He spotted a pink toenail broken from the struggle, and his heart crowded his throat. "Oh, please forgive me."

Crawling across the damp carpet, he seized her foot. He raised her toe to his lips and kissed the broken nail. He wished he could take it back, this terrible blemish he'd left on her new form.

"I'm sorry," he said. "I made a mistake."

He had been surprised by the fight the sorority girl put up. How she stomped her feet and gouged at his face and bit his fingers. She was thin yet fierce. She'd twisted free and opened the door. For one horrorstruck moment, Louis watched her shirt tear from his grip and her hair slide between his fingers.

Then Oksana had done her thing, shouting a stream of curses that rearranged the walls and staggered them both. It was all he needed to grab the girl, yank her back into the bedroom, and finish her off with the hammer.

He had been so careful not to ruin anything below the collar.

But this broken toenail... How had he been so clumsy?

So, here he was, kneeling at the feet of his love. Sliding her toe past his lips as he kissed her split nail. He would kiss every perfect inch if she let him.

"Please," he said. "You need to heal. You should keep resting."

Oksana planted her other foot on his forehead and pushed him away. He thought of windchimes as she spoke. "I've been resting for years."

Then she stood, stepping delicately around the mess on the floor. She laid a finger on the doorknob, tracing the facets of the glass handle. Her gaze was a sunbeam, warming his cheeks and watering his eyes. Distantly, he knew he was crying.

Because of what she was going to ask.

"Do you love me, Louis? Do you want me to be happy?"

"More than anything."

"Then do me one final kindness."

She leaned in, his body tensing as her lips touched his ear. Her words poured in, honeyed whispers raising the hairs on the back of his neck and hardening him in that place of great shame.

Then she kissed him, her lips soft against his. She was in him, always, ever since that first morning on the boat in the bay, the best day of his life. He felt every cell beginning to sing.

"Thank you, Louis."

He was nodding and crying now; he knew what needed to be done and was proud of his part.

He just needed the strength.

chapter forty

Cindy was disgusted, but not really.

After finishing off a bag of pretzels, she found the real score, a few pints of Ben & Jerry's buried at the back of the freezer and unlabeled. House rules: always write your name on your food.

After a half hour she was sugared up and giggling as Adam Sandler turned his angry hockey skills into long drives on the golf course. She rested her feet on the sofa. Like June, Cindy was all legs and a thin neckline. A few more pounds wouldn't kill her, might even size her up a half cup. She never cared for the Kate Moss look.

But the sorority had a certain standard of appearance, one unspoken but expected. A standard that meant ice cream and pretzels were never free from the judgmental glare of her sisters, most of whom weren't blessed with Cindy's fast metabolism. Indulgent nights like tonight were a rare treat.

Which made her sad when her spoon hit the bottom of the pint.

She reached for the remote, waiting to pause it until Bob Barker and Adam Sandler stopped fighting. She was halfway to the kitchen when she heard the noise: a low thump that rattled the old house's ceilings. A door quickly opening and slamming shut.

A faint melody echoed down the halls. June was listening to music. And beneath it, something like a bed squeaking and moving.

Oh, Cindy realized. So that was what she meant by her friend paying a visit. At least one of them was getting lucky.

Cindy was a half dozen spoonfuls into a fresh pint of Cherry Garcia when the phone rang down the hall. She waited. Was she still required to answer the phone over vacation? Probably so.

Savoring the cherry and chocolate, Cindy strolled down the hall, a skip to her step. On the eighth ring, she picked up. "Theta."

She never heard what the caller said.

There was a crackling sound over the line that made her think of Geiger counters and those hazmat suits from *E.T.* Her skin grew oddly warm for late November.

She turned to see June walking down the stairs, one checkered Keds after the other. Something seemed to shift and slither beneath her shearling jacket. When she turned, Cindy felt that warmth turn to a fierce itch under her skin.

That wasn't June.

Or, rather, that wasn't June's head on her body.

Despite the hole where her left eye should be, there was a beauty to the woman on the stairs, a carnal power. The phone slipped from Cindy's fingers. She felt time shatter into fragments, discordant memories that would linger in her mind for the rest of her life. Some would bring a smile to her lips. Others that would tear her from her dreams, sweaty and gasping.

For now, the heat caressed Cindy, then left as the stranger's gaze broke. She descended the stairs. There was a click a floor above and one below—doors, Cindy realized distantly—and then her breath returned in heavy gasps, faster and faster.

She thought of gnarled things with long fingers that had lived in her childhood closet. She thought of all the monsters she'd dismissed as imaginary, now crashing through her subconscious, as real as her skin.

Most of all, she thought of June.

That woman had come from her room. That woman had—impossibly—walked just like her.

Cindy told her body to move, to walk forward. *Go now. Do it.* She forced herself up those stairs. She made it as far as the bathroom before she stopped in her tracks.

June's music was loud.

A crimson pool leaked from under her door.

And something leaned against the hallway trash can. A ruined mound of wet violet, wreathed with black hair dyed blonde at the tips.

Cindy did not remember running, nor wetting herself. She felt no shame. She felt only a deep wind rising in her chest as she threw the front door open and the cool night embraced her, a wind now leaving her lips as a guttural scream.

chapter forty-one

Megan parked in the visitors lot and started walking across the university's dark quad. She'd never been to an Ivy League campus and didn't know what to expect. Posh buildings with gold domes. Students seated near fountains while aged professors lectured from leather-bound tomes. Perhaps a statue garden of great thinkers.

But it wasn't that different from Tenbury, just larger.

She found a payphone and spent a quarter paging June. She never responded. She called the sorority but the connection was bad and each redial ended in garbled hissing. So she followed the campus directory, noting the blue emergency poles with phones that had been recently installed. She also noted the car passing by, the driver turning and studying her, slowing down.

And then pulling over.

"Meg?"

Her concern gave way to frustration and a curious relief. "Adam? What are you doing here?"

Brushing hair from his face, Adam stepped out of his 4Runner. "I should ask you the same thing."

She eyed him skeptically. When he'd shown up last week with a vague story about weird dreams, she hardly listened. All she could hear were the unanswered phone calls she'd made, the unreturned letters she'd written. That pain had become anger. She'd wanted him to feel scorned and alone, worthless like her.

But that was wrong.

There was something new growing now, a sadness perhaps at what could have once been. And an acceptance, too, that their past would always connect them.

"I'm picking my cousin up for Thanksgiving," he said. "It's her first semester and she lost her license. Figured I'd pressure-check the party scene, maybe join the Skull and Bones." He scratched his neck. "What about you?"

"I'm visiting Chunhee," she said. "Actually, she wanted me to come up."

"Really? Cool, cool. So, how's she doing?"

"Well, considering I haven't seen her since Tenbury, I don't know. But I have some questions and she has some answers. Figured it's time for a little reunion."

He tilted his head. "Answers about what?"

"It's hard to explain."

"Well, get in. I'll drive you to her sorority."

"You've been there?"

"What? No, this is my first time on campus."

"Then you'll be driving in circles. You can't get to sorority row from this side of the river. At least that's what the map says."

He reached back in the 4Runner and activated the hazard lights. "Then we'll hoof it."

"That's a fire lane."

He shrugged and locked the door. "I'll take the ticket. Consider it back payment for being a dick."

"In that case, I'd rather just have the money."

His cheeks stretched as he grinned that same grin she once found irresistible. "I'll cut you a check right now. Name the price."

"I'm not sure the trust fund could take the hit."

She regretted her words as they left her lips. In her head, she had rehearsed endless barbs that would cut him to the bone. She carried them like arrows. Now she saw them for what they were, petty comments forged in the fires of disappointment and sharpened by time.

"Sorry," she said. "That wasn't nice."

Adam gave a wistful rise of his shoulder. Something about his gesture struck her as tired and defeated. Maybe the years had wounded them both.

They walked in silence, the campus damp, the evening breeze cool on their skin. A curtain of fog turned the lamps into amber halos. When the quiet felt suffocating, he finally spoke.

"You're driving again. That's great."

"Gotta rejoin civilization sometime."

"Isuzu. It's a good car."

"It's my boyfriend's." She wasn't sure why she said it until she already had.

"Hmm. Sounds like a lie."

She stopped. "What?"

"Joe Isuzu, hello? That commercial where he races a bullet? 'The Isuzu Trooper: it can hold the whole state of Texas. Sounds like a...'" He gave her a nudge. "'Lie?'"

Megan had a vague memory of those commercials during the Super Bowl, the slick man in the suit making outrageous claims about a car. "Ah, right."

Two joggers ran past, reflective strips glowing down their windbreakers, shoes going *thuck-thuck-thuck* on the gravel path. A few blocks away, voices were shouting out. Vacation was close, but there were still a few parties to be found.

Adam zipped up his jacket. "So, these answers you're looking for, what are they?"

"You'd never believe me."

"Well, last time I came to you with a story, you said I was crazy."

"I never said you were crazy."

"You implied it with your eyes. I think the term you used was 'delusional.'"

"I was frustrated and I have a limited vocabulary. You're the English major. Grab a thesaurus, swap it out for something else."

They started across a footbridge over a river, where wood frogs croaked and cackled below. The distant voices were growing now, a far-off siren mixing in. She sensed they were getting close to the fun side of campus.

Megan said, "I'm here because there's a girl I can't quite remember. And yet I can't seem to forget her, either. Lately, she's been rattling around in my thoughts."

Adam nodded. "Oksana."

Megan swallowed. That name was a stone on her tongue, and her mouth was trying to find balance between spitting it out or choking it down.

She said, "It's like those stupid Magic Eye posters at the mall. Every time I focus on her, I can't see her. But then sometimes my brain goes cross-eyed and it just comes."

"You were never good at those posters."

She speared him with a nervous glance. "Adam, what did we do?"

Adam drummed his fingers along the railing. "What do you mean?"

"I mean, something bad happened, didn't it? What was it?"

They reached the other side of the bridge, and Adam was still silent. She could see the gears turning, his mind laying the words out before him, calculating. He wasn't the smartest one in their group of friends; that had always been Chunhee. But he'd always been the cleverest.

"Nothing," he said. "We didn't do anything. I did. Oksana had a crush on me and she made a move."

"When?"

"A few nights after graduation, at Desi's summer house. I was drunk, and like the idiot I am, I kissed her back. I wish I could take it back or forget it, but I can't. Anyways, I told her to stop, but you saw it. You were pissed, and I mean *righteously* pissed. That's when you sped off in the car. We found it a few miles down the road, just barely clinging to the side of the cliffs. Your head was all..."

He motioned to the crescent scar on her forehead, which was throbbing now. She nodded slowly, letting his story align beside the empty holes and wounded tissue of her mind. It seemed to fit, some of it.

And yet...

"You never told me that."

"I know. I should have. I didn't want to add more condiments to the shit sandwich you woke up to."

According to the records, there'd been too much alcohol in her blood for the doctors to stitch her up immediately. She fell into a coma for seventy-two hours. By the time her name hit the medical database, the police were tracking her down.

Because her home was a smoldering ruin.

Because her parents were gone.

She asked, "So what ever happened to her?"

"Oksana? Who knows and who fucking cares? I dumped her ass in Hartford, and that was that. We were done with her, all of us. We tried to be friendly all semester and she'd just turn on us, hold things over each of us, like leverage. You most of all."

"Me? I barely remember her."

"Well, she idolized you. Started dressing like you, talking like you. You know what a zero-sum game is? It's where one side only wins if the other loses. Everything was a zero-sum game to her."

They continued along the campus path, the dorms and buildings on the far side of the river giving way to old colonial houses and tree-lined streets. Megan's head spun. Some of the memories were now settling into place, a satisfying click like a bone in a socket. Others were still scattered, rogue pieces on some puzzle she wasn't sure would ever be solved.

"I used to think that if I just waited it all out, you'd remember," Adam said. "If I hadn't kissed her, you wouldn't have taken off. And if you didn't remember, it couldn't hurt you, right? And then, I dunno, maybe then it wasn't my fault. But it was, and I saw it etched on your face every time you visited. Chickenshit excuse, I know."

Megan didn't answer. Instead, she listened to the damp earth beneath her Doc Martens. Adam was right: it was a chickenshit excuse. But it was one she understood. When she started falling behind in art school, she'd lived in denial. She told herself she just needed inspiration, a change of location, something always just out of grasp. She told herself raw talent would make up for consistent work. And yeah, she'd lied to herself as the bills and assignments piled up, learning to ignore each letter: the scholastic warnings, the academic suspensions, the expulsion.

Until it all collapsed under the weight.

The footpath brought them onto a spacious, tree-lined street where the colonial houses were wide and tall. Megan said, "I just wish you'd..."

She never finished her thought.

The cop car blew by them, sirens squawking, lights painting the columns and hedge rows blue and red. Another cop car zoomed past.

Several houses down, the street ended in a cul-de-sac. Greek letters flew from flags and adorned stately homes. The two houses on the left were dim. A few lit windows on the second and third floors, but otherwise quiet. A crowd gathered outside the house on the right.

"Theta," Megan said. "Guess Chunhee joined a real Animal House."

Adam smiled. "You know she goes by June now, right?"

"Get out of here."

"Swear to God..."

The amusement drained from his eyes, replaced by a confused scowl. Megan understood it too. Those weren't partygoers stuck on campus and seeking out a good time. Their voices weren't happy but carried nervous murmurs. At the lawn, police were setting up a perimeter and waving students back.

Because of the man, Megan realized. The man standing on the roof.

The man covered in blood.

chapter forty-two

Adam braced himself for another fight. He knew that Chunhee would be angry to see him; she'd told him not to call and to leave her alone. She had good reasons. Now here he was, nearing her doorstep.

Yet the scene before him didn't make sense.

The man standing on the roof. The cops at the hedges and the fence of Kappa Alpha Theta. The sorority house with the cruiser's spotlights aimed upward, smearing the third-floor balcony and roof in bright yellow light.

The crowd filled half the cul-de-sac, a growing crescent of students, neighboring sorority sisters, and a few curious fraternity brothers clutching beers. Adam and Megan squeezed closer to the front. They would not be heading into Chunhee's house, not any time soon.

Two cops were shouting at the students to step back. A third huddled with a young woman in a silver tank top, her eyeshadow smeared down her cheeks. A fourth burst from the house and vomited into the hedges.

"Hey, what's going on?" Megan asked a group of guys with frisbees.

"Dude, so we were on the sixth hole and that chick comes screaming out of the house, saying all this crazy shit." The guy tapped his frisbee nervously. "Then homeboy up there steps onto the balcony and scales the roof with that rope. He's been tying it ever since."

Adam glanced back at the young woman with the silver tank top. That was hard trauma misting in her eyes; he knew that look well. Her body was in the midst of the shakes.

Megan was whispering now, "No. No, please. No."

Then the crowd shuddered. "Yo, is he... Is he pointing at me?" frisbee guy asked.

Atop the roof, the bloodied man stretched out a hand and gestured. Below, the crowd turned their heads to the left, to the right, then behind them. A few stepped aside. Even frisbee guy was looking back now, his gaze falling on Adam and Megan.

Because the haggard man was pointing at them.

He curled his wounded hand to his mouth and shouted, "I see you! I see both of you now. I've seen such *perfection*."

The crowd parted, stepping away from Adam and Megan as if they were toxic. Someone asked, "Do you know him?"

Megan didn't answer, didn't say anything, and for that, Adam was grateful. He wasn't sure he could form a single word. Not while that man was glaring across the cul-de-sac, his crimson face a mad rictus.

"It's okay," the man on the roof shouted. "She wants you to know that your secret is safe."

The man wasn't talking to him, Adam realized. He was talking to Megan.

Did she know him? Adam studied her reaction, reading her for any glimpse of recognition. Instead, her eyes widened and she shouted, "No, please! Don't!"

Screams rocked the crowd. Adam turned back, catching only flashes. The glinting blade drawing horizontal. The wet handle falling from the man's hands. The ribbon opening from his neck like a red Cheshire grin. The man smiled as he leaned forward and let his feet slip from the roof.

Next came the whipping of rope tied to the chimney. Then the snap and a groan as the red bricks shifted, but only slightly.

Adam wasn't sure what the poor man had planned. If he'd wanted the rope to be so long, or if he'd meant to cut his throat so terribly deep. Perhaps it was part of his plan, a way to ensure the noose didn't fail.

With a damp thump, the man's body hit the hedges. His head bounced across the grass, a few feet away.

chapter forty-three

Now

Sipping his sparkling water, Anwar savors the crisp finish. He has to admit, it's a hell of a story, one that she's selling well. The silent tear down her cheek, the subtle pauses. Even that pained smile that softens her eyes when she speaks the name of her dead high school friend, Chunhee. To think, he'd been worried Mrs. Monroe might hold back.

Now he's more worried about his recordings and how much time he has left.

The tape recorder stops with a click. He ejects the cassette and labels the side. He spots tissues by the microwave and passes her the box.

He says, "Awful business that night."

She dabs her eye and offers a weak nod.

He gives her a moment. Then, "Do you mind if I use your restroom? The desert always makes me thirsty. I don't know how y'all do it."

"Down the hall, second door on the right."

He hesitates at the edge of the kitchen. There she sits, Megan Monroe, at her posh kitchen table with its colorful Mexican tiles. The sun has gotten lower and warmer, the shadows stretching across those desert hills. If he squints, he can almost see her trajectory, those bloody days in the mid-nineties becoming the long calm that followed. No wonder she settled far from the haunted vales of New England.

Walking through her house, he tells himself she's not a bad woman. She has donated time, taught classes, used her art to raise money for charity. Hell, she's an assistant coach for her kids' baseball team. The photos hang on these walls.

But that doesn't excuse her part in what happened.

Nor does it absolve him of his duties. To the truth, sure, and to his listeners, to whom he owes a good story. And to his advertisers and the merchandisers. He can almost see the stickers and mugs: *I Know What You Did Last Decade.*

Well, not a perfect fit, but a good place to start.

He uses the toilet and lets the sink run for a moment. He checks the spy microphone clipped inside of his sleeve. Three-quarters of a battery and another seven gigs of uncompressed audio. Good. It's impressive what you can order from China.

He wolfs down a protein bar in four bites to lift his blood sugar. Another trick of the trade: keep yourself fed while the interviewee grows hungry. Most subjects never want to be the first to break for a snack.

Yes, Anwar is using every strategy he knows against Megan, because she is using hers against him. She's stalled and told a few meandering anecdotes. She's still playing loose with the truth.

Does she really think he believes half this bullshit?

No, of course not. He's not a fool.

He'll have to pore over the transcript with his attorneys, sorting fact from fiction and checking the dates. Perhaps they'll impanel a grand jury if he's lucky, like Robert Durst.

But one way or another, he'll get his confession. He always does.

Another idea rises while he washes his hands: he could hire a team of shrinks to analyze her psychosis. Make it a real roundtable event.

Yes, the pieces are coming together. This isn't a single episode or a special. It's not a show but perhaps a whole season. Eight episodes, maybe ten if he stretches. Mix in some dramatic music, a brooding narrator. He'll need another ninety minutes of her talking; everything starts with these recordings. The one on the table, which he paused, and the other under his shirt, always listening.

Smiling to himself, he opens the bathroom door and heads down the hall. Damn, he's going the wrong way. Then something stops him from turning back.

Several paintings hang on the walls, each set among recessed molding and subtly lit. There's a classic Verduci with bold shadows and light. A colorful stencil from Shepard Fairy's early days. And a third painting, one that catches his eye.

"No shit."

There, in three feet by two feet of oil and canvas, hangs a surreal collage of several motifs. Photorealistic children skip down a curved sidewalk beneath a familiar white chapel floating on an island of dead grass. A warm house rises from a cold beach, its walls merging with the sand. Some sort of power plant tower belches blue light. And there, to the left of the frame, two women stand holding hands in an homage to Kahlo's famous painting, *The Two Fridas*.

The woman made of smoke and cindering wood is a teenage Megan.

The other woman is formed from wet seaweed and dark coral.

Anwar never saw a photo, but based on the descriptions in his uncle's journal, he knows who it is. He snaps a picture, realizing a moment too late his smartphone isn't on silent. The shutter click echoes down the quiet hallway. A moment later, a door opens.

Megan's eight-year-old son Symon pokes his head out of his bedroom, eyes locking onto Anwar. "What are you doing?"

"Me?" Anwar casts a mock glance over his shoulder. He never really warmed to children, finding them squirrelly, either too silly or too serious. "I'm just admiring your mom's art, buddy. She's talented."

Symon stares out from his bedroom. Then another door opens, and now Sofiy is looking out as well, eyes like spotlights on this stranger in their hall.

With a wink, Anwar heads back. *Message received, you* Village of the Damned *little creeps. Enjoy your remaining time with your mom.*

He finds Megan laying out two charcuterie trays and adding sliced apple beside the meats. A fresh glass of sparkling water waits at his place. A bowl of nuts sits between them. He chews a few almonds, making a show of switching the cassette but not pressing *record*.

"Look, off the record, I have to ask: why lie about Oksana?"

The question stops the knife in Megan's hand. A deep breath. She gathers the apple slices then runs the blade under the faucet.

She says, "What do you mean?"

"Earlier, you said it'd been years since you thought of her name. And yet, there's a painting in your hallway that says otherwise."

She arranges the walnuts and almonds in a flower around the fruit. "Ah, you were snooping."

Yeah, he supposes he was, but how could she prove it? He says, "It's a big house. I got turned around."

With a crinkling rip, she seals both trays with shrink wrap. She gulps down a long sip of wine. "Make your point, Mr. Fariz."

"Look, I'm not an artist or a psychoanalyst or whatever. But you thought of Oksana enough to put her in one of your paintings. That one by the bathroom, it's part of that new series, isn't it? I saw them on your website. I didn't make the connection until now."

She spots a scuff on the table and scrapes it away.

"So, I guess my point is the following." He leans in, giving her his best It's Just Between Us look of concern. "I know something bad happened. Something a lot of people wanted swept under the rug. If you need to keep your family protected, well, let's keep a few parts off the record. Just as long as we're working our way there."

"Working our way... where?"

"To the truth, Mrs. Collings. To your version of it. That's all my listeners want. They're smart. They know you're not the bad guy here. Besides, this was decades ago. They just want your take on what happened."

Her gaze drifts to the window. He can see it starting to crack, her mental defenses, her resolve. His interviewees aren't all the same, not exactly, but they all have similar traits. Beneath years of practiced calm, something always cries out for absolution. Guilt bubbles to the surface in the most curious of ways.

Like a painting of a missing girl made decades later.

She whispers, "How much stays off the record?"

He pushes the tape recorder away, leaving the slot open and empty and easily seen. He flashes his best salesman's smile. "As much as you need."

part four

Can't Stop This Thing We Started

chapter forty-four

1996

Graham shadowed the handler and his cadaver dog, a droopy bloodhound named Radar with a tail strong enough to leave bruises. For an hour they meandered along the perimeter of Louis's property, giving Radar ample time to stop and sniff. But he didn't, not even once. By the second pass, the handler had his doubts. By the third, Radar was losing interest altogether.

And so were the neighbors.

Some had been watching the operation since sunrise, when the sheriff's department, county search and rescue, and the remains recovery specialist all pulled up to Louis's house in tandem. Now, with the dew burning off the grass, most of the looky-loos were heading inside or off to church. Graham had to agree with their assessment: the operation was spinning its wheels.

"Well, that's about it." The handler gave Radar a scratch and a few treats from a pouch at his side. "I'm not saying there's nothing here, but Radar's found remains under concrete, even in water. Odds aren't looking good."

They walked through the gate that split Louis's backyard from his front. There was Bill, flushed and sitting on his porch, bitterly sipping from a mug that didn't hold coffee. Graham gave him a solemn nod.

"This would have been two, maybe two and a half years ago,"

Graham said. "Is there any chance it could have been buried in different parts of the yard? Maybe to spread out the scent?"

He didn't like calling a missing girl "it." She was a woman, someone with parents, a life, a story. She was eighteen, on exchange from Ukraine. Her name was Oksana Samarina. Even if no one was looking for her now, someday they would.

And yet, he wasn't certain she was connected. Hell, not every missing person was a crime. An abusive partner, a domineering family. Some people had good reason to vanish.

"Well, dismemberment's a pretty common method of disposal." The handler gave Radar a pat. "Thing is, the body produces a spectrum of smells during decomp. Days, months, even years later, they all outgas. The dogs are trained on those scents. So, if there was a limb here or an old bone there, Radar would be on it."

Great, Graham thought. Another dead end. He should take a clue from Radar, stick to one scent.

Maybe this case was basic and he needed to refocus. Yes, and maybe Louis was just a down-on-his-luck bastard who killed his neighbor's dog over a spat. And maybe the necklace was a piece of found jewelry he was hoping to pawn off for some much-needed cash.

And yet, his instinct said otherwise. The assault. The bag Louis carried. The one that he was mumbling to. The one that seemed to be moving. These questions whispered beneath Graham's busy thoughts, little burs stuck in his subconscious.

And yeah, he was probably about to catch hell for wasting county resources on a cadaver hunt that produced nothing. Which was probably why his lieutenant was pulling up to the curb in the cruiser.

"Graham," Rourke shouted and pointed to Louis's porch. "Let's have a little pow-wow."

Graham said goodbye to the remains recovery team, who were packing up and probably disappointed. He gave Radar a quick pet, the bloodhound regarding him with eerily human eyes. Then he hurried across the driveway and prepared his ass for a chewing.

"What's the story, LT?"

Rourke motioned to the front door, where one of the deputies was opening the house and letting them in. The deputy said, "They'll be calling any moment, sir."

That raised Graham's eyebrow, but Rourke didn't say anything, so he knew better than to ask.

Inside, Rourke waited until the door was closed and they were alone, by the very kitchen table where Graham had been assaulted. Rourke checked his watch. "Good, we've got a few minutes."

Rourke pulled Louis's phone off the wall and placed it at the center of the table. The man looked oddly pale, Graham realized. Something was eating him up.

"Look, I'm going to be honest," Rourke said. "When you called the corpse hound out here, I thought it was a stretch. But I trust you. I respect your thinking, even if it's a little hard to follow at times."

"Well, I appreciate the vote of confidence, LT, but it looks like I fumbled."

"Not so fast. I just got a couple of messages that're in your wheelhouse."

The chair squeaked as Graham leaned forward.

Rourke continued, "Last night out in Litchfield County, some mountain bikers came across a fresh body."

"Litchfield," Graham said. "That's western Connecticut, right?"

Rourke nodded. "They found her out at one of those prep schools. Victim was a groundskeeper out on a maintenance call. Someone caved her face in, dumped her body in the woods, and made off with her truck. They're still trying to find her jaw."

"Jesus." Graham stiffened. "That wasn't the Tenbury School, was it?"

Again, Rourke nodded. "It was. And I'll give you one guess whose Ford Taurus was parked on campus, not a thousand feet away from the corpse."

"Louis. No shit?"

"No shit."

Graham considered the pieces, the trajectories, the timeline. He could see Louis rumbling down the county roads and rural byways, driving west with that shifty expression, a man running out of time. Okay, so the necklace, the missing girl, the boarding school, they really were all connected. And Beatrice? Graham had read that psychopaths often hurt animals, so maybe it tracked.

But murder...

Had Louis been hiding something terrible for years? Had the dog been some sort of trigger? Graham sensed strobe-lit flashes, pieces of a larger puzzle still cloaked in the shadows.

"LT, I know squat about boarding schools, but Thanksgiving's on Thursday, so that campus is probably empty, right?"

A third nod from Rourke.

"Maybe our pal Louis figured he could switch cars out, but something went sideways. Hell, he could be in the Florida Keys by now."

"Or New Hampshire," Rourke said. "I got the call, twenty minutes ago. Campus PD up in Darrington found the groundskeeper's pickup. It was parked behind a sorority."

"A sorority?"

That was when he noticed the color leaving Rourke's face.

What he said next floored Graham, rendering him momentarily numb. His first thought was that he'd simply misheard. His next thought was that he'd been wrong about Louis, so terribly wrong.

He spoke slowly. "What do you mean he cut off her head?"

Rourke twisted his wedding band. "Louis turned up at the house and found some poor girl. He knocked her face in with a hammer and sawed off her head. Used hedge clippers to excavate her lungs and heart. NHSP are still trying to figure out what he did with her body."

"He's not saying anything?"

"Oh, he said a bunch of things, according to the witnesses. Things that didn't make a whole lot of sense. Some film student got it all on tape. Then our pal Louis took a leap off the sorority with a rope tied round his neck. Gave himself a long drop too, popped his noggin free like a cork."

Graham scoffed, his brain sifting through each gruesome fact. Perhaps it was the concussion that was slowing him down. Perhaps a part of him still struggled to believe what Louis had done. With grim detachment, he realized they were now sitting at a dead man's table, inside a dead man's house.

Then the dead man's telephone rang.

Rourke slid it toward Graham. "That's New Hampshire State convening a task force. I told them you're handling Louis's case from our end. And that you'd help each other make sense of it all. I sure fucking can't."

Two gruesome killings. A task force. This had gone rogue, grown beyond what he could have ever imagined.

Metastasized.

He shuddered at the word and steeled his fears. Then he answered the phone.

"This is Detective Graham."

For the next several minutes, he listened and took notes, his eyes drifting down to the kitchen floor. A few brown flecks of dried blood were still spattered on the linoleum tiles, a reminder of Louis's hammer. Graham had been lucky; he'd woken up. The world before that blow now seemed impossibly distant, a dream fading with each brutal new fact.

He hung up the phone and took a moment to steady his nerves. Outside, Rourke was sipping his coffee and staring off at the trees, looking older and worn down in the gray light of the morning.

It was so much worse than he thought.

Graham had a long drive ahead.

chapter forty-five

"This is bullshit," Adam muttered. "What's taking them so long?"

He had been adamant that they didn't have to talk to the police. Officially, they weren't suspects or people of interest or witnesses, really. They had merely shown up when a madman butchered their friend and leapt from a roof. They were doing the investigators a favor by sticking around; that was what they said.

Still, Megan couldn't believe it: June, her friend Chunhee, gone just like that.

And her body... What was the phrase they used? 'Unaccounted for.' Another way to say it was missing.

Megan pushed the thought out of her mind as a young officer brought them some more coffee. Like the station itself, the chairs were uncomfortable, molded plastic with little concern for human posture. She hadn't been able to sit still for hours, and the ringing phones weren't helping. Occasionally, a curious reporter wandered in and poked about the waiting area until that same young officer waved them off.

Adam rubbed his eyes. Last night, they had gotten a motel room. Separate rooms, of course, until she'd awoken in a panic and knocked on his door. She hadn't felt safe alone. So she crashed on his floor, listening to the hum of the freeway, sleeping in fragments as her mental theater replayed the events.

The glint of the knife and the crack of the rope.

That mad glare across several hundred feet of strangers. "Your secret is safe."

The hysterical girl in the shiny tube top. "She was *wearing* her body!"

Now, with morning stretching into noon and the investigators delaying, Megan was starting to agree with Adam: this was taking forever.

Knees popping, she went to the friendly cop's desk, a smooth-faced deputy named Sams. "Officer, how much longer will this take?"

"I'm sorry, ma'am. All I know is they're waiting for someone from out of state. They're on their way."

"Which state, Utah?" Adam shouted.

Sams shrugged. "Beats me."

Megan thanked him and returned to the seats. "Fucking government," Adam said. "Should change its motto to 'hurry up and wait.'"

When they had agreed to be interviewed, he insisted Megan go first. She knew Chunhee best, after all. But if her statement ran long, they could be stuck here another night, which meant another motel and more food, things she could barely afford.

Still, questions scratched about in her mind.

"I'll tell you everything, I promise. I've been meaning to tell you for years."

The last words she'd ever heard from her friend.

Megan was nearing the bottom of her coffee when she sensed a change in the air. The officers and clerical staff perked up. A few stood, taking on a somber posture and removing their hats. She walked to the balcony that looked down upon the lobby.

Oh God.

Megan didn't know Chunhee's parents very well. On the restaurant menus and billboards, Mr. Chang always smiled that wide, toothy smile, eyes uplifted and closed. At Parents Weekend, he'd gleefully passed out egg rolls and bowed. Here, now, he stumbled through the lobby, his wife at one shoulder, his son at the other. His sobs echoed off the station's brick walls, guttural for such a small man.

Megan's stomach twisted at the procession. She wanted to run down the stairs, to hug the Changs and tell them how sorry she was for their loss. Yet her feet remained planted on the tiles and her knees refused to unlock.

Then the doors opened, the noon light engulfed them, and the Chang family was gone.

"Ms. Megan Monroe?"

The voice was warm and older, more seasoned than the nervous campus police and the somber state troopers. A man with a *Magnum, P.I.* mustache tapped his clipboard and a curious blue notebook. He might have been good-looking if it weren't for the scruffy hair and the gray blazer that hung from him a little too large. He smelled like the road.

"I'm Detective Nolan. I'm sorry to keep you waiting."

She glanced back at Adam, who was lighting up another cigarette and circling the ashtray. He nodded and said, "See you on the other side."

chapter forty-six

With a gentle hand, Detective Nolan guided Megan through the station's labyrinthian halls. He paused occasionally, seemingly lost before resuming. They found a back office with frosted glass walls and a view of a river.

"I'm so sorry about your friend," he said, closing the door. "She sounded like a neat woman."

Her stomach knotted as they settled at a messy desk. It pained her to think of Chunhee as gone. That was for people far beyond college, those in the latter half of life, when ailments and illness became regular and pills lined their bathroom sink. Chunhee was too young to be condemned to the past tense.

Don't go there, Megan told herself. *Think, but don't feel. Remember, but don't ruminate.*

"And I appreciate your patience," he added. "I just drove up from Bristol County."

"You're from Massachusetts?"

He nodded, pushing several folders to the side of the desk and opening that blue notebook. "More of a transplant, as the locals keep reminding me. I'm surprised you know it."

"One of my friends has a summer cottage on the coast. Beautiful area."

"Must be nice."

She nodded. It was a nice house. So nice that she'd gotten drunk and drove off in a rage she couldn't remember. Her lawyer had assured her the DUI was struck from her record. Still, panic wormed its way up her back as Detective Nolan flipped through his folders and notes.

"You and the deceased were boarding school classmates," he said without looking up. "When was the last time you spoke to her?"

The deceased, Christ. It really happened. "Yesterday afternoon around two."

"At two? You're sure?"

"Give or take. I left New Bedford at two and the drive took three and a half hours. I stopped for lunch in Northampton."

He compared the clipboard to his notebook. He made a quick note in it, seeming to agree with whatever was written. "And the nature of your conversation?"

"The nature?"

She had prepared for these questions all morning. Practiced ways to talk around why she didn't have a good answer. She had sought out Tenbury because of her dreams. She had sought out Chunhee because new memories had emerged. And Chunhee had promised her answers.

"What I mean is, was the conversation happy or angry?" Detective Nolan asked. "Did Ms. Chang seem worried? Did she say anything that led you to believe she was in danger?"

"No, I'm not sure."

"No?" He lowered his glasses. "Or you're not sure?"

The caffeine and lack of sleep were making her anxious. Which, in turn, made the silences uncomfortable. She felt a compulsion to fill them in. "I don't know. She said she couldn't speak over the phone. I thought..."

Again, with that stare over his glasses. She liked the detective, but she also felt her diction was on trial. She was an artist, not a wordsmith. Perhaps Adam could clear up any doubts.

"I was in a car crash, right after the end of high school. It really messed with my head for a while."

She told him about the accident, about the fire that claimed her parents. About how she sometimes woke up, certain they were still alive and awaiting her call. He nodded and listened politely but seemed disinterested. Most people usually were.

"And this man?" He slid over a photograph of the man who had stepped off the roof. That monster who had butchered Chunhee. "Have you ever met him before?"

"Louis? No."

"And you've never spoken to him on the phone?"

"Never."

"No mutual friends or secondhand contact?"

"None that I know of."

"How'd you know his name?"

"One of the cops said it this morning. Louis... Hardy?"

"Mmhmm, Harding." He made quick little tick marks in his notebook and compared it to his clipboard. There was a knock at the frosted glass door, and a friendly officer in her late thirties poked her head in. "Detective Nolan? Press conference starts in thirty and the chief wants to know if you'll have anything to add."

"Just that he should postpone it until after five."

She laughed. He didn't. "Wait, you're serious?"

"If he holds it now, it'll be the top story on the five o'clock news. Your switchboard will be busy until Christmas. You'll get a thousand concerned mothers and half as many useless tips. Or you can wait until tonight, keep the line from getting clogged up and your one operator happy."

She scrunched her eyes and studied him. "Huh. That's pretty clever."

"I've stepped in a few cow pies over the years."

Megan sensed a flirtatious tension between them. Two adults with all the subtlety of kids. On most days it might make her smile. Today, it just left her sad.

The officer left and Detective Nolan took a long sip from his coffee, reviewing his notes. "So, this guy Louis, he has zero reason to know you, correct? And yet, there's a video tape of him calling out you and your boyfriend. 'Your secret is safe.'"

"Okay, first, Adam is not my boyfriend."

Detective Nolan raised an eyebrow and crosschecked his notes. "No? This photo was in Chunhee's room."

He slid her the photocopy, but she knew the image before she turned the page over. The chapel at Tenbury. Their semiformal attire, probably hanging in closets or rotting in boxes these days. Tom and his *hang loose* gesture. The five smiling friends.

"*Tri. Dva. Odeen.* Cheese."

"This photo is ancient history," Megan said. "We broke up two years ago."

More like he stopped returning my calls, she thought. And she realized they had been apart longer now than they'd ever been together. Why did it feel recent and raw?

"I'll make a note of that. No... longer... dating." Detective Nolan scratched down the words and turned a few pages. "So, you call your old high school friend. She tells you to drive up. You live in Connecticut so you hit the interstate—"

"I don't live in Connecticut, not anymore."

"You said you left New Bedford at two."

"I was visiting our old school. I live in Philly. I'm an art student."

His posture shifted and his eyes bounced from his notebook to Megan. It was as if his chair had become charged. "Hold on. New Bedford. You were at Tenbury yesterday? That's what you mean?"

She nodded. "Yes, that's what I said."

Now he was really leaning toward her, studying her. "What time?"

"Noon. Why?"

"Who were you visiting?"

"My old Spanish teacher."

"And she'll vouch for that?"

"Vouch?" Megan sensed something moving at the edges of her understanding. "Of course she'll vouch. Why does that matter?"

He drummed his fingers along the edge of the table. She could see his jaw clenching. She didn't need to be an investigator to know he was playing his cards close to his chest. Then he nodded to himself, settling on a decision.

"Louis Harding, I've been tracking him ever since he killed his neighbor's dog and clobbered me with a ball-peen hammer."

"Clobbered? Like—"

"Your friend, yeah. Maybe it was the same. Maybe it was different. I don't know. What I do know is this: Louis was also at that boarding school of yours, yesterday. There's reason to believe he killed a groundskeeper, swapped vehicles, and headed up here."

Megan went to speak, but the coffee that had brought speed to her thoughts was now gluing her tongue to the roof of her mouth. She could feel the baseboard heater blowing warm air on her ankles.

She said, "I'm sorry, you're saying Louis was at Tenbury yesterday."

He nodded.

"So, he was, like, stalking me, or...?"

"I don't know. So far the timelines don't match up."

"What was he doing?"

"See, that's the sixty-four-thousand-dollar question, isn't it?" Detective Nolan leaned back in his chair. "Why would Louis drive from eastern Mass to western Connecticut, then head up here and... well, you know the rest. What's the connection? Best I can figure out, it's this boarding school of yours."

Megan swallowed. "I'm sorry, Detective. I'm confused. Am I in some sort of trouble?"

He blinked, those fierce, focused eyes suddenly becoming soft and wide and a little bit protective. "Oh no, no no no, of course not. I'm sorry, I'm not trying to be ominous or anything."

Megan exhaled. It felt like she'd been holding her breath for the past half hour.

"Breathe, young grasshopper," he said. "Breathe."

She took out a cigarette and tapped the pack. He stretched out and fumbled with the window. Then the cool breeze off the river and the nicotine did their tricks, sharpening her mind and calming her heart. That was the same river they'd crossed last night. If only she'd gotten here faster.

After a few drags, she wiped away a single, stubborn tear. "I'm sorry, it's just been a rough day."

They spent the rest of the cigarette and the one that followed going over Chunhee's details: what Megan remembered from high school, rumors she'd heard in the years since. Megan learned a thing or two.

Chunhee was on track for summa cum laude. She occasionally dated. And she really did spend the summer and part of the fall interning with the Clinton reelection campaign. She'd been inside the White House.

Chunhee...

June...

That shy, quiet girl remade into a confident young woman. How Megan would have liked to see her friend's evolution.

The detective circled back to Louis a few times, and Megan shook her head at every question. She didn't know him, or how he knew Chunhee. But she was glad he was dead.

Then it was over, and the detective gave her his card and wrote down a local number. He led her to the door and then hesitated. He said, "This is probably a long shot, but have you seen a woman named Oksana Samarina lately?"

Megan licked her lips. "Oksana?"

"She'd be about your age. She—"

"No, I mean, I know who she is. We were roommates."

He told her about the necklace, the empty apartment. None of it made any sense, and he admitted as much.

A flash of Adam's words: "A zero-sum game."

The two of them kissing.

Headlights cutting the dark night as her tires left the road.

"No, I haven't seen her," Megan said. "But when you do, be sure to give her a message. Tell her she can go straight to hell."

After reapplying her makeup in the bathroom, Megan returned to the winding halls of the station. She found the second-floor waiting area and took a seat, waiting for Adam to finish his interview. *Days of Our Lives* droned on the nearby TV. Bo and Hope were having their perfect English wedding and exchanging vows. Megan remembered watching it as a child, thinking maybe one day she'd live in a castle.

But here she was, in a police station, running on a few hours of sleep and dozing off. During a commercial break, Detective Nolan emerged from the hall. He cast a quizzical glance around the room and asked, "Where's Adam?"

Megan shook her head. "I thought he was with you."

After searching the station for twenty minutes, Megan found a payphone in the lobby. She poured in several quarters, fingers dancing across the dial pad on instinct. It was odd what phone numbers remained in her head over the years. On the fourth ring, a familiar woman's voice answered, Adam's mother. Megan lowered her voice.

"Hi, I'm trying to get in touch with Adam. He was just here in Darrington and we got split up—"

"Darrington?"

"Yes, ma'am, Darrington, New Hampshire. He—"

"What on earth is he doing up there?"

A knot formed in Megan's gut. "He said he was picking his cousin up, and I was hoping you had their number—"

"Cousin?" A pause. "I'm not sure I understand. Adam doesn't have any cousins at Darrington."

Megan closed her eyes. No, of course he didn't. She'd met his aunt and uncle over the holidays once. They lived in Virginia and only had dogs.

"Is... Is this Megan? Have you—"

Megan hung up.

Outside, she found Adam's curbside parking spot now occupied by a news van, the meter recently fed. She went around back to where she'd parked Corey's Isuzu to avoid paying. Her walk turned into a jog as she saw the truck tilting to the left side, rims touching the asphalt.

Three of the tires were slashed.

chapter forty-seven

Graham watched the press conference from the sidelines of the lobby with morbid amusement. The New England State Police Compact, as well as NESPIN—the New England State Police Information Network—helped state and local law coordinate without stepping on each other's toes. But sometimes that coordination required knowing when to step back.

Graham had handled press interviews, but these days he preferred to stay away from the media. *Unsolved Mysteries* and *America's Most Wanted* made the public twitchy and impatient. Real police work took time and was often solved at a desk in some office. The Darrington chief of police, however, seemed to enjoy the media attention.

Until the questions started coming.

Now he was holding out his hands, asking for calm and getting only a barrage of questions from the indignant reporters. Graham chuckled. Some cops got so used to barking orders they ended up surprised when people didn't always take them.

"What evidence do you have that the murderer has been apprehended?" asked a man whose press badge identified him as a reporter for *The Eagle-Tribune*.

"And how do you know we don't have a serial killer in our community?" shouted a journalist from the *Concord Monitor*.

"Any comment on why the victim's heart and lungs were still

attached to her head?" asked a man from *The Boston Globe*. "Was this some sort of Satanic sacrifice?"

The chief beseeched calm but the questions came rapid-fire now, both from the press and the scared citizens. Shaking his head, Graham bowed out of the rest of the conference. He had time to make a few calls.

The first was to an old liaison at the state department. He wanted to run the name Oksana Samarina by him and see if anything came up in their systems. Nothing did, just another student on an overstayed visa.

The second was to the Ukrainian consulate in New York City. It was Sunday, so he left a message.

At a quarter past two, his stomach rumbled. Good, he had enough time to grab a bagel before his appointment with the medical examiner.

Like most college towns, Darrington was walkable with wide sidewalks and a pleasant canopy of trees. After getting directions from the bagel shop, Graham cut across a small park and followed Whitman Street past the courthouse. A blue butterfly flew beside him for a moment and then followed the breeze east.

He used the walk to review his thoughts.

Fact one: There was some connection between Louis and Chunhee still waiting to be uncovered. Was Oksana that link? Perhaps.

Fact two: Chunhee, Megan, and Oksana all attended the same school. Had Louis been obsessing over them for years and building a kill list? It was certainly possible.

Fact three: Megan hadn't necessarily lied but she'd kept something hidden. When he'd asked about Oksana, she turned as pale as a ghost.

Graham finished his bagel and hurried across the street. He would have liked to talk to Adam, but the guy was under no obligation. Besides, he'd struck Graham as moneyed, which meant he knew to consult a lawyer before talking to a cop. Clever kid.

What mattered most was that Louis was dead and cold. This was a remains-recovery operation now, and he pitied whoever found Chunhee's missing body, that terrible V cut through her shoulders and chest.

The medical examiner's suite was chilly and sterile, but the man was cheerful and warm. He reminded Graham of a hobbit.

"I was worried you'd stayed for the press conference," the medical examiner said and gestured to a radio near the dissection tables. "I've been tuned in since it started. Much more interesting than looking at dead bodies, I'll tell you."

"I'll take your stiffs over reporters any day," Graham said and put on a pair of latex gloves. "They're better behaved."

The medical examiner chuckled and opened the cadaver shelf. "God help us if that changes."

In Graham's experience, the myth of the somber medical examiner was just that, a myth. Some of his best conversations had been with men and women who worked with the dead. They were a chatty bunch who knew the silence of death and appreciated the noises of life.

"It's not often that you see a long drop decap." The man slid the cadaver rack out. "They tend to stick in your memory. I saw one in Da Nang, sixty-five. ARVN caught a Viet Cong sympathizer and wanted to make an example. They stole some rope from my unit but messed up converting feet to meters."

"Yeah, that pretty much sums up that whole mess," Graham said, adding, "First Battalion, Forty-Sixth Infantry. I was only in-country for the end."

"Glad you made it home. What a waste of lives."

"Charlie didn't think so."

"And that's why they won, son. Never pick a fight with an enemy you don't understand."

"Roger that."

While the medical examiner unzipped the bag, Graham consulted the death certificate on the clipboard. Here it was, the final facts of Louis Harding's life. His height and weight, his sex and race, the culmination of fifty-some years reduced to lines and checked boxes.

"You prefer to stay above the neck or want to go below?" the medical examiner asked.

Graham consulted the clipboard. "Below. He was missing a finger when I last saw him."

"Well, he's missing more than one now." The medical examiner rolled the bag down to the dead man's chest and hoisted a pale wrist. Graham took it all in. The head, resting against the neck but clearly separated. The mottled chest. And the fingers, two were cut down to the knuckles. The third, his left pinky, was missing its distal phalanx.

Yep, this was Louis all right.

Graham checked the box and signed, verifying that he had witnessed the body. His part in this mess was over.

Then something shifted.

"What was that?" He glanced at the body, focusing on that torn rut that separated Louis's jawline from his neck. "Did you see that?"

"Yeah." The medical examiner took a step back. "Yeah, I think I did."

The two men squinted. There was something moving now, a shadow rustling in the dark plastic of the body bag by Louis's shoulder.

"Is that..."

Then Louis's head lolled to one side.

Graham found himself struggling to understand what was beneath it. An insect, perhaps, or an animal. Something small and wet and—Jesus Christ—it was *crawling*.

From between the torn muscle and fat at the nape of Louis's ruined neck, an oily sheen spread itself out. Pink fibers inched toward the edge of the bag. Little tendrils lashed out and pulled, lashed out and pulled. It reminded Graham of a shivering hand stretching and contracting.

"The hell is that?" he asked.

Eyes wide, the medical examiner said, "I... I don't know."

Not a good thing to hear from a doctor.

It was a dimpled pink puddle at first. Then it stretched and frayed to webbing, sending little roots to the edge of the body bag. Tendrils straddled the open zipper, glistening in the sterile light. Graham was both disgusted and transfixed.

Disgusted, because he could see bubbles forming in the substance, pushing hairs and skin to the surface, ligaments and veins and something that looked like a tooth.

Transfixed, because it was changing before them. Its surface rippled, stiffened, and darkened. It was mimicking the PVC vinyl and zipper.

"Are you seeing this?" the medical examiner whispered, leaning in closer.

Big mistake.

A tendril sprouted from the webbing and stretched out for the medical examiner's curious face. Graham pulled the man back hard, and they both fell to the floor.

"Christ on a crutch."

The pink webbing spilled down the body bag, oozed over the gurney, and hit the tiled floor in a pancake-sized puddle. Clumps of gristle and hair glistened as it rolled like oatmeal. Then it did something that drove the men back even farther.

It mewled.

It fucking cried like a baby.

The puddle grew speckled, taking on a shimmering reflection of the floor tiles. Quivering lumps pushed themselves to the surface and opened. Distantly, Graham realized, those were two puckering lips.

"*Cray... cray-sssssst... onna... crrrrrruuuudge... Craystonnacrutch.*"

The mass oozed and undulated in ways that no liquid possibly could. It stretched and it crawled and it shivered. All the while, that cry echoed out, wet agony and madness.

Two braided tendrils twisted, pulling the puddle away. A third piece split down the middle, inching it forward.

Toward the drain, Graham realized. "Catch it."

"*CASHEET,*" those lumpy lips burbled. "*GASHEET... GAJOOD...*"

Both men scrambled. The medical examiner went for a metal tray, and Graham for his clipboard. They were going to block it in.

They were too slow.

With a shuddering lurch, the puddle spat its way toward the drain's stainless-steel holes and began sliding through.

Well, half of it.

The other half was split by wood and paper where Graham drove the clipboard through the pink mass. He felt the resistance, as if somehow this was more than just liquid. It had the density of blackstrap molasses and a strength like the jaws of a pit bull.

With a wet slap, it folded back and lanced out a tentacle, climbing a third of the way up the paper and clipboard. Its surface shifted, taking on the complexion of the death certificate, white spotted with dark lines and text.

It was coming for Graham's hand.

He did the only thing he could think of, more of an instinct than a plan. He unholstered his gun and fired three times at the puddle.

The gunshots boomed in the refrigerated room. His eyes watered, and gunpowder shook his senses and spattered his cheek. The clipboard was blown clean from his fingers.

Then the medical examiner was grabbing him, pointing to the clipboard and the paper upon it. Flames licked up the side, entire pages of carbon copy smoldering from the muzzle flash.

Pinned beneath the cindering clipboard, the wet thing twisted. Blisters erupted on its surface. Hissing and sputtering, it squirmed away from the flames.

"The fire," Graham said. "Get something that burns."

"Copy that."

The medical examiner moved fast. Graham had barely pinned the clipboard underfoot when the medical examiner twisted a bottle and poured out its contents.

The isopropyl alcohol ignited, driving both men back. The fiery puddle blackened the clipboard and curled the pages, burping ash and smoke. Within, the webbed thing bubbled and twisted in on itself. Layers peeled, first raw and pink, then mottled gray and cindering to ash.

"*KEEBY DAD... KOOBY THAD... COPY THAT...*"

With a twitch, those rotten lips emerged from the mound of ash, wheezing out a final sound. All they heard was a low buzzing, a thousand flies thrashing against glass. Graham could feel himself slipping, stumbling, sliding down a steep cliff of madness, his fingers scraping at the loose rocks and roots for traction and sanity.

Then it was over. The mound of ash collapsed, smearing the tiles beside the smoldering clipboard and papers. There was nothing left that could burn.

With a hiss, the fire-suppression sprinklers went off, soaking the room and bringing Graham and the medical examiner crashing back to the present.

As Graham wiped his eyes, the medical examiner whispered, "What in good God's name just happened?"

chapter forty-eight

It was the third hour of the dumb bus ride, and Willy Watson hated every stupid minute. Except, of course, when he was playing his Game Boy. He was further along into *Donkey Kong Land 2* than ever, all the way to Mudhole Marsh. He'd collected most of the bananas, jumped from alligator to alligator. He almost acquired the last letter to spell K-O-N-G and earn a 1UP.

Then the Game Boy ran out of power.

Willy tapped the screen as it faded and dimmed. He tried turning down the volume to preserve the power. It was too late. Diddy Kong, the bananas, the whole swamp and its precious pixels all faded to a green void. Willy was ready to scream.

But screaming was bad manners, according to Mother. Screaming meant he wasn't in control of his emotions, but his emotions were controlling him. Big boys didn't scream, they didn't cry over Game Boys, they didn't have tantrums. But still... all those points he'd accumulated, now forever lost.

Well, at least he could use his save slot and make his way back.

"Mom, batteries."

"Hmm?" His mother stirred in the window seat. Like most of the passengers, she'd nodded off the moment the bus started moving. Willy was envious. He could never sleep in a car or a bus, especially when they were traveling all the way to Upstate New York. The farthest he'd been outside of Maine was to the Boston Museum of Science.

"Batteries," he repeated. "My Game Boy is out."

She shook her head. "I didn't pack any, hon. Sorry. I told you to bring extras."

A dark fear murmured in Willy's nine-year-old mind: the AA batteries, had he remembered to bring them? He had taken them from the drawer, yes. He'd put them in the plastic baggie along with his cartridges for *The Lion King* and *Mega Man V*.

But now his fingers touched the bottom of his backpack. There was no plastic bag, no click of cartridges, no spare batteries.

A low moan rose from his lungs and he burned with fury. He could see the stupid bag sitting on the kitchen table, a few hundred miles away. The bus driver needed to turn around, now, but would he listen? Probably not.

Perhaps sensing her son's frustration, his mom asked, "William, what is it?"

William. That was his Serious Name, his Let's Be On Our Best Behavior name. "I... batteries... I left them back *hoooome*."

Her nostrils flared so he knew she was choosing her words. Adults had a bigger vocabulary, so it sometimes took them a while to find the exact perfect word. "Well, I suppose this is a learning experience for both of us. You learned that it's important to double-check that you brought everything. And I learned I need to check that you checked."

Willy considered it as the bus changed lanes on the highway. "So, it's not my fault?"

"No, it *is* your fault."

"But then why's it a learning experience for both of us?"

She smiled her We're Done Talking About This smile, which meant that Willy had frustrated her. He didn't like frustrating Mother because sometimes that made her sad, and S-A-D was B-A-D. He preferred Mother when she was H-A-P-P-Y.

But his Game Boy...

Diddy Kong and those bananas...

He sank down in his seat. "How much longer?"

She glanced out the window for a moment. He thought she was ignoring him or had forgotten the question, so he tugged on her blouse and repeated it twice.

"Hold your horses," she said. "I'm trying to figure out where we are."

The road signs. That was what she was looking at. Just then, a big green one passed. *Cobbs Hill Country Club, Ontario County, NY.*

"Not long," she said. "Maybe another three hours?"

He felt the moan rising in his throat and the little angry bugs crawling in from the corner of his vision. He needed to be careful. If he got too worked up, he could trigger another episode where he didn't remember stuff 'cause his brain was rebooting. He didn't like the other word the doctors used; the S-word.

But three hours?

He slid down further into the seat, knees scraping the chair in front of him. He made little pedaling gestures, trying to imagine he was helping the bus move faster, like Fred Flintstone and his car.

"William, off the floor," his mom said. "Big boy time. Here, I brought one of your favorites."

She handed him a fresh *Goosebumps* paperback. A book? What was she thinking? Kids needed real entertainment, not stupid pages with stupid words he didn't always understand. She might as well give him homework.

He opened the book and tried reading, but he couldn't stop thinking of Diddy Kong and the bananas. He wished he could make save points and restart his own life. He'd make a save point back at his house. He'd restart so he could get those stupid batteries.

Willy's eyes drifted across the aisle to the woman with the empty seat beside her. Like Willy, she wasn't a sleeper. He could see one of her eyes was open, watching the landscape of rivers and covered bridges drifting by.

Her other eye was covered in a bandage.

Willy tried not to stare at the woman. Prolonged eye contact was considered rude, according to his teacher. In nature, some animals took it as a threat.

But he wasn't a threat to the woman; he found her quite pretty.

Actually, she was one of the most beautiful things he'd ever seen. Her hair hung past her shoulders, somehow black and brown and even red in a few places. It reminded Willy of shimmering oil. Her hands looked soft and precise.

Occasionally, she twirled a pen through her fingers. She was writing or doodling in a notebook.

Willy knew that it was bad manners to snoop on other people; you needed to ask permission. But he didn't want to because she might say no. And then he wouldn't have anything else to keep him entertained and the bus ride was already taking for-ev-er.

Folding his feet between his butt and the seat, he stretched up, peering across the aisle. He was right; she was writing or drawing. But what it was didn't make any sense.

He could see letters and numbers, lines of them running vertical and horizontal. There were sentences that stretched down the whole page and words running across it that were little more than three letters. There were strange letters too. Not the real alphabet but maybe something foreign and curved, like markings found in a wizard's book of spells.

The woman snapped her head in his direction. Willy sat down immediately and pretended to look out the window. He tapped his fingers for added effect and counted to sixty. He hummed the chorus of "Cotton Eye Joe."

When he looked back at the woman, she was slowly tearing the page from her notebook and folding it. She placed it in an envelope and wrote down some sort of address.

Then she took out another piece of paper and began scrawling that same gibberish. He stole a glance at her bandaged face. Gauze and cotton stretched across her eye and down her cheek to keep out the dirty stuff, like when he skinned his knee on the pavement. He wondered what was beneath the bandage. Probably nothing.

Or maybe something so terrible she had to conceal it.

"It's not polite to stare," she said without looking at Willy. He gasped, wondering how she'd seen him. He caught a glance of something shifting and coiling beneath her jacket.

"Sorry," he whispered.

"It's okay," she whispered back. "I always stare at things too."

Willy swallowed. Was she being friendly? Mother said not to talk to strangers, but that was out there in the real world, not here on a bus where the strangers were also travelers and no one could run.

He asked, "What are you making?"

"I'm not making anything." Her hand moved across the page quickly, scribbling that bizarre pattern, *scrikity-scratch*. It reminded him of a crossword puzzle if the boxes were gone. "I am preserving."

"Like, making jams?"

"I suppose." A coy smile tugged at her lips. He saw freckles blink to the surface of her skin, then fade just as fast. At some point he had started leaning out of his seat and into the aisle. Her voice reminded him of gravel and cotton candy. He tasted cherry Zotz on his tongue.

"So, why are you making preserves?"

"Why are you breathing?"

Willy scoffed. What a stupid question. "Because if I don't breathe, then I die." He almost added a "duh" but decided not to. Mother said he was a very clever boy, and sometimes other people didn't like being told they were less clever.

The woman smiled and said nothing.

Try as he might, Willy couldn't resist stealing another glance at the gauze and tape that covered her eye. Because something had moved beneath it, hadn't it? Yes, something had pressed against the bandage from the inside.

Slowing, the bus rumbled along the highway off-ramp. The speaker crackled as the driver said, "Next stop, Rochester."

Then the woman twitched.

Her pen scratched across the page and her fingers clenched and dug into the seat. Her whole body stiffened. With a shudder, that one good eye of hers rolled up to whites. Willy thought of a satellite dish locking onto a signal.

She sat like that for a moment, fingers digging into the seat, squeezing the armrests. He squinted, mesmerized by her nail polish and how it reflected the pattern of the fabric. Something wet slithered and retreated under her collar.

A thought bubbled forth in Willy's mind: that bandage wasn't there to keep the dirty stuff out of her injury. Maybe it was to keep the dirty stuff in.

He glanced at Mother, who was sleeping now, head against her folded jacket and the window. He wanted to wake her up and tell her that something was wrong with this woman, something for which he was still choosing his words. Angry? Rotten? Infectious?

"Hey, kid," the woman said, leaning a little bit closer. She was no longer concentrating and her eye had returned to normal. "You'll remember me, won't you?"

Willy nodded. He sensed he would remember her for the rest of his life.

She said, "That's what I thought."

Then her hand rose to the bandage and her fingers dug in. There was a quiet *scrich* as the tape peeled away.

Willy wasn't sure what he was looking at. A hole, yes, but something more. A well of memories and flesh. He now stood at the precipice of that well, his balance collapsing as the chorus of "Cotton Eye Joe" echoed and stretched. With a wet squeak, his feet slid past the edge. He tumbled forward, into the hole, into the void, into her.

There was no water at the bottom but a vast sea of undulating letters and words—her patterns and designs drawn upon this darkness. It washed over him. Waves of letters, waves of memories. Warm, hot perhaps, now scalding. Fingers fell upon his skin, and he wondered, how did she have so many hands?

From a distant place, Willy heard the squeak of brakes and a rumble as the bus pulled to a stop. He heard the driver announce, "Rochester, ladies and gentlemen. This stop is Rochester. We'll take a thirty-minute break."

And he sensed people gathering around him now, faces looking down with worry and concern. How had he gotten down into the aisle? And why were his arms and legs dancing?

"It's okay," Mother said, assuring the other passengers. "This happens sometimes when he has a seizure. Don't worry, he'll be okay."

And she was right. This sometimes did happen. As for today, he couldn't say why.

A stranger departed the bus, a woman with a bandaged eye and a modest smile. Willy watched her go, sensing from a receding hole in his mind that he knew her. Yet he never thought of her again; he never remembered her face.

And he never had another seizure.

chapter forty-nine

The mechanic was totaling up the estimate when the sensation hit Megan, sent her lurching against the wall of the automotive center and stole the words from her mouth. She held up a finger and wandered off, in search of some water. She found the cooler and gulped down several cups.

Was it true what that detective had said? There was no record of Oksana moving out of her apartment? That Louis had something of hers at his house?

But that meant...

No, she put that out of her mind. Locked it away in the same place that she put that starfish-thing from the library archives, her scattered fears, her nightmares. She would deal with each of those dreaded facts soon. For now, she needed to deal with the pain rattling around in her brain.

Letters formed at the edge of her vision, that errant radio station deep in her mind now buzzing to life. Like a week ago, she had an urge to draw or paint or create. And something else...

The squeak of heavy brakes coming to a stop.

A cold breeze off a vast lake.

Letters beneath an icon of a greyhound: *Rochester Bus Station*.

She let her heart slow before returning to the mechanic. She had two questions she needed answered.

First, she asked, "How much longer will this take?"

He glanced at the other cars. "I'd say two hours, maybe? Give or take."

"Two hours? To replace three tires."

"Well, it's four tires. You can't replace them odd-like. Otherwise, you'd have balance and traction issues with the treads not matching."

Megan wasn't sure if that was a thing or if she was being taken advantage of. She'd gotten spoiled living in such a walkable city. The last time she checked oil, she realized, her parents were alive and her head wasn't home to intrusive thoughts.

"Plus, I got two cars before yours." The mechanic rolled over to his tool chest and dug through it. "Yep, it wouldn't be Thanksgiving if everyone wasn't in a damn hurry."

Next, she asked, "Is there a payphone nearby?"

She found the phone by a Dunkin' Donuts. This was silly, she told herself. She was still in shock from Chunhee's death. Her mind was reeling and scratching for answers. And yet those doubts whispered.

Why had Adam slashed her tires? And why was she seeing the name of some random city in New York?

Because something is on the way.

She pressed her fingers against her throbbing scar. That was impossible, she told herself. Louis was dead. That detective said he was going to verify the corpse.

A flash of that poor girl at the sorority, screaming to an officer just loud enough for everyone to hear.

"She was *wearing* her body!"

Megan reached into her purse and opened the photocopies from Tenbury. She found the two names that stuck out. Tom Frenning, page ninety-two, and Desiree Chastain, page ninety-eight. Underneath both names were the same six words:

Attending this fall: University of Rochester.

No...

Megan fed the payphone several quarters, playing 411 roulette and hoping that Tom or Desi kept their numbers listed. Desi's wasn't. But the operator found five Tom Frennings, so she gave them each a try.

The first never answered. The second was a man who grumbled he didn't know her and quickly hung up. After four rings, the third went straight to the machine.

"This is Tom—"

"—and Desi."

"Do your thing after the beep—"

"—and we'll do ours."

When the machine chirped, Megan found the words retreating down her throat. *Tell them. Tell them about Chunhee. Tell them you're not sure why but you think they're in danger.*

So that was what she did. Swallowing, she stuttered and sputtered and meandered her way to the fact that she missed them, she was worried, and these weren't just bad feelings but something more. Premonitions or warnings or some terrible zeitgeist she'd tapped into. A spliced cable connection of the mind.

Then the answering machine cut her off.

After a moment of stunned silence, she realized she hadn't made her point. She dialed again, the phone ringing four times. She told herself to focus.

"Desi, Tom, it's me again. It's Megan from Tenbury. I'm not sure how to say this, but Chunhee's dead. I'm... I am *so* sorry to tell you all this. I just... I needed you to know because..."

She could feel herself choking. *Say it.*

"Because I think you're in danger. Both of you. I think we're all in danger. And, well, I need you to be careful. Just keep your eyes open, okay? Maybe go somewhere, out of town. If you see Adam—"

The answering machine cut her off yet again. She dropped in several more quarters and redialed. A double beep as the greeting finished, then a new warning: "Messages full. Please try again later."

She hung up knowing just how insane she sounded. An old high school friend, reaching out after two years with bad news and a conspiracy theory she couldn't quite explain. Was this what it felt like to slowly go crazy? To believe in something deeply, devoutly, and yet have little evidence to show?

Perhaps. Probably. But she still had to do what she could.

She only needed a quarter for the next call.

"Darrington PD, Homicide."

The voice that answered was a little too high for Detective Nolan's weatherman diction. Megan hesitated.

"Hello?"

She told the woman she was trying to reach Detective Nolan. The woman insisted there was no one at the station by that name. After some explaining, Megan could almost see the woman nodding, saying, "Yeah, yeah, that masshole from Bristol. What's the message?"

"Tell him I have some information he needs."

The woman chuckled. "And what information is that?"

"It's confidential."

"Got it, confidential. Writing it down now: top... secret... information."

There was something in the woman's voice that Megan found discomforting. Like she was rolling her eyes and picking her ear with a pencil. Megan asked, "You'll tell him Megan Monroe called?"

"Yep, sure will. I'll have them put out an APB. You take care now."

Then she hung up. The cop, she hung up on Megan; she didn't believe her.

And why would she? Megan doubted herself. Doubted her own eyes, her own mind. And if she couldn't convince herself something was wrong, how could she convince others?

A flash of a silver moon rising over the waves.

Those amber doors slowly opening to shadows.

A rusty shovel among dirt.

Megan shook off the images and returned to the garage. She opened her wallet, fishing out the last of her cash. She had her checkbook in hand when the mechanic looked up from the hood of a blue Volvo.

"I'll pay you whatever you want," she said. "But I need my tires fixed as soon as possible. Now, actually. And I'm not taking no for an answer."

Then she gave him her best Please Take Pity on Me Sir look, which she'd learned from Desi at Tenbury and always felt awkward to use.

But it worked.

Thirty minutes later, she had a cold bottle of Josta cola between her knees, the Isuzu and its fresh tires merging onto the freeway, driving east as fast as she could.

chapter fifty

Shoes echoing off the linoleum tiles, Detective Graham Nolan hurried through the east hall of the Darrington police station. A deputy waved him toward the conference room. Hazelnut coffee filled his nostrils and he tasted pizza before entering, probably Little Caesars. He was sad to see he was right.

The briefing was already underway, the task force present and half the department lingering at the edges. There were Grafton County sheriffs, NH state, even a serious man in the back with a navy-blue windbreaker that Graham pegged for a fed.

It really did take a village.

He stood toward the rear while the chief went over the five-o'clock update. No, this wasn't a serial killer. No, there was little evidence to suggest Louis was part of a cult. No, they didn't need to keep an eye on their daughters, but locking doors and windows was always good practice, even in a quiet college town.

Graham was mid-sip of that hazelnut coffee when the chief gestured to him. "And we owe a special thanks to Detective Nelson on loan from Bristol County in Mass. He helped kick this whole thing off."

Graham couldn't tell if he was joking or serious. Likely the latter, based upon the polite clapping and nods. Compared to the small station down in Bristol, Darrington felt like the ninth precinct.

"Hell, the man took a hammer to the head just to flush out this monster. That's dedication. Why don't you give us an update, Detective Nelson?"

"Nolan, sir." Two dozen pairs of eyes were upon him now. Graham cleared his throat. "Well, I'm afraid I don't have any leads on what Mr. Harding did with the victim's body. But I just spent several hours with your ME and I'm not sure where to start."

"How's Jerry handling all of this? Busy day for him, I imagine."

Graham nodded. And it had gotten even busier. "We found some... irregularities on Mr. Harding. In addition to the wounds on his fingers, we discovered something unusual with his neck."

"Yeah, it was missing his head," a young cop said, glancing around with a grin.

"Besides his head," Graham said. "Actually, inside it. At least that's where we think it came from."

He reached into his briefcase and began passing out the photos the medical examiner took after they'd shut off the sprinklers.

"The lab could only rush-print thirty-six of these. I hope you don't mind sharing."

Murmurs as the photos made their way around. "What is this?" asked one of the older state troopers. "Looks like someone burnt their tacos."

"Looks like something my cat would cough up," someone added.

"That was inside Louis Harding's neck," Graham said. "Based on some deep-tissue damage and bone scarring, the ME thinks it was wrapped around his spine. Specifically the cervical vertebrae. That's at the base of his skull."

Another cop asked, "What, like a tumor?"

Graham paused to consider his next words. He was pretty sure he should stop here.

Except, they needed to hear it; they needed to know. This was another piece of the puzzle they were solving together. Another piece that didn't quite fit. If he left out the disquieting and uncomfortable, he was just choosing the facts.

"Yeah, like a tumor," he said. "One that crawled out of Louis."

Silence. Every eye at the conference table turned from the photos to Graham. Even the chief's eyebrows crinkled. "Crawled out?"

"Oozed. Slithered. Slank. I'm not sure there's a word for what it did. But it moved toward us. It made noises. It… imitated us."

"Jesus, you really did get hit in the head." It was that same young cop who'd cracked the joke. Now it was Graham's turn on the other end.

"Maybe, but that won't change what we saw. Check with Jerry. He'll vouch. As for what it is, I don't know. He's running some tests, but he doesn't expect much. It's mostly ash and mud at this point."

The chief asked, "So how'd it get toasted?"

Graham swallowed. "Well, like I said, it moved toward us in a threatening manner. I discharged my firearm. Jerry used rubbing alcohol. This… is the aftermath."

He slapped the photos against his fingers. An hour ago, it had felt like he was holding a sure hand. Now it was all jokers. The human mind had a way of pushing back at the unsettling, quarantining it, relegating it to dark corners. In the jungle, Graham had seen evil and a few miracles too. But mostly, he'd seen good men shrug them off in equal measure. He wasn't sure where this fell, just that no one around him wanted it in their lap.

"Folks, I know how this looks, so make of it what you will, okay? Maybe Louis had some weird virus or the world's nastiest goiter. I dunno. Just file it away or—"

"Wait, you think he had some sort of virus?" The question came from the back of the conference room. "Was he, like, contagious? Like Ebola?"

"No, no, there's nothing to indicate anything like that."

Arms shot up as a half dozen questions overlapped. Graham could see a familiar concern wrinkling the chief's forehead. This was getting out of hand.

So he said, "Look, I've said enough. I'll keep you all updated."

But he doubted he would.

AN HOUR LATER, Graham sat in the spare office, the phone warm and his ear ringing. Word about the conference had gotten back to Bristol, and Rourke was curious what his detective was up to.

"No, LT, there's no evidence it's a pathogen or anything. I'm just... I'm just telling it like I see it, that's all."

A clinking of glass and a quick burble of poured liquid from the other end. Rourke was probably having a bourbon about now. Graham couldn't blame him if it was his second or third.

"Well, make sure you don't spook the locals," Rourke said. "That welcome mat ain't etched in stone."

There was a tap on the door and a distorted form beyond the frosted glass. Graham sensed it was a navy-blue windbreaker.

"I'll brief you tomorrow," Graham said and hung up.

A second knock and he called out to come in. As the man entered, Graham revised his earlier assessment: the man in the blue windbreaker didn't have the cocky swagger of someone that hailed from a three-letter agency.

"Detective Nolan, can I have a moment of your time?"

He was tall and lean, his features sharp and severe. His nose seemed a bit crooked, perhaps broken a few times. But it was his voice that Graham noticed most. Sure, his English was good, but few things could hide a Balto-Slavic accent.

"My name is Petro Kurkov, and I am private investigator."

He produced a card and handed it to Graham, then offered a firm handshake. Graham gestured to the chair and pushed aside an ever-growing mountain of paperwork. The clipboard and fiery pages might have saved him earlier, but the water-damaged reports and discharged pistol would plant his ass at a desk for a week.

Graham said, "I didn't know Darrington gave PIs free roam of the station."

Petro's lips rose to a flat line. Graham suspected that was as high as his smile went. "A wise man once said, 'Chaos is a friend of mine.'"

"Dostoevsky?"

"Bob Dylan."

Graham chuckled. "*Investigator* Kurkov, what can I do for you before I have that big cop down the hall toss you out?"

Again with that flat smile. He was even nodding now, perhaps agreeing with Graham's latent frustration. "I was most curious about what you say in meeting. With, uh, specific regard to *anomaly* found in Mr. Harding's... neck."

Graham gestured to the chair again, and he realized Petro was waiting for him to sit as well. So he did. "Yeah. That. Well, you saw the photos, right? To be honest, I'm still wrapping my mind around what happened. It was kind of a blur."

"Ah, a blur." Petro leaned forward. "But it happened, yes? You *remember* it."

Graham nodded. He did. Yet there was a faint haze to the memory, frayed at the edges and sheening in the center, grease smeared upon his mental lens.

"Did you come into contact with it? Through a wound or an orifice?"

"I didn't eat it, if that's what you're asking."

"Yes, of course."

The curious man spread his hands flat on the desk. Graham sensed an excitement beneath that placid face. He said, "Mr. Kurkov, that accent is a bit thick for a PI in New Hampshire. I can't imagine it helps you blend in."

"It is, and it does not. My clients are mostly immigrants or overseas. Err... Russian, Ukrainian, sometimes Belarusian. It is a... How do you say? A sword of two blades."

"A double-edged sword," Graham said, thinking, *Ukrainian. Now that seems to track.* "You work for the consulate?"

Petro offered a slow nod. "From time to time, I assist. Sometimes, a citizen overstay visa or go missing and I look into it. Sometimes, they have run away, and sometimes, they have been married. But every now and then..."

Graham didn't like how Petro didn't finish the sentence. Nor did he like the way his eyes were gleaming, waiting for Graham to make the next move. But Graham wasn't having it. It was after five and the Steelers were playing the Dolphins in a few hours. He was hoping to tune in by kickoff.

Petro sighed. "Very well. I suppose it is me who needs to make jump of faith. In your investigation with this man, this Mr. Harding, have you perhaps come across a woman named Zorianna Romanko?"

Graham shook his head. "No."

"Or perhaps a Katarina Zubokev?"

"Nyet."

The man raised an eyebrow. "Ah, Russian. In Ukrainian, no is *ni*."

"Ni, nyet, nada. Sorry, buddy, I can't—"

"Oksana Samarina." Again, his gray eyes gleamed. "Ah, I see by expression that you have. Good, this will save us both much time. I was hired by my client to search for their Ms. Samarina. She... failed to return home. This was at beginning of summer, two years in past. I look, but all I find is nothing."

"Case went cold, huh?"

"Coldest. Is like she no longer exist."

Graham's stomach rumbled. Too much station coffee and not enough real food. He sighed, suspecting he might miss the kickoff. "Petro, tell me two things, honestly now."

"Okay."

"Do you think Louis had something to do with Oksana's disappearance?"

Petro picked at his tobacco-stained fingers. He was trying to gauge Graham. "Maybe, or maybe not. But there is, eh... What is word? Entanglement. Yes, he knew something of it."

"How could he know something of it without being involved?"

Petro shrugged. "You are the detective. Was that second question?"

"No, it wasn't," Graham said. "Petro, I'm starving, so where are we grabbing dinner?"

chapter fifty-one

Graham found a corner booth in the diner with a view of the police station, every office window still lit into the evening. He tamped down the coffee jitters with a tuna melt and a bowl of clam chowder. Petro rolled the dice on the house borscht with a side of pirozhki. He winced after each bite.

When the waitress was out of earshot, Graham leaned in. "Here's the thing, Petro. Do you mind if I call you Petro?"

The private eye considered it, nodding once. "Is fine."

"If we're going to cooperate, then I need to know what cards you're holding. Let's start with your client, which I assume is the Samarina family, correct?"

Petro's head bobbed and his bottom lip jutted out. "Yes, and no."

"Yes and no? Okay, who cuts your checks?"

"For now, my work is... How do you say? Speculative."

"Speculative." Graham could feel his nostrils flaring. "See, this makes cooperation hard. Trust is a two-way street, give and take. You know what that means?"

"Yes. You scratch me and I scratch you back."

Graham smiled. *Close enough.* "Okay, so you have a nondisclosure agreement? I can respect that. But if that agreement impedes an investigation, that becomes obstruction of justice. Clear?"

"Is understood."

"Good."

Graham gave the man a moment to consider it all. Obstruction wasn't that simple, of course, but he'd made a calculated bet Petro might not be legally versed in interstate investigative procedures. Heck, Graham was always learning new things. And this case was growing more complicated in part because everyone seemed to think it was over.

But he wasn't so sure.

Petro pulled the ashtray over and reached for some matches. Graham wasn't a smoker—not after spending months in the cancer ward—but he kept a pack of Marlboro Reds in his jacket for such moments.

"So, Louis Harding and Oksana Samarina." He placed the cigarettes on the table between them. "What's the connection?"

Petro's fingers found their way to the pack. Without asking, he plucked one out, struck a match, and lit up. He exhaled through his nostrils. Graham thought of Alice's caterpillar on his comfortable mushroom.

"I think maybe he kill her."

Graham was quiet for a moment. Then, "Yeah, I think maybe you're right."

"And yet, if he kill her, where? At this school for boarding? No. And if not, then why he return?"

It was an angle Graham had been considering, one he'd set aside after the incident at the medical examiner's office. "I've read that serial killers often return to the scene of their first crimes to relive the excitement. Maybe Oksana was just that."

"You think Mr. Louis is... serial killer?"

"Three or more killings over an extended period of time, that's the definition. If Oksana was the first, the groundskeeper was the second, and this sorority girl June is the third, then yeah, that tracks. You look skeptical."

"Is nothing." Petro waved the thought off.

"See, this is the part where we build trust, Petro. My cards and yours."

Petro had smoked the cigarette almost to the filter in only a handful of drags. The man liked his Virginian tobacco, and Graham couldn't blame him. He'd smoked Belomorkanals once, Russia's version of Marlboros. He'd rather suck on a tailpipe.

So he held out another cigarette for Petro. He supposed one day they'd start closing down the smoking sections and sending customers outside for their nicotine fix, like they were proposing out in California. But for now, light 'em up, which was what Petro did.

After another moment of consideration, Petro said, "And what if Oksana is... not dead?"

Graham tilted his head. "What, like she ran away?"

"Yes, maybe. Or maybe she is... make cooperate. With this Mr. Harding."

The waitress returned with the bill, which Graham quickly paid. It bought him a moment to consider Petro's angle, which his mind had rejected on reflex. Never a good habit to indulge. Especially for an investigator trying to make sense of the senseless.

He asked, "Why would she cooperate?"

"Is my understanding Ms. Samarina can be... persuasive."

"Persuasive, huh? Give me an example."

"Example, okay. This girl—a nobody from Ukraine—maybe she convince her family to let visit America. Maybe her plan is don't return. And maybe somebody know where she is hiding. Where it is that she... went."

"That's a lot of maybes, Petro. I feel like maybe you're not telling me everything."

"This... *thing* you find in Mr. Harding's neck, is only one?"

"That pink gunk? God, I hope so." Graham realized he'd been nervously touching the back of his own neck at the mere mention of the thing. Like yawning after someone else.

"And you find nothing else? Nothing strange."

Everything about this was strange, Graham thought. But Petro's senses were right. It wasn't the only odd thing they'd found. Just an hour ago he'd gotten a fax from Rourke, sent from West Bedford PD via the Connecticut State Police. He removed it from his case file and laid it out on the table.

"They found Louis's boat bag at Tenbury School," he said as Petro studied the fuzzy black and white image. "CSP said it looks like some sort of basket made out of antler or bone. See how it punctured the fabric of the bag? I saw that same bag at Louis's house a day before. He was carrying it right after he hit me. It didn't look like that."

"Like how?"

"Like he was growing a nest inside it."

Graham noted the way Petro reacted to each word. Not his face, which remained placid and unreadable. No, it was in his eyes. Something flickered within. Something like fear.

He was about to offer him a third cigarette when the waitress returned. "Detective Nolan, is it?"

Graham studied the homely woman. "Who's asking?"

She nodded back toward the register. "There's a phone call. Said they'd been looking for you at the station."

He sighed, knowing the routine. The messages passed around from one to another, often lost in the shuffle. Little Post-it notes and interdepartmental envelopes with the wrong names crossed off. And yet, this conversation was flaring his instinct, a needle pushing into the red.

He took the fax back from Petro and returned it to his case file. "To be continued."

While he made his way to the phone, he kept a watch on the Ukrainian. He didn't trust him. Especially not after that flicker in his eye.

He put the red phone to his ear. "Detective Nolan."

After a few minutes of listening to third-hand information, he was almost ready to hang up. Then something caught his attention and he pulled out his pen. "Rochester," he repeated. "As in Upstate New York? You're sure that's what she said?"

He opened his notebook and started writing.

Two follow-up calls later and he returned to the table, where Petro was on his fourth cigarette. Graham said, "What kind of car are you driving?"

Petro blinked. "A Geo Metro. Why?"

"That's too slow. We'll take mine. C'mon, Petro. You're in charge of the map and the lights."

"Where we go?"

Graham peeled off a twenty and left it on the table. "It seems you're not the only one looking for Oksana."

chapter fifty-two

Tom spent most of the dinner poking at the salad and dividing his steak into increasingly smaller portions. He'd hardly eaten because he was grumpy; he was grumpy because of the location. Everything about the country club restaurant was too formal, too white, too posh for his blood. It was the first time he'd worn a blazer since high school. He was bummed to discover it fit a little too tight around the stomach.

Most of all, he hadn't gotten high all day. He was nervous by lunch and jonesing by dinner. Now, after ninety minutes of awkward talk, Desi's parents were finally relaxing. Two bottles of wine did the trick for them, but God forbid he spark up on the sly.

"I don't understand why you two just can't come with us," Mrs. Chastain said, almost hiccupping. "There's plenty of room in the back, and Dick's driving. We'll get there by midnight."

Dick was the Chastain family servant, chef, and chauffeur all rolled into one. When he wasn't running errands or cooking meals, he resided in a cottage at their Greenwich estate. Desi spoke about him the way others spoke about their grandparents. The whole arrangement weirded Tom out.

Desi said, "Thanks, Mom, but we prefer to drive there ourselves."

"I know that, sweetie, but I worry about you on the road," she said. "Especially late at night."

"Statistically, that's the safest time to drive. Unless it's Saturday from nine to midnight." That was Tom, trying to offer reassurance but sensing he'd come off as condescending. Who was he to lecture the Chastains? They had financial advisors and estate planners, probably a whole firm of attorneys on speed dial. He was just some middle child from a middle-class family in Middlebury.

"Yeah, Tom's right," Desi said. "I read that statistic as well. Besides, he's an excellent driver. We'll take it slow. If we get there after you've gone to bed, we'll let ourselves in."

Mrs. Chastain's merlot gaze lingered on Tom. "Mmhmm. Like I said, I worry."

Was this really what he wanted to marry into? He caught glimpses of Mrs. Chastain's ring sparkling like the stars. He could feel the engagement ring in his jacket pocket, small and pathetic. And yet, whenever Desi smiled, it made the awkward dinners worthwhile.

"They're just being independent, love," Mr. Chastain said, his Ike Behar tie now loosened and a cool sheen in his eyes. "Independence is an important part of maturation. It's encouraging. Frankly, your brother could learn a thing or two. We had to wire him funds just to bring him home for the holidays. The Western Union was in Ibiza."

Desi's eyes lit up. "Brandon's coming?"

Mr. Chastain wiped his lips with a napkin. "Tomorrow evening. Dick's driving to JFK to pick him up."

Tom could see Desi's mood lift. Brandon was the black sheep of the family, a backpacker who traveled the world and worked odd jobs in countries Tom struggled to find on the map. He was carefree and easygoing, a welcome buffer against Desi's parents.

Mrs. Chastain sighed. "I just don't understand why we can't drive together. It's so *simple*."

"Mom, you'll be asleep within ten minutes."

"That's not true."

"You literally slept the whole drive to the beach house this summer. You were snoring before we left the driveway."

"Well, I certainly don't *snore*."

It was more than just logistics, Tom suspected. It was about control. If Dick drove them in the Range Rover, they wouldn't have their own car for Thanksgiving at the Finger Lakes. Which meant they couldn't leave without asking to borrow a set of keys. Mrs. Chastain planned out every holiday, scheduled every activity down to the hour.

Lunch with the Warburtons.

An afternoon at the spa.

Dinner at Harbor House, where she would gossip a little too loud and the other wealthy families would pretend not to listen.

Tom sipped his coffee. "Hey, you can always crash at our place if you like. The pullout is super comfortable."

He regretted the joke the moment it left his lips. Mr. Chastain curled an eyebrow and Mrs. Chastain looked appalled. Even Desi nudged him, her elbow digging into his side and bumping up against the ring box.

"Or not."

An hour later and they were back at their apartment, Desi flopping onto the couch, removing her heels, and rubbing her sore feet. "Well, that was a fun evening. Not."

"Why does it always have to be the country club?" Tom removed his tie and tossed his blazer over a chair. "Would it kill them to pick an Applebee's or Chili's?"

"Chili's, seriously?" Desi turned the TV on and flipped through the channels. "Could you see my mom eating an Awesome Blossom? She'd probably melt."

Tom hesitated by the bedroom. "Hey, we're not really driving up tonight, are we? I haven't even packed."

She gave him a knowing smirk. "No, of course not. Something came up."

He furrowed his brow. Then he got it. "Ah, right. Yes, 'something came up' indeed."

"Didn't you have an article that needed a last-minute retraction?"

"Dude, why do I take the fall?"

"Because my dad likes you. He'll cut you some slack."

"Yeah right." Tom dropped his cufflinks on the dresser.

Desi lowered the remote, settling on MTV's *The Real World: Miami*. She had a thing for reality shows, and Tom had to admit he was getting sucked in. Thankfully, it was a rerun of last week's episode, when that bitch Melissa finally moved out of the house.

Tom asked, "Wait, what do you mean he likes me?"

"You're serious?" Desi asked. "He smiles at your jokes. He always asks about you. He never does that, not with me and definitely not with Brandon."

"No shit?"

"Duh."

Tom lingered at the door to the bedroom, letting that thought wash over him. He'd always thought of Mr. Chastain as cold and distant, but maybe he was starting to thaw. It'd only taken six years.

"Okay, so I'm going to go take a dump and process this turn of events."

"That's my man."

The bathroom bulb didn't brighten past a candle's glow no matter how many times Tom toggled the switch. He didn't care. He was still buzzing from Desi's revelation: perhaps he wasn't persona non grata to the Chastain family, not entirely. And a revelation like that called for a celebration.

He opened the medicine cabinet and let his fingers dance over the row of film canisters. Labels displayed tonight's choices. Northern Lights. Purple Haze. Chronic.

He settled on something special, a new strain straight from the Dutch coffee shops, Jack Herer. He got comfortable on the toilet and popped the film canister open. He was breathing in its skunky goodness when something moved in the bathtub.

A cockroach, he realized. He could see its little brown body peeking out between the shower curtain and the rim. A big one too. Its limbs clicked against the acrylic tub.

Pants around his ankles, he reached for an issue of *Scientific American*. He slowly rolled it up. There was another cockroach now, a bigger one emerging next to the first.

Then two more cockroaches peeked out, their chitinous bodies lined up like little viewers over a fence. He'd never seen cockroaches stand still like that. Jesus, he'd need to bug bomb the whole place.

Then a new thought bloomed as cold fear skittered up his spine.

Those weren't cockroaches.

At least, they weren't anymore.

Those were four fingernails between the shower curtain and the rim of the tub. Then the hand rose, the curtain parted, and Tom found his mind going numb as he beheld a quivering body unfolding before him.

"Oh," he murmured. "What are you doing here?"

chapter fifty-three

During the commercial break, Desiree uncorked the bottle of white wine and poured herself a healthy glass. She gulped it down fast and poured another.

Yes, she knew she was self-medicating, and yes, she didn't quite care. Apples didn't fall far from their trees. At least that was what she told herself to get through another holiday; that was her mantra. *Drink, don't think. Just smile and nod and let the judgmental barbs slide off like ice.* It was only five days.

Another deep sip to calm her nerves. It wasn't just her parents that had her on edge. Nor was it Tom's odd behavior and her suspicion he was getting ready to propose. She should be happy; it was about time.

No, there was something deeper, wasn't there? An old brick knocked loose from the wall of her mind. That guilt they'd all walled over and forgotten.

Then she noticed the cordless phone and its blinking red light. It hung on the wall in the kitchen, next to the dry-erase board covered in doodles and pizza delivery coupons. Usually, she got anxious checking the messages, but tonight the white wine did its trick. She pressed *play* and listened.

Mailbox full. Seven new messages, nine saved.

The first was from Brandon, asking if she could remind their parents to wire some more money. The second was Ray, wishing them a happy Thanksgiving and vowing a rematch in *Mortal Kombat*. He would have his revenge for her crimes.

The third was ten seconds of silence followed by a voice from the past. One that bristled her back and sobered her mind.

"Hey, it's Adam from Tenbury. Long time, right? Listen, we need to talk. I'll be in town soon. It's... well, you know what it's about."

Stunned, she rewound the message and listened again. Her shoulders were tight and her tongue tasted dry. When had her knees started to tremble? And that loose brick in the wall of her mind, it was no longer alone. Others were shifting, the mortar dusty and crumbling.

Desiree never heard the rest of the messages.

There was a sopping thump from the bathroom, something heavy hitting the tub. She swore she heard the distinct clink of shower curtain hooks snapping apart. Then came the burble of liquid draining down the apartment's old pipes.

Crossing through the living room, she did not notice the TV flickering static. Nor how the lights had all slightly dimmed. She did notice the cockroach skittering along the floor's molding. But not how its wings were painted red fingernails.

What had her attention was the glow emanating from the bathroom, a radiance brighter than any bulb should produce. It shimmered and subsumed the door's edges, outlining the dark door like an X-ray.

Only the old keyhole remained, a shadow passing back and forth, back and forth.

Trembling, Desi bent to that keyhole and peered through.

The eye peering back was Tom's. She recognized the amber-green of the iris's edge, the twin speckles beneath his pupil, motes in an emerald sea. And yet she knew the eye gazing back was not her boyfriend's, her best friend's, her beloved.

Tom never stared with such spite.

The door opened inward and the floor embraced her. Somehow she had fallen, and her hands rose up to shield her face from the light.

She perceived whitewashed glimpses of a terrible rending. A pile of oily gauze and bandages discarded by the toilet. A torn shower curtain. Tom's body askew in the tub, legs protruding, his pants around his ankles. Tom's face, a stiff mask of surprise, his right eye rolled up to the whites.

From his left socket, a raw well descended into darkness, bubbling and steaming. His foot spasmed only once, final and weak, and then never moved.

But the woman standing before her did. Gracefully, lithely, she stepped out of the bathroom and into the hall, her fingers beaded crimson, the aftermath of this terrible consumption. Desi beheld those beads and how they slithered up her wrist, draining into her skin like rain into the soil of a grateful desert.

"Oksana," she whispered.

Oksana's lips curled in a demure smile.

There were familiar features upon her, pieces of the past condemned to that walled room of Desi's mind. Now the final bricks were tumbling, the mortar falling to dust.

And she saw new features too. A jaw that seemed sharper. A body slightly different. And that left eye, her dear Tom's eye. Oh God. The green was blending to match the icy blue of her right, as if they shared the same palette.

Trembling, Desi averted her stare. She couldn't meet what remained of Tom's stolen gaze. She had made a mistake with her life, made a terrible assumption. She believed all these days and nights were theirs to live as they pleased.

But she had only borrowed time, she realized. Borrowed every second for the past two and a half years.

And now it was over.

"Hello, Desiree," Oksana said. She bent down and ran a warm finger along Desi's trembling leg. "Ah, how I've missed you."

Desi felt a door against her back, the coat closet. At some point, she'd scooted all the way down the hall. And her bladder, she could feel it beginning to boil.

"Desi, look at me."

Desi bit her lips, willing herself to meet Oksana's eyes. There was a tenderness in them, a glow from her skin as if every pore promised soft kisses.

"There we go, dear."

Her hand slid up Desi's arm and lifted her chin. Desi whimpered, "I'm so sorry. I never meant to hurt you."

"Of course you didn't. I know," Oksana whispered, her voice breeze-like and as sweet as a peach. "But you didn't stop it."

The tears were coming now, dripping down Desi's cheeks, warm, perhaps a little too hot. She choked out a question. "Will it hurt?"

When Oksana smiled, there was no end to her teeth. "Terribly."

Then she stretched out her arms and embraced her. Desi felt her old friend's breath beside her ear, whispering not to worry. That it would be over soon. That she'd always envied her complexion. That she didn't need much to make things even, just some of her skin.

Their two hearts drummed together now, faster and faster.

At first Desi thought the lights were dimming. But it was Oksana's skin that was glowing, radiating, brighter and brighter, until the very air leaving Desi's lips was a fast-blackening smoke and her screams became embers.

chapter fifty-four

With the cool wind in her hair and canned coffee surging through her veins, Megan stiffened as she pulled up to the College Terrace Apartments. Ambulance lights painted the concrete facade a stuttering red and white. A crowd gathered by a Waldenbooks at ground floor, mostly students.

She left the Isuzu by the curb and rushed over, hoping for the best but suspecting the worst. Earlier, as she crossed into Monroe County, she had secured Tom and Desiree's location from a phone book while gassing up at a Wawa and scarfing down a hoagie. Now her heart sank as she compared the apartment building to the address. No, not twice in two nights.

There was a rattling clatter of wheels and a low moan. Someone shouted from the building's entrance and the students stepped back, clearing space. An EMT pulled a stretcher while another followed.

And there, upon sheets soaked a sickening pink, lay the blistering ruins of a woman she knew. A friend who had swapped secrets with Megan, who had asked her nervous questions about first sexual experiences, who had shared her most intimate dreams.

As far as Megan could tell, Desiree Chastain appeared to be melting.

But that didn't keep Megan from her. She pushed through the crowd, right over to the side of the stretcher. The EMTs shouted to step back, but Megan ignored them.

"Desi, it's Megan, from Tenbury."

"Meg-an?" Desi gulped as she spoke, lips leaving gummy strands as they struggled to form words. Her eyes were two curdled marbles. "Meg-an Mon-roe? I can't see ver-y well."

"Ma'am, you need to get back, now!" The EMT gestured to the crowd.

"Wait!" Desi wasn't having it. She shot out a gnarled claw, latching damp fingers onto Megan's sleeve. God, Megan could feel the heat coming off her, like meat smoked for too long.

"Oh God, Desi. I tried to get here sooner. Where's Tom?"

Desi moaned and shook her head. Megan sensed she was trying to mouth the word "gone" but could only form a wet burble.

Then she sat bolt upright, rattling the stretcher and leaving a web between her neck and the sheet. Vertically, her entire structure was beginning to droop. One of the EMTs stumbled back and made the sign of the cross.

"Meg-an, I... I'm so sor-ry for... eve-ry-thing... we did."

"What did we do, Desi? I don't remember."

"Ma'am, step back."

Desi ignored the EMT and twisted her lips into familiar shapes. Distantly, numbly, Megan realized those were teeth sliding down her chin.

"You are a good... per-son. We... weren't good... peop-le. This is my... kar-ma."

"Ma'am, I am ordering you to step back."

Desi's hand tightened on Megan's arm. She could feel the heat transferring, her own skin beginning to redden. Desi coughed. And her eyes, they'd taken on an oblong drip as gravity slid them from her sockets.

"Meg-an... Wait."

She drew in a deep, burbling breath, one that Megan sensed cost every ounce of her willpower. It was the final breath her smoldering lungs could muster.

Although her words were wet, her pronunciation was flawless.

"She bound us to each other, together, Megan. Each of us... a part of her whole. She knows where we are and will never stop looking. We should have... list-en-ed to... you."

One of the big EMTs was grabbing Megan now, yanking her away. Desi's fingers dug in, desperate and fierce, grabbing for a friend she could no longer see. There was a sound like tape tearing from a box and Desi rasped as the ruined flesh slid from her arm.

Megan was screaming now and so were the others. One of the students simply fainted. Hands fell upon her, strong and tight, pulling her back and begging her to calm down, to stay focused. All she could see was Desi being wheeled into the ambulance, skin pouring down the wet steel of the stretcher, down the bumper, and down Megan's wet leg.

The big EMT passed Megan off to someone else, a man whose embrace was strong yet soft and supporting, bear-like arms hugging her tight as much as holding her back.

"Ms. Monroe, please, let them help her."

She recognized that husky voice, the scent of coffee on his breath. She had heard it earlier, some three hundred miles away.

It was Detective Graham Nolan who held her as she cried.

chapter fifty-five

Adam loathed the behavior of crowds. The lack of control, the confusion, the contagious hysteria. A group only had the IQ of its dumbest member.

Still, he was glad the onlookers were gathered on the windy sidewalk and screaming. It made it easier to blend in. All he needed was a beanie and his hood and a spot near the back. He even stifled a gag when Desi degloved her own arm.

And Megan, poor Megan. He was about to push through and offer his help but that detective showed up.

Fuck.

So, Adam hung back, observing with detachment. Calculating. They loaded Desi into the ambulance, but he knew the truth: she was already dead. The detective took Megan in his thick arms and led her away from the mess, comforting and compassionate.

Lingering by the bookstore, Adam took stock of his options. That Megan and the detective hadn't shown up together was one comforting fact. But they were still putting it together. What else would they find?

The voicemail he left. What a stupid mistake. He'd been scared, not thinking straight after Chunhee. Then, on the drive, he'd come to his senses. His message hadn't said much, but it would raise too many questions. It would only be a matter of time before it made its way to that detective.

So he needed that tape.

The good news was that the College Terrace Apartments were just that, a terraced building for college kids and recent grads. He could see at least two entrances. One, here by the bookstore. Another, just past a bar crowded with observers.

Hood up, Adam hurried that way.

Inside, he found the tenant directory. He was pleased to see Desi and Tom listed on the third floor, just a quick jaunt up the stairs. He didn't need to guess which way to turn down the hall. There was another paramedic heading out of the apartment and a pair of neighbors wiping tears from their eyes. Within minutes, Desi's apartment would be swarming with cops.

He needed a diversion.

It took him three tries to slam down the fire alarm handle. There was a crunch of glass and a delay, then the whooping shriek of sirens. White lights blinked over the hall's exits.

Adam hurried, holding his head low and whistling. When a young woman emerged from her apartment, he asked, "Sparky? Sparky? Have you seen Sparky? Little thing, maybe this big."

The confused student shook her head.

"Shit. Sparky!" He called out for his nonexistent dog until he was at the open apartment and able to peek in. "Sparky?"

No answer. But there was movement near the bathroom, a flash and a pop. Someone was taking pictures of something inside.

Tom, Adam realized. Poor fucking Tom. If only they'd all listened and done what he said. Well, he could mourn them later. Now he needed to act fast.

A quick scan of the apartment revealed two likely places for the answering machine. One, by the entry. A second, by the wall that divided the open kitchen from the living room.

He crouched and stepped inside the apartment.

The entryway was a bust. No phone or answering machine, just an end table where keys sat in a bowl. Above it hung a familiar painting, a modernist piece Megan created her senior year when she was experimenting with colors. For a moment his heart ached with the weight of all they had lost.

The paint freckling her fingers and forearms.

The kiwi-scented shampoo that lingered in her hair.

How she used to laugh often and generously, as if every joke were the best she'd heard.

He shook off the past and focused on this moment, stepping lightly and making his way to the kitchen. Here it was, a cordless phone with a Sony answering machine. He didn't need to press play; he knew how it worked. He held *erase* until the phone chirped its confirmation. "All messages deleted."

And that was that. One crisis averted among a dozen others.

He was back in the living room when the reflection stopped him in his tracks. Through the hallway door and off the closet mirror, the man in the bathroom crouched and snapped photos. Each pop of the flash revealed something new.

Tom, sprawled in the bathtub, the shower curtain clinging to him like a robe.

Tom, who had always been childishly naive and earnestly sweet.

Tom, whose hollow eye socket glared at Adam, as if cursing him now. See what ruins we made with our lives.

He backed toward the door when a noise stopped him in his tracks: a shrill tritone chirp from a purse near his feet. Slowly, carefully, he lifted a cellular phone from Desi's bag. He extended the antenna and pressed *answer*. He said nothing.

There was a faint clicking on the other end, the hiss of static. Then a song emerged, "No Excuses" by Alice in Chains. Beneath the jangly guitar riffs and crisp drumming, Layne Staley's vocals harmonized with Jerry Cantrell's, infusing the lyrics with the pain of broken friendships.

That song.

Their song.

She had played it when—

No. He hung up and removed the battery, dumping it all back into the purse.

He heard the police and the EMT a second before they entered. He was trapped. So he twisted his face into a mask of confusion and pain and cried out, "Oh God... Oh dear God, what happened to Tom? Is he... Is he...?"

The cop grumbled at the others. "Christ, keep someone posted outside." Then, more apologetically, he said, "Buddy, you can't be in here."

Adam wasn't certain he could cry on command, but his eyes were sure getting misty. "I… I was just returning a movie… The fire alarm… I wanted to see if… Oh God, is he really gone?"

The cops convened for a moment. The EMT wanted nothing to do with this and squeezed into the apartment and retrieved his stuff. Then the youngest cop escorted Adam out into the hall, placing a gentle hand on his shoulder and murmuring condolences. By the stairs, a building maintenance man waved a flashlight, ushering the residents toward the exit. Adam quickly fell in line.

Outside, he joined the crowd, then ducked into the bookstore. He wiped his eyes and let the mask fall from his face.

This was going sideways so fast his head was beginning to spin. And his neck, the tension had worsened. He squeezed his nape and steadied his thoughts.

The detective had left, probably taking Megan along. She was gone but not far; he could sense her presence.

And he could sense another, growing stronger, one he hadn't felt in several years.

Shaking, he got in his 4Runner and drove off as fast as it went.

He needed a weapon for what would come next.

chapter fifty-six

The sign for the Cozy Rest Inn promised HBO, an in-room fridge, and a breakfast buffet. What Graham cared about most were the adjoining rooms and their proximity to Rochester PD three blocks away. He booked two rooms on his credit card, making sure the outer doors were thick and double-locked, the ones inside open and connected. He instructed Petro and Megan to stay and to call with any questions. If they left, he'd have arrest warrants out within the hour.

It wasn't his best threat, nor his most honest, but it worked. They both nodded and locked the door behind him.

He touched base at the station with a young local detective named Harringer, whom he'd spoken with earlier over the phone from New Hampshire. Then Harringer had brushed off Graham's concerns. Now, after the scene at the apartment, he was muttering and squeezing his shaking fingers.

"I just came from the hospital," he muttered. "Her skin... it was just falling off the bone. There was hardly anything left. You didn't say anything about *that*."

"I didn't know about that," Graham said. "I still don't."

"And that Tom fellow? Forensics said something hollowed out half his skull. You ever seen anything like this?"

Graham shook his head. It was the truth. Megan's message had included vague worries. Suspicions that something terrible was headed toward Rochester, toward Thomas Frenning and Desiree Chastain. She had gone light on the details.

Why?

Because she was hiding something, he suspected. Or perhaps she was involved and now trying to stop it. Maybe she was the key to all this, the center around which this twisted case swung.

Louis Harding. The Tenbury School. A missing girl named Oksana. Chunhee Chang and now Desiree and Tom.

"I need to ask you a favor," Graham said, which snapped the detective out of his stupor. "NHPS is going to send over prints pulled from an ongoing in Darrington. I need them compared against the ones found at College Terrace, pronto."

"Sure, we've got AFIS all set up."

AFIS, the Automated Fingerprint Identification System, connected state and federal agencies, allowing them to compare fingerprints against known databases or those found in the wild. It was far from perfect, but with a good set of eyes on the screen, it was accurate and faster than mailing a tenprint card.

"Good," Graham said. "It'll be latent against latent. Can you have a technician on standby?"

"Yeah, sure." The detective nodded. His eyes were on Graham's legs, where a pink smear marred his jeans. He was still wearing some of Desiree's skin.

After calling Darrington and getting the systems arranged on both ends, Graham scrubbed his pants in the station washroom. He left his pager and motel phone number with the detective and stopped by a 7-Eleven. He bought a half dozen Big Bite hot dogs and some snacks he hardly remembered. When he returned to the motel, he checked the bag, embarrassed that he'd forgotten condiments or drinks.

No one seemed to care. Petro unraveled his hot dog and placed it on the silver foil, silently cutting into it with a plastic knife and a fork. Megan devoured two hot dogs by hand, hardly blinking.

Graham knew the look in their eyes. The distant stare, numb detachment. They were shellshocked and still processing what they'd witnessed, each waging their own internal battles. With what they didn't know, what they did, and what they were all keeping from each other.

After finishing his dinner, Graham said, "I'm going to take a shower. I suggest you do the same. Then we're all going to have a long talk, all of us. Coincidences might be twins but they're never triplets. Sound good?"

Megan nodded. Petro mumbled, "Is good idea, I think."

chapter fifty-seven

Megan could still feel Desi's grip, warm and itchy against her wrist. No amount of scrubbing or scouring under the shower removed it. Even now, with the cool air seeping in through the bathroom window and raising goosebumps across her damp body, that last, desperate grasp tugged at her skin. Her friend, beseeching her with frantic, wet lips.

"You're a good person."

"We weren't good people."

"She knows where we are and will never stop looking."

Megan wiped the steam from the mirror and studied her reflection. That scar bisecting her face, it was there, always there. And so were the answers beneath it.

She had just been too scared to look.

But no more. She owed it to her friends.

She found Detective Nolan and that Slavic man, Petro, both waiting in the adjoining room. The television was on, the evening news reporting vagaries about the incident. God, this was getting worse by the day. Detective Nolan muted the TV as she joined them.

"Okay," she said. "I think I need to go first."

Petro nodded. The detective said, "I'm all ears, Ms. Monroe."

They waited, looking at her, really seeing her. And for the first time, she felt that she knew them as well. Maybe it was a trick of her wounded brain, a way to convince herself she wasn't jumping into the unknown. Or maybe she was just tired of denying a truth she didn't understand in her head yet felt in her heart.

"Remember when I said something happened to me two and a half years ago?"

Graham nodded. "Your car accident. The fire and your family."

"Yeah, busy summer." The bed squeaked as she sat down. "I think something else happened too and it involved Oksana. I think maybe she was hurt." Her jaw tensed, the words heavy on her tongue. "Or worse."

"Or worse?" Graham repeated.

She noticed Petro's eyes darting about, as if he were calculating something. A flicker of recognition glistened within.

"I think maybe she was killed. I can't prove it, but I think... Well, maybe it was our fault."

Graham inhaled. It seemed to last forever. "What, like in the car accident?"

"Maybe before. Maybe after. Maybe we did something that I don't remember. For two and a half years I've had this void at the center of everything. I used to paint and draw and then I couldn't. A few weeks ago I couldn't even tell you Oksana's name. I mean, I literally didn't know that I knew her. And now—"

"The memories are all flooding back in," Petro said. "First a drip, then a trickle, then soon it's a river, yes? What about your dreams? Are they vivid as well?"

It was a curious thing, Megan realized, how Petro's inflections had shifted. His accent wasn't gone, not entirely. But the thickness and strength of it had given way to a subtle precision. Even his diction had changed.

"Yes," she said. "Sometimes I'm not even asleep."

"I see. And Oksana, you were classmates with her at this boarding school, yes?"

Megan nodded. "And her roommate."

A small gasp left Petro's lips. "For how long? A week, a month?"

"My senior spring, so three months at least? Maybe longer."

Petro took a napkin and wiped his sweaty forehead. His right hand went for one of Megan's cigarettes. "May I?"

"Sure."

While Petro lit up, Detective Nolan held his hands out. "Okay, pause. This little group therapy session needs to have a come-to-Jesus moment, all three of us. And that means you too, my foreign friend." He bored into Petro with those investigator's eyes. "You know what that means? A come-to-Jesus moment?"

Petro exhaled. "Yes, I'm not an idiot, Detective."

"I never thought you were. But a minute ago you never spoke perfect English, so I'm not fielding plays with a full roster, am I? Who are you, Petro? Who are you really?"

"Petro is my name, not my only name, of course. And yes, I'm also an investigator, in a sense."

"What sense is that?"

"I'm a clinical researcher in the field of pediatric molecular oncology."

Detective Nolan clicked his pen. "Oncology. That's cancer."

"You're familiar?"

Graham nodded, something soft flickering in his eyes before they hardened.

Petro continued, "My research focuses on the somatic mutation of cells. That is non-heritable mutations, those not acquired from our ancestors but from external factors."

Megan asked, "What, like lung cancer?"

Petro gave her a grim smirk and exhaled. "My postdoctoral research focused on the survivors of Hiroshima and Nagasaki and the long-term effects of ionizing radiation. They are possibly the most studied cohort in human history. I published several papers and the Soviets took notice."

"Russkis," Graham said. "I thought you were from Ukraine?"

"I am, but this was before the collapse. I was working in Pripyat in April of eighty-six when it happened. The number four reactor at the Vladimir Lenin Nuclear Power Plant—what people call Chernobyl—exploded, covering the area in a radioactive haze. I saw the sky turn blue. Within thirty minutes I was evacuated. And I was fortunate. Others, less so."

He stubbed out the cigarette and removed his glasses. Detective Nolan offered him another one, but he declined with a wave.

"This was only a decade ago, but you have to remember the desperation people felt. Our economy was stagnant. Citizens were losing faith in the politburo. You could see the cracks forming, the distrust, the anger. So, when the meltdown occurred, some saw opportunity. There was a ten-year-old girl, Zorianna, whose father was one of those opportunists. Pripyat hadn't even been evacuated yet and he filled his truck with plundered metals: copper and steel, spent fuel rods and cobalt-60, all ejected from the blast. Some of it was covered in corium, what we call the Elephant's Foot."

"Christ," Detective Nolan said. "I saw a photo of that. Looks like lava."

"Indeed. But to Zorianna's father, that scrap was money, a means to help his family. He was a nobody, a Romani thief with no education and no understanding of radiation. Corium, it generates eighty grays of energy an hour. Eighty grays. A lethal dose is four and a half. This was the poison he brought back to their home. Within hours their hair fell out, their skin blistered, and their bone marrow cooked from within. The family was dead before dawn."

Megan remembered hearing about Chernobyl in school, a few months after watching the *Challenger* explode live on TV. She had been eleven. It had felt like a parade of tragedies that year. And then, like all news, it faded and the world moved on.

"You said it killed them," she said. "But what about the girl?"

"She was different."

Detective Nolan's chair squeaked as he leaned forward. "Define 'different.'"

"I mean different. Her body, it adapted, mutated at new rates. Intestinal epithelial cells, for example, are the fastest-regenerating cells in your body. They divide and renew within days. But with the right nutrients, hers took only hours."

Detective Nolan said, "You're telling me this girl was some sort of *X-Files* freak?"

"I'm telling you that girl spent two years living in the Red Forest, surviving off mushrooms and mugwort and stealing from scientists. She was feral when we found her. Her skin was bark. She had vines growing from her fingers and lips circling her eyes."

"Mugwort," Detective Nolan said. "Like wormwood, the plant?"

"Yes," Petro said. "That's what Chernobyl means, wormwood."

Detective Nolan sketched something in his notebook. A flowering shape that Megan vaguely recognized, as if from a dream. "Is this it?"

Petro glanced at the drawing. "That's the flower, yes."

"Oksana had a jeweler make a necklace like this."

"It's a common tea," Petro said. "Zorianna's mother gathered and sold it before the explosion. She drank it every night when I nursed her back. And she healed. I watched her grow into a vibrant young woman, smart and full of curiosity for the world."

Detective Nolan tilted his head. "Yeah. Or maybe you kept her in a lab."

Petro's eyes dropped to his shoes. "What you have to understand is her family were Romani—what you call gypsies. Not easy to track. There were very few records, and believe me, the Soviets loved their records. After the collapse and Ukraine's independence, I... Well, I hid her and I destroyed any records. By the time the dust settled, she was my niece."

Megan had kept quiet through most of this, not because she didn't believe it but because she did. She sensed it in her flesh, in her bones, no different than an instinct to pull her hand back from fire or to lean toward warmth when cold. And she sensed where this was headed.

"Zorianna, Oksana," she said. "So how'd she get to Tenbury School?"

Petro's tongue traced his lips. "It's complicated."

"More complicated than a radioactive zombie?" Detective Nolan tapped his fingers on the table, jostling the hot dog wrappers. "C'mon, Petro, you're holding back. Is it complicated or embarrassing?"

"Both." Petro closed his eyes. "I made a mistake. There was a family we knew at our apartment in Kyiv. Their daughter was a dancer who was going abroad. Zorianna became... obsessed. She started imitating her, listening to the same music, speaking in her voice. At first she didn't want her friend to leave. Then she begged to go with her."

His eyes were moistening now, and a pink flush filled his cheeks. He reached for another cigarette and lit up.

He said, "I don't know when Zorianna killed her. But I do know when they found the remains in the sewer. It was five months after her friend left for the U.S. and never returned. Five months after Zorianna ran away."

"Ran away," Megan repeated. "And came to my school."

Petro's tired eyes met her own. "Her friend's name was Oksana."

Megan's mouth had gone dry. She wanted to reject it, to deny every word and walk out of this room. Yet she sensed it was true, knew it deep in her bones.

Then the phone rang, startling her and bringing a curse to Petro's lips. Only Detective Nolan seemed undisturbed. He answered it, spoke only his name and a few words. "Tell me what they found."

She heard a male voice on the other end, too muffled to make out. She could see by Detective Nolan's stiffening posture that he had learned something new. The silence stretched on until he thanked the caller and hung up.

For a moment he said nothing as calculations whirred behind those brown eyes. "They found fingerprints at Desiree and Tom's apartment that matched the sorority," he said. "They were Chunhee Chang's."

chapter fifty-eight

Graham paced the hotel room, struggling to feel the carpet beneath his shoes. Struggling to reconcile what he was learning. Oksana, an eighteen-year-old Ukrainian girl who had vanished while heading abroad. And Zorianna, some irradiated freak who had taken her identity, taken her place, perhaps taken her face.

Like the groundskeeper's jaw.

Like Chunhee's body.

Like Tom's eye and Desi's—

No, it was all too confusing, too bizarre, too fucking weird.

And yet that instinct he trusted—the one that had whispered Louis was up to something shady—was now nodding from the dark halls of his mind. The puzzle was coming together, a few pieces about the right shape and size.

Still, he needed more. He didn't trust Petro, who had lied about his identity. And he didn't trust Megan's memory. Hell, he didn't trust his own eyes, until he reminded himself he watched a young woman melt only six hours ago.

"What she cannot quickly regrow she can take," Petro said. "Like a parasite embedding itself in another organism, a host it can use. Those are Ms. Chang's fingerprints, but that is no longer her flesh."

"And Desiree," Graham said slowly. "Was that some form of radiation poisoning?"

Petro nodded. "I think so, yes."

"You think so? I thought this was your field."

"It is."

"You're supposed to be an expert."

"I am. Even experts don't have all the answers." Petro fidgeted with a bag of vending machine chips. "I've biopsied her cells and watched them divide. Sometimes they build a tooth or hair follicle, or sometimes they die. There is no handbook for this, Detective, no guide."

He pointed at the TV, where the news had given way to *The Tonight Show with Jay Leno*. Jerry Rice sat on the couch while Huey Lewis belted out a muted song.

"Take this TV, for example. The cathode ray emits trace radiation, yes? If you lined up enough of them, built a large array with enough power, you could start a fire, cause cancer, unravel the very DNA in your cells. I think that's how her body works."

Megan whispered something so quiet she had to repeat it. "Could it cause memory loss?"

"Absolutely. The brain is eighty percent water. Superheat its cells and you can provoke a variety of symptoms: discomfort, nausea, time dilation, even hallucinations over great distances. It's like gravity; it affects us even if we can't see it."

Her eyes took on a distant stare. Graham sensed a battle being waged behind them, beyond. He pitied the girl. If this story was even half true, she had spent months exposed to Oksana and soaking up radiation. Worse, she and her friends had crossed the wrong woman.

If that was what Oksana was anymore.

Megan asked, "So am I... I'm going to die, aren't I?"

Petro's eyes brightened. "Actually, in my experience, length of exposure has an inoculating effect. The closer one is, the longer they're exposed at low levels, the more they can recall. A sort of mental vaccine."

"And that thing in Louis's neck," Graham said, "that was a piece of her controlling him, wasn't it?"

"A parasite, yes. Like a fluke worm, attaching to its host's brain and hijacking its impulses, from snail to fish and on up the food chain."

A shiver ran up Graham's spine. "Christ, it's like *Aliens* was a documentary."

"The yearbook," Megan said. "On her senior page, there was this collection of words, like—"

"Mmm, like a crossword puzzle," Petro said.

Graham rubbed his tired eyes. "If you tell me it's a magic spell, I'm going to lose it."

"No, no magic. More of a mnemonic trick we developed. Even her brain cells sometimes regenerate too quickly for stable retention. She uses such diagrams to store memories, like a floppy disk or an insurance policy."

"She stores her memories," Graham said slowly. "You realize how that sounds?"

Petro turned the pack of cigarettes over and gestured to the bottom, where a series of black lines sat in a rectangle. A UPC code. "One can convey a lot with mere symbols, Detective. Just ask our young artist here."

"And the photos," Megan said. "At Tenbury, all the photos of Oksana had these artifacts, blooms of light like they'd been overexposed."

Petro was already nodding. "Yes, yes, of course. Like an X-ray."

"Of course," Graham repeated dryly and looked at his hands. He'd been squeezing them so hard he'd left little crescents in his palm. "This just gets better by the minute, doesn't it? Assuming you're not full of shit—and that's a big assumption—this girl has been mindfucking her way across New England like a pissed-off Charles Bronson."

"You still don't understand it, Detective," Petro said. "She is not a girl. She is the sum of many experiences and memories, a collective of all that she's encountered. She doesn't just regenerate; she integrates and assimilates."

Graham slumped into the chair, stomach acid burning the walls of his gut. It was almost midnight now. The adrenaline was fading, leaving halos at the edge of his vision. "So what you're saying is, she could be anywhere."

"Yes," Petro nodded. "And in enough time, she could be anyone."

What came next wasn't from his lips or Petro's. It came from

Megan, who had teetered upon some great precipice and finally decided to jump. Her eyes hardened.

"So then how do we stop her?"

Graham considered it. "Fire worked on that thing inside Louis."

"Yes, fire always works," Petro agreed. "Starvation as well. It provokes a sort of larval regression as her body consumes itself to survive."

"Yeah, well, I'm not about to dig a Buffalo Bill pit in my basement just to starve your dear niece. No offense. And another thing, how do we track her? If I put out a BOLO and get the force involved, I'll be on psych leave by the end of the hour."

Petro offered him a knowing smirk. "Now you understand why I wasn't more forthcoming, Detective. Front-load the human mind with the improbable and we reject it. Our mental defenses, they keep reality balanced. Fortunately, our best chance to track her is already here." He turned his tired gaze onto Megan.

"Me?"

"Yes, you, dear. Did your waking dreams coincide with Oksana's reappearance? Did your inspiration return?"

A flash of those midnight hours spent filling empty canvas with paint.

Six finished compositions before her.

And a feeling that countless more lurked within.

Megan gave a weak nod of her chin. "Yes."

"Because she is fixated on your friends and you. Positive or not, you are all emotionally bonded. And that bond runs both ways."

Graham said, "You want to use her as bait?"

"I want her to help build a trap."

Graham held his tongue. This wasn't his decision to make. And hell, he wasn't sure he even wanted to confront this Oksana woman, this thing she had become. He was a human, after all, and humans got the shakes and jitters. Petro was right: humans feared the unknown.

And yet, he had a job to do and justice to be seen. So he tamped down that fear and turned his dry eyes toward Megan. "What do you think?"

For a long beat, she just stared off into the corner of the room. Off into the past. She rubbed her scar and he wondered if it itched or bothered her. It didn't bother him. He thought it was beautiful and gave her a fierce strength.

Then she nodded and looked into their eyes. "She killed sweet Chunhee and Desi and Tom. I say we catch this bitch and burn her alive."

chapter fifty-nine

Now

Anwar is disappointed in himself.

At some point during the interview, he started leaning forward, and now here he is, nearing the edge of the chair. He re-centers himself and takes a long drink of sparkling water. Then he scoots back.

"And you believed him?" he asks. "This Russian scientist you only met a few hours before."

"Ukrainian," Megan says. "And no, I didn't believe him. Not entirely. But I didn't believe myself either. Memories are fallible."

"Yeah, but even a lie points the way to a truth. Or someone's version of it."

Megan lets her gaze drift to the window and those sage-dotted hills. The sun has begun its descent, the light taking on a majestic hue. Golden hour soon.

Inwardly, Anwar is smiling and proud. The recorders have captured some excellent clips, enough for a whole season now. Maybe enough for a lengthy investigation. And maybe a conviction, if he's lucky and her words bring warmth to a few cold cases. He thinks they just might.

He shuts off the recorder on the table. "So, help me understand something. You and Oksana, you had this connection, right? What, was it like psychic or something?"

She gives him an amused tilt of her head. “Psychic? No, don’t be silly.”

“Right, of course. Radiation sickness and parasites, makes perfect sense. But let’s draw the line at ESP.”

“Now you’re being sarcastic.”

“In my line of work, it’s a healthy defense. You wouldn’t believe how many people contact me saying they had a vision or God told them to do something.”

“And you don’t believe them?”

Anwar’s lower lip juts as he gives a slight lift of his shoulder. “They believe it, so that’s what’s important. But come on, something up there pulling strings, moving us around like action figures and giving a few precious glimpses behind the curtain? I’ve seen no evidence of that.”

“No evidence, of course not.” Her eyes drift down to the old journal and the yearbook between them. “Did evidence bring you here?”

He smirks. “No, it didn’t.”

“Then what did?”

A good story, he thinks.

A scandal hidden in these quiet suburbs he can sell to his listeners.

A woman who ran from her past but still hasn’t paid.

What he says is, “Instinct.”

“Instinct, yes.”

“And inspiration.”

“Something inspired you to drive out here? Something set you on this path and pushed. And sometimes that push comes from outside as much as from within.”

Anwar does his best to avoid cringing. This new age stuff, it always rubs him as hokey. What’s she going to do next, discuss essential oils and yoga?

“Do you have children, Mr. Fariz?”

Anwar blinks, unsure of where this is going. No children, not that he wants any. And no partner, at least not that he hasn’t paid for or coerced with his status. Even his acquaintances are few these days, most having retreated into parenthood and school events, that black hole called family that swallows so many his age. Lately he’s realized his closest friend is his agent.

“No children,” he says and gives her a smug smile. “But I do have a career.”

“A career,” she repeats. “Well, if you decide to become a parent, you may notice your senses changing. You learn to read the patterns in noise, the scamper of feet. You anticipate the sound of a falling body, the cry of distress. Your ears understand silence and the danger it implies.”

“Being a parent isn’t some sort of superpower. We’ve been doing it since the beginning of time.”

“True. But some are more in tune with the patterns than others. Instinct and inspiration, Mr. Fariz. Outside and within. Oksana and I shared something similar.”

Before Anwar can say anything, the kitchen partition squeaks and slides open, revealing Sofiy. She studies Anwar with those curious eight-year-old eyes. He smiles at her and does not get a smile in return.

“Mom, can I have a snack?”

“Dinner’s in a few hours.”

Her hands root around in her pockets. “But I’m starving.”

“You’re starving? Are you literally dying due to lack of nutrition?”

The girl smiles and nods, her ponytail bouncing.

“And your brother, is he starving too?”

“Super starving. It’s bad.”

“Well now, we can’t have our guest thinking I malnourish my family, can we? Open the fridge. I made you some snacks. Bring them to your brother, okay?”

She runs past them and opens the fridge, removing a tray of fruits and nuts, meats and cheeses. A smile stretches her face as she pulls it out.

As she passes them, Megan says, “Sofiy, my friend here had a question. Maybe you can help us.”

She studies Anwar, still not sure about this stranger in their house. “Oh-kay.”

“How’d you know Symon was hungry?”

She blinks as if she’d never considered it.

“Did you ask him?”

She shakes her head.

“And did he tell you he was hungry?”

Another shake of her head.

"So how'd you know?"

She shrugs. "I just knew."

Megan smiles and gives her daughter a kiss on the top of her head. "Good girl. Now don't ruin your dinner, okay?"

Then she's gone, squeezing through the partition and disappearing into the house, feet pounding on the hardwood. Megan slides the door shut.

"Does that answer your question?"

"Not really. You and Oksana, you weren't twins. You were just roommates."

Megan takes their empty glasses and heads to the sink. A moment later she returns with the other tray of meats and cheeses and two glasses. She places a glass in front of Anwar and leaves the tray between them.

"The deepest bonds are elemental, built upon the friction of opposition. Water and fire, night and day, life and death. The transition from adolescence to adulthood lives at this nexus. It's why you remember the chapped lips of your first kiss and the songs of the summer. Why true awe is your first trip to Fenway Park, with your friends. And why nothing ever tastes as delicious as that hotdog they bought you."

She closes her eyes and sits back in her chair. For a moment, she says nothing. Just lets the sun warm her skin and the cool breeze from the fan jostle a few hairs.

"I can hear them whispering to me. I can see time through their eyes. And sometimes I can reply, like the wind rolling over the hills and shaking the leaves."

Great, he thinks. So on top of everything else, Megan Collings might just be crazy. At least it'll play well to the listeners.

She opens her eyes and that smile leaves her lips. Something is changing. A steeling behind her eyes. A yearning for all that has passed.

"I didn't want to admit what my body already knew. That Oksana and I were bound to each other. But Petro taught me to listen for that bond. To feel it. And to follow it, like your instinct, wherever it led."

She pierces him with that wizened gaze that glints with regret.

"Can you truly not guess how our bond was created?"

Anwar can feel his heart fluttering now, the sweat beading his back. This is it. He's getting so close to her confession. He pushes the tape recorder aside and stares deep into her eyes. He aims the hidden mic up his sleeve toward her.

"Yeah, I can guess," he says. "But why don't you tell me?"

part five

Tonight, Tonight

chapter sixty

1996

A hard rumble snapped Megan's eyes open as the cruiser struck a pothole at the New York–Massachusetts border. She was in the back seat, doing her best to focus and follow her thoughts. To listen for inspiration as Petro had insisted.

"Are you sure that's what you see?" he asked from the front. "Two amber doors?"

She rubbed her temples, the morning sun scalding her tired eyes. They'd gotten a few hours of rest, sleeping in shifts before hitting the highway at dawn. Detective Nolan insisted they drive together. His red and blue lights cleared a path and made short work of the traffic. She supposed she'd have to bus back to Rochester for Corey's Isuzu.

That was assuming any of this worked out. Assuming she didn't end up in jail. Or worse.

"Yeah, two amber doors," Megan said. "It's Desi's family, their summer cottage. I know the doors and the porch. We had our grad party there. I think that's it."

"You think?" Detective Nolan's dry eyes met Megan's in the rearview mirror. "How're you feeling?"

"Like a radio tuned between stations. I can smell the coffee on your breath and taste salt water on my tongue. When I close my eyes, I... I can hear a loud engine and traffic."

Detective Nolan clenched his jaw. "Petro, this better work."

"It might if she can maintain the connection."

So Megan closed her eyes again and refocused. Behind the dark walls of her lids, the whipping wind of the speeding car gave way to something else.

The low rumble of waves against a long wash of sand.

A half-swallowed fence leaning in the breeze.

The creaky wood deck with its old gray railing and view of the bay.

"Follow your senses," Petro said, his voice a distant murmur. "Your memories might be damaged but some neural pathways remain. What does it sound like? What can you smell? What emotions are flowing through you when you walk through that house?"

Megan pressed her scar, really tried to dig in, but it wasn't working. All she could see were strobe-lit glimpses: Tom and Desiree dancing to Culture Beat's "Mr. Vain"; Chunhee nervously lifting her first joint to her lips; Adam, seen through frosted glass as he leaned in and kissed—

No. No, her mind refused to go there. Sweat bloomed down her back and her gut twisted. Rust coated her mouth and...

And then something else.

Her tongue circled a sandy lump near her molar that wiggled and twisted. Wincing, she spat into her hand.

A black snail squirmed and fell from her fingers.

"What the hell?"

Detective Nolan glanced in the rearview mirror and Petro turned around. "What is it?"

"I... There was..." She studied the dark floor mat, the clumpy fibers worn and dirty. She felt her tongue, throbbing and salty. But there was no snail to be found.

"There was what?" Detective Nolan asked.

The sharp, jagged shell, the crumbling sand, and the brine on the back of her tongue. It hit her, floored her, knocked the words right out of her for several moments.

"Megan, what is it?"

Dean Henry's words echoed down the locked halls of her mind.

"We must be fearless."

"We must confront what truly scares us."

"Have you been brave these past two and a half years?"

No, she hadn't been brave then, and she was still tiptoeing now. Yes, she was doing this wrong. She was still seeing with her eyes and thinking with her mind but not feeling with her heart. The only time she was truly happy, truly connected to something else, was when she was creating her art.

She said, "We need to pull off at the next city."

"Why?"

"Because I've figured out how the two of us talk."

THIRTY MINUTES LATER, Megan emerged from the arts and crafts store with a fresh sketchpad under one arm and a tin of colored pencils in hand. Detective Nolan regarded her skeptically, hot coffee and a box of donuts waiting on the hood of the cruiser. She handed him a mailing envelope she'd purchased. He removed that curious blue notebook and scribbled a final entry.

"I never pegged you for a fan of Inspector Gadget," she said.

He glanced at the notebook. "My daughter got me into it."

"Ah, a girl with good taste. And Penny?" She pointed to the young character on the cover. "Penny's the best."

"Yeah, she is." He gave the old notebook an affectionate pat before sealing it inside. He affixed a few stamps and scribbled an address on the cover.

After a moment of silence, Megan whistled the opening notes of the theme song. "Do-ta-do-ti-do, Inspector Gadget. Do-ta-do-ti-dooo..." She eyed him, waiting.

He added, "Woo hoo."

"God I miss those Saturday mornings." Her smile faded. "It doesn't get any easier, does it?"

"No, it doesn't," he said. "But you learn how to take a few of the hits."

Petro finished his call at the payphone and hurried back. "My wife's going to kill me. She still thinks I'm in Manhattan. Shall we?"

Caffeinated and sugared-up, they hit the road, Petro up front and

Detective Nolan behind the wheel. And Megan, in the back seat, twenty-four colored pencils in her lap and a blank page open, hers to fill.

chapter sixty-one

Todd Dollanger liked the pretty young thing in the passenger seat of his Peterbilt 377 big rig. She made him feel young again and a little nervous. Like those beauties he used to chat up after the high school games, when he could still throw the ball and his back wasn't all bent. Those were the days.

This doll beside him, he'd spotted her outside the truck stop, thumb raised to the road and dawn glistening in them peepers, one a cool blue, the other a minty green. But it was her smile that pumped his brakes. As if it was meant just for him.

When she climbed in, he could see she wasn't some lot lizard, that was for damn sure. Not with a body like that. Not with that fresh, velvety skin. So when she asked for a ride, he kindly obliged. When she offered to pay, he shook his head. He'd take her where she wanted, so long as he was headed the same way.

And yeah, Todd was a man, a man with eyes in his head and blood in his veins. Some of the long-haulers stuck to the old maxim: *Grass, gas, or ass*, but Todd was a gentleman. If she wanted to throw some skin his direction, well, his truck was a sleeper and the bed comfortably fit two. If not, he was just pleased to have company.

Which was why her sudden outburst concerned him.

She hooked a finger and pulled something out of her mouth. He swore he saw wood speckling her lips, like she'd been nibbling a pencil.

Then it was gone and she said, "Turn around."

It was the first time she'd spoken in thirty minutes. Her gaze had been alternating between the road ahead and something she was scribbling in a notebook. He'd pegged her for some sort of writer or poet.

But now she was swinging those peepers around, not to the road ahead but behind them. She repeated, "Turn around."

Todd chuckled. "What, missy, you forget something?"

He gave her his best grin, hoping there wasn't something stuck in his teeth. She was pretty. Actually, she was stunning.

And fierce.

"Turn the truck around and go back."

His grin faded. "Seriously? Go back where?"

"East, I think. Cold waters and sand. Bresden Bay, Massachusetts. Drive now and don't stop until I give you permission."

He let out a low chuckle. Turn around? Permission? It took him a moment to understand she wasn't joking. And Massachusetts? Hell no. He was bound for Cleveland and St. Louis and then on to Dallas.

"Look, lady, I'm sorry to break it to you, but we ain't taking requests."

"Todd Jeremiah Dollanger, turn the truck around this instant."

He blinked. He'd introduced himself, sure, but he hadn't told her his last name or his middle. What'n the hell?

"I can't just... Hold up a second. What is this? What's going on?"

This was a prank or a trap; it had to be. Perhaps she was an undercover who'd blown past the other cops and he was about to get cited for picking her up.

Then he noticed the skin bubbling around her neck.

It was the weirdest thing, the way the jacket slid from her shoulders and her flesh revealed itself. He'd wanted a glimpse and now he got more, too much. Her collarbones slouched and her arms fell to her side, limp and twitching. Her head turned and rose, a dog hearing a distant whistle.

But it was where her neck joined her chest that planted a bur in his mind. Her skin stretched and frayed and a seam opened up. With a tilt, her head snapped backward like a Pez dispenser.

There was no candy in that yawning crevice above those splendid breasts. But there were plenty of mouths. A half dozen or so, all babbling and chattering and mewling out words.

He could hear his mother in there, mocking his choice to marry that slut he'd knocked up. He could hear his ex-wife cackling, then his daughter screaming the way she had in the weeks after her birth. And his dad and his prick of a boss and that old cat Franklin, meowing when he wanted supper. A chorus of blistering lips, twisting and puckering and all shrieking out, "Turn around. Turn around! TURN AROUND!"

So that's what he fuckin' did.

Todd knew the Peterbilt 377 like the back of his hand. He pumped the brakes and swung the wheel to his left. A red Miata trying to pass him nearly went under. He caught a glimpse in the side mirror as the little car spun out like a toy.

The median rose before them, tall grass and reeds all dewy and brown. Then he plowed the truck right through them, executing the best emergency turn of his life. With a dozen bumps and furious horns, his westbound journey along Interstate 490 became an eastward retreat. He didn't know his hands and his feet could move that fast.

The morning sun was in his eyes now. He straightened the Peterbilt out, grateful to feel the asphalt underneath. The road before him was stable.

But inside...

He forced a great lump down his throat. After several minutes he stole a glance in his passenger's direction. She was buttoning her jacket, her skin smooth and her face a placid mask, calm and modest.

"Uh, where... Where are we going?" he whispered, not surprised to find that he was crying.

She told him again in that angelic voice, slightly husky, slightly accented. He knew that she'd told him earlier, but that was a lifetime ago, divided by what she'd been and what she'd become. He could sense his sanity on the far side of the median, still driving west.

"Bresden Bay, Massachusetts," he repeated. "Got it."

She finished buttoning her jacket and leaned toward him. A whimper flew past his lips. He felt something warm on his cheeks: a gentle kiss. He was blushing now, smiling deep inside and with great pride.

"Thank you," she said.

They drove in silence for a while, the road going *bumpity bump* as the little hula girl his daughter had given him did her dashboard shimmy.

Todd mumbled, "I gotta pee."

His passenger ignored him, reaching out and delicately tuning through the stations. Static filled the cabin, then talk radio, then disco.

"I really gotta pee," he repeated.

"Then go."

She settled on an alt-rock station playing Better Than Ezra's "Good," which brought a smile to her lips after a few chords. He found himself tapping his toes along too, his boot filling with urine. Normally, he would've scolded his rider for touching his stuff. But she'd kissed him and thanked him and somehow that made it all right.

chapter sixty-two

The sun hung low and cold as they crossed into Bresden Bay, population 147. Graham tasted salt water in the fog and it reminded him that in some ways he'd come full circle. Another thirty miles south, and he could knock on Louis's door.

Maybe Megan was right. Maybe something had happened to Oksana at the summer house and the tides had carried her down the coast.

And maybe Petro was also right: they were connected, Oksana and Megan. He sure as hell hoped that they were.

Because otherwise they were fucked. What they planned wasn't just illegal; it was insane. Breaking into a house that none of them owned. Baiting some irradiated mutant. Setting a trap.

"Turn around and go home," he mumbled to himself after giving the gas station attendant ten bucks for the number four pump. "You're going to wind up dead or in prison. Turn around, you big idiot."

Instead, Graham returned to the cruiser.

He filled three plastic canisters with 87 unleaded. While fueling the car, he watched Megan in the back seat, her fingers moving fast over the sketchpad. She'd filled half the pages since noon.

"You really think this'll work?" he asked.

The chewed pencil paused mid-scratch. She studied her composition, that same beach house she'd described, opened up like a doll's house to show every room in impossible configurations. Doors leading into stairs that twisted upward and became parts of the wall. Shadows embracing each other, fighting each other, fleeing. A wrecked car clinging to the side of a cliff.

"Do I think this will work?" she repeated, as if emerging from a trance. "Maybe. Maybe not. But I've remembered more in six hours of drawing than I did in two years of therapy."

"What else do you remember?"

She looked up at him. Those were the eyes of someone older, he thought. Much older than the twenty-one years she'd spent on this earth.

"I remember the fight with my parents," she said. "A real Monroe family blow-out. I told them I was going to art school and they told me they wouldn't pay. I remember telling my friends I just wished they'd go away. I think the last words I ever said to them were, I didn't need them; they were holding me back. And that sucks, you know?"

"They knew you didn't mean it."

She gave him a flat smile and a tired shrug. "Too late for take-backs."

"Being a parent is hard. You learn as you go."

"Yeah, well, being young isn't much easier."

He wanted to tell her she was right, but he wasn't sure his words carried much weight. She held a quiet wisdom, the kind born from regret and sharpened over time. He recognized its shape.

He said, "You get older, you start to forget what it's like being young. Everything so raw and uncomfortable."

Megan nodded, that scar taking on a long, ponderous shadow beneath the dim station lights. She waited for him to say something, but he didn't. "I've only known you a few days, but you seem like a good dad. Your daughter is lucky."

Is.

He smiled at that word.

The pump clicked and he topped off the tank. "Your parents knew that you cared."

Her jaw tensed as she fought back the tears. She glanced down at her sketchpad. "I should probably..."

"Yeah, no, keep at it. We're all in on this plan, right?"

"All in."

Petro returned with a map bearing an address circled in red. As they drove off, he passed out little plastic baggies. Graham turned one over. "Earplugs?"

Petro nodded. "Oksana will use your senses against you. Sounds, lights, things you may think that you're touching. Even your memories aren't safe."

"And these will protect us?"

"Protect? No. But if we're lucky, they might dampen her attacks." He turned back to Megan. "Now, tell us everything about your friend's house."

As Graham drove, Megan filled them in about the Chastain family summer home. As students, they'd gone there over the years, mostly when Desiree's parents were away, always to party. It was three floors of old wood and stone with acres of privacy and a view of the bay.

"Sounds like the entryway is the choke point," Graham said, taking a long curve around a hill. "We'll stage the ambush there and seal off the other entrances."

"What if she tries another way in?" Petro asked. "Like a window?"

"She won't." Megan turned her sketchbook toward them. The page was covered in a dozen amber doors from her dreams.

They followed the road deep into the late-autumn woods, fog blanketing the brown earth and rendering the trees into thin fingers. The rumble of the ocean grew closer, closer.

Megan perked up. "Up ahead. Pull over."

"Why?"

"Just do it."

Graham guided the car to the side of the road where the bushes and rocks leaned down the bluffs. They'd hardly stopped and Megan was already out, passing through the headlights and off to the shoulder.

Petro glanced at the empty road behind them. "What's she doing?"

"I don't know." Graham stepped out, loose pebbles crackling under his shoes.

He found her standing at the edge of a scraggly cliff descending into tide pools and fog. It shocked him how high the road actually was.

"I remember this place." Megan followed the shoulder until she came to a turn where the trees and bushes thinned out.

Graham traced her gaze down the embankment. He could see it now, the way he could see an old game trail in the woods, distressing the reeds and nudging the saplings. Below, battered trees and scarred trunks clutched the rocks. Further, a gash marred the slope, one not formed by the slow erosion of earth but something heavy and forceful.

A crash.

"That's where they found you?"

She nodded.

"Christ, you were lucky. Five feet in either direction and you'd be down on the rocks."

She stood there at the edge of the road, at the edge of her past. A young woman and her fragmented memory, yesterday's scars still etched in the present.

"It's weird," she said. "I always got scared on this road. I'd ask Adam or Tom to drive it for me. So why did I drive it back?"

chapter sixty-three

The old summer house stretched from the bluff, a fog-wrapped thing of shadowed brick and creaking wood. Casement windows winked in the headlights. A brown rat scurried down the porch and into the dry brush. Gulls scattered as Detective Nolan parked in the crescent driveway. His gaze rose to the wrap-around deck with its third-floor view of the bay.

"You said it was a cottage," he grumbled. "This is a mansion."

Megan closed her sketchpad. "That's what Desi's family calls it."

Petro hoisted his bag from the trunk. "New money shouts, but old money whispers."

It had been years since her last visit, and fear gnawed at her thoughts. What if the Chastains had sold the property? What if they'd changed the locks or moved the key? But the house was dark, its windows shuttered. She found the key where Desi always had, at the base of an antique hitching post in a little wood box.

"Okay, let's hope this works."

She stood before the twin amber doors, heart drumming, fingers trembling over the handle. This was it, what she feared to open.

The crackle of blackening wood.

The taste of ash on her tongue.

The glint of a shovel in the moonlight.

With a deep breath, she inserted the key. The old door yawned before her.

Inside, curved forms crouched in the foyer and lurked in the corners, tables and high-back chairs and loveseats all draped in velvet canvas. The air was redolent of dust and latent dampness. With clicking paws, another rat scampered among the high ceiling beams.

"Nothing," Petro said, toggling the light switch. "No power."

"There's a breaker," she said. "It's in… I think it's the pantry, past the kitchen."

"I'll toss it." Detective Nolan's flashlight panned across the parlor, finding the open kitchen and the pantry beyond. His right hand hung near his holster, always.

While he disappeared into the kitchen, Petro's gaze rose as he took in the moonlit ceiling that stretched up to the second and third floors. Crossed oars and old life buoys decorated the walls. Nets and spears and shelves with the occasional ship in a bottle. High above, an old helm hung from tasteful chains, repurposed into a chandelier.

Squinting, Megan could almost see the cigarette smoke rising up to the rafters and beams. Long gone laughter echoed off the walls. She could hear the jokes and the dares, the beer bottles clinking and rolling. She could feel the first tequila shot to hit her lips, the first hangover to scramble her brain, and the thunderstorm when she and Adam lost their virginity together in that loft room at the east end of the house. She had been determined, and he had been nervous he'd underperform. And yet, in the end it was tender and sweet and quite delightful. Funny, how much people built it all up.

"Power should be on," Detective Nolan called out.

Megan found a lamp and its power cord. She held the plug in her hands, inches from the outlet. *Do it*, she told herself. *It's just rubber and wires.*

"What is it?" Petro asked.

"Nothing," she said and slid the plug into the outlet.

The lights buzzed as dust burned off the warming bulbs. Detective Nolan spread out groceries and jugs of water in the kitchen. "First things first, what kind of timeline are we looking at?"

Megan turned to Petro, only to find him returning her stare. "Me?" she asked. "How should I know?"

Petro asked, "How do you feel?"

"Like I've been eating junk food for two days and forgot how to sleep."

"Nothing else?"

"What, am I a radar or something?"

"No, of course not. It's just... In my years of exposure, Oksana and I, we developed something of a connection. You know how the air changes before a storm? It felt like that when she was close."

Detective Nolan cast a dubious glance toward Petro and passed out pastrami grinders that had cooled. "We should eat."

They ate in silence, three dim forms in a dusty kitchen, serenaded by the rumble of the ocean. After a moment Megan asked, "What was she like?"

Petro's jaw slowed and his eyes drifted to a dark corner of the kitchen. "Scared." He chewed another bite, then swallowed. "She didn't have any family or friends. She didn't understand what was happening to her body. No one did. It took us a year of work before she could leave the clinic in Kharkiv, but only at night."

Detective Nolan chased his hoagie with a creme soda. "I thought you said you were in Kyiv."

"We had to move often." Petro wiped his mouth. "We should probably get ready."

Megan wasn't certain, but she thought something darkened on Detective Nolan's face for a moment. He shook it off and said, "Right. A reconnoiter is in order."

She followed them through the house, the men discussing things like choke points and funnels. They pointed out back doors and side entrances. They used words like *flank* and *breach* and *area of engagement*. She had no strategy or insight to offer, but she helped slide tables and stack couches in front of doors. They even rolled a piano to block the side porch.

They did the same with the second floor and the third, checking rooms and obstructing points of ingress. Windows already shuttered were concealed behind flipped mattresses and tilted shelves. Bookshelves were emptied and tilted to block halls, dusty hardbacks dumped in awkward piles. Occasionally, Detective Nolan or Petro took a step back to admire their work and reconvene.

Next, they emptied Snapple bottles into the sink and tore rags from the dishtowels. They filled a quarter of each bottle with shredded Styrofoam from their coffee cups. Petro stuffed cloth wicks into the bottles as Graham poured the gasoline.

"Molotov cocktail," he said. "Be very careful."

"We'll handle them," Petro said to Megan. "You keep our guest talking."

"Okay." The thought of fire worried her and the fumes irritated her eyes. Her lungs craved fresh air.

Outside, trees and cliffs suggested sharp rocks behind a curtain of haze. The sea murmured beyond. She breathed in the salty fog, fingers curling around the wood railing of the old balcony.

If she could truly quiet her mind, she could feel her friends here. Chunhee, wrapped in a thick blanket and watching the sun rise, their mostly sober guardian. Adam, cooking hotdogs and steak over the grill. Tom, dropping a beer down the stairs. And Desi, shouting to be careful, that if her parents thought she was using this place to party, they'd change out the locks.

Chunhee. Desi. Tom. All gone.

And Adam too, in his own way. Checked himself out of her life, out of everything she'd once hoped to build. It was okay, she told herself. In life, friends came and went. But it didn't fill the hole they left. Would she ever know anyone as deeply as those she grew into adulthood with?

She followed the balcony, tracing the curious mix of wood that made up the railing. Most was old and weathered by the ocean and seasons. Not here. A section of wood was newer, shiny and imbued with deep browns, neither aged nor salty and gray.

The balcony groaned as she peered over. Far below lay a rocky escarpment, the fallow gardens, and the patio swaddled in mist.

Vertigo struck and her fingers clamped the rickety railing. Something cold hummed deep in her mind. That same connection she'd felt over the past several weeks. First, rattling around the edge of her dreams, then clawing its way into her waking life. A flicker, a moment, and now a whole memory bloomed before her.

She had been standing right here. Yes, she had. There was no fog but rather an endless summer ocean. The moon looked down upon them, a tired eye in a sea of stars, unblinking and indifferent.

There stood Adam, his eyes locked on his shoes. He couldn't look up. Why couldn't he look up?

Because it wasn't Megan that was talking. Nor was it Chunhee. Nor Tom or Desi.

It was Oksana.

Her form breathed cool radiance, an X-ray developing before them. And in that shape, Megan could hear words. Yes, Oksana's words came back to her now, each syllable rich and smoky and dripping like wax.

"I don't understand," Oksana had said. "Isn't this what you wanted? You have your whole future ahead."

Megan squeezed her temples, trying to bring that bright memory into focus. She was there. She could almost see Oksana just past the edge of the light.

Megan stretched out her hand.

And then Tom was standing up and shaking his head while Desi was yelling. Chunhee hugged her own chest, drawing the blanket in over her shoulders.

Megan stretched out until the light swallowed her fingertips and someone asked, "Meg, what are you doing?"

Then it was gone. The radiance, the memory, the echoes of her friends. The starry sky of three summers ago collapsed behind tonight's curtain of fog and the hum of rollers and latches.

Detective Nolan was opening the sliding glass door. "Everything okay?"

No, everything's not okay, she thought. *And it hasn't been for some time.*

But she said, "She's getting close."

chapter sixty-four

Adam parked his 4Runner under a wind-shaped cedar at the side of the road. He reached into the back and unzipped the rifle case. His fingers knew every inch of the Remington Model 7400, a faithful thing of warm checkered walnut and etched metal. He had cleaned her, sighted her in, and now he loaded the magazine and checked the chamber. Ten rounds ready to work with, and four spare magazines in his pockets.

God help him if that wasn't enough.

Slinging the rifle over his shoulder, he followed the road's edge where the shadows were longest and the gravel didn't crunch underfoot. After a quarter mile, his eyes adjusted to the darkness. He savored the sea breeze and the memories it brought.

Megan and him, entwined in the cool sheets of the loft. Or was that Oksana?

Yes, Megan was pulling him back in, lips soft and sticky against his.

But then Oksana lay on her back, smiling and blissful, the necklace glistening around her bare neck. Adam was muttering, "What did I do? What have I done?"

"What we both wanted."

He waved off the memory and checked the empty road before darting across. Something rustled in a bush and went silent as he passed.

Oksana. Megan. That whole fucking weekend. Didn't she understand what a gift he'd given her? Jesus had been wrong. It wasn't the meek that were blessed; it was the ignorant.

Megan was blind and numb and dumbly swiping at the past. She'd bring everything down. Everything they'd all built together.

He had to stop it.

So here he was once again, stalking the shadows and plodding down this old coastal road. Praying another car wouldn't drive past. Praying he could fix things yet again. The dew underfoot and the distant lights of scattered homes, slowly growing closer and closer. Then came the dark turnoff to Desi's summer house.

And behind him: a car struggling up the hill.

Adam threw himself into the bushes, the burs and thorns biting his skin. Adrenaline warmed his ears and spiked his heart. He worried someone might hear it.

Headlights smeared the road yellow, followed by a rumbling hiss. It wasn't a car but a truck, a big rig without a trailer. Adam kept flat in the bushes as it drove past. What the hell was that doing out here?

Unless...

Brake lights bloomed red in the mist. The truck slowed and turned down that long tree-lined driveway.

Shit.

The truck idled at the mouth of the driveway, lights painting the trees and the engine purring. The world held its breath, and so did Adam.

A form broke off from the cab and passed the headlights. A dark, feminine shape stretched against the foggy glow. She rose to the driver's side, whispering. It was *her*. Finally. He sensed it, knew it in every bone and cell of his body.

Which meant she might as well.

Two silver eyes turned to him, glaring across several hundred yards of haze.

Adam buried his face in his hands and flattened himself against the embankment. He bit his knuckle, willing himself to hold still, to not shake the bushes, to not shake in his own skin. He sucked in his breath. *No, not here*, he thought and squeezed his tense neck. *Please, not now.*

In that quiet, he waited. The whispering wind. The murmuring bay.

The engine now rumbling several hundred feet off. Wait. Yes, if he waited and drew closer, he might have a shot.

With a squeal of brakes and the clatter of gravel, the truck reversed and accelerated away from that dark driveway. He peeked over the embankment as it rumbled past. A glimpse of a middle-aged trucker, ashen and wide-eyed, white-knuckling the wheel.

Then it drove on, fleeing down the coastal road.

After counting to one hundred, Adam emerged from his bushy hideout, hands damp and shaking. He could see her, Oksana. Even in the darkness, he could make out her form down that tree-lined path.

As if she were just out for an evening stroll.

As if she were coming home after all she had ruined.

As if.

He drew in a deep breath. Yes, he knew what he must do, but he doubted the angle. If he could get closer, he'd have a shot.

He gave Oksana another fifty count, then crossed to the driveway and stuck to the trees. There she was, nearing the twin amber doors of the summer home a hundred yards off.

He edged closer, closer. Eighty yards now. Seventy.

At fifty yards, he dropped to a kneeling position behind a mossy oak. This was it. He wound his left arm through the rifle strap, making a hasty sling to keep the stock tense against his shoulder. He wiped dew from his eyelashes and took aim through the scope.

It had been two years, five months, and twenty-two days since he'd last seen Oksana. And yeah, they'd both changed. Her hair, her skin, nearly everything about her was different. Yet he sensed her presence like the body sensed a resurgent cancer, a foe known at the cellular level.

He held his breath as the reticles settled over her glistening hair. He tracked down the base of her skull. He waited for his heartbeat to slow.

And he told himself to squeeze between beats before she got too close to the house. *Squeeze before she opens the door. Yes, take the shot now and end what should have been finished.*

He never squeezed.

He sensed motion to his left a second before it was on him: a shape stretching out from the trees. He swung his rifle too late. A gloved hand grabbed the barrel and pushed it away. An arm hooked around his throat and yanked him back.

Adam kicked and flailed and dug his fingers under that grip. It was strong, too strong to break. He saw something before unconsciousness overtook him: a man in tactical black, eyes hidden behind night-vision goggles. The man raised a finger to his lips—*shh*.

Then his world sank into a deep ocean of shadows and he cursed himself with his dimming thoughts.

Should've... taken... the shot.

chapter sixty-five

Megan squeezed the banister and breathed deep, focusing on the front door below. She felt like a glove, something molded to other hands. A doll posed at the top of the stairs and waiting for that knob to turn and the doors to creak open.

Please don't open.

Distantly, numbly, she acknowledged Detective Nolan behind the pillar to the entryway's right. His flashlight and gun, both down but drawn. Several bottles sat near his feet, wicks dangling. And Petro, here on the second floor, crouching behind an open door to her left.

According to them, they had the tactical advantage. Once Oksana was inside, Graham would hit her with a Molotov cocktail, cutting off her retreat. Petro would follow up, raining down secondary cocktails once Graham got clear. And here Megan would stand, drawing Oksana's eyes to the top of the stairs.

Megan wasn't a tactician, but it seemed like a good plan. And it was.

Until it collapsed.

The knock reverberated through the dark house. She closed her eyes and thought, *Come in*.

With a click, the doors opened and moonlight poured into the foyer. A jagged shadow stretched out. Megan's hands shook as the dark shape stepped in. First came her legs, then her body, then her fog-dampened hair. She wiped a strand from her face, eyes twinkling as her gaze wormed its way up the stairs.

They saw each other and they knew each other.

"Meg."

"Oksana."

"It's been quite a while." She paused at the edge of the rug, her mismatched eyes scouring the pillars and shadows. "You're not alone."

"I never said that I would be."

"No, you did not."

Megan could feel Oksana's smoky voice penetrating the shadows and clawing its way into her ears. A warm finger slid up her spine and straightened every hair on her neck. She was drowsy and wanted to yawn.

Shit. Her hand had risen to her cheek, fingers digging to pull out the earplug. She sobered up and pressed the plugs in deeper.

At the bottom of the stairs, Oksana's eyes narrowed.

"I suppose I should be used to it," she shouted. "Never being alone. These days, I have so many old friends tagging along. I envy your... solitude."

She made a retching cough, her throat swelling and then falling. When she spoke, it was as if Chunhee were right here. "I'll tell you everything, I promise. I've been meaning to tell you for years."

A twist of her neck, a wheezing gag, and now Desi's voice filled the foyer. "Sometimes I like to think that school never existed."

Another wet cough, and another lump stretched her throat. Tom's voice passed her lips. "We did what we needed to do, okay? If we had to do it all over, I'd do the same thing."

It took every ounce of Megan's willpower not to run screaming. Instead, she let those stolen voices wash over her, remembering the laughter they had once carried. If she made no reaction, she held all the power.

"Megan, Megan, Megan." Oksana sighed, something sinuous twisting beneath her black pants. "I was mad at you. For the longest time, I was *furious*. Do you know what fury tastes like? How it sits on your tongue? How it poisons your thoughts until it's the only warmth that you know?"

"No, I don't," Megan said. "But your English has improved."

"You were a good tutor. But I have others now. Or is it 'now I have others'?"

Oksana smiled, and Megan thought it might be the most beautiful smile she'd ever seen.

"I thought that's what kept bringing me back. Our friendship, our connection, but most of all, that fury. I thought it *preserved* me. But then Chunhee showed me her memories. Well, what remained after..."

She mimed a hammer blow and something breaking with her hands.

"So I took a little stroll inside Tom's and Desi's memories as well. Like Mr. Daly's English class, always check your sources, yes? And a funny thing happened. That fury, it gave way to something else. Call it envy or pity, I'm not really sure. Admiration, perhaps. See, I think you've been too harsh on yourself, Meg. I think it's time we have a long, friendly chat."

"You're a monster. We have nothing to discuss."

"I beg to differ."

"You murdered them."

"I settled *our* debts." Oksana gave a dismissive wave of her hand. "Now they're with me forever. Maybe one day we can bring them back. And that scar, you poor thing. I can help you erase it."

"Who said I wanted it gone?"

Oksana took one step onto the stairs, and Megan took one step back. Then they waited, calculating their next move.

"Meg, I forgive you. But you need to forgive yourself."

Megan's lip quivered. "I'm not asking for your forgiveness."

Oksana's eyes narrowed. "Then why are you here?"

It happened so fast. First, Oksana's glare shifted to her right. Then the dim light pulsed and brightened. A flare filled the foyer, chasing the shadows and painting the walls a fiery red.

Oksana covered her eyes as Petro emerged from behind the door, waving a road flare back and forth. He shouted something but not in English. To Oksana's right, Graham was peeking out, confusion scrunching his face.

Lowering her hand, Oksana widened her eyes. It was all gone: the calm poise, that confident stare, those full lips always hinting at a smirk. Her face twisted into a bitter scowl as she stepped back down the stairs.

"You. What are you doing here?"

"Sweetie," Petro said, "it's time to come home."

chapter sixty-six

Graham tensed when he heard the distinctive pop of the flare. When the walls reddened, he risked a quick peek. And when he saw Petro waving it and shouting something like Russian, fear straightened his back.

Because this wasn't part of the plan.

Because he hadn't thrown the first bottle.

And because Oksana's face was twisting in anger or fury or—

No, he realized. That was recognition.

"Sweetie, it's time to come home."

"No." A childish fear wavered in her voice. "No, no no no, I won't go back to that *cage*."

Graham had a second to consider her words before he heard the *plinkity-plink* of the canister as it rolled past his feet. He recognized its shape: an M84 stun grenade. It had come from the window.

He turned and took two steps before it went off, searing the walls and his retinas, filling his ears with a thousand ringing bells.

Three more stun grenades detonated in quick succession. He stumbled over the couch, grasping for traction as the world faltered. Shadows stormed in from the edge of the house. A side door folded beneath boots and battering rams. Two figures descended from the third-floor balcony, moonlight streaming through shattered glass. Flashlights beamed down gun barrels aimed by men in ballistic armor.

For a moment, Graham was relieved the SWAT team had arrived. But where were their patches? And why weren't they speaking English?

Because of Petro, he realized. He wasn't here to stop Oksana. He was here to capture her.

Graham went for his firearm too slow, too late. One of the mercenaries grabbed his wrist, wrestling him onto the couch. Another rushed over with handcuffs. He kicked and twisted, catching glimpses of more men entering from the front door. They wore protective earmuffs and carried poles with metal hoops at the end. Someone jammed a cattle prod into Oksana that loosed a shriek from her lips.

Graham curled, tugging his assailant's hand against his chest and rolling. He felt something break underneath—perhaps the man's wrist—and he wrenched the gun free.

Another strobe-lit glimpse of the foyer. Megan, hoisted and dragged from the banister. Animal control poles with metal hoops latched around Oksana, two on her neck and one on her wrist. Petro, pointing at Graham, "There, be careful! That one's armed!"

Graham raised his service pistol and swung, sighting the man with the broken wrist. He looked back with frightened eyes, shouting, "*Nyet! Nyet!* No shoot!"

Graham hesitated a moment too long.

He wasn't sure which blow knocked him unconscious. He caught a sidelong glimmer of light down a black polymer gun stock. Then he was on the floor, sliding, being pulled, and despite the earplugs, the screams drew closer. Something feral, something pained, something furious. Head swimming, he blinked blood from his eyes and tried to wipe his face, but his hands were cuffed.

Another shape stumbled through the front door, shoved by the men in tactical black. Graham recognized the preppy young man from the police station in New Hampshire. Adam. Yes, that was his name. Somehow he was here and handcuffed as well.

Over Oksana's guttural shrieking, Petro directed the men to place Graham and Adam on a couch near the base of the stairs. Next came the ball gag, two mercenaries nervously stuffing it in Oksana's mouth and covering it with duct tape again and again. They brought Megan down, cuffed and kicking, and shoved her onto the couch.

Only Oksana was putting up a fight, swinging and lashing out at the animal control poles locked onto her limbs. Her body contorted and twisted, snake-like and slippery. In a blur between flashlights and shadows, Graham swore something like barbed vines whipped out from under her jacket.

They were all trapped here now, Megan on the couch, hands holding her down by the shoulders. Two mercenaries carried wood and books, tossing them under the couch. A third carried the gasoline canister. Graham's eyes widened.

"Yes, good, I've got your attention." Petro snapped his fingers before the detective.

"So, what, you're with the Russkis now?" The tang of iron filled Graham's mouth. He spat on the floor. "Let me guess, KGB's your client."

"The KGB is long gone. Another casualty of the Cold War. The private sector pays better now. Long live capitalism."

"And Oksana, what, she's your runaway experiment?"

"I'm afraid you'll never know, Detective. But forgive me, it's like you Americans say: time is money, and there're too many loose ends to ignore. If I have to ask twice, Vitali here will cut off your finger."

Adam struggled but those gloved hands clamped his shoulders, pressed him back into the couch. Graham counted six men in total: three restraining Oksana, and three here before them. He pegged Vitali, the one with the gas canister, as second in command.

Graham centered himself. "So, what, you burn our bodies if we don't play along. You thought of everything, except good interrogation technique."

"Oh, Detective, you are mistaken. You will all burn. Whether you're alive or dead, in one piece or in several, that depends on your answers."

Before Graham could say anything, Petro turned to Adam. "What happened to Oksana? Where did she go?"

Adam blinked. Graham saw defiance crystalizing in the young man's eyes. *Don't lie to them, kid. These are hard men. Don't feed them some bullshit.*

But that was what Adam did.

"I... I don't know what you're talking about."

The words had hardly left Adam's mouth when Petro nodded and Vitali produced a knife, took ahold of something behind Adam, then jerked upward. The scream left Adam's lips and scrambled Graham's thoughts.

Vitali held out the severed finger, wagging it in Adam's face. He jerked away, but the hands clamped him back to the couch.

Petro cleared his throat and pointed to Megan. "We'll try again. What happened to Oksana? Where did she go? Who was hiding her? Who else knows?"

Megan blinked. "Me? I don't know. What do you think I've been trying to figure out?"

For the longest time, Adam said nothing, just whimpered and let the tears streak down his cheeks.

Petro scowled. "Vitali, when I reach zero, take out her left eye. *Pyat... cetyre... tri... dva...*"

"I told you, I don't know."

"Lies!"

"Wait, wait." A twitch ran up Adam's spine and straightened his back. "There was an accident. Oksana... She told us some things that she did. Terrible things. She..." His eyes rose to meet Megan's, wet and embarrassed. "She started the fire. At your house, Meg, your parents. That was *her*. She said she was setting you free. That it was her gift to you."

A whimper left Megan's lips. "What?"

Adam's head sagged. "I'm sorry. I should've... We should have told you. But we couldn't. Because if you knew the truth, you'd know what we did."

Megan swallowed. "What did we do?"

Adam met her eyes. "You killed her. We all did. We all killed Oksana."

chapter sixty-seven

It was as if a key had slid into an old, dry lock, and all the rusty pins moved into place. Megan had sensed this answer for weeks, lingering just past the edge of her fears. Now, hearing Adam's words loosened her muscles and brought a slouch to her shoulders.

"How?" she asked. "How did we kill her?"

Only Petro seemed amused, a smirk tugging one side of his lips. "Yes, I'm curious. How did you kill her?"

Megan could see the confusion spreading across Detective Nolan's face. Then the acceptance. Maybe he'd already made the connection. Or maybe not. But he must have suspected, and now he knew.

A missing girl.

A fisherman who went on a rampage.

Six friends connected by this very house.

When Vitali raised the knife, Adam flinched and whimpered. "It was an accident, upstairs. She told us what she did to Meg's parents. The fire, she *bragged* about it. She said it was her gift." He turned his wet eyes on Megan. "You were on the balcony. She said you were overreacting, that it was a good thing that she'd done. She was hugging you and... You pushed her away. You pushed her, hard, and she went through the railing."

Megan closed her eyes. In the fog of past seasons, she could hear the crack of the old wood. She could see Oksana stumbling back, her eyes widening as fingers grasped at the mist. A cry from her lips echoed through the years.

Then she fell.

Then nothing.

"It took us ten minutes to find her body. When we dragged her back up, she was all… crooked and bent. This pink stuff was pouring out her nose. And her bones, it was like she was rearranging. She wasn't dead but she wasn't really living, just spitting out words that got into your head."

There they were in the dusty corners of Megan's mind, a dozen fractured glimpses.

A twisted back, crackling as the vertebrae reset.

A mottled leg with too many joints.

And beneath it all, a rattling scream, endless and maddening.

Adam blinked away tears. Even Oksana settled momentarily, her chest heaving, eyes boring into him from across the dark room.

"I mean, what do you do?" He sniffed. "None of us knew what she was. I tried to help, but she kept talking, kept screaming, kept saying such horrible things… So I hit her. With the shovel, I hit her again and again until she stopped talking."

The shovel blade in the moonlight. The handle speckled red. That maddening shriek, finally silent. From a deep cave of Megan's mind, acceptance spread as Oksana's broken body lay quiet and still.

"And you thought she was dead because she stopped breathing?" Petro grinned. "Tsk. Tsk. So, what then? You buried her body, yes?"

"No, not buried." Adam shook his head. "Tom and I, we took Desi's boat and dumped her in the bay. We didn't know what she was or what else to do."

"Didn't know?" Megan swallowed. "Didn't know? We should have gone to the police. We should have—"

"Yes!" His eyes sparkled. "Yes, that's what you said. When we got back, you said you were going to the cops, that you *needed* to tell them. You said you'd take the blame. We couldn't talk you out of it. None of us could. You were getting into your car. That's when it happened."

"What happened?" she asked. "Adam, what happened?"

"When I hit you."

Megan blinked as the darkness stretched back through the years. There was a shadow crossing the driveway on that warm summer night. She was that shadow. She had been angry, yes, because they had done a terrible thing. And worse, they had agreed to cover it up. All except her. She remembered the sorrow, how it hurt that she had to do the right thing all alone.

Yes, she was in the driveway, walking to her car. What had she said?

"It's my fault, so don't try to stop me."

And yes, Adam was running after her, and what was he shouting? "Hey, Meg, wait up. I want to come with."

Then she had turned and caught a glimpse of all of them there. Desi and Tom and Chunhee, sadness etched on the faces of her dear friends. They all looked so much older that night.

The shovel glinted in the darkness as Adam swung from the side. The stars divided and fell. That bitter moon looked down on it all, silent and still.

"You..." The words caught in her mouth. "You... tried to kill me, too."

"We all did," Adam said. "I killed myself that night. I loved both of you but I couldn't have either. So we put you in the car and drove down the road. We put you behind the wheel. And then I put it in drive."

Megan sensed them all, every little doubt that had skittered about in her mind. The bourbon on her clothes, even though she hated hard liquor. The rocks rattling beneath the wheels like a hailstorm. The trees scraping at the windows, clawing the hood, drumming down the car until the faces of her friends vanished and everything tilted and fell.

"You... sent me over the cliff?"

"We all did," Adam said. "But we fucked it up. There were too many trees. Then someone drove by and saw us and they had a car phone. Next thing we knew, there were cops and rescue services descending on ropes. I couldn't stop any of it, so I lied. And when it was over, you... you didn't remember a single thing. You got a do-over. You pushed Oksana. You made her fall. *You*. And you never remembered. I *hated* you for that. I think we all did in some way."

Megan tried to wipe her eyes, but her wrists were cuffed and the hands on her shoulder pressed her down. "Stop. Just... don't touch me."

"Easy now," Petro said. "Easy."

"Fuck you," she snarled at Petro. "And fuck you, Adam. You lied to me, you coward. And you..." She turned to Oksana. "I barely remember you. But fuck you for what you did to my parents. They weren't perfect, but they were my family."

Megan sank against Detective Nolan, exhausted. She had nothing. No more gas in the tank. All those hours wasted in therapy, scratching her way to this moment, and what had she gained? She was a criminal. Her best friends had lied to her, tried to kill her. Her ex had been in love with two women. And her family...

That was her fault. Not because of some heater or overloaded power cord, but because of a careless comment she'd made to a friend.

"I wish my parents would just go away."

Petro bent down, eye to eye with Adam. "So, Megan's bond with Oksana brought her back and Mr. Harding found her. And the necklace? That was your gift to her?"

Adam gave a weak nod.

"Yes, she is quite persuasive." Then Petro clapped his hands. "Okay, I think we can fill in the rest. Ready?"

He whistled to the mercenaries and made a quick gesture. *Time to wrap up.* Several men hoisted their guns. Vitali swapped his knife for the can of gasoline. Detective Nolan twisted and tugged.

This was it, a rain of bullets if they were lucky, and then searing heat. Megan closed her eyes and accepted it.

Only Adam remained still, his head bowed as a curious giggle left his lips. Across the room, Oksana stared at him, unblinking.

"You... still don't... get it," he laughed.

Petro took Adam by his hair and hoisted his face. "Something final to add?"

"None of you... get it." Adam's eyes fluttered at the edge of unconsciousness.

Through tears, Megan noticed Adam's severed finger. Wormlike, it inched its way across the floor.

"It wasn't Megan who brought Oksana back," he said. "I've been inside of her. Which means she's been inside of me for years."

He sprang to his feet and leapt onto Petro. Despite the handcuffs, the two spilled over backward, tangled and twisting.

Megan wasn't sure what happened first. The gunshots, perhaps. Or the guttural cry from Adam's throat. Or maybe the ruby fissures that opened down his cheeks as his jaw dislocated and his teeth sank into Petro's tender face.

So many teeth.

Adam pounced and thrashed like a dog on a rat. His hands broke themselves and slid through the cuffs. His back arched and twisted. But it was the lump that held her attention.

A swelling blister at the base of his neck.

Puppet-like, Adam snapped his head back, peeling Petro's face with his teeth and leaving lidless eyes staring back. He spat the red mask at the mercenaries, who opened fire with their submachine guns, one first, then two, then several joining in. Megan never knew something could sound so loud and end so abruptly.

Adam was simply shredded.

As well as one of the handlers gripping Oksana's pole.

Acrid smoke filled the air. In the confusion, another handler found herself pushed into the mercenaries, reeling backward as Oksana charged. Bony hooks sprouted from her fingers.

Detective Nolan seized on the chaos and tackled the nearest mercenary. Megan rolled to her right, kicking and helping to pin the man down. The detective pressed a knee on the man's neck and twisted.

"*Nyet!* No! Stop!"

The commando gestured behind them, where Adam rose again, now dotted with rubies. That blistering mound on his neck hoisted him up. Shaking, swelling, it grew to the size of a grapefruit as the skin stretched and became transparent.

Then it burst.

Megan wasn't sure what emerged. At first it was a tentacle or a snake. Then it was ringed with a dozen glistening beaks, all shrieking and cawing. Whiplike, it lashed out and struck a mercenary, leaving a raw hollow across his throat.

On trembling legs, the Adam-puppet shambled forward, arms loose at his sides. His broken fingers made phantom gestures. His lips sputtered curses that made Megan cover her ears. All the while, that whip-thing wriggled and lashed out. Beyond him, Oksana was crab-walking her way up a wall, one pole still tight around her neck.

"Key," Detective Nolan said, pulling the handcuff key from the mercenary's pocket while he kept a knee to the man's neck. "Turn around."

Megan turned, feeling the click and the precious release of the cuffs. Her wrists screamed in freedom. "Your turn."

She uncuffed him. In seconds he was pushing her to the stairs, grabbing a gun and laying down suppressing fire. This was chaos, battle, something Megan knew nothing about. So when Detective Nolan said, "Go, upstairs, run!" that was just what she did.

Below, a faceless Petro squirmed across the floor. The Adam-puppet skittered toward a nervous mercenary, who fumbled with a fresh magazine. And Vitali, Megan saw him spilling over a chair as Oksana scurried down the wall. His boot caught the canister of gas as he took aim at the Adam-puppet.

Megan and Detective Nolan saw it at the same time. The fallen flare and where Petro was crawling. Petro's hand, desperately reaching for the overturned can. And the gasoline, burbling onto the floor and spreading.

Detective Nolan hugged Megan and whispered, "Get down."

The blast blew out the lower windows and turned the walls a blazing blood orange. The air singed her nostrils.

Then secondary explosions went off. The Molotovs Petro had left crackled and spun. Within seconds the curtains were burning. Megan shielded her eyes from the heat as the bottom floor became a furnace of horrors.

Fully engulfed, Vitali shrieked and crashed off the walls.

Oksana tore the gag from her face and grinned a shark's grin at a wounded mercenary. Cornered, the man put a gun to his own head and squeezed the trigger.

By the base of the stairs, the Adam-puppet mewled and scampered in fiery circles before collapsing in a blistering heap.

Upstairs, a secondary blast knocked Megan back, one of the Molotov cocktails exploding. Another went spinning toward her, its fuse already lit. Detective Nolan kicked it back across the parlor, where it burst against a cloth-covered piano.

He shouted, "We need to get out of here!"

Megan studied the second floor. The dining room, where the view of the bay was now barricaded behind smoldering couches and chairs. The halls, where cindering mattresses were flipped against windows. They had moments before the air became toxic. But there wasn't a way out, not on this floor.

"Upstairs," she said. "The patio, the balcony, then down the stairs to the garden."

Detective Nolan nodded. "Go."

They took the central stairs up, the ashy air battering their cheeks. They were on the third floor now, coughing and pushing forth. She could see the way out, the sliding glass door behind that sofa stacked at an angle and the balcony beyond.

Thirty feet. Twenty feet. Ten.

They threw the sofa aside, reaching for the glass door and the promise of cool fog and precious air. Megan caught the red-yellow reflections of fire stretching up the halls and curling the wallpaper.

She took the handle and slid the door open.

And then the whole house rearranged.

chapter sixty-eight

Graham wasn't quite sure what just happened. He'd pulled the couch aside and pushed Megan toward the sliding glass door. They were inches from escaping. She had opened it and—

And then everything *changed*.

The walls shifted, the floor buckled, and the ceiling moved to the right. He was no longer pushing the sofa aside but was crouching beside Megan after the gas canister exploded. They weren't on the third floor, but back on the second.

Some sort of reset.

It was the concussion, he told himself. He'd finally taken too many blows to the head and his eggs were all scrambled. And if they didn't move quick, they were soon to be cooked.

"Did the house just change for you?" Megan asked. "Tell me I'm not crazy."

He wiped soot from his eye. "Oh good, you saw that too."

A Molotov cocktail went spinning toward her, its fuse already lit. Graham kicked it back across the parlor, where it burst beside a cloth-covered piano.

Okay, that was strange.

He studied it all: the fiery dining room, the smoke climbing the walls, the air swirling with cinders. And then came Oksana's voice.

"You're too harsh on yourself, Meg. You made a mistake but you weren't alone. We all made mistakes. We lied to each other."

Graham spun, searching the shadows for Oksana's shape. She was nearby. Had to be. Her voice was everywhere. A whisper over his shoulder. An echo down a fiery hall. A murmur scratching at the back of his eyes.

Megan took Graham's hand. "We need to get out of here."

He gave her a confused nod. Hadn't he said that a moment ago? Still, he followed her, waving off ash as they raced up the stairs once again. Was this what smoke inhalation felt like? Were these the dying visions of his oxygen-starved brain?

"Adam wanted to end it with you. Do you know that? He was too scared, of course. Always too timid. Instead, he just drifted. Like all of you, just drifted apart. And you thought you were friends."

"We were friends," Megan said. "And you killed them, you cancerous freak."

"Mmm. Do friends keep such secrets from each other?"

Coughing, Graham turned the corner. There it was, the hall and the upturned sofa, the sliding glass door just beyond. They could make it. He pushed Megan onward.

Then the doors opened on the left side of the hall.

Megan's eyes drifted inside the loft bedroom, where two bodies lay entwined in the sheets. Adam and Oksana. As their lips locked and their bodies merged, Oksana's fingers slid across Adam's dimpling skin.

And then slid underneath.

"He was never going to tell you, Megan. He didn't want to hurt you. But the others suspected. Chunhee, of course. She was always the smartest. And Desi whispered to Tom. Yes, I see their memories now, all that they kept to themselves. Do friends truly deceive one another?"

"No, they don't," Megan shouted to the smoke and the devouring whispers. "But Adam beat you to death, so how'd that turn out?"

Graham snapped his fingers in front of Megan. She was fixated on that empty bedroom, smoke rising through the floor vents. "Megan, c'mon."

Covering her face with his hand, he led her to the end of the hall.

They dug their fingers into the sofa, throwing the cushions and tilting it over. There, just beyond the glass: the cool air.

And the house shifted.

They were back downstairs, hands wrapped around each other. Megan blinked it off. "Again?"

"Yeah, seems like it."

An ember landed in Megan's hair and sent up tendrils of smoke. Graham slapped it out. Then he saw her ear. "The earbuds, shit."

He dug a finger into his canal. It was empty, damn. Same with Megan's. He had a memory of the mercenaries removing them, but it was distant and dim. How long had they been in this house?

"She's in our heads," Megan said. "She won't let us leave."

"Hell, we're probably just running in place."

A Molotov cocktail went spinning past her, its fuse already lit. He went to reach for it, but Megan kicked it over to a ransacked bookshelf.

Okay, wait a second. Maybe he could figure this out.

"Upstairs," he said. "Fast as we can."

Oksana's voice chased them, booming down the smoky halls and scratching at their ankles. Every word shook something loose. A floorboard buckled and rose. A painting slid down the wall. Something crunched underfoot and his boot lost traction. Hundreds of snails carpeted the floor.

"Do you know what it's like to have nothing? To be reduced to the barest scrap of existence? To eat desperation? Of course not. You and your friends, you whine about hardships, but you've never tasted misery. You're a tourist to suffering."

They made it to the long hall as the air thickened. There, at the far end, the sofa stood behind a curtain of smoke. Megan doubled over and retched. He gathered her in his heavy embrace, dragging her toward that barricaded door and the promise of fresh air.

Then the doors opened on the right side of the hall.

This time, Graham came to a stop.

Because what stood inside had no business being there.

Here was his daughter's bedroom, just as they'd painted and decorated it through the years. The wall by the crib, that salmon pink he'd bought from Lowe's a month before she was born. Another wall, painted that racer blue she'd loved as she learned colors in preschool. By the desk they bought her in third grade, there was wallpaper now, dancing clowns and dogs and endless balloons.

At her empty desk sat that blue notebook he bought from the hospital gift shop. A gift she would never get to open.

And then, closest to him, the walls were stripped and repapered. Gone was the color of childhood, the cozy bed, and the bins for toys that would no longer feel her hands. Gone was the touch of life. Only a subtle brown remained, the hue of a spare room, a place of pain he had learned to walk past and forget.

The name left his lips. "Jennie?"

She stood there at the window, his daughter, just as he'd seen her on that last day of summer. She said, *"Look at all those butterflies."*

And there had been so many. Black Swallowtails with their marigold spots. White Peacocks that fluttered brown in the breeze. And a Summer Azure, its delicate wings shimmering as it settled on the window and took rest in the shade.

Distantly, he knew Megan was pushing the sofa from the door. That her hand was falling on the handle and sliding the glass open. He wanted her to stop, to wait; he needed this moment.

Then the house reset.

He was no longer reaching for his lost daughter, but was reaching out for the Molotov cocktail as it went rolling toward Megan, the fuse already lit.

He grabbed the bottle and hoisted it. *Careful. Careful now.*

They were back on the second floor, the wood slick with ash and the halls crawling with flames. Megan raged at the smoky shadows. "Oh, fuck you, Oksana. All these gifts and abilities and you're just a parasite, some scared little girl. You know why no one remembers you? It's because you're not worth remembering!"

The walls shuddered and the floor buckled. Megan squeezed her temple, and Graham felt it too, the buzzing of a million flies inside his skull. He stifled a gag, worried he might just spit up maggots.

This was it. He needed to do something, to stall her. To draw her out.

Jennie...

Graham held up a hand to Megan. *Wait.* It wasn't a plan but instinct, that same troublesome murmur that kicked off this whole wretched affair. Damn, it really would be the death of him.

But it needed to be done.

So he turned back to the fire and the balcony. He shouted, "Jennie? Is that you? I can't see you."

Megan's scamper came to a halt at the stairs. "Detective... What are you—"

He held up a fist, silencing her. He gestured to step away, back, to get the hell out of here. *Go,* he mouthed. *Run. I've got this.*

Then he shouted, "Jennie? What are you doing here?"

"Dad?"

"I'm up here, sweetie. Is that... Is that really you?"

"Dad, I'm coming. Don't leave me, please!"

Megan was right, he realized. About Oksana. She was more right than she knew. Beneath the fury, she was wounded and angry. At surviving. At being trapped. At being alone and abandoned.

If she was wounded, it meant she could be hurt.

And if she was angry, she could be tricked.

Here she was now, his daughter Jennie, climbing out of the scalding smoke. Her hair wasn't patchy and thin from the treatment, but full of those vibrant curls from the years before. Her skin was no longer chemo-swollen but soft and creamy and warm to the touch. And her smile, the pain behind it was gone. Her smile bloomed with life so vibrant it nearly blinded him.

"Dad?"

"Hey, sweetie. It's me."

Coughing, Graham stumbled forward. He waved away smoke and cinders and wiped his eyes with the back of his hand. The air sizzled the hair on his arms. He had to see. He had to see her.

"Dad? I'm scared."

"Don't be, sweetie. I'm here now. There's nothing to be scared of."

And he was here, before her, before the daughter whose memory he had consigned to the broken rooms of his heart. She was no child but a young woman now, the very age she should have grown into. On her way to becoming a doctor, an astronaut, a teacher, or whatever future that disease stole away.

All he could say was, “Oh, how I’ve missed you.”

He fell into her arms. He wanted this moment, this embrace. He needed it for so long he’d taught himself to forget.

He placed ashy fingers under her chin and studied her face.

“Look at you. All grown up.”

She blinked one blue eye, one green. Her smile was endless and consuming.

Then he said, “But you’re not my daughter.”

There was a click as he fastened the handcuff to her left wrist. Another as he attached it to his own.

Gone was his sweet Jennie, her face crumbling like dry bark as Oksana’s eyes bulged from the mask. Her cheeks split as a jagged sneer widened. The very air warped as she screamed.

With two clicks of a second set of handcuffs, he chained them both to the banister. She slashed and snarled, fingers gouging ribbons down his arm. Her neck stretched as something like a crab’s mouth opened from her ribs.

Graham felt the pincers dig in, lacerating his leg, his thigh, his sides. Something hot and long coiled its way under his skin, penetrating him. He didn’t care. He just needed to reach out, to stretch his fingers and take that flaming bottle. To raise it up over them both.

“Don’t be afraid, sweetie,” he whispered. “We’ll do this together.”

chapter sixty-nine

Megan realized what Detective Nolan was doing too late to stop it.

The crack of glass at his feet, the blossom of flames. In the space of one breath, the Molotov engulfed them. Oksana, shrieking and thrashing and pulling away. And Graham, grunting and squeezing and bringing her into his heavy embrace.

Megan raced toward them, but they were already wreathed in fire, bodies twisting and merging in a whirling dance of cinders and ash. The world around them ignited. The dry plants and old books. The fish netting on the wall. The rug smoldered underfoot, a thousand snails becoming hot coals.

Coughing, retching, Megan retreated up to the third floor. She stole a glance below. There, at the banister, the two burning bodies strained against each other. The railing cracked. One body tumbled over the ledge, pulling the other by a sizzling handcuff. They teetered at the edge of the blaze.

In ten racing steps, Megan reached the end of the hall. Flinging the couch aside, she slid the glass door open. There was no reset. No rearrangement of fiery walls or smoldering wood. No flies buzzing deep in her mind.

"Help me!"

Don't look back, Megan told herself. *Don't do it.*

She looked back.

Blackening fingers scratched at the rug, sliding back, backward toward the edge and the inferno below. With all her strength, Oksana clawed at the cindering floorboards and stretched out a desperate hand. "*Help me! Please, Meg! Don't leave me again!*"

And there Megan stood between the blistering heat on her cheeks and the cool fog on her back, the past still reaching out and screaming to be heard.

OUTSIDE, the breeze hit her lungs, so salty-sweet and cool she almost threw up. She limped down the stairs, gulping in the moist air until she collapsed in the garden, coughing and spitting up ash. She never thought air could taste so full of life.

Behind her, the house crackled as something collapsed deep inside. A wave of heat caressed her tender skin. But she was safe now. She rolled onto her back, not sure whether she was laughing or crying or perhaps doing both.

Warmth on her cheeks and cool air in her lungs. Moisture and heat, reborn from them both. Above her spun an endless black sky, that cold, indifferent moon, and a single star now shining down through a fog that was slowly, mercifully, beginning to lift.

part six

Don't Look Back in Anger

chapter seventy

Now

With a click, Anwar shuts off the tape recorder, letting the silence punctuate the end of her story. He gives Megan a moment to compose herself. It's been a long afternoon. A *weird* afternoon.

Outside, the sun is low, the kitchen painted in those golden tones that whisper of nostalgia. The hills are darkening, ochre lumps beneath a fiery sky.

Yes, he has to admit, there is a charm to the desert, a desolate beauty. And perhaps an unspoken promise: the desert doesn't care about your dreams or your deeds, your future or your past. The desert can devour you.

And maybe, if you go deep enough, if you're strong enough and stay long enough, then maybe you can emerge a new person. It's a nice enough thought.

Until someone like him comes around and digs it all up.

"So that's it?" he asks. "You didn't stick around for the fire trucks or the cops?"

Megan shakes her head. "No."

Good. He read that it took the first responders thirty minutes to arrive. Fueled by the wind off the bay, the blaze spread to neighboring houses and acres of forest, burning for over a day. The whole thing was a mess.

He sips his sparkling water and studies her face. The sharp eyes. That soft smile at the corners of her lips. The shadow of that scar, smoothed by the years. Like the desert, there's something about her he finds alluring. Something he's starting to respect.

It's a pity what will have to come next.

"Boarding schools. Cancerous mutations. Friends killing each other. I have to say, it's quite the story, Mrs. Collings. There's just one thing I'm curious about."

Megan lifts her gaze from the wine. "One thing?"

"The bodies," he says. "I've checked the report; I've got it right here. They only found a couple of bodies inside. Two, maybe three, all beyond identification."

"It was hot. I hardly made it out."

"Hot enough to burn bones?"

"I'm not an expert on combustion."

"I'm not either. But I got curious so I looked it up. Turns out, at around thirteen hundred degrees, calcium phosphates—bones, basically—fuse and become brittle. Now, the average house fire can reach up to fifteen hundred and this was a whopper. But still, even crematoriums have to break bone into ash. Otherwise, you get little pieces of grandma's femur in that nice urn. Nobody wants that. So, it makes you wonder, doesn't it?"

"Wonder what?"

"Like, what happened to the dead Russians?"

Megan's head tilts and her gaze narrows. "You think someone covered it up? What, like people who worked for Petro?"

Anwar feels his toes curling. My God, this is too much. She's really going to make him say it.

"Or maybe no one worked for Petro."

Her posture straightens as her lips part in protest. She catches herself and shifts. There it is, he thinks. The realization that she's spent three hours with this stranger, letting him into her home, into her kitchen, feeding him and giving him water and talking, talking, talking.

Yes, he can see that epiphany dawning on her face. He needs to press ahead, as fast as he can.

"See, maybe there were no Russians. And this Petro person? My uncle's journal mentions him, but only a little. Certainly nothing about Chernobyl or escaped Ukrainian gypsies."

Megan's jaw tenses. "She wasn't a gypsy."

"Right, whatever it's called. My point is, it wasn't written down."

"We didn't have much time."

"Yeah. Or maybe it never happened."

Defiance sparkles deep in her eyes. "Not everything that happens gets written down."

"And conversely, not everything written down happens as such." He leans closer, lowering his voice. "C'mon, we both know it's been decades. Time plays tricks on us; you said it yourself. Your memory was a bit *off*. Mrs. Collings—Megan—I know you're holding back. That instinct? That *investigative* instinct? My uncle isn't the only one with it."

She's about to speak when the kitchen door opens. Symon pokes his head in, his eight-year-old eyes lingering on this stranger who's taken the whole afternoon with his mother.

"Everything okay, Mom?"

"Of course, buddy. Hey, I've got an idea. Why don't you go play down the street until daddy comes home? Show R.J. that new basketball you got?"

"R.J.'s grounded."

"I bet if you ask his mother to use their hoop, she'll let him out on parole." She gives him a wink. "Go on. My friend and I have business to discuss."

Symon gives her a weak bob of his head, eyes lingering on Anwar. Of course the boy can sense it. Anwar doesn't care for kids but he respects their intuition; they've got good bullshit detectors.

Megan closes the door after her son and takes a moment to pace the kitchen. She's working up the courage to push forward. But he can sense her hesitation too, the push-pull he's grown used to with cornered interviewees. She'll need a nudge in the proper direction. Sticks and carrots.

"Mrs. Collings, I've been picking this case apart for nearly three years. I know what happened. But it's the truth—*your* truth—that matters. Help me understand it."

She runs a finger along the kitchen counter and wipes off a scuff.

He'll give her another beat to get her thoughts in order, he supposes. Heck, he doesn't mind the view. Her, in the late-afternoon light. That posh, middle-aged confidence giving way to youthful nerves. The successful artist reverting to a scared student and now doubting her words.

She whispers, "You knock on my door... with the names of my dead friends dripping from your lips. You come into my home and you stir up these memories. You... *insinuate.*"

He gives her his most agreeable nod with each point.

"And for what? To get some clips for a lousy podcast?"

Fear tickles his skin, but he forces himself to keep that calm mask from slipping.

"What, you thought I wouldn't figure it out? I looked you up while you were in the bathroom. Anwar Fariz of *Suburban Murders*. Or was it *The Killer Next Door* that won that trashy podcast award?"

He holds up two fingers and gives her a smug smile. "Two-time winner."

"You dig up people's pain and sadness. You process it like a sausage and profit. You don't create; you regurgitate. You're a vulture, a merchant of misery."

"'A merchant of misery.' I'll have to remember that." He claps his hands together. "But you're right, Mrs. Collings: I'm a storyteller. All the terrible things people do to each other, that's my jam. Like what you and your friends did to Oksana. And what Adam did to your friends."

There it is, he thinks, a twitch on her face and a sharpening of her gaze. As if she's just bitten something bad and can't wash it down. He lives for that twitch.

"What happened to your friends?" he continues. "What *really* happened?"

"I told you."

"No, you told me part of it. The rest you dressed up. You even had me convinced, in places."

The last vestiges of hospitality fade from her lips. "Why don't you tell me, then? What really happened?"

He sighs and makes a big deal of removing the tape and putting it into his jacket. He does his best to look disappointed. "Off the record?"

"Off the record."

"I think you were a young woman with a head full of trauma. I think you and your friends made a mistake. That mistake became your shared little secret. And like all secrets, it became harder to keep. There's no statute of limitations for murder."

Her jaw tightens. Maybe she knows where he's going with this. Maybe not. But in the end, it really doesn't matter.

Because this has never been about innocence or guilt. It's been about the story, where her memory meets his truth. And that truth, well, it can be whatever he wants. Splice the audio, mix in dreadful music, or add a voiceover track. *It was with this revelation that Mrs. Collings asked me to leave. And that was how I last saw her, hands crossed at her kitchen table, denying the past and the part that she played.*

Yes, it has a nice ring to it. Still, he has to try for a confession.

"Yeah, you fed Uncle Graham some bullshit about Oksana coming back. And yeah, he wrote it down in his journal, just like I've been recording. Neither makes it true. But Oksana's death, that secret you all shared? That was true. And it was too much for Adam, wasn't it? Like an infection, it got under his skin. It *festered*. So he started cleaning it up. First Chunhee, then Tom and Desi. Maybe Louis found a piece and connected that necklace to Adam, so he had to go too. But eventually Adam came after you."

Megan says nothing, but she doesn't need to. He can sense her struggle, every muscle holding back, which means he's touched the right nerves.

"Adam wasn't kicked out of Brown for bad grades," Anwar says. "He roughed up some freshman, put the kid in the hospital. Now, maybe you cooperated with Adam's purge. Or maybe you were next so you fed my uncle some bullshit. But in the end, *cui bono*? Who benefits? If there were two of you, one could always talk. Best not to take that risk, right?"

And then she whispers, "Yes."

Anwar almost plows ahead but catches himself. "I'm... I'm sorry?"

A single tear streaks her cheek. "Yes."

He meets her eyes and takes a quick breath. His heart thrums against the hidden recorder. *Hold it together.*

"Yes to what part?"

"Yes. Yes to all of it. Is that what you want to hear? Yes, that's how it happened. That's *exactly* how it occurred. Too many people knew the truth and they had to go."

Something shifts in her body, a great release of tension. It's as if her shoulders have been pushed down by decades of weight and are suddenly free. For a moment she looks older, ancient. No, he realizes.

She looks defeated.

This is it. Holy shit. Not just a partial but a full admission. He's captured it all.

Anwar has only a few seconds to celebrate this victory before the front door opens and footsteps echo through the house.

"Hellooo?" A man's voice drifts in, warm and friendly. "Megan, babe?"

She rises, her face shifting from exhaustion to performative warmth, perhaps a bit manic. She wipes the tear away quickly. "Hey, welcome home. How was your day?"

Her husband strikes Anwar as a nearly forgettable man, broad-shouldered and square-jawed and a little soft in the sides. Perhaps a few years older than her but not much.

"You know, ups and downs. Who's this?"

"Oh, Anwar, this is Corey. Corey, Anwar is a... well, a friend of a friend. I'm afraid he was just leaving."

"Corey?" Anwar shakes the man's hand. "It's nice to meet you. She's said so many good things."

Corey's smile is wide and white and almost bashful. "Well, don't believe them all."

"No, I certainly won't."

Megan almost winces but it flies right over Corey's head. Anwar wonders when she'll tell him the truth. Probably soon. They'll have to prepare.

Or maybe she'll deny it to the end. No matter.

"Well, I need to get going. Thanks for the water and thanks for the chat. It was nice catching up on old times."

He runs a finger over the hidden recorder while they walk him to the door. Warm and secure, good. He hoists his bag over his shoulder and stifles a grin.

At the door, he casts a final glance back into the house, where Sofiy sits on the couch, engrossed in a book. Warm light spills across the living room, the entryway, the hall. And the walls, where paintings add splashes of color and beauty. Just a snapshot of the perfect American home.

Perhaps he'll come back and get a photo, right here. Dial the colors down to an ominous gray. Photoshop some yellow police tape across the front door. Yes, that would make a good picture for the podcast.

But one thing at a time.

"Goodbye, Anwar."

"Goodbye, Megan."

And that's how he leaves them, Corey smiling his white smile from the porch, Megan's cheeks flushed in the sunbeam, her eyes seething, betraying that placid mask she's worn for so long.

chapter seventy-one

Waving off the heat, Anwar settles behind the wheel of his rental car and cranks the AC. He's nearly vibrating with excitement.

The interview, while occasionally meandering and far from perfect, has given him more than he'd hoped for. Enough juicy clips to keep his audience's attention. Enough ambiguity to fuel conspiracy theories. And maybe, if he's lucky, enough evidence to get the wheels of justice rolling once again. Hell, a few super fans might even raid this gated community, convinced they're helping the cause.

Wouldn't that be nice?

Smiling, he checks the time, pleased to discover he's got several hours until his flight. He connects his phone to the display and types the airport into the GPS. It's a two-hour drive, which will give him time to review some of the audio.

For now, he just needs to leave. So that's what he does.

Marigold Drive becomes Ivy Lane, which merges into Rose Way. The community sign reads fifteen miles per hour, but he climbs to thirty. He fumbles with the recorder, disconnecting and reconnecting the Bluetooth audio. He turns up the volume.

Nothing.

No.

He turns the volume up even more.

No, no.

Still nothing.

Wait. There it is; he can hear something, thank God. Heart racing, he twists the knob, maxing out the volume.

But there are no voices. No ambient hum of the room as heard from inside his jacket. No Anwar asking endless questions, nor Megan with her implausible answers. No confession.

No, no, no. Please...

He drives past another sign for Marigold Drive. His eyes leave the smooth, curving road. He taps the recorder, skipping through minutes, hours, desperately searching for something, anything.

All he hears is a wall of hissing static laced with a persistent clicking. A tangle of noise that makes him think, oddly enough, of old video tapes and dead radio stations.

And radiation.

Zooming past yet another sign for Marigold Drive, he grabs the other recorder, shoves the tape in. He fumbles with the buttons, eyes leaving the wheel and the road. He doesn't look to his right.

The basketball bounces high off the driveway and out into the street. A red-haired kid follows, sneakers leaving the curb. Anwar looks up just in time to recognize Symon in the driveway, his face a calm mask like his mother's.

Then the brakes squeal, the ball pops, and the red-haired boy disappears beneath the car.

For the space of five breaths, Anwar sits, frozen, hands gripping the wheel. From a far distant place, he realizes the stereo is still on, "No Excuses" by Alice in Chains warbling behind a chorus of static.

Numbly, he feels his finger hit *mute*. The warm desert dazes him as he steps out of the car. Distantly, he watches himself move around the dented hood to the back of the car. He knows what he'll find: a child, injured or worse.

He thinks of the flight he'll probably miss. The call to his lawyer he'll need to make soon. And all those missing minutes he captured...

The red-haired boy lies on his back, eyes fluttering and focused on the fluffy pink clouds filling the sky. His lips make little gasping gestures.

But it's the boy's broken arm that has Anwar's attention.

"Shit, kid, you came out of nowhere."

Then the boy moans. Or rather, that's what Anwar perceives. Fish-like, his lips make little O's as he slaps his hands and feet on the asphalt. Then comes the mewling scream that shocks Anwar, sends a shiver up his spine and a dribble down his leg. Little flies buzz behind his eyes.

Symon watches it all from the driveway, a coy smile on his lips.

Clutching his temple, Anwar steps back from the thrashing boy. His gaze falls to the bruised flesh and the shattered bone bulging beneath skin. A lump that moves, twists, and straightens itself with a crack.

Anwar doesn't hear the click of opening doors, nor the hum of sliding glass. He only senses the neighbors when they're all closing in.

A woman with a bulge in her belly and a sparkling ring on her finger.

A man in his forties with mousy-brown hair.

Despite a few wrinkles, Tom and Desiree have kept the shining eyes of their youth and their playful demeanor. And their smiles, ageless and unblemished and infinitely sour.

Another door opens. Another figure emerges from a perfectly bland home. Chunhee Chang in yoga capris, getting ready for an evening run.

It goes on as such, doors opening and feet moving, their walks turning into jogs and then sprints across lawns and down smooth side-walks. There is Adam among them, hands dirty, knees grassy, garden tools hanging from a belt.

No, it's too much. It's impossible. Anwar's mind retreats inward while his body struggles to catch up. *Go. Now. Run.* He ducks into his rental car and puts it in drive. He stomps the accelerator.

The wheels squeal as bodies smack against the side windows, the mirrors. With a meaty thump, someone with a wide smile and too many teeth slides under the hood.

There are too many bodies, too many hands. Anwar fights the loose steering, the tires struggling for traction. The car swings left, right, left before crashing into a fountain upon a flawless green lawn. With a pop, the airbag deploys, turning his world to powdery nylon.

Then come the hands.

Some break glass and some tear open the door. Others tug at his seatbelt, his clothes, and his face. They pass him off, from one group to the next and on and on. Dozens of warm hands and more every second. There's not a closed door for blocks.

A man with a silver mustache reaches into Anwar's back seat and retrieves the blue notebook. "I've been looking for this." Uncle Graham gives his nephew a jagged smile before the crowd swallows him up.

All the while, Anwar shouts, "Let go of me! No! This... isn't... POSSIBLE!"

He can only watch from his upside-down perspective as the bodies part for one woman. And he wonders, had Megan's eyes always been two different colors? Had Megan's scar always quivered and moved? Perhaps it's the light. Yes, that's what he tells himself in this moment; it *must* be the light.

She runs her fingers through his hair. Like being touched by the sun. And when she speaks, her words bloom deep in his mind.

"We've both learned a few tricks over the years, haven't we, Mr. Fariz? You've been inside my house, taking my life apart. But I've been inside you since we first sat together."

She traces a fingernail across her palm, where a seam opens up. Anwar moans and closes his eyes. He can see it now, a flash of her memories bubbling up inside his, mixing until he can't tell which is which.

Her kitchen counter with that damp cutting board.

That ceramic knife slicing fruit and then sliding across her palm. Her hand passing over ice cubes, squeezing a single black bead into his sparkling water. Anwar raising the glass to his thirsty lips.

Megan says, "Shh, Mr. Fariz. I think you'll like it here; everyone does. We'll make a few changes, of course, but I'm glad you're sticking around."

Then they pass him off, from one group to another, his screams following, lawn by lawn, house by house, until he is carried through an unremarkable door, one no different than all the others here, in this quiet community beneath a warm sun at the edge of the desert.

epilogue

Pretend We're Dead

On a cool Tuesday in December, the clouds gathered and fattened with the season's first snow. There were jagged flakes and thin pebbles of sleet. There were flurries that spun in the breeze.

One flake in particular, an unbalanced particle of lumpy crystals and dust, hung around longer than most. It twisted and turned, twinkling red and green in the holiday lights until its earthbound journey ended on the warm shoulder of a young woman who thought, *I'm done with the cold*.

Inside O'Bannon's, the regulars were filling their yuletide cheer at the bar. Junior was playing darts with a boozehound named Betty, a Santa hat slung low over her eyes. Senior lounged in the corner, watching Bob Saget ham it up on a holiday edition of *America's Funniest Home Videos*. A half dozen hands nursed eggnog and mulled wine and candy cane cocktails at half off.

And Corey, on the other side, poured generously tonight, keeping the pretzels refilled and smiling often. Because it was mostly the lonely who came here on Christmas Eve. Those with distant family or none at all. Those of few connections. And sometimes they had the most interesting stories to tell. He was doing his best to listen more these days. He was trying to be better.

The door opened, bringing with it the silver light, the breeze, and a few fast-melting flakes. And it brought in someone else, a woman who'd run off with his car and left a hole in his heart.

Megan wiped the snow from her hair and met Corey's eyes. It was the strangest thing, he thought, how they flickered a dozen different colors beneath the lights and the holly. And how she seemed almost nervous to see him again.

"Holy shit, now here's the real Christmas miracle," Junior proclaimed, marching over. "Halle-fucking-lujah. Where the hell have you been?"

"I'm sorry. I had to catch up with some friends."

"Friends?" Junior blinked. "Where, in Egypt? That's it, no more. You're fired."

For a moment Corey wasn't sure whether Junior was going to shout or keel over from a heart attack. The vein on his forehead bulged. But Megan met his stare, her face a calm mask, strong and indifferent.

A long beat passed between them. Then Junior's leathery face stretched into a smile and those big hands waved it all off. "Ah, what do I look like, the fucking Grinch? Merry Christmas, Megan. But you *are* working tonight."

"I'll help out for a bit."

"Help out. You kids, always lazy." He gave her a friendly smack on the back, the fresh scars from the fire still tingling at his touch. "Help out for a bit."

As Megan sidled up to the bar, Corey did his best to keep his emotions in check. He was pissed, hurt, and confused as hell. Mostly, he was glad to see her.

She said, "I owe you an apology."

There was something about her, a luster or shine. Something he had to admit was ladening his tongue and slowing his words. She stood straight and with purpose.

"And I also owe you a car."

He swallowed. "Hold up, I'm still processing that first one. Jesus, Meg, no one's seen you for a month. Are you okay?"

"Yeah, I really think that I am."

He believed her. There was something definitive to it. Something strong that he had glimpsed when she was deep into her art. Now she wore it all over. "Well, I'm glad to hear that. Really."

"And I also realized you were nice to me. I think maybe I took that for granted, you know? I'm sorry, Corey. Life's too fragile."

His cheeks flushed. "Nah, you were fine. I just..."

"You caught feelings."

"Yeah, I had a few." He glanced down and wiped a glass. "And maybe I still do. But I guess that depends, doesn't it?"

"Depends on what?"

"On what happened to my car."

He looked into those endless eyes. She returned it with a smile, confident and raw with strength and mischievous implications.

"Oh, that. I will make it up to you, I promise."

"You're here, so you already have."

Her eyes grew misty, but then Junior stopped by, tapping an envelope against his hand. "Ah, get a room, you two. But after we close." He slid the envelope to Megan. "This came for you a few weeks ago."

Corey studied the envelope, the bar's address written in a curious scrawl. A few of the letters looked almost foreign, and he thought of languages from the far side of the world. There was no return address.

He asked, "What is that?"

"Nothing." With precise fingers, she tore it and dropped the pieces into the trash. "Just some junk I didn't need." And that was that.

Within minutes they were back to their old routine. Corey mixing the drinks and pouring generously, Megan carrying them to the tables and chatting with the regulars who were rough around the edges but mostly polite. He found his eyes could hardly leave her. She smiled often and looked like she meant it. There was a curious lilt to her speech.

A song came on over the house stereo, Better Than Ezra's "Good," and her eyes sparkled as the tinny speakers came to life. First the catchy guitar riff and the ringing cymbals. Then the upbeat bassline and those good-time vocals.

Megan bobbed her head and swayed as she neared the bar. She surprised Corey by reaching out a warm hand, and he surprised himself by taking it. He found himself drawn toward her, a curious rhythm in his feet that mirrored her own.

And she said, "Dance with me, stranger."

afterword

Ah, the nineties.

That weird time of quiet after the Cold War's nuclear hysteria and before America mired itself in forever wars in the Middle East. Sometimes I think it was just a decade of dreams.

Nostalgia can be one hell of a drug.

I didn't intend to set *Head Like a Hole* in the nineties when the seed of the story took shape. And yet, like characters and themes, settings themselves often emerge organically. This one crawled out of a foggy bay I once visited in high school.

I was seventeen in 1996, the year of this novel. You can do the math to figure out my current age now. Regardless, some moments of that year are still so sharp in my brain it's like they happened yesterday.

The reelection of Bill Clinton.

My first taste of freedom behind the wheel of a car.

The Unabomber.

My first beer fresh from a keg.

The death of Tupac.

My first summer love and my first heartbreak. Spoiler alert: she wasn't the one.

Writing *Head Like a Hole* became a time capsule project, one that taught me as much about my own mind and memories as it did about the shattered psyche of poor Megan Monroe. Memories are formed through a confluence of sensory, environmental, and emotional inputs. Neuronal connections are strengthened with concentration and recollection, moving them from short-term to long-term via repeated retrieval. Memories are not fact; they're adjusted every time they're re-encoded.

Sometimes I wonder why I can recall the freckles on the cheeks of my first serious girlfriend. Did she really have freckles? Or did my mind paint those on her skin over the years?

As an author, it's easy to get lost in rumination; it's basically what we do. And yet, as I revisited the nineties while writing *Head Like a Hole*, I had to fight my desire to look back on the past with a love-drunk gaze.

Didn't those summers feel endless?

Weren't things simpler back then?

Well, yes and no.

Our measurements of time were different. Our perceptions of the world's complications were narrowed in scope. No mortgage or child-care to worry about. No careers or midlife crises. Things weren't simpler; we simply weren't aware of all the things we didn't know.

Ignorance can sometimes be a bit blissful.

I also had to triangulate my memories against the actual facts and hard dates in history. It was sometimes unsettling what I found.

I was *certain* Princess Diana died during the Bill Clinton reelection campaign. They weren't related, but they were associated in my head.

Wrong. She died in 1997.

I was also certain Britney Spears came before the Spice Girls. And that Alice in Chains's masterful performance on MTV's *Unplugged* happened the same night as Nirvana's. They were a two-for-one special; I was so certain of this.

Wrong again.

And despite my love for nineties gangsta rap, I'm sometimes certain that there's more crime today and the world is far more dangerous.

Still wrong.

Crime has fallen dramatically. By every metric, we're far safer than at any point in the nineties.

My memories were quite fallible.

There were also certain cruelties growing up in the 1980s and 1990s that are no longer tolerated. Language has drifted. The meanings of words change over time.

I do miss the era of no cell phones and few internet distractions. Sometimes, it feels like we have too much access to information... and certainly plenty of *bad* information.

Yes, change can be scary as one gets older. I feel it too, that siren song of "Weren't things just simpler back then?" Nostalgia serving up another cup of that addictive Dandelion Wine.

But change can also be good. It means we're evolving as individuals, and as a culture.

I hope I'm evolving too.

Just not as fast as Oksana.

Thanks for reading!

Andrew Van Wey
August 2022

about the author

A child of the eighties, Andrew Van Wey was born in Palo Alto, California, came of age in New England, and lived as an expatriate abroad for nearly a decade. He currently resides in Northern California with his wife and their Old English Sheepdog, Daeny.

When he's not writing Andrew can probably be found mountain biking, hunting for rare fountain pens, or geeking out about D&D and new technology.

For special offers, new releases, and a free starter book, please visit andrewvanwey.com

instagram.com/heydrew
facebook.com/andrewvanwey
goodreads.com/andrewvanwey
bookbub.com/authors/andrew-van-wey
amazon.com/author/andrewvanwey

also by andrew van wey

Novels

Forsaken: A Novel of Art, Evil, and Insanity

Head Like a Hole: A Novel of Horror

Beyond The Lost Coast

By the Light of Dead Stars

Tides of Darkness

The Clearwater Conspiracies

Blind Site

Refraction

The Last Shadow

Collections

Grim Horizons: Tales of Dark Fiction

Made in the USA
Columbia, SC
26 February 2024

a48dc787-5721-4f64-b0d8-f8fd0da59436R01